Dawn of the Construct

Book 1 of the Soul Machine Saga

Dawn of the Construct

Book 1 of the Soul Machine Saga

Eric Lard

COSMIC EGG
BOOKS

Winchester, UK
Washington, USA

JOHN HUNT PUBLISHING

First published by Cosmic Egg Books, 2022
Cosmic Egg Books is an imprint of John Hunt Publishing Ltd., 3 East St., Alresford,
Hampshire SO24 9EE, UK
office@jhpbooks.net
www.johnhuntpublishing.com
www.cosmicegg-books.com

For distributor details and how to order please visit the 'Ordering' section on our website.

ISBN: 978 1 80341 078 4
978 1 80341 079 1 (ebook)
Library of Congress Control Number: 2021949890

A CIP catalogue record for this book is available from the British Library.

Design: Matthew Greenfield

UK: Printed and bound by CPI Group (UK) Ltd, Croydon, CR0 4YY
US: Printed and bound by Thomson-Shore, 7300 West Joy Road, Dexter, MI 48130

This book is dedicated to God, family, and friends. Without their support we'd achieve little and enjoy far less. Specifically, I'd like to thank my lovely wife, who provides order and sensibility to my life, my boys who encourage and inspire me every day and all my family and friends who have contributed to pull this story from the void between worlds and pound it out into ink, paper, and digital print.

One

The Astrig Ka'a

19.004329 AC (After Construct)
Age of the Half-Orc War

The hail of arrows seemed to hang in the darkness above – vivid arcs of green flame tracing their paths from further upriver. Eyes heavenward, the party squinted against the driving rain when a jagged slash of light seared their vision. Thunder boomed so close it felt like a mule kick to the chest. Deaf and blind they scrambled for cover.

D'avry slid hard into the mast, his pulse pounding as if to count down the seconds till impact. But even in that moment of chaos and terror, he could feel that overwhelming presence drawing down on them. Feel its power…its hate. Then the volley of arrows that had been lost in the blast hammered the shoreline around them. Arrow split rock. Unholy fire bubbled below the surface of the surging river — And still, the craft stuck.

Less than an hour earlier…

The bull caribou's head swung to the side, antlers *whooshing* gently as the scent of danger or…perhaps something else, drifted on the barely perceptible breeze. He listened intently. Water like liquid light streamed from the long white hairs beneath his muzzle. Something clodded clumsily away further down the trail from which they'd come.

The seven cows of his harem grazed idly, knee- and thigh-deep in the milky azure waters of a river he knew as a dot on a skein in a tapestry of pathways that was branded on his psyche, or perhaps, even deeper on some generational memory.

Wait, *seven* cows…?

A few yards away further downstream, the current tugged

at D'avry's haunches as it washed over a shallow section of cobble. His head buried in the water, he was single-mindedly focused on a clump of stringy river grass. He was amazed by the texture and the complexity of the flavors. How did he not know that grass could be this good? D'avry raised his head from the soothing riffles of the high-mountain runoff to consider this experience when he sensed a change in the mood of his companions.

Suddenly alert, he scanned the herd to find the bull caribou staring directly at him.

Oh no, he thought. *It's happened again.*

The pull. The compulsion had been at play.

How exactly did he get here? What was he doing with a herd of caribou? A jolt of panic broke the serenity of the moment as he strained to recall the moments leading up to this one.

Last he remembered there were...men...*he* was a man, not a caribou, and it was dark. The town...felt unfamiliar. And there was a dim alleyway. And it smelled putrid in the warm, breezeless inner recesses of what he recalled as a trading outpost along an overland route.

D'avry recalled he had been running. Before that there was gold. Not much. And silver. Quite a bit of silver, and other bits too. He'd been winning. A lot. There'd been a sketchy looking tavern he'd felt compelled to enter. Pulled as if by an undeniable force. And then he'd felt compelled to wager, and to drink. Things he did not often indulge in, since he was barely of age to do such things in his homeland, but he did much of this, nonetheless.

He recalled a malty, porridge-like concoction that made his nose tingle. And then there had been winning followed by more winning until the smiles and laughter grew less and less and a darkness descended upon the faces around him with much the same force of presence as the stench that filled that final alleyway.

That's when he'd run. Stumbling and clawing, leaping over unknown obstacles into further darkness, down narrow streets, and a multitude of narrow, seemingly exitless byways until he'd found the one alley. And then the compulsion called to him again. He was terrified to listen, but he knew that these things had an expiration date and as awful and daft and completely impractical as the compulsions were, they were always right. And they were never as expected.

Even as the sounds of pursuit drew closer, D'avry had stopped, picked up what appeared to be a semi-dried nugget of maybe, possum scat, and drew a barrel-sized circle on the wall. And, as bodies tumbled into the alley behind him brandishing cudgels and long-bladed daggers, he just — stepped through.

Glancing back through the blackness into a space only slightly less dim, something had caught his eye. In the darkest corner of that alley. Something was watching, something blacker than black, with searing red eyes.

D'avry felt the subtle shifting of the Astrig Ka'a and his footing failed him. He went down flailing. The last thing he saw was his now human hand swinging wildly through the air before his head went underwater. Unimpressed, the bull and the other caribou cast their heads away and began to graze again as if nothing strange had occurred at all.

How he'd stepped through a wall as a human and then into a river as a caribou was unclear. What time had passed was also uncertain, but those details were quickly washed away by the frigid water, tumbling him like a dislodged chunk of flotsam.

He was uncertain what to do now. Other than *not* drown and *not* freeze to death and *not* get washed downstream. Bobbing and splashing across the current toward the shore with its grapefruit-sized cobbles and intermittent patches of sand, he struggled to find traction enough to haul his soaking, thankfully human body from the current.

His normally blond shoulder-length hair was dark with

moisture and plastered flat about his angular face. His similarly angular frame, hints of it just visible beneath his finely tailored but well-worn long jacket, tunic, and trousers, all hung in a dark, muddled mess under the dim light of a dismally overcast sky.

As he climbed from the water onto the beach, each step squished slightly less than the last. He shivered and stumbled and slipped his way over the larger rocks, around the few scattered boulders and between scraggly branches of what bushes remained with bits of moss and refuse worn like badges of honor from the last time the river had risen that high.

D'avry looked about him at the barest spit of flat land gathered at the foot of an alpine forest. The tree line, breaking abruptly up on both sides of the river, formed the rugged notch of a long, J-shaped valley. Upstream, the river simply meandered away and out of sight. Further down it careened wildly left, tumbling over cottage-sized boulders, down and away into a thin, ghostly mist. The moist air echoed with the throaty *thrum* of what D'avry could tell was a meat grinder of a section of rapids.

In his estimation, there would be no exit upward from either bank. The mountains were too steep. Where he stood was most likely a portage if any trade moved through these waters, though, of that, he was skeptical. As it stood, he would have to choose either upstream or down or count on the compulsion to whisk him away elsewhere.

But that was not the way of the Astrig Ka'a, the Luck Magic. He had been brought here. From one place to another, for a purpose. Never his own, but a purpose, nonetheless. All that remained, he surmised, was to make do and let fate find him.

D'avry quieted his mind, silencing the discomfort of the cold. He made about the business of seeking a suitable place to light a small fire to dry his clothes and hopefully cook something for a morning meal, if he could catch it. Searching his person for any remnants of the previous night's escapades he found nothing. Nothing except a lone copper, and apparently a seam to stitch in his inside left pocket... But that's how the compulsion worked.

He would like to imagine that all those errant coins and gems had found their way into the pockets of orphans and widows, but reality rarely seemed to work that way. And the results of all the swirling eddies of cause and effect borne into existence by the Astrig Ka' were quite remiss to reveal themselves.

D'avry had called it *Luck Magic* for he had no other name for it. He'd never heard of any such form of sorcery or enchantment. Even in all those texts, though he had not been looking for it then. He considered himself a poor kind of magician anyway. In fact, he had never really wanted to be a mage at all.

In his lands, the title Mage was more of a political term applied to those who dealt in the business of nations and interpreting the dreams of rulers or really *bending* the intentions of those rulers whom they affected to enlighten. In fact, he had had another life entirely but then, that life and all the possibilities it held were as much a memory as his escapades of the night before. And held as much meaning when one was wet, cold, and hungry, with no supplies or the vaguest idea of where one was.

Welcome to Druesday, he thought and forced the frigid muscles of his face into a slightly maniacal grin. Of all the things he didn't have at the moment, knowledge of which day of the week it was, was the least of them. Druesday, Pinnick's Day, Nander... meaningless. It was Lost-in-the-Middle-of-Nowhere's Day at a quarter to Soaked and Starving as far as he was concerned.

A fledgling fire sputtered to life all on its own within a small, ash-filled circle of rocks. D'avry opened his eyes and seeing that it didn't dwindle away, turned his attention to the copper he had unconsciously been worrying in his hand. Closer examination yielded nothing of interest.

It was plain, worn, made round from sixteen or so flat edges, and had a square hole in the middle. Markings were unimpressive but it was remarkably heavier than he had expected...but for all intents and purposes it was tipping cash from some unknown principality. Likely it would not be exchanged in local trade other than accompanied by a great deal more of similar, more familiar coin. D'avry resisted the urge to draw back and huck it into the river. Instead, he bent over stiffly and placed it, precisely, atop one of the larger half-buried stones of the fire circle.

He'd no sooner set it down than a flash of black and a *whoosh* of wings spirited it away with a caw and a click as a raven winged across the spit and continued away, north, toward the river's headwaters.

Well! That's that, I guess, D'avry thought resignedly as his eyes strained to follow the quickly diminishing speck; his heart still pumping from the encounter. Nothing but the still dripping clothes on his back to show for his endeavors over the last few months' time.

His kit, he'd lost running from brigands, who in turn were running from King's Guard, who, in their own right, were little more than the thugs they pursued. His pony, Nesbit, lost to ogres who apparently didn't know they were only supposed to inhabit swamps.

His staff? Now that was a truly miserable thought. *Taken by beavers!* Beavers with a nearly impenetrable dam, so it would seem, thanks to the nascent properties of the enchanted jewel impressed upon the exquisitely carved handle of what had been his most prized possession. Among its many virtues, the staff had been especially good for walking with. Something he'd been doing a lot of lately...

He thought all of this, and his misery deepened. It was going to take some serious meditation to manage the quagmire of funk he now found himself wallowing in. By chance, D'avry glanced back the way of the raven-thief and caught a glimpse of light. Dimly. A barely perceptible twinkling in the muted gray of this most miserable morning.

What was it? A fairy in the middle distance? The last fading embers of a funeral pyre? Maybe an orc raiding party using the flaming corpse of a likely weaponless farmer as a standard?

D'avry's thin, not-quite-delicate features framed a frown. His cobalt eyes, tattooed dark along the lower rims in the way of his people, fixed on a space between himself and the offending light.

Standing erect, motionless, as if to fool the trees themselves, only the fingers of his right hand moved, twitching in small, abrupt swishes and swirls at his side. And then, balling into a fist, they splayed out like water dousing a fire. And the fire, already struggling to summon heat from the ash pile it'd been summoned from, put up little resistance. The flames winked out, the beggarly warmth disappeared, and smoke tendrils grew slowly skyward. D'avry noticed this and his hand, still close by his side, twitched again. The tendrils slowly circled in tighter and tighter spirals until, in a pitiful poof, it was as if they never were.

A blast of cold air whipped up, causing him to shiver involuntarily, and spit out sand while blinking away grit through bleary eyes to see the concerning light more clearly. The wind had come from up valley and carried with it the faintest smell of...pork? Perhaps it was the workings of the Astrig Ka'a that caused his senses to be more highly tuned at times but even this seemed entirely unlikely.

However, D'avry felt a tug, but this time it was not a compulsion of the Luck Magic, it was his stomach, which now remembered it was hungry. But it would have to wait.

Too often the unwary, looking for a meal, became one.

He smiled sourly, remembering the old monk who'd taught him that maxim. It was at the tail end of a week-long fast when he'd found himself hanging from his ankles in the forest, shaking stars from his vision and wondering why everything was upside down.

Again, his hand moved, this time sliding softly from side to side as if wiping away symbols in the sand. And, as he did so, he appeared more and more to be nothing but a lesser part of the greater forest.

Two

A Sign

The party, drifting at the whim of the chilly azure waters, was being pushed along by an increasingly fervent wind. And yet, they lay about the craft like rags about a laundry. None stirred but a man named Trask, a librarian, recently unemployed he mused to himself, who was fervently working to warm a sausage over a fire held in a large bronze bowl.

Crudely crafted, the bowl was suspended by rusty, soot-covered chains hanging from what looked like the craft's solitary mast but was more likely some sort of rigging for lifting goods or fish nets. In fact, the craft was intended to be driven by oars rather than sails though none were evident except at the stern. There, a steering oar had been lashed in place to keep the craft moving in a straight line. It kind of worked. Sadly, the state of the craft bore a keen resemblance to that of its passengers.

A choking snort rose from what had been a steady choir of snoring and the rail-like man, whipped his head in its direction. Eyes wide, it took a moment for the look of prey-animal terror to drain from his face and to be replaced with a snarky smirk.

The man's gray-blond hair was little more than a ragged stubble, except above his largish ears, where it was shorn to the scalp in three very peculiar but precise horizontal lines. He looked fairly acquainted with the elements for an academic but, his skin was oddly pale, at least that which could be seen beneath the grime of mud-ash and dried streaks of blood.

In contrast, his light blue eyes were clear and bright and seemed to burn with what some would describe as a zealous fire. To add to the set of seeming contradictions was a set of nearly perfect teeth that rested below a gnarled hunk of driftwood for a nose. The inevitable conclusion being that it had been broken and reset on more than one occasion. The previous night being likely the most recent such event since some of the dried blood still resided there.

To an untrained eye, his garments and those of his companions would suggest a boatload of refugees from a tavern fire, but a keen observer would pick out a powerful, soldierly form here or intricate scrollwork on a hasp-bound tome there, or maybe a blade, peeking from a scabbard throat, glowing faintly in the flat gray light.

Trask looked over his would-be rescuers. Gearlach, the towering man with a face like a granite slab was their leader. Dark, brooding, keen, he was a force of nature with an axe. It was because of him they'd gotten this far. The other three, men of the isles he understood, had an oddly confrontational relationship.

It seemed that the ranger and the thief had a problem with the mystic, or priest. Trask couldn't be sure what the issue was since the subject of his occupation seemed to be entirely off limits. *Odd.* He'd only known them for a couple of days now. Except Liggo, the thief. He'd been sneaking into the chieftain's camp in order to plan Trask's rescue which had culminated only two days prior.

Out of a newly formed habit Trask scanned the water and shoreline behind him. He scanned the sky and then any bits of thinning vegetation on the hillside and then he scanned again within the shadows in between. The wind whipped, and he squinted in a quietly menacing way.

It was one of a short list of sour expressions his face adopted as a response to almost any circumstance. But, for the time being he was satisfied and turned back to the work at hand just as a flurry of feathers blinded him, pummeled his face and in an instant made off with his breakfast, squawking twice before perching atop the mast. The librarian's slender hand flashed, and a dagger tip buried itself within an inch of the top of the mast. Intentionally of course.

The raven scrambled, squawking with outrage and in its haste dropped its prize. Without so much as a second glance, Trask's hand stretched out casually and caught the falling object. But, to his surprise, it was not a sausage. It was a coin. And yet *not* a coin...a sign!

A bright trickle of new blood gathered on his cheek, as his eyes, burning anew, drifted downstream, surveying the great boulders at the far end of the notch-shaped valley and the bare spit of cobble-ridden beach that lay like an altar before it. Slowly, a faint semblance of a smile touched his face before fading into a kind of burnished resolve. It was the look of stone if stone could be angry. Angry, spiteful, and filled with an insatiable lust for vengeance.

Bedraggled, worse for wear, the party trudged in silence. The single-masted river boat, through no small effort, was now safely beached and laying over on its shallow keel on the shore. And, though it was only late morning, a haunting gloom had impressed itself upon the valley, punctuated now and then by the chill of a gusting wind.

Trask, his weather-worn cloak whipping like a flag on his gaunt frame, mounted the small rise to the head of the portage trail and then dropped his heavy rucksack with a *thud*. On his heels, an almost impossibly huge man with dark, ruddy skin and darker eyes did the same. The angular shapes protruding from beneath his heavy woolen cloak suggested armor, but it was clear that raw muscle accounted for the bulk of his frame.

He was terrifyingly huge. Anyone with any sense gave him a wide berth, except children, who to his infinite amazement found him irresistible. Smiling broadly, his outsized jaw moved to reveal similarly oversized lower canines. The man, though brooding and beastly in appearance, spoke with a clarity and insight that betrayed an unlikely intellect.

"Trask. You see a dragon for the shadow of a mouse," said Gearlach, his deep voice at once easy and precise. The librarian crossed his arms and shot him a look but said nothing. The scratch on his cheek was now dried dark and faded into the background of dirt, dried blood and ash that covered all the party members.

Another man completed his trek and joined them. Dropping his heavy sack, he pulled back the hood of a close-fitting leather tunic. He had a thick black beard and greasy black hair slicked back to hang just above his shoulders in wisps that evoked the image of a pudgy, black hawk.

Thadding Liggo, looked a decade younger than both men and was shorter by a head than Trask and easily by two of the larger man. Though heavier set, his movements were smooth and efficient like a dancer or circus acrobat. A long knife with a worn stagwood handle and full bronze guard materialized in his hand as he casually began to tidy up the stubble on his neck where his beard ended and the grime of campaign began. A trick of the eye, most likely, seemed to cause the edge of the blade to capture more light than it rightfully should.

"A sign ya say?" he asked in a husky, almost drawling voice that was clearly not suited to the dialect of his two companions. They looked at him but said nothing, content to let the question hang in the brooding silence. He seemed unoffended.

The moment dragged on until Thadding Volkreek and Gemballelven Farn reached the others and, too, dropped their gear in a heap. Volkreek, light of hair with green eyes and an auburn-gray, mid-length beard, wore heavier garments and light leather armor. He also wore a longbow and hand-and-a-half sword upon his back.

If he appeared the ranger, the other newcomer, Farn, with his bald head, blond beard and stockier build was more the fighting priest. Farn, the third from Thadding was from the far isles rather than the main island like the other two. He had an ironwood mace hanging from his hip and rather than britches tucked into knee high boots, he wore a long leather tunic that ended in foot long leather strips just above his shin plates. The garment, much like the three men, looked tough and agile.

Like Trask and Gearlach, these three wore a layer of filth that suggested calamity for days before and probably more ahead, else they'd pursue at least a modicum of hygiene. With that, the circle of companions was complete. All eyes were on Trask.

The light-haired Volkreek stretched extravagantly and then, removing his black leather gloves, began to work the ends of a reddish mustache that was prominent above the rest of his auburn, grey and white speckled beard. He cast a meaningful look at Farn and then at Liggo before resuming with his mustache.

Trask's eyes darted to the hawk-like Liggo and then Volkreek and Farn before finally settling back on the towering warrior. It was clear that his word was the final one within the small, dangerous looking band.

"Well, I don't know what it means. But it defies logic that a bird would steal a sausage...from out of a *flame*...and leave behind just this coin, or whatever it is." Trask burst out, while scrutinizing the copper-looking object closely and then again at arm's length.

"Not enough?" the priestly Farn asked. "You're right. I'd give *fifty* copper for a sausage right about now..." His warm brown eyes smiling at his own joke. He rubbed his bald head and seeing the dirt and dried blood looked up and began gingerly poking about for any injuries from the previous night's activities that might still need attention. His accent was oddly light in comparison to Liggo. Volkreek didn't seem to speak at all.

"Let me see this coin," said Gearlach, motioning for Trask to toss it over to him. The scarecrow-esque man paused from inspecting it, eyed Gearlach skeptically, and then flipped it across the open gap between them.

The coin stopped mid-flight as if hitting an invisible wall and fell to the ground with a quiet *clink*.

The men shifted uncomfortably, but Gearlach remained stoic, "I knew you were here, somewhere," he said, his voice conversational, lacking the menace one would expect from his appearance.

"You smell alone...Is that so?" he asked while staring at the empty space in the middle of the circle.

Seconds stretched on but then a thin, dark-eyed young man with wet sandy hair and even wetter garments materialized in the center of the group. D'avry stooped woodenly to pick up the coin.

"Th-th-thank you for returning this to me. I-I s-s-seem to have l-lost everything...else," he said, looking about himself and patting his pockets for effect. He was drenched to the bone and his lips and skin were shades of blue-gray. Obviously, he had been standing there, quite still, for some time.

"S-so, you guys, l-l-looking...f-for...a mage?" he asked, wondering if this was what the Astrig Ka'a had plopped him in the middle of a freezing river for. He looked at each of them but purposefully avoided looking at the tome poking out of Farn's sack.

"A sign!" Trask said triumphantly, pounding his hand with his fist.

Gearlach rolled his eyes and returned his attention to the wet, magician pup. "Others...I asked," his voice a low, menacing rumble.

That seemed to spark the others into action, heads swiveled as they scanned the deeply shadowed woods. Weapons materialized in their hands; Volkreek his bow, Liggo now with two of the heavy woodsman's knives glinting in the wan light and Farn, mace in hand and tome cracked to imbue his face with soft light that set his eyes deep in shadow. His lips moved feverishly as he whispered unintelligibly to himself.

"Hmmm? Oh, yes...Uh, no." D'avry replied absently. His gaunt features accentuated by the onset of hypothermia causing him to resemble a shivering cadaver.

"Now, that we're all, h-h-here, do you...do you mind?" He asked motioning in the direction of a clear space just a bit further beyond the trailhead. It seemed to be the intended campsite for the portage, complete with its own fire circle and rocks to sit on.

Working his hands with starts in obscure figures and patterns, without waiting for permission, he shuffled rigidly in that direction. Trask cast a quick glance at Gearlach and seeing him raise his eyebrow appraisingly but refrain from drawing steel, allowed D'avry to press by. Just then a couple pops and sparks burst into a vertical column of flame filling the fire circle ahead.

Stripping while he walked, he laid everything but his underclothes on the closest rock and turned his skinny backside so close to the wall of flames that he appeared almost to be a shadow within them. His shoulders drooped as he rolled his head side to side, soaking in the heat.

"Please, m-make yourselves useful," he said, jerking his head toward the wooded hillside. "This spell won't last forever. It'll need fuel...event...eventually," he struggled out.

Liggo rolled his eyes and leaned over to Volkreek, "The stones on this cub...," he murmured. "He's as bad as Trask." This caused the ranger to suppress a smile and shake his head.

D'avry looked out past the party of adventurers, something caught his attention. If his eyes weren't failing him, it seemed a second light had appeared at the end of the valley. A shiver went up his spine and if it was possible to feel a more bone-chilling cold, he did. Only now, instead of aching ears, toes, and fingers, he was preoccupied by a deep foreboding and a renewed sense of his own mortality.

Sometimes the Astrig Ka'a, when not directly twisting

events as they unfolded, would manifest itself in the form of a heightened awareness. Other times the pull itself felt as though imbued with a character of its own, the way that a single word could convey humility or caustic spite. Only now, the pull of the Astrig Ka'a felt thick and cumbersome, like a raspy bowline tugging at D'avry's ankles, indeed, at the entire party. And in this instance, the bowline was whipping overboard. Tied to the heaviest of anchors. Driving to the bottom of a very deep and very dark end.

"What have you done?" he whispered, staring into empty space. And then burning holes through Gearlach, teeth gritted, "What have you *done!*"

D'avry snatched his still soaking jacket and britches and whipped them on, hopping and pulling on his boots, half stumbling as he drew up square to Gearlach, his head barely even with the man's breast plate. The mages' eyes darted to Gearlach's great axe, the edge of it glinting wickedly in the diminished light, now only inches from his face.

Still, he pressed. "Do you *feel* that?" he asked, pointing upriver, eyes feral, each word dripping with meaning.

The wind, forgotten, whipped now like a trumpet's blast, and all eyes shot upriver to the way from which they'd come. To a glimmer, now easily identifiable as firelight but nothing that could have been mistaken for something so mundane.

It was at that moment, in the uncertain silence, that the weather broke. Sheets of water and lightning romped in the sky making it feel a thing alive and the band broke for gear and weapons. Slipping and scrambling on what moments ago was dry and well-packed trail.

D'avry yelled out, "To the boat!"

And each of the companions drew up short from their scrambling. Their faces, finally visible for the showering rain scouring layers of dirt and ash, stared at him jaws slack.

"This is a portage for a reason, cub," Trask spat over the din of wind and rain and thunder. "That way is impassable," he said, pointing to the section of river that was just out of sight but whose roaring filled the air with a constant drone. He returned to his gear.

"To. The. Boat!" D'avry yelled, "or die on this hillside!"

He spun, slipping again before catching himself and then strode back down the trail. The trail that even now was beginning to wash out with muddy streams pushing mats of pine needles from the tree line.

Gearlach's eyes followed the odd young man stomping across the cobbles. The chaos in his mind a dark mirror of the now hemorrhaging sky. It seemed at first that he would turn to the portage trail but then he paused. His attention drawn to the single-masted river craft. Beached less than twenty minutes prior, it was pitching wildly now. Heaving up on its keel and then slamming down hard against the rocks. Indeed, the sudden downpour had seemed to reinvigorate the river, its waters swelling, rising visibly.

"Maybe the mage is right," he said in a voice unheard over the din of marble-sized drops angling down to explode against the snotty hardpack. But Trask saw, Volkreek, too, as he paused from his preparations, the muscles tensing in his jaws, the barest shake of his head telling Trask that this was a madman's errand. He returned his gaze to see only the dark-eyed giant's back, his feet moving with purpose to follow the misguided mage.

Liggo and Farn followed without pause. They steadied themselves on the glistening rock outcroppings, treading carefully so as not to lose the contents of the heavy sacks slung over their shoulders. They picked their way down to the sand of the quickly diminishing shoreline. Already water sloshed over cobbles near the hillside creating an island from the spit of rock where they'd left the boat.

Sign indeed! thought Trask darkly before following suit. He took up the rear behind Volkreek the ranger, whose hooded cowl still lay about his shoulders. His face cast heavenward while streams of water poured over his brow and cheeks, blurring the varied colors of his beard into one dark, glistening mass.

In that instant, Trask had a vision of that same face, only with streams of *blood running down it*. An expression of serenity cast by lifeless, unblinking eyes still staring upward, but at a blood red sky. His chest tightened. Trask swallowed deliberately, forcing himself to inhale deeply through his battered nose, the charge of electricity detectable within overtones of mud and moss. And on his lips the faintest taste of blood, reconstituted by the pouring rain, now running in steady streams from the gray stubble on his scalp.

Three

Last of the Long Rifles

00.000001 BC (Before Construct)
Dawn of the Construct

Capt. Maj. Rutker Novak could not pull the trigger. Not yet...

Sweat had long ceased pouring down his face and the former dull ache between his temples has been replaced with a full-blown New Year's parade shoe-horned into a steel drum. He was beyond dehydrated. Now flirting with heat exhaustion, his skin felt sticky-dry, and he struggled to focus on the crosshairs and the sliver of daylight beyond.

Unfortunately, it was only going to get hotter. They didn't call the Novak Long Rifle the 'Widow Maker' for nothing. Its baffles would allow him the stealth he needed to hide from the merc in the Osiris mech — read as seventy-five tons of robotic firepower. But that same stealthing ability would just as likely fry him if he had to wait too much longer. It wouldn't be the first time that had happened to a pilot, he thought bitterly.

He needed one clear shot.

He would only get, one clear shot.

With the sniper mech's single 20mm Emag Cannon he could have nearly disabled the medium transport his family and the rest of the delegation had crash-landed just hours north of his present location. But it was the manual-feed that presented the problem. Unless *merc boy* and his buddy further up the canyon lined up in front of one of the narrow crevasses he could see through from this vantage point, he'd be loading the next round while the entire cave came crashing down around his head in a fiery avalanche of rock, particle beam and rocket fire.

He proceeded to wait. A crackle of static burst through the

mech's comms. They were jamming him. Shoving a multi-band pulse through the air, trying to find where they would sink; invariably, his receiver. The cave should have provided adequate protection, but his thumb brushed the electronics 'All Kill' button, just in case.

Now, he was completely cut off. If their buddies showed up, Colonel Dexx wouldn't be able to notify him that he'd have party-crashers. Worse still, his wife Katherryn wouldn't be able to fill him in on the hunt for their presumed saboteur either. She imagined it was the Colonel. She was sharp, stunningly clear-sighted, but that would be a quarter Daywork he *didn't* want to lose. Not with his family and the Epriot-Delvadr peace treaty on the line.

The landing bay explosion was no lucky shot by ragtag privateers. Nearly an entire platoon of Marines had been annihilated with almost zero collateral damage to the delegation transport, *Xandraitha's Hope*. He thanked Maker for the safety of his family, and the truce-critical cargo they so carefully jettisoned, but claiming that it was something other than sinister intervention would be beyond naive.

Rutker grimaced, straining through the pain in his head while struggling to maintain focus. He wasn't immune to ignorance at times, but rarely of *that* magnitude. Still, they were in the dark. Fending off curiously ineffective bandits while feigning major repairs to the grounded transport. He had been the obvious choice for retrieving the jettisoned packages due to his familiarity with the only serviceable mech in the hangar. And that was liberal use of the word *serviceable*.

The Long Rifle, aside from its illustrious heritage, was a death trap. No armor to speak of. Minimal sensors except for a handful of hummingbird-sized drones, and one cannon, fully as long as the mech was tall (when fully extended), which was to say a little more than twice his own height. Thankfully the cannon folded in half. Still, the mech was not something he wanted to be in while picking a fight with a mercenary horde on an unknown planet.

Why can't this creep hurry up? he thought while feeling the heat pressure in the dark silence of the cabin continue to climb.

Dust and rocks spilled down the haphazard stack of boulders that made up the east wall of his spider hole. The ultra-low rumble of hover-buckets told him that merc two was making his way over the bluffs edge and down to his partner who was slowly picking his way towards the wide, pale, scar of a canyon below. The second mech was a dragoon-class, medium mech. He'd spotted it early due to its garish, neon-punk paint job. That's how he'd known they were mercenaries rather than standing army. He'd never truly been fooled by the pirate ploy.

Rutker backed out the magnification to give his eyes a break and stretch his neck, knowing it'd take a moment or two before the other mech was close to lining up. A few glowing dust motes danced in slow motion between him and the darker shadows of the far wall. Suspended in the angular columns of light, they twirled near the edges and then quietly winked out of existence.

Rutker tried to swallow. The click and pop of thick saliva assaulted his ears and seemed to fill the space inside the mech's cramped cockpit. He cracked his neck and leaned forward, hands back on the controllers. Blinking his eyes wide, he brushed the 'weapons hot' button though he could have just used the HUD's ocular recognition or simply whispered the command.

Rutker adjusted the zoom manually, not leaving anything to chance. Judging by the speed of the second mech there was a chance that the two could, *possibly*, line up as the Dragoon reached the farthest opening. The worst, shittiest angle. The last *clean* shot without having to move and possibly give away his position.

Rutker focused even more intensely. There was nothing else he needed to see. The big mech moved again and stopped. Again, static burst through the cockpit. But to Rutker, the world didn't exist outside of a three-by-three square centimeter patch of sun-faded metal, high and left of the Osiris' rear bucket vents.

He imagined his father in this exact same model but years before. Eyes focused, drawing in a slow, deep breath and letting it out in one smooth stream. Waiting to squeeze the trigger in a complete union of man and machine — brain and body.

To Rutker, it felt like it was his father's ghost that was driving the Long Rifle now. Who's to say it wasn't?

Suddenly, a blur of movement crossed the magnified field of view. Merc One, the big guy he'd seen earlier in the Osiris was moving again, but Rutker couldn't see Merc Two yet. Panic pierced his gut.

Wait...was that pink? Did I see pink!

...can't tell...

At the last possible moment, he eased the trigger back in the control stick hoping against hope that it *was* pink. That the Dragoon had entered the gap behind the Osiris. And then... silence.

Of course, the pause was only in his mind, adrenalin-juiced into hyperdrive, racing faster, making the seconds stretch out like minutes.

But then, without warning, the concussive blast of the Emag charge exploded through the cannon rails, propelling a hyper-dense armor piercing round to unimaginable speed. The violence of the explosion was compounded by the close quarters. It rattled his insides and knocked loose bowling ball sized chunks of rock that filled the partially shadowed cave with billowing clouds of dust.

Shafts of morning sun, once crisp and crystalline, now barely pierced the vaguely luminous mass of swirling dirt and grit. He couldn't see through the glowing haze if he wanted to. Instead, he toggled the zoom out as he heard armor and engine bits still falling to the ground outside, thrashing drought-stunted trees and littering the twisting canyon stream with half-molten debris.

"Baffles off," he gasped through parched vocals. Luckily the mechs onboard intelligence would recognize his whisper from fifteen meters. Two quick flips of harness buckles and the antiquated sniper powered down, opening like a tri-petaled lotus flower forward and down toward the floor. No sooner did his feet touch the sandstone floor than he was running, pistol in hand, sandbag legs pumping towards the thin chalky crack that made up the entrance of his rock shelter. It took a highly specialized machine to fit into a space that tight. Rutker could barely see through the dust and crystallized sweat caking his eyes. But all he could think of was water.

No. Personnel and comms first. Keep it clean, he thought and forced himself to do things the way his father and granddad had taught him. The ECD, too, though they were late to the show. Much as always.

He leapt two bodies on the way to the larger half of the wreckage, and then realized that there was no use coming back to check vitals. It was the same body.

The Osiris, also, was sheered into upper and lower halves.

But no pilot?

That was unfortunate. And there was trace power showing up on his wrist display, which meant that conceivably a beacon could still be operable.

I'm not going to hang around for the sequel, he thought while watching thick, acrid smoke spiral into the sky above, making it a moot point.

Still, he had to get water every chance he could get. His headache returned now with the pause in the action. Head pounding with crisp peals, he squinted through the pain as he made his way to the stream. Still, something felt out of place...

Just then, heavy footsteps thudded from behind him, and his vision exploded into white hot shards. Propelled into the side of what was left of the Osiris' foot armor, he clung to consciousness, but numbly, straining to clear his head. His attacker slammed him hard from behind again. Warm breath was on his neck and ear and the pungent stench of fungus attempting to colonize a flight suit filled his nostrils. He felt kind of certain that it was his missing pilot, but his brain wasn't clear, and his face was busy smearing a crimson Rorschach splotch on the metallic plating, making it hard to confirm his suspicion.

His odds of surviving this matchup were quickly diminishing but years of training inhabited a small, still functioning part of his mind. There, was kept a library of martial drills, lifetimes of hand-to-hand combat — all too many with real lives in the balance.

As his face slid toward the wreckage of the mech's hover bucket, the increasing sensation of heat through his cheek created the linkage to reality that his brain needed, and training took over. Dropping one shoulder he pressed his blood-smeared face hard against the mech and made a tiny gap as he cleared the quad-barreled muzzle of his Rawling Midget from its holster and buried it into folds of flesh and squeezed off two rounds, mass-center of his attacker.

It is my pilot! he thought in a happy stupor even as his legs buckled, and he had to lean against the wreckage of the mech to stay vertical.

Amazingly, the man sat back up from his new position, meters away. The second charge clearly had brought him off his feet. Rutker saw now that as well as being nearly round; the pilot was easily a head and a half taller than himself.

How'd he fit into the cockpit! he wondered. Rutker, himself, was a solid two meters tall.

It was clear that the merc had had the sense to wear electro-shield body armor. Which also meant that he'd soaked up a substantial amount of the Midget's energy cell.

Not a problem. He'd seen two still attached to the other merc's vest, though he didn't relish the task of scavenging gear from just a torso.

Meanwhile, the massive bulk of the stunned pilot was still sitting there. It didn't mean he'd be getting up though.

The man's eyes rolled back, resembling two glowing dust motes set in carbon and blood-streaked flesh. And then he fell back and began to twitch.

An entire pirate army combing the landscape for him, his wife and kids holed up in a crippled starliner. An interplanetary war hanging in the balance over the retrieval of two jettisoned packages...and he was sitting now, chest deep, in a creek not fifty yards from the smoldering remains of two renegade mechs and the twitching body of one their pilots. Yeah, that seemed about right...

Rutker's mind drifted to his dad. How his father had done it. Played sleight of hand with fate for all that time. But as good as he was, it still didn't matter in the end. The Godsend that Rutker's grandfather had created had helped save a young republic and made Willem Novak a hero. But then it also killed him. Which, killed them *both*, really...

Sometimes, all it takes to bring a strong man down is a single blow. Willem had taught Rutker that...as well as a thousand other things. He took solace in the fact that his father had lived his forty some-odd years well. If not well, then at least with purpose. Protecting your family from an alien invasion was purpose enough, Rutker thought. And now, *he* was going to go make peace with them... That, too, seemed purpose enough, if not a little bittersweet.

Three wars in forty years on five separate planets. Well, one was a very large moon, but that didn't really change things much. He wondered when the quality of life you were fighting for finally succumbed to the kind of life it took to win it. But he didn't have an answer for that.

Yet here he was just the same. Living in the aftermath of so-called victory. He would have given anything for a fully loaded Phalanx trans-orbital fighter right then. That would make this a fair fight... instead of a *bug hunt*. He didn't appreciate being the bug either.

Right then, Rutker could hear only the clamoring stream. As far as his eyes could see was nothing but boulder-strewn hillside with a few scraggly trees upon it. The hillside tumbled down to a wide valley that was hazy with dust suspended in the heat emanating from its sunbaked, pale-alabaster surface.

It was almost serene in the wake of the battle but the hairs on the back of his neck were beginning to crackle. There was something still out there. Man, or machine? Creature? He wasn't sure. The hillside was full of pockets and stretched for miles. Each fold, each buckle...who knew what could disappear out there. The whole place had a spooky feeling to it, like an unholy blanket laying over the top of it all.

Now I'm just creeping myself out, he thought.

On the other hand, it could be the fact that he'd been sitting in the freezing water for several minutes and was actually beginning to feel the cold.

He stayed a few more minutes just to be certain that he'd lowered his core temperature as much as he could before the ride down the canyon and whatever lay beyond. Once he got down to the valley floor, there was nowhere to hide. He'd have to run in stealth mode for sure, otherwise he'd be visible on scans from the air, from orbit, from well-equipped ground units...

Rutker hoped beyond anything that Katherryn would make the first comms rendezvous. She'd promised him every six hours. He had had to *make* her promise. She wanted nothing to do with the possibility of bursting out radio static while he was running and hiding from half of the pirate horde that they had watched streak into the sky after their impromptu grounding. She'd radio if she could. Otherwise, he'd worry. And that wasn't good either. *Time to go.*

At least the cold water was keeping the split over his eye from swelling.

Entering the cave caused that creeping sensation to return. He did a quick recon, arms full of goodies he'd scavenged, with the ominous hulk of the Long Rifle standing, hunched, in the corner. Maybe it was the scarce lighting, but the cave looked like a temple to an ancient deity. And he was the priest not knowing what kind of creature he'd woken.

He ignored the feeling of sacrilege as he stepped up and strapped in. The dash came alive with backlit, red-on-black contortions and landscapes. Why this particular model was trimmed in Delvic, he didn't know. Being that it was the language of their sworn enemy. He'd have to muse on that later. Not coincidentally, Delvic was one of the few Rim World languages that he could struggle through. Maybe there was a thread of luck still winding its way through this impossible situation…

His eyes glanced across a set of markings hand etched into the overhead console above the heads-up display, but he couldn't make it out. They looked like mad scribblings on the wall of a long-forgotten prison, but it could have been that it was just a long time since he'd seen handwritten Delvic…

He was doing it again, he realized, subconsciously forestalling the inevitable. He needed to get going, his family and the treaty hung in the balance and every hour on this planet made success less likely.

Each whirring step felt infinitesimally better, as his body conformed to its new home in the mech. He was sure he'd be walking like it was the day after rodeo for a month when this ordeal was over.

First mile's always the hardest, he thought and flicked his left wrist back to wind the Novak up to redline. It started gliding forward in that oddly graceful manner he was accustomed to seeing. The mech was amazingly agile for all its albatross good looks.

It was time to check scans. Rutker flicked a switch, heard the pneumatic *thump* of dual air cannons as two coffee can sized projectiles shot a hundred meters into the air and splintered into twenty-four tiny whirring shadows. Suddenly, his horizon display tipped down for a scrolling 3D perspective on the surrounding terrain, the Novak's gliding gait stretched out further, more efficiently assessing the terrain ahead with the enhanced resolution.

Rutker scrutinized the image and was surprised to find a city of some sort, or at least a colony. A good-sized colony, actually. *Quiet, though,* he thought. This bore inspection. He held his breath unconsciously as a pair of trans-orbitals buzzed through the high valley haze and disappeared to the north, their passing followed seconds later by a low, distant rumble. Great, he thought, *mechs weren't bad enough, now I've got fighters just aching for a good ground-and-pound...*

Minutes later, a tight, gravelly voice reached out of the static haze in his ear buds, "Negative ROV1. No time. Christmas is northeast of the city, in the foothills... pretty broken up. We'll refer to this delta as Mongoose. Copy?"

He didn't respond. Colonel Dexx wasn't breaking up too badly, but Rutker deigned to keep the good colonel in the dark at least half as much as he did his second-in-command.

He was irritated that he still hadn't heard a peep from Katherryn. The six standard hour mark had come and gone without contact. He didn't waste time imagining all of the reasons why she wouldn't have reached out. That'd have to wait till later. He couldn't do a thing at this point and knew she could take care of herself and that the boys were with her. They were just as squirrely and drawn to mischief as he himself had been, if not more.

He threw out a quick prayer, hoping someone would hear it. Having it answered would be nice. Being back in the cockpit of his Phalanx fighter right now, doing Mach six, two hundred meters off the hard deck would also be good. Instead, it was going to take him a solid four or five hours before he was within visual of the next delta; Mongoose, he thought it was. And that was if he ran straight across the valley. *That'd be a short trip!* he thought.

There were no gulley's to speak of. No escarpment to follow. Just flat, vulnerable no-man's-land between his present location and the first of two, all-important 'diplomatic' packages, whatever that meant. Whether Katherryn was right or not, Rutker didn't believe the Colonel when he said he didn't know what was in them. With all this interest, he could only guess...

Rutker slowed the mech's pace, retarding the throttle to forty percent. Just enough to maintain operations and limited surveillance. He'd have to throttle up in a hurry to charge the cannon if, when, something came up.

What little cover he had dwindled into a couple of low hills and scattered groupings of long since burned out tree trunks. Even the, heretofore, clamoring creek had given way to a wide rabble of river rock the size and shape of human skulls. He didn't look too closely. The sheer number made it impossible, but he still couldn't bear to disprove his morbid imagination. Further on, the dry creek bed spilled out into a plain thirty kilometers across and that stretched even farther north and south. There was a vague brownish haze hanging over the whole thing that obscured the mountains in the distance.

The complete absence of scrub brush was an indicator of either high mineral content in the soil or of intelligent activity. The kind of environmentally negligent behavior that could have caused a whole city to turn into a ghost town...? Perhaps not. Still, he had to wonder what kind of ghosts lived there.

Eight standard on this planet, and he was ready to leave. Time was not a luxury he had at this point. No blips. Nothing but that creepy feeling that he was being followed, or maybe sized up? He spread the drones out, casting the net wider. Nothing but the beginning of a kind of web pattern to the flat waste of the valley floor before him. It was a vaguely unnatural pattern.

A closer look and the pattern seemed to emanate outward from the colony at the north end of the valley. And, if he wasn't mistaken, it looked as though there were some darker bits to the web, like maybe there was a subterranean feature, rather than a series of dried-up streams or canals like it had first appeared. Rutker zoomed in. The dark spots could actually be holes in the surface... If that was the case, he could end up doing some inadvertent spelunking if he didn't step with caution. The clock was ticking. Diminishing options.

"Let's get this over with. Hammer down," he said out loud to no one but the Long Rifle's SortieNet AI.

Four

The Torrent and the Lantern Door

19.004329 AC (After Construct)
Age of the Half-Orc War

The mast lurched up and then down again. Lightning burst all around, casting everything in stark white contrast, and burning the after image into D'avry's eyes. Instantly, thunder cracked so loudly it was hard to tell the difference between what he felt in his body and the deafening rumble all around him.

The stern of the boat began to slip downstream and looked as though it would depart without them until it struck hard against rock. It held, but tenuously. Cold water poured into his boots as he clung to the railing with both hands. Unconsciously, he darted a look back toward the torchlight upriver and felt a jolt of panic as he realized the unearthly firelight was *much* closer than expected.

Somehow, this pursuing craft would clear the valley in half the time than Trask and Gearlach's party had. Whether by rower's back or sail was irrelevant. He didn't guess at what it was that pursued them. He *felt* it.

The product of death and vengeance was a twisted creature. The more in life, even more so in death. *Revenant* was a term he'd heard only whispered in the halls of academy. Somehow, the idea was as certain as stone in his mind though. Still, he spared a glance downstream, towards the impassable rapids whose roaring was only obscured by the torrent of rain and thunder breaking upon their heads.

D'avry knew desperation and this is what it looked like. He didn't know why he knew that staying on the trail would end in tragedy, but he did. It was a certainty. This present course of action however seemed even more of a death wish. And, as much as he could still feel the Luck Magic, as tangible as taste or smell, it no longer felt like a pull. In fact, it felt quite the opposite.

For the first time that he could recall, it was a desperate imperative to be anywhere *but* near the source of that eerie, ghoulish light. But then, the light, too, seemed to have developed a character of its own, a now overwhelming force of presence; tainted, twisted, bitter with longing, energized by malice.

D'avry turned his attention back to the railing just as the boat lurched and ripped out of his hands. It reared up and then rocked back down just as he lost his footing. He braced to be knocked senseless in the sloshing water but was snatched back by the scruff of his neck. Only his boots still splashed in the rising waters. A huge hand gripped the rail, and the boat steadied somewhat.

"Try again now, mage," Gearlach said and pushed him half up the side of the craft, leaving D'avry to scramble the rest of the way, which he did but with little grace.

At once, gear bags began flopping over the side to land on the deck all around him. D'avry, seeing Farn struggle to board the craft much as he had, reached down to grasp his cloak, but when he pulled, the boat shifted again, landing both of them on deck in an undignified heap.

The two struggled to gain their feet, eyes locking momentarily. Farn clearly perturbed and ready to share his mind when a moment's lapse in the wind and rain carried a deep thudding rumble of something that was definitely *not* thunder.

The rhythmic booming was the not-so-distant sound of drums. Pounding in time, it was mesmerizing, out of place in the chaos. But there was something else that captured D'avry's attention. Somehow, he could tell that the drum skins were new and that they were...*human*. He lurched for the rail, struggling against the urge to vomit. Bile filled his throat, and he screwed his eyes shut hard against the rising sickness when a new sensation took over. A cool, clean rush of energy that coursed through him and then vanished just as quickly.

He looked around. The boat lurched wildly, but with renewed clarity he realized that it was fortifying magic that had bolstered him. *Was it the priest?* He turned to see Farn, cross-legged on the deck, his hood pulled over his bald head, bent over to protect the pages of his book from the rain and splashing water.

D'avry wasn't sure that the water would affect the pages but maybe the tome was only waterproof when it was closed? He realized something else, the buff had dulled the effect of terror and revulsion that had gripped him. Too many things were going on to have to worry about dark magic aiding whatever unholy power was bearing down upon them.

The boat bucked but still it seemed pinned to the shore, stuck as if by anchor. All the companions were on deck as far as D'avry could tell. Except for Gearlach. The huge warrior was pushing with all his formidable strength, chest-deep in the storm-swollen waters and being thrashed like a child's toy.

The drums grew louder, and the glow of unholy, green fire brightened through the fog of rain. D'avry's blood ran cold as he saw the light shoot upward and then separate into individual streaks across the chaos of swirling carbon that was the sky. The dozen or so comet-like streaks seemed to slow as they drew overhead and then quickly began to grow again as they plummeted down in their direction.

"Cover! Cover!" he screamed mere seconds before a volley of flaming arrows buried themselves in the deck and the water and rocks of the shoreline.

The arrows boiled in flame whether stuck in the boat's deck or struck through rocks beneath the rushing waters. D'avry's eyes grew wide but he only had seconds to think before another volley rent the heavens.

The companions seemed locked in place, staring heavenward

now at the second wave of incoming missiles. Rain battered their faces as lightning burst again from the clouds, casting everything white and then abruptly into darkness. The arrows, lost from view, still coursed with certainty toward them.

Thunder exploded and the boat broke free with one last heave from Gearlach, struggling to keep his head above the frothing current. He leaped for a drain hole at the deck-line and was pulled away with the craft just as the volley came crashing down, thudding into the shore where the boat had been just a heartbeat before. The massive warrior pulled himself, with his waterlogged armor, the rest of the way over the railing and crashed to the deck, eyes wide and sucking lungsful of air.

D'avry almost breathed a sigh of relief but then movement caught his eye. Farn scurrying backward, away from the tome he'd only just used as a shield from the onslaught of orcish arrows. There was one stuck dead center in its metal bound cover. It crackled and hissed violently, alive with the dark energy. The book itself seemed to shudder on the slick deck, or maybe it was a trick of the eyes in all the chaos and failing light? D'avry couldn't be sure, but then the boat rocked, casting them all against the railings as it crested a shoal and then dropped into faster moving water.

They'd got their wish, now what? D'avry wondered as he scanned the deck and realized that there were no oars in sight. They had nothing to guide them or protect them from oncoming rocks!

The antiquated craft gathered speed toward a precipice they all knew was there but couldn't see. Gliding forward, another volley of flaming arrows peppered the waters leaving ominous glowing beacons below the surface as they passed.

D'avry tried to account for all the crew once more before the next volley arrived but felt like he was missing something. He saw Gearlach of course, now standing with one hand on his axe hilt and the other gripping the mast, easily taking in the wild undulations beneath his feet.

Suddenly, it struck D'avry, something that should have been obvious but maybe had been obscured by Gearlach's civil, almost introspective demeaner. He was half-orc or something to that effect. That could account for his size but there was much, much more to the picture before him besides the obvious contradiction of his nature.

The realization made him wonder again at their pursuer and the nature of that malevolent presence. Still, time was of the essence. He scanned the craft again. Farn was there, seated with his back pressed against the railing, eyes transfixed on the book with the flaming arrow stuck through it, terror, and fascination warring on his bearded face. To his right, the other two, Liggo and Volkreek, were positioned at the stern, each grasping a rail and standing in a low crouch to let the boat rock beneath them. Their attention was wholly upriver, on the light that had grown close enough to easily distinguish an individual torch but somehow had become much too bright for that now.

D'avry, too, fixed his eyes on the pursuing craft, just as bodies began to hurl themselves overboard to every side. Some trailing flames that he knew could not be quenched by the rushing waters. It looked as though the substance of the flame had somehow ignited the craft itself, along with its crew. In fact, it appeared that the entire craft was engulfed in the blazing greenish flame.

D'avry was dumbfounded at the luck, but then he had an intimate relationship with luck. This was by no means over. As soon as the thought crossed his mind, a movement in the deepest shadows of the flaming craft caught his eye. Not the frantic flailing of yet another unfortunate orc, but something else.

A darkness pressed forward from within the flames, surrounded by their intensity but still somehow cloaked in shadow. A figure emerged, stepping forward to grasp the mast.

Half again the height of any of the ill-fated crew, though it was hard to tell from this distance of maybe two-hundred yards. The dark silhouette was still clearly larger than even Gearlach. In fact, D'avry thought, there was a striking similarity of form to the half-orc, as if Gearlach himself stood aboard the flaming craft.

The boat lurched, and D'avry lost track of their pursuer as the rain redoubled its effort and was followed by yet another crash of lightning and instantaneous peels of deafening thunder. He wondered if he'd ever hear again.

The heart of the rapids was drawing close now. Still, something nagged...Trask! The Librarian, where was he? And beyond that, what was his role anyway? D'avry had still not been able to sort out what it was exactly that he was there to do.

The boat pumped up and down, tossing in the waves as D'avry's mind raced to pull the pieces together. But as much as he tried, nothing would connect. He gripped the rail and pulled himself toward the half-man, half-orc known as Gearlach. Knowing that at any moment they might crash into a boulder or drop over a falls, he inched cautiously.

Indeed, as if reading his thoughts, the bow arced upward, paused, and then crashed down again as the craft rolled over a larger rapid and smashed into a boiling wall of white that cascaded over the bow of the craft. The vessel, though, was made for the river and allowed the flow to wash over it and spill out the sides by way of the large oval drain holes in the rails. D'avry only hoped that the hull would handle things as effectively...

He resumed his trek toward the bow, hand over hand until he was within shouting range of his beastly companion.

"Why?" he yelled. Gearlach didn't turn but spoke in a voice that carried easily over the chaos as his eyes continued to scan the waters ahead in the near blackness of what was now an epically miserable morning.

"If you mean the craft behind us, it's complicated."

"Try me," D'avry yelled. "And where's Trask?"

The boat lurched again as it first slammed into a large rock shelf, and then, while being pushed upward with the force of the river behind, began taking water over the stern. Liggo and Volkreek scrambled forward as it seemed that the boat might sink right then and there, when suddenly it shifted. Sliding portside, it crashed back down, grinding the length of the starboard side before slipping back into the main current. Water sloshed on the deck boot-high as it gushed from the drains that D'avry now silently thanked the builder for. How much more the craft could take was anyone's guess.

D'avry returned his attention to Gearlach, who smiled as the wind whipped sopping cords of thick black hair across his rock-hewn face.

"Trask is a God!" he yelled over the gale, smiling almost maniacally.

"A what?" he asked, a look of shock etched on his face as he tried to maintain eye contact while desperately clutching the rail. The craft bounded down a short section of rapids.

"A Ghodt! And a Librarian." Seeing the anticipated look of utter confusion, he continued, "Graeburn Trask is... *was*, a librarian for a powerful orc chieftain." He motioned with his head back upriver.

"Ghodt are considered to be gifted with," and he paused as if weighing words, "awareness... of future events. Not foresight, but something close to it. They see signs," he said this last shaking his head in resignation.

Another series of whoops and dips interrupted the conversation before he continued.

"Trask has been in the employ of the chieftain N'Bruyyh for years. Forced employ. The chieftain has won battles and made advancements using Trask's insights. You probably wouldn't know, but there has been an unsteady peace between the Orcish clans of the Northern Sweep for a moon cycle now, about twenty-four winters. Trask has seen a sign that that peace could end. N'Bruyyh means to capitalize on that knowledge. Position himself as the head of *all* clans. Something forbidden for as long as the orc have kept chronicle."

Gearlach's grip tightened on the mast in the dim light.

"If that happens, the peace which required much effort on behalf of all the clans will be nullified. Replaced with a single focus. The annihilation of mankind in its entirety. The only thing that orcs hate more than other orcs, it seems, are humans…and maybe drougehnn," he said this last as an afterthought. "This is the only end by which N'Bruyyh can hold at bay the differences amongst the clans and draw them together long enough to solidify his reign."

Gearlach fixed D'avry with a level stare, scratched at a spot on his neck where wet leather was wearing the skin raw. "We thought we had ended that possibility."

"When you freed Trask," D'avry put in.

"When I slayed N'Bruyyh!" Gearlach growled, lip curled in disgust and frustration, revealing the first hint D'avry had seen of the beast within.

"Whatever darkness he's pledged himself to, he's much more than a ghost. Though, I suspect, Goriahh had a hand in this. She's grown strong in the years since I began my search for her," he said, cooling down to just a simmering boil…for now.

The pause in the conversation gave them both a chance to cast their eyes aft. The green glow, which had been growing closer, now seemed a far way off. Perhaps still at the top of the rapids behind them. And then the light blinked out as if on cue as the rapids careened away with the canyon, leaving them to stare at indistinguishable tree shapes on the dimly lit hillside beyond.

Apparently, the dark power that protected the orc chieftain hadn't extend to his boat and crew. There was silence for a minute as the two separately registered the fact that they had somehow, not only avoided an encounter with the revenant chieftain but had also managed to not be smashed to pieces or drowned in the process of blindly navigating an impassable section of river while bearing the brunt of nature's impressively malevolent whimsy.

D'avry sheltered his eyes with one prune-like hand, squinting through the wan light to make out his surroundings. He was haggard, still freezing, but in the moment that had been somehow forgotten. He was reminded now. The emotional void that remained where terror had held sway for what seemed like hours drained away to leave little to consider but the physical.

"She sits lower," Liggo offered with his usual thickly consonanted speech. He still had to raise his voice to be heard only now it was just the din of rain, rather than the roar of the rapids. Stepping away from the stern of the craft towards the other two, he swept the hair out of his face with a deft flick of his hand, causing it to flare out at his neckline which in turn made him look once again like a pudgy bird-of-prey as he glanced from one to the other and back again.

"Sinking," he croaked, crouching slightly, and padding his hands downward to simulate a settling sort of movement. Gearlach and D'avry locked eyes and then scanned the river just beyond the railings. It was evident that the man was right; the river was running just below the drain ports at the gunnel. *Much* higher than before. Not a good sign.

Though the river had smoothed somewhat, the sky was still not entirely quiet. A steady rain had replaced the torrent from before, but at least now there was enough light to navigate properly. D'avry hoped to see sky again soon. He hoped to dry off, warm himself by a fire and fill his hollow stomach with brook trout or hare or grouse or ground squirrel even, though he found them to be mostly bones and fleas. He still had the taste of river grass in his mouth he realized with irritation, though now it was decidedly less appetizing than before.

He doubted that any of those thoughts of comfort were likely, though. The revenant warlord was certainly not going to be deterred by some foul weather and turbulent water if death itself was not an obstacle. They really should put a lot of river between here and where they finally stopped long enough to regroup.

But, with the condition of the boat, they could not carry on long. They had to put in now. However, they still didn't have oars, just the steering oar strapped to the stern, which he doubted even worked.

And then there was the issue of the Ghodt; Graeburn Trask.

"Gearlach. Where again did you say the librarian went?"

"For my coin, I'd say that it was Trask that instigated that bit of mayhem upriver." The muscles in Gearlach's jaw tensed so that the striations were visible even through heavy, black stubble and the dim light.

"I'd expect that he'll be making his way down the portage trail. We should do our best to join him and be on our way," he said in that low, smooth, serious tone.

As an acolyte, D'avry recalled mimicking one of the older brothers of the soldiery who had a similar voice. At the time he'd found it comically self-important. And perhaps it was. But coming from Gearlach, a man that was literally half-monster and could have likely used that other man as a toothpick, it sounded different.

D'avry's mind idled on Gearlach's words but didn't quite comprehend them. In that moment, the pull, the Astrig Ka'a was moving.

"What's your... affiliation, with the two? Trask and N'Bruyyh?" D'avry asked. And then, "Can this be stopped?"

Gearlach, who had moved to the stern and was untying the steering oar, paused, and then returned to his work in silence.

It was Farn who spoke next. His voice was anything but the

cool, measured calm of the group's leader.

"We must ashore. Make sure N'Bruyyh doesn't get a hold of Trask again, and…something must be done about this," he said, this last while looking pointedly at the book of spells laying in the middle of the deck.

Here it quite clearly *did* shudder under its own power, most likely because of the still flaming and hissing arrow stuck dead-center in its metal-bound cover. How they'd managed to ignore that in the intervening time was unclear. Sensory overload was the only thing D'avry could think of.

Farn's hands were clasped tightly together, he breathed warm air into them, rubbed them together and then shook his head as if passing judgement. "This will not hold. And I don't know what will happen when one or the other magics wins."

D'avry had to agree. The book bounced and jittered now with increasing fervency. Liggo and Volkreek had flanked the priest in the intervening time, making the three look like a matched set. Their attention, too, transfixed upon the flaming tome.

The Astrig Ka'a twisted in D'avry's gut like a tapeworm, though he tried to ignore it. Again, the *feel* of the compulsion seemed to illuminate the direction that things would go. It was a sickening sensation now, like the moment when you realize that your most recent meal has turned on you and you'd best make a mad dash for the bushes and hope there's some lamb's ear in the underbrush.

Since D'avry couldn't recall his last meal, it was the compulsion for sure. But part of him wondered if it wasn't something else as well. The thought that a war for the ages might be stirring. An all-out human and orc battle for supremacy.

The gravity of that thought… He wasn't sure what idea he liked least. That he would be forced to band together with this tattered band of adventurers set against an unkillable enemy with an army of orcs at his disposal and allied to who-knew-what kind of dark magic? Or the idea that he might not?

In the intervening three years since the Astrig Ka'a had whisked him away from betrothal to a runaway girl-who-would-be-queen, he'd seldom been left to choose his own destiny and would be stunned beyond reason if it actually came to that. The irony of it left a bitter taste in his mouth...

D'avry found his mind wondering to the events of that night but was interrupted by a feeling, an almost imperceptible shift at the core of his being. *Something...* was different. He couldn't place it.

As Gearlach worked the steering oar to coax the vessel toward a sandy stretch of shoreline just ahead of a confluence of two forks of the river, D'avry began to take a mental inventory. First, of his surroundings, the creaking mast, ropes wet, knots thudding softly with the boat's gentle rocking. Then his garments, the chafing around his knees, thighs, armpits, and neck. The weight of his drenched jacket and hooded tunic dragging against aching muscles. He looked at his hands and then at his square-toed, black leather boots; the way that water bubbled out between the soles and uppers when he shifted his weight. And then he sensed it more firmly.

His stomach dropped a little as he pulled open his jacket, grabbed the overlapping hems of his tunic and pulled them aside, baring the lean muscles of his chest and stomach to the bitter elements. And there, in the middle of his chest where his heart should be, he found a window of sorts. It was like a lantern door made from some kind of crystalline material that was mostly translucent with soft angular lines running through it, interspersed with hairline veins of gold.

It was seamless where the door frame connected to his skin, bone, and muscles. So much so that there seemed to be no clearly defined point where one stopped and the others began. But there was no mistaking what it was; a window into what should have been his heart. *Irony again*, he mused darkly.

The craft grew quiet as the other companions took in the

oddity of the moment, shifting nervously where they stood. But D'avry noticed something. He saw that the window was in fact a door, *exactly* like what would be found on a box lantern. Inset in the frame on one side was a small golden circle for a handle. So, he opened it.

And inside was darkness. Not in the sense of evil, but in the sense of complete void, like a starless night. His mouth was bone-dry. He licked his lips and choked a little while trying to swallow. His eyes darted to the book with the arrow stuck in its cover, still shuddering but now beginning to blacken the deck around it for the heat of the flame that was no longer squelched by rain or sloshing waters.

Before anyone could protest, D'avry dove for the book, grasping both the binding and the flaming shaft imbedded in it and squeezed them impossibly together. No one budged. He fought with every sinew of muscle to compress the articles into a smaller and smaller package until, once the conjoined pieces were just the size of maybe a large apple, he pulled them into the gaping void in his chest, and slammed the crystalline door shut.

D'avry gasped with exertion, lying on his back on the slick deck, eyes staring at his palms to assess the damage. They widened with amusement when he realized they weren't scored to the bone. His hands flopped to the side as he stared up at the gray turmoil of the post-storm sky, just lightening as the clouds thinned.

The rain had stopped, replaced by a hard mist, and staring back down at him were the companions. All but Trask, who was presumably on the portage trail, even now making his way back to the party after sabotaging the undead, revenant, orc chieftain's boat, or his archers, or both. Apparently, librarian meant something else entirely in Trask's culture than it did in D'avry's.

No one spoke. Each just stared down at him. It was an odd

moment to realize that Volkreek, of all the companions, was the only one whom he'd never heard speak in their short but meaningful acquaintance.

He continued that streak. It was Liggo who broke the silence with a whisper,

"It's inside," he said, and then finding his voice, "I can see it still...still burning?" he observed, his accent even thicker than usual as if he was using all his cognitive ability to comprehend the sight before him.

D'avry dipped his chin to look down at his chest. The thief was right. The burning book was clearly evident behind the window. It shivered and jolted violently but seemed somehow suspended, tumbling slowly end over end as if falling down a never-ending shaft into the core of the earth itself.

Farn's jaw tensed, his eyes narrowing as he spoke, "Why would you do that?" And then shivering and shaking his head in shock and anger he repeated "Why, would you do that!"

"I don't know," D'avry answered honestly. "It's the Astrig Ka'a; the Luck Magic. It does what it wants. I'm just along for the ride. I mean, I participate or I'm a conduit of some sort, but I don't direct it. I wish I could make heads or tails, but to be honest, I can't divine a purpose," he said breathlessly, shaking his head in futility.

Farn stared at him flatly. "Is it contained then? You have dark magic and light magic; that's a very ancient..." His eyes clouded a bit, "...a very important, very *holy* book. It's... ancestral," he finished, seeming to bite the words off as if choking down essence of bitterroot.

Clearly there was an emotional component to the value of the object. In the present moment D'avry was uncertain how to tease out that convoluted thread but he supposed there'd be time enough for that later. He hoped there would be.

Though D'avry had barely seen two decades in his lifetime, he'd learned the lesson of time. All things waited on it. And in time, all things *could* be revealed. But only if you worked at it.

"I will be a...proper...steward. As best the Astrig Ka'a will allow," he assured him, but inwardly, secretly there was the barest thrill.

There had been a certain energy that poured into him with the transaction. And, as odd as this present incarnation of the randomizing force he'd come to accept, maybe even embrace, was, he couldn't help but wonder what the long-term effects might be. Was he just a vessel, or was he participating somehow?

Words sprang into his mind unbidden.

Unity. Bond. Balance. Framework. Focus.

D'avry wanted to understand but he knew that there were other, more pressing issues. Where was Trask? And even more importantly, where was N'Bruyyh? What could they even do against something that couldn't die, or at least, not die in the traditional way?

He couldn't recall anything from his studies that spoke to disposing of a revenant soul. But then, this chieftain seemed to have tapped into something else and beyond that, there was a feel of inevitability to the entire situation. And he still didn't know how Gearlach fit into all of this, or how the other members of the team came to be involved.

So many questions. Not the least of which was this new twist, the magical lantern door and the thing that now resided within it. Inside of him.

Five

Gains and Losses

The boat lurched as it slid along the coarse sand of another small spit clinging to the base of the forest, every bit as vertical as the take-out upriver. Only here, they were in the protected waters of an eddy current, the fast-moving water closer to the far shore.

The remaining members leapt over the railings, splashing through the shallows to push and pull the river craft ashore the little that they could. They had no rope to secure it. No anchor but the belly full of water that made it near impossible to move. All they could hope to do was beach the craft as best they could. Someone would have to mind the boat. Maybe two of the companions as no one but Gearlach could manage it alone.

Farn put his shoulder to the work but without conviction. His greatest weapon had been destroyed. Or stolen, depending on how you looked at it. He may not have any magic ability outside of the power of the tome. D'avry felt a pang of sympathy and not the least bit of guilt. He hadn't really had a choice and the likelihood was that the tome was destroyed already and quite possibly could have destroyed the party if left untended.

D'avry surveyed their new location. To one side was a small clearing right before the tree line and a formation of rock that flanked the trail. Though it was wide enough to accommodate a wagon, it was steep, deeply rutted and choked with tall grass, which caused him again to question whether much trade moved through here at all. Lack of use was usually an ill-sign.

D'avry was, however, pleased to see that the miserable, driving mist had diminished somewhat and with it the wind. Still no sunlight and none seemed likely, but he would take what he could get. Puffs of vapor drifted from his lips as he contemplated the gnawing ache in his belly. Something new lived there. A warm energy inside him that seemed to smooth out the bite somewhat. As he jumped ashore, he'd felt a sensation, almost as though the ground itself had lurched up to meet him. He could imagine tiny shockwaves shooting out from where he landed, like ripples in a pond. No one else seemed to notice, so D'avry just tucked this thought away.

The forest smelled damp as he scanned the shoreline for Trask, but the ex-librarian to the undead revenant orc chieftain was nowhere to be found. He was also only mildly surprised to see that Liggo, the dark haired Thadding man with the thick accent, was gone. Volkreek the Silent, as D'avry now thought of him, had jogged down to the far end of the shore where the other fork met this broader stretch.

Gearlach had gone upstream to scan the water and the trees for any sign of danger there. His axe still hung at his hip but the formed leather covers that protected its wicked crescent blade and fang-like spike had been folded back to provide instant access.

The axe did indeed have an ethereal glow about it, but darkly, the way of moonlit stone between shadow. It had been harder to see before but now D'avry had no problem making out every line of scrollwork, every curve, the line of each overlapping leather strip, knot, tassel, even the tiny charms dangling from the axe handle, the many-sided geometric cage that held a gem within it.

He was drawn into that gem, felt himself being pulled towards it as it glowed with greater intensity, a warmth surrounding him. He shook himself to snap out of what felt like a dream. Heat rising in his cheeks, D'avry glanced around quickly to make sure that no one saw him standing there dumbly. This band of adventurers seemed to operate as a pretty slick unit, and he was definitely the outsider. He didn't want to appear anymore useless than how he was feeling just then.

Luckily, no one appeared to notice or care, so he allowed

his thoughts to return to the experience from moments ago. There was just no way that he could have seen that far with that amount of detail. Gearlach was an easy hundred paces away but somehow D'avry could sense the magic inside the axe. Feel the emanating waves of power reaching out to tussle each tiny hair of his body like… *Whoa, not again,* he thought, forcibly pulling back this new layer of perception.

Even as he did so, he felt something else, something further beyond the trailhead. D'avry took in the river, he was surprised to notice that it was full of debris now… tree trunks, planks, driftwood. Too, it appeared transformed from the clear, almost tropic blue to something resembling dirty milk. Probably the same ash, he realized, that had coated the band at their introduction. Apparently, the maelstrom that had exploded over their heads earlier had not been relegated to just the immediate valley but spread further upriver as well.

Maybe the storm had just been a coincidence and not some part of the dark power aiding N'Bruyyh? He put that line of reasoning aside for later. His eyes darted from water to shore to tree to trail and then settled on the shadows obscuring the far side of the river.

He saw no sign of the revenant chieftain. Perhaps he was waiting for a better opportunity or possibly gathering forces. That would be a mixed blessing. It meant that maybe he respected his quarry a little more than D'avry had initially thought, or maybe it meant he'd got what he came for — Trask. That thought was beyond worrisome.

He hadn't come to any conclusions on what that might mean, but Gearlach seemed to be quite certain about it. The ushering in of a new era, one where mankind was either eradicated, or at best a slave-class to the orc. Whether or not that would be the case, it certainly meant a new era of warfare, and where there was war, there was death and pestilence, starvation, and injustice; atrocities perpetrated by both sides. A dark new era indeed.

The thief-spy, Liggo reappeared as from the ether. Apparently, he did have a knack for being quiet, in spite of his bulk. It reaffirmed D'avry's suspicion about his vocation. Thief, by profession of course, not opportunity. Though that would remain to be seen.

There was a difference he was told, though where D'avry was from there was no guild for thieves. They were hung, plain and simple. Whether it was for stealing a loaf of bread or the King's own daughter. D'avry winced at that thought. Still, his people would starve to death before they took something that did not belong to them, possessions not people, he corrected himself. Still, D'avry had grown accustomed to how different cultures could be from place to place.

D'avry studied him as he was tending to his gear. He was mildly surprised that for the first time, the knives he had sheathed behind his back seemed to be traced by a now familiar glow. He knew that this new awareness was not the Astrig Ka'a directly but some new imbuement, a by-product of the lantern door or its contents, which was of course a direct product of the Luck Magic. But his sense told him that the door served another purpose. There was more to unlock there. Words flooded his mind again:

Unity. Bond. Balance. Framework. Focus. D'avry massaged his temples as if the action would make it stop or make all the meaningless sensory input resolve into focus. Maybe he was still just a little hung over? Or maybe the rush of danger was just wearing off and he was feeling a bit rummy?

Gearlach returned from the upper strand, striding over rocks stacked above the water's edge in large black and burnished metal boots. His matching greaves gleamed darkly in the low light, his black cloak, flapping like a banner, hung from hammered bronze pins on his chest armor. Volkreek, too, approached but swiftly, in silence, from the lower stretch. He seemed to flow like mercury over the obstacles, unbothered by the hand-and-a-half sword and bow crossed upon his back. They were two very different figures, but both, unmistakably deadly. D'avry breathed in an anxious sigh, wondering what kind of company he was keeping.

It was then that he realized Farn was still waist high in the frigid water, minding the craft in case they needed to make a hasty departure — as depressing as that would be with a hull full of water.

He appeared even more glum if that were possible. The loss of his ancestral tome seemed to have robbed him of his sardonic wit. With the vigorous scrubbing they'd received over the course of the last hour and a half, D'avry now saw that the priest was perhaps in his late thirties, on the old side for an adventurer, which meant he was either very good at his vocation or had been forced into it late in life. D'avry could empathize. However, neither of the two observations felt proper. The man, though bald, was handsome in a hardy way, and had the bearing of a soldier though he was obviously of a religious order of some kind. He was too rigid to be a mystic. D'avry assumed priest but that was not necessarily a foregone conclusion.

There was an inner fortitude to the men from Thadding that seemed to be less of a product of culture as something borne from hardship. D'avry had no recollection of Thadding or Far-Thadding as places where he'd been an accidental tourist, borne along by the whim of the Astrig Ka'a. But there were a dizzying number of instances where he received very little insight as to his exact location before popping back out of that reality and into another. He had no proof that it was anything as exotic as that, different realities, but they might as well be, as different as one place and circumstance seemed to be from another.

D'avry, for a time, had been convinced that there was no actual relevance to anything he did. That he was simply the victim of magic gone wrong, or maybe a curse of some sort, possibly at the king's behest... That thought made him twinge inside in a place where his heart might have been if it wasn't now the domicile of a miniature burning book and flaming arrow, behind a magical door made of crystal and gold... The Astrig Ka'a was certainly strange of ways.

Nevertheless, he was secretly holding a thin hope, that there was some corrective action in effect. That the universe and time itself were somehow being mended, one story at a time, moment by moment, until the mechanism could be set right. A romantic thought but one that D'avry was surprised had taken unlikely, if not substantial root, like a pine tree growing from a cleft in a cliff wall.

The luck mage looked again to Farn when suddenly a glimmer caught his eye. Or maybe it wasn't even something he saw, but there was definitely something in the river. He felt himself drawn in again, saw the faint glow and instantly knew what he was looking at.

He spun towards Volkreek and pointed to a floating mass of driftwood just clearing the edge of the spit. The ranger nodded affirmation and with the efficiency of movement borne from a lifetime had his fishing line affixed to an arrow for that purpose and was charging into the shallows to get a closer shot. D'avry rushed further down shore, ready to leap in if Volkreek's arrow went awry.

The arrow arced through the air, line whipping behind it and in the span of seconds the ranger was pulling in his line, masterfully managing tension to ensure that the arrow persuaded the drifting debris shoreward without pulling it apart. D'avry rushed forward toward the swift water, deeper and deeper until he was at the point that he'd need to swim to continue and at that moment the pad of drifting refuse, made up of hacked logs and branches, caught the eddy and spiraled inward, losing the arrow and line but now captured by the contra current.

It floated, first shoreward, then toward the boat where

Farn was standing, turning just a bit blue. D'avry waded back to shore, not giving the object of their effort a second glance. Instead, he looked at Farn. "Perhaps we are even for now."

Farn, his face screwed up in obvious skepticism, looked over the pad of refuse, which was not actually *hacked up* branches, but rather *chewed up* branches and logs. Slowly a look of comprehension crept across his face. The other companions seemed as confused as he had been, all but Gearlach who as usual seemed a man apart. His arms folded across his barrel chest, one eyebrow raised and a shadow of a smile betraying his normally stoic composure.

Farn's face broke into an amused grin. He waded through the flotsam and grabbed one of the longer sticks. It was as long as he was tall, the circumference of an axe handle except at one end where the last foot-and-a-half was roughly wrist thick. As he pulled it from the water, darkened symbols could be seen to adorn the length of it and there was a blue-green gem, the size of a man's thumb and vaguely opalescent, set prominently in the head of what was now clearly a staff.

D'avry smiled stiffly, battling the urge to change his mind and keep it for himself. "Do you think you can make use of this?"

"Is this what it seems to be? If so, I have to admit that I have no training for this." The priest pondered the staff in his hands looking somewhat dumbfounded and then his expression turned oddly subdued. "This form of magic is not rightly... *condoned* by my order."

He darted a furtive look at Volkreek and Liggo. D'avry would have to sort out the meaning of that later.

"I can teach you some. I believe our circumstances demand a certain amount of... adaptation. Besides, I know this piece."

Farn's eyes widened again but retained a hint of skepticism.

"I thought it was lost forever. Beavers," he said amusedly, assuming that that cleared it all up. Farn didn't take the bait.

He was much more intent upon the possibilities, good and bad, before him.

"What's it's, um, purpose?" he asked, seeming uncomfortable in having to ask the younger man for information about things magical.

"It is an aid for casting, of course. You will have to memorize your spells from here on out. But it also has some defensive properties. Against magic mostly and *some* physical damage which is why I was unable to re-acquire it once it had been taken from me." D'avry cocked his head, thinking. "There must be some latent arcane ability within those flat-tailed river pirates... I should make a note to look into that at some later date. But, regarding the staff, objects of power are largely influenced by those who wield them. There may be...properties to the staff that you interact with in a way that I could not. And vice versa."

"So, you really don't know," the man said, making his way out of the shallows with long slow strides and then shaking water and grit out of his sandals.

"No. That's not what I said," D'avry replied, crossing his arms across his chest. "I just don't know what it will do for you."

The priest nodded with understanding though D'avry guessed he was wondering the same thing that D'avry himself had been. There was no certainty that he'd even be able to wield the staff. As with all things magic, there was a chance of failure. And failure, as it pertained to magic, was often fatal, or worse.

"Don't worry. If a beaver can do it, so can you," D'avry provided with a disarming smile.

Farn shot him hard look.

Gearlach stepped in, his voice easy, authoritative, certain as stone. Liggo. Establish a perimeter and then scan up the adjoining river a ways," he said, pointing in the direction of the fork. "Make sure there are no landings or crossings we need to consider in defending ourselves. The main fork here may force most to the trail but the other could deliver an overwhelming force in minutes. Farn. Before, you were able to conjure wards. Work with D'avry to see what you can do to provide us an early warning against any threats. However, I do not wish to snare our librarian if he manages to find us. But do not harm yourself in the process. Trust your own self. I think our young mage here is too familiar with forces most might fail to apprehend..." He said this last looking at D'avry, fixing him with an expression that was either amusement, disdain, or concern. D'avry found it hard to tell which. Maybe it was all three?

Gearlach turned to look back up the trail, "I will seek out our lost companion. If I'm not back by nightfall tend to your people, for dark times will indeed be upon us." He arced an open palm in front of himself and glanced heavenward — an abbreviated version of the moon prayer, a plea for mercy against injustice.

"I do not think the chieftain remains in the valley, but he will not be gone long. N'Bruyyh is nothing if not shrewd. He will use surprise, terrain, and overwhelming force to achieve his ends." The sun was still too shrouded by cloud cover to distinguish direction, so Gearlach unwrapped a leather thong that was tied about his wrist with a murky stone attached to it. He held it to the sky sifting right and then left until it lit up when aligned with the sun's position. Not man's magic, just nature's own way of providing assistance to those shrewd enough to seek her wisdom. It was the tool of a seaman, a navigator. He wrapped it back up with speed and precision and trotted off toward the trail.

D'avry was still trying to unlock the specifics of this band of adventurers, and the idiosyncrasies of its leader. He was clearly well-educated and carried the manner of many campaigns about him. Where would a half-orc, half-man receive the opportunity for that manner of training, D'avry wondered? He would have been shunned by both races. And shunned would have been a polite reaction in most kingdoms.

As the thoughts tumbled through his head, he was vaguely aware of a growing weight in his upper pocket. D'avry reached inside his jacket and was surprised to find the odd coin was still there. He was sure it'd been lost during the chaos of their flight down the rapids. It seemed strange to him, but the coin felt almost alive in his hand, however, he did not bring it out right away. A suspicion was forming in his mind, and he wanted the opportunity to bring it to light.

"Gearlach. Wait..."

The monstrous black form paused and turned to face him again.

"You'll need this," he said, pulling the coin from an inside pocket of his jacket and flipping it casually in the soldier's direction. *Soldier*, he'd decided, not warrior.

Without delay, a flash of black whipped between them and whisked away with the coin in its claws. The raven flew up slope, coming to rest atop a barren, sun-bleached pine several hundred paces away. Not toward the portage trail, but uphill.

Gearlach masked his surprise by smiling slyly back at D'avry, a look that was both endearing and terrifying. He gave a curt nod, and then jogged off silently into the forest in that direction.

Totem, spirit, familiar... harbinger? D'avry didn't know what the bird was exactly but felt a surge of hope. Maybe the fates were conspiring in a way that would have some visible result this time... He dashed that thought and gave it a good stomping before it took root. His experience told him differently. And yet...? One thing was for certain, the lantern door had changed things in what seemed to be a positive way.

His way with magic had always been one of intuition, usually a foolish musing followed by foolish action but sometimes, those actions paid off. He'd discovered most of his magic out of necessity and in the moment, such as the spontaneous flame and the invisibility spell he'd used earlier. The Astrig Ka'a was an entity all its own.

He felt that that had very little to do with him or any innate ability he possessed. Usually, he felt it more a curse than anything else. But its effects were surprising and sometimes, though few and far between, even enjoyable. It just meant that he was doomed to a life of uncertainty and for the most part, aloneness. An image of a girl with freckles on her porcelain skin and tightly curled strawberry-blonde locks flashed through his mind and burst into vapor. The after image was of her standing alone at the base of a vast, spreading oak.

He rubbed his eyes as if to clear away the grit of sleep and breathed in deep through his nose and then out. He pried his thoughts away from the past. Struggling over the hollowness that had abandoned his stomach and was now occupying his chest. That thought reminded him of the lantern door. There was some untapped potential there.

With it, he felt energetic, almost restless in a subtly powerful way. And there was darkness there, too, like a too visible trap. Was that the real danger or just a distraction? A treble hook with an invisible string. He'd have to be very aware of any attachments before deciding on a course of action.

The ability to discern magical instruments was intriguing. He believed it was the workmanship that he could see, not the magic itself. That would be like seeing gravity. It was everywhere, so how could you see anything else? Or maybe it was density, an aggregation of magical power? He wondered these things, but his mind moved elsewhere when he found no purchase for his arguments.

D'avry spared a glance away from the forest. He realized now that he had been staring into it vacantly again, hand resting on the crystal and gold lantern door beneath his tunic. Blinking with surprise he cinched his jacket tight, pulling it close about his neck as he brought his hood up. His breath, clouds of vapor leaking into the chill air. Night would be coming in due course.

A dozen steps away, Farn had laid the staff on a large rock

and was cautiously inspecting it from top to bottom. He had an expression that matched D'avry's feelings exactly — wonder, fear, tempered excitement. It was time to see how adept Farn would be as a pupil, he thought, chuckling inwardly. He was certain that the priest would hate every minute of it.

Set up the wards, don't get killed in the process, he thought. Simple enough. The mental heavy-lifting of what the Astrig-Ka'a was doing, how to utilize this newfound power or curse and what part he'd have in circumventing the annihilation of his race would have to wait until later...

Six

Collapse

00.000001 BC (Before Construct)
Dawn of the Construct

The Long Rifle was taking long, loping strides across the exposed valley floor. The smooth, flat surface along with high-res drone imagery allowing it to push upwards of thirty percent over max speed. Rutker didn't know that that was possible until just now. With the mech doing all the work and still having to close another forty kilometers, he was taking a minute to perform something of a personal inventory.

Putting the pieces together from the initial attack on the *Xandraitha's Hope*, and then the speed at which the attackers followed them into unknown geo-political territory. It was clear why they were forced down here; there was no one around. That was beyond unlikely in the universe as he knew it.

Intelligent beings claimed real estate. It was a physical law as certain as gravity. War, strife, and danger were the only deterrents for any length of time. This planet surely had a history that deserved some sorting out. In fact, it might not be smart to wait for some more convenient time. There could be pressing matters that they were just not privy to. Another unknown. Well, he needed to get his focus back.

The first package was across the valley and north into the hills, still about a four-hour jog. Hopefully, Katherryn would have gotten in touch before he got there but, if not, his concerns about how things were going back at the ship were not looking very positive. Rutker cursed under his breath. He hated being stuck out here while all this was going on.

Scanning the SortieNet data, he realized that two of the

twenty-four drones were still offline. He'd have to wait and see if they were just out of range or if something more sinister had occurred. Meanwhile, he cast the net wide to scan the area between his current location and the colony and, as far as he could see, out towards the first package.

Might as well take the opportunity to collect intel while I can, he thought.

The fact was, it wouldn't be hard to track the missing mechs and draw a conclusion as to the direction he was heading. He could expect a whole lot more company in the very near future. Air support first, followed by units on the ground. If they had any reserves in orbit, he could expect some serious ground support in ten minutes or less. Rutker was beginning to get the sense that the 'pirates' assumed this would be a one-and-done sort of affair and didn't bother leaving any backup off planet. He hoped he was right...

Either way, he was faced with the fact that he didn't have the luxury of time. Rutker headed toward the colony at the north end of the valley, covering ground in an efficient gait, sorting imagery compiled by the drone net as he traveled.

The structures of the colony were largely industrial. There was a minor space port but mostly it looked like material processing for what was probably a mining operation. That could account for the spider web effect on the valley floor, perhaps tunnels. Analyzing the drone imagery through the SortieNet, he zoomed in on one of the larger dark spots in the barren valley floor. It was now quite evidently an opening. It looked like some of the intersections within the web pattern had openings going down quite a ways, as if there were multiple levels to the cave structure below. He wondered if the spider web extended into the hillside.

Rutker peeled out two drones to scan the tunnel network for any kind of activity, recent or otherwise. He also wanted to determine if it was a safer option to navigate the distance underground rather than drawing attention to himself on the surface. There was a part of him that harbored serious apprehension about that tack. He'd been to some ghost towns that seemed more alive than human habitations. This place was like one of those. The eerie sense of being watched back in the canyon still had never quite subsided. He wasn't certain that he was just being paranoid.

Peeling out two more drones to scan the colony in greater detail didn't provide any new insights but it did allow him to build a virtual map in the Long Rifle's SortieNet. The SortieNet was a battle computer that acted as a nexus of all sensory input and communications. It utilized a 3D map as its main interface. When operating independently, such as Rutker was now, the AI would populate that map with high-probability kill zones, hideouts, and retreat pathways.

Depending on identified threats, Rutker could map out multiple ambush and fighting retreat scenarios. Fighting one-v-many, the SortieNet would be exactly the sort of tactical advantage he needed to stay alive. He peeled back one more drone to the colony for good measure.

He was just beginning to receive footage from the tunnels when one of the drones dropped offline. That could have been a host of things, but the first concern, of course, was that it had been eliminated. Usually, a drone would notify if it was under fire, in which case, Rutker could playback footage of the attack to get an idea of what danger was out there. Not so, this time. It could have also been interference from the tunnel itself. Or machinery. Or even certain minerals. Another reason not to go down there.

He was due for the next comms rendezvous with Katherryn and the last thing he wanted to do was to be out of radio range when she finally did reach out. He was making good time across the valley floor. Another ten kilometers would get him to the colony. Probably about the same time that he could expect to see another pair of flyers if this group of so-called pirates was as organized as they were beginning to appear.

Out of instinct he scanned the horizon and sky by sector and was surprised to note that the sun was still barely past peak. It had been early to mid-morning when they had crashed. Which must be close to nine standard hours by his count. It had taken him the better part of an hour to gather his family, assign defensive positions within and around the *Xandraitha* and get the sniper mech out of deep storage. Luckily, it was designed to go long periods of time with very little maintenance. Thirty more minutes to load up and slip out. After that, he had managed to evade the pirate search parties for two or three hours before making contact in the canyon.

Based on those observations, that meant that daytime on this planet was roughly twenty-two to twenty-eight hours long. His second discovery was that there appeared to be at least a partial eclipse in progress. The shadows in the drone imagery had a distinct scalloped appearance to them. He really couldn't guess as to how much of an eclipse to expect — diminished light or full black, and how long.

Things were getting more complicated. Beside the fact that he'd been running and gunning for the better part of a day and slowly turning into jerky inside the hot box disguised as a mech, there was still a huge amount of local knowledge he yet needed to sort out. The kind that could get him killed without even seeing it coming.

No sooner did he drop his gaze to the colony ahead than alarms started screaming through the cockpit. Multiple drones had picked up orbital entry. It looked like two small signatures but small was relative. It could have been transorbital flyers, or, just as easily, fully loaded drop ships. The composite image coalesced into shapes that were all too familiar; Thune drop ships. Or, more precisely, Thune made drop ships.

The Thune didn't like to fight their *own* battles, but rather profit from others'. They'd been influencing Ring World policy for decades and providing the machinery to back it up for as long. Given the Kirgen fighters, this was looking to be a very well-funded little operation. Rutker began to wonder if the drop ships were held in reserve or if they were actually reinforcements from a larger contingent just arriving in theatre. There was no time to dwell on it. He had party crashers inbound and didn't like the odds.

Rutker dropped the Long Rifle into shooting position and sighted on the lead drop ship. It was time to swap projectiles. The concussion round he'd loaded previously would do little in this instance. He didn't have a lot of options in his arsenal but maybe a couple surprises. The initial attack on the *Xandraitha's Hope* may have taken out nearly all of the marine contingent aboard but it was a little too precise. The armory had stayed mostly intact, and he'd taken advantage of it.

He perused his inventory and opted for the Triple Threat. It was hard to argue with a round that could shrug off shields and armor and deliver a hefty payload, especially at the velocities that the sniper mech's Emag cannon was capable of generating. He cycled the breach, ejecting the used carrier, then slid the new round into the receivers loading ramp. The spring loaded ramp door snapped into place. Placing the next round in the on deck position for easy access, he swiveled back into position.

The lead drop ship was now scary close. It was jumping all over his screen, but the reticles were interlocked and glowing red. He eased the trigger back as the cannon folded out into its fully extended position for maximum velocity and accuracy, charging the Emag fully in the process. As he got near the end of the stroke, the round exploded from the cannon. It was less than a second later that the second drop ship was flying through the debris field of the first.

Rutker grinned evilly. No time for a victory lap, he jumped up and started sprinting toward the colony. There was no way he could make it but the closer he got the better. Standard Thune drop ships were capable of carrying up to four heavy mechs, like the Osiris from earlier. Getting caught in the flats here would not end well.

The mech was spooled up and humming at full sprint even while Rutker was loading the concussion round and placing an incendiary in the on deck slot. Racing over the silty, white-tan hardpack of the valley floor with only ten kilometers to go, the drop ship slammed into the earth midway between Rutker and the outskirts of the colony. The ground shuddered with the impact as dust clouds billowed from the craft. He was amazed to see that the ship actually stuck into the valley floor, forced into a drunken lean. He guessed that it must have collapsed one of the tunnels below.

Normally, the side walls of the drop ship would fold out like drawbridges and act as ramps for the mechs to exit: four doors, four mechs. But, with the drop ship half submerged, only two of the gates were able to fold down and even then, not fully. Whether the mechs inside were capable of dismounting at that angle was another question. He realized that now was his chance to take out all the mechs at once. He skidded to a halt and dropped prone in a thin depression in the valley floor just a kilometer away from the ship. The back of his mind registered that this depression may have been one of the tunnel intersections that didn't open to the surface above. But his attention was fully on the drop ship and its defenses, still live regardless of the functionality of the rest of the ship.

Rutker knew he needed to close the baffles again in order to avoid being targeted by the ship's defensive systems. A twinge of panic rippled through him, but he flipped the switch before he could have a chance to think twice about it. The internal temperature jumped instantly. Sweat beaded on his face and hands as he, again, began to swap out the concussion round for a standard armor penetrating round. He was getting faster at it.

As he swapped it out, he remembered that his drone feed was also cut off with the baffles closed. He cursed under his breath for not locking on target first.

"Manual optics!" Rutker barked, and then he was maneuvering the extended cannon arm to sight in the reticles rather than letting the computer utilize the drone net imagery to do it. Willing the gray lines to converge into the glowing red reticle on the lower center mass of the Thune orbital transport. He only heard a quick chirp of a beacon before something slammed the ground hard behind him. Rutker's mind raced with possibilities. Debris from the explosion? Or worse, a jump-mech? That would make sense as the drones would have announced dangerous debris as much as any other threat, but a jump-mech with stealth tech would be near to impossible to detect.

Rutker pulled the trigger then saw a vortex-like hole punch through the cloud of dust high and right of the drop ship — *no joy*. He was about to spin to deal with whatever it was that landed behind him but the concussion from the cannon must have loosened something below him. The chalk white dirt began to crumble. He felt his stomach rise as the mech fell through.

Out of desperation he twisted and fired the grappling hook at the remaining bit of roof. It caught clean and he swung spinning into the near wall of the cavity, twisting just enough to get one of the Long Rifle's feet to contact it. The auto-deployable talons did the rest, holding the mech fast in place against the wall.

Rutker realized that the talons deployed upon impact when the grappling line was in use. *Made sense.* Another thing he hadn't known until today. He choked back equal parts shock and pride even as he hung there in the silence, suspended by the grappling line and one foot that was stuck to the cave wall. He stared down the chasm below and saw nothing but darkness.

The tunnel wall across from him was barely discernible through the glowing wall of dust. The collapsed roof crashed faintly into the water far below. *That was quite a ways down,* he realized. Looking through the haze of glowing dust he saw that the roof had been only about two meters thick where he had been resting on it above. It was a wonder it hadn't collapsed decades ago or when he first dropped into position for the shot. Regretfully he recalled that that shot had not hit its target. That meant that there were at least a couple combatants in play still, plus whatever it was that caused him to miss his shot in the first place.

Sweat rolled into Rutker's eyes and he had to blink away the sting of the salt-choked moisture while listening intently for movement above. His heart was still pounding. Pulsing in his temples. The mech was almost unbearably hot with the baffles closed. He was unable to use the enhanced imagery from the drones for the same reason. He would have the SortieNet virtual model once he got to the colony but in the tunnel system with the baffles closed, he was effectively blind. He couldn't even try to re-sync with the lost drones to help him find his way. He certainly wouldn't be going topside.

From his vantage point the tunnel was plenty big enough for his sniper mech but would prove problematic for a mech the size of an Osiris. Unfortunately, that didn't preclude a medium mech like the Dragoon. And then there was the thing above him. He hoped against hope that it was not a jump mech. Only Elites could drop orbitally, and only *some* of those had effective stealthing ability.

Rutker slowed his breath and made his thoughts small and focused. If it truly was an Elite, it could have far more sophisticated sensory capability as well. He was hoping that whatever was concealing the signal from the drones he'd sent below earlier was hiding any trace signatures he might be giving off with his antiquated equipment.

Rocks and dirt crumbled from the edge of the cave-in above, and quickly passed into the enveloping darkness. Seconds later he heard the telltale chunk and whoosh of jump engines as the mech peeled out. He assumed that it was probably going to assess the damage to the drop ship but that was pure speculation. He was struggling with whether or not he should open the baffles when one of the drones came sliding into view from further down the tunnel. It looked like it was headed toward the colony, but the layout of the tunnel system was anything but intuitive.

Rutker's skin was prickly under the fabric of his flight suit. He realized that he was no longer sweating. That was quick. He'd either have to drop the stealthing baffles or be too weak from heat exhaustion to carry on, or to fight. There was no time to consider options, he had to risk it. The drones' signals dropped off almost instantly upon entry, so it should be safe, he thought. Plus, if he could gather the drone, he could download the raw feed which would be more detailed if less comprehensive than the compiled data from the Drone Net.

Seven

Catacombs

Rutker spoke and the Long Rifle baffles retracted. Hot air blew through the ducting but began to trend warmer. The drone, however, synced almost instantaneously. The other one didn't come online but he did now have a beacon signal which appeared to be several levels below and in the direction of the colony. The question was whether to hunt it down to get a better picture of what was down there or just go directly to the colony to hopefully slip out the back, away from the action. Or even better would be if the catacombs continued beyond the colony into the foothills, getting him closer to the first package without having to expose himself.

The drone download provided a reasonable map of the upper three levels of the tunnel and about halfway to the colony. He was hopeful that the other drone would complete the picture. He realized then that he'd already decided to go deeper and find the missing drone. The thought of what lurked above the surface, he was ashamed, was terrifying. He was a decorated pilot, a veteran of two hard fought campaigns and while he'd had some scrapes, he'd never been in a battle where he felt so outmatched on every level. And this playing field was anything but even.

Rutker sprang off the wall and fast rappelled into the darkness below. Using the mech's night vision and the drone's second set of eyes he was able to avoid the jagged shards of exposed rock and construction materials that poked into the gap at awkward angles. He reached the end of the grappling line at a hundred and fifty meters and had to reset his anchor in order to go any further. It was possible that he'd have to repeat this step to get all the way to the bottom.

He sent the drone down ahead to check it out. As he descended, the tunnels structured appearance gave way to something altogether more natural and free flowing. It was definitely a mining operation above, though in serious disrepair and not from time and natural processes. Much of the destruction appeared to be from battle as there were some scattered fortifications and areas that were clearly destroyed by ordinance.

Something unexpected though was what appeared to be groupings of natural features that weren't natural at all. He had no frame of reference for them, but he noted the anomalies and instructed the Long Rifle's SortieNet to recognize the features as he explored further.

As he drew near the end of the line, he saw that there was water at the bottom. His reflection appeared as a dark shape drawing closer with a thin slice of sunlight in the far distance behind it. The surface was glassy now, but the pool still seemed to be clearing from the debris dropped into it earlier. He turned on the search lights, but they didn't penetrate deep enough to find the bottom; it could be ten meters, or it could be hundreds. He didn't expect to find out. Instead, Rutker paused a few meters above the pool to allow the mech to swing back to the wall and then spring off to land on the tunnel floor behind him.

The drone beacon was about three-hundred meters further on. Closer to the colony, which was good. But he didn't like the fact that the drone hadn't synced yet. That meant that it was offline. He could have sent his one functional drone ahead to scout but something, call it instinct, suggested that he should leave it behind to watch his rear in case he was walking into a trap.

He instructed the drone to follow fifty meters into the tunnel, until the pool was barely visible before rounding a corner. The drone attached to the tunnel roof and powered down to sleep mode. It would only come back online if it sensed movement.

With the modicum of assurance that that provided he turned to track down his missing drone. Just as he did, he could swear that he saw movement from the tunnel beyond the pool. Rutker continued forward as if nothing had happened, but his mind was frantically replaying what he just saw. It was not a mech, not a creature. It had looked like a man standing there. But then as he moved, the figure faded back into the darkness... The drone picked up nothing. Neither had the mech. Rutker was forced to believe it was just his nerves, but he knew better than that.

Rutker hydrated as the mech glided slowly forward. He was surprised again at the agility of the Long Rifle. Urging the display to enhance audio he listened intently and still there was barely more than a muffled crunch with each step. The cavern's cooler air had done much to expel the mech's stored up heat so the thought of closing the baffles seemed less suicidal but still, he needed to be mindful of the mechs physical needs as well as his own. The Long Rifle could still handle a considerable amount more abuse than he ever could. His headache was still a dull ache in the background, but at least he could think through it.

He was thinking clearly enough to recall that every second down here was one that he wouldn't be able to get an update from Katherryn. He forced himself to compartmentalize the torrent of thoughts and emotion. Feelings were for later. He yearned to know that she and the boys were okay.

And then there was that part of him, the side where the righteous anger lived. That part wanted to know if she'd made any headway on uncovering the saboteur, the one who'd put his family in danger and who threatened to destroy the possibility of peace for not just him and his family, but for his entire solar system. Worry was for later too. But anger was a useful tool and he could use it to focus and to persevere, which was what he needed to do now.

The cavern floor descended slowly as he rounded yet another

corner. The next section looked as though it was going to double back and descend below what had been the water level where he'd started. That was a little disconcerting.

The tunnel did indeed double back, only another spur cut to the right and up, while yet another just beyond it cut through a gap and intersected a separate tunnel in complete disregard for reason. The area appeared to have been one of the failed fortifications as twisted metal was strewn everywhere, partially blocking progress in all directions but down. It was a perfect place for an ambush.

Rutker realized that he'd unconsciously slid to the side of the tunnel as he was making his observations. Taking partial cover behind one of the larger unrecognizable bits of metal fused rock. The Long Rifle's optics were one of its most advanced features and even by present standards, it was pretty solid. He scoured every pocket and felt confident maneuvering forward through the wreckage. He would have to follow the switchback to head down toward the stronger beacon signal, which could only be another seventy-five meters or so. That was his estimate at least.

He rounded the corner and continued a little further before the tunnel opened into a larger chamber that was largely submersed as the cavern continued down below the water table. The chamber was roughly forty-five meters across, with scattered, rusting hunks of machinery that were partially or fully submerged. It was apparent that some of the wreckage was mining equipment, but that some of the other equipment were transports of some kind. Some of those had improvised weaponry mounted to them.

Rutker really couldn't make heads or tails of who had been fighting who, though. None of the equipment's positioning appeared to be engaged with one another but, instead, was all facing vaguely down tunnel. He didn't look too closely at first, not really wanting to see in gruesome detail the combatants that might still be rotting in place where they had died. But something was nagging at him. Like he needed to know. Like it was an important piece of the puzzle.

He scanned the carnage again and realized that there weren't any bodies... anywhere. All of the vehicles were empty. And all the former fortifications were absent of any bodies as well. No weapons, no uniforms, nothing. This was clearly not drone or robotic warfare either. All indicators pointed to biological combatants. At least on the losing side...

His mind flashed to forms of biological warfare that might eliminate organic material. Chemical and biological warfare could account for that. Some types of nuclear weaponry, though the Long Rifle's sensors would have picked up most if not all those options. Barring something truly exotic, only one plausible option remained, gruesome as it was.

While he pondered this, he realized that the approximate location of the signal from his missing drone matched up with what appeared to be an opening to yet another chamber at the end of this one. The fully submerged end of the main chamber. Rutker thought it unlikely that, though capable of such an endeavor, his drone would have seen the value of venturing underwater, as it was unlikely that the mech would. That it would somehow fail mechanically, right at the foot of a submersed cavern entrance, seemed beyond likelihood.

The feeling of being watched soaked his subconscious again. Only, this time, it felt palpable. Twinges of fear twisted in his gut, and he was surprised to hear himself take a couple of slow breaths to fend off the sensation. It was something he'd never felt in combat, not like this. This was actual terror. The sensation settled in, building a base from which to squeeze every bit of sanity from his thoughts, every bit of certainty from his actions. A couple more breaths and he strode forward, afraid if he stayed too long, he might never move.

He eased the mech into the water so as not to disturb the silt and destroy his visibility. Once fully submerged, he looked around again. Thirty-five meters beyond, two annihilated transports appeared to have been casually pushed aside. The opening lay just beyond. Rutker craned his head to take it all in as he drew closer. There was a huge metal door off to one side, hanging from its track. Darkness lay beyond the opening but the door itself, ten meters tall and equally wide was covered in a script that was entirely foreign. The message however was easy to comprehend:

Danger! Do not Enter.

As he drew closer, bobbing weightless across the cavern floor, he saw the drone laying on a low outcrop of rock just before the massive, ruined door.

The drone had been torn, quite literally, into two pieces. The components required to maintain the beacon, however, were still functioning. A message to Rutker that was as clear as the ten meter graffiti wall beyond.

Every step forward now was a magnitude greater in terror. His throat felt constricted. His pulse was racing and, as a fighter pilot, he was shocked to see that even his hands were trembling slightly. He focused back on the door and on the drone. A wave of panic over the loss of mastery of his own body jolted him, though, and he realized that he had just stopped. He was physically unable to move forward.

This moment was unequivocally the most terrified he'd ever been. His body screamed at him that any movement forward would end in some fate worse by far than death itself. He struggled to remember why he even needed to retrieve the drone, but somewhere, in the inner core of his psyche, he just knew that it had to happen. His thoughts turned to Katherryn and Mads and Macq, and it all came back in a tidal wave.

The fear retreated ever so slightly, leaving a filthy residue on his mind. The sensation was something that he couldn't describe and couldn't imagine ever trying to. This moment should die, rot, and never be exhumed from his memory. Seizing a shard of clarity, he pushed forward the remaining meters to the destroyed drone. He grabbed the two pieces in one hand and turned back the way he'd come. He didn't want to know what was in the chamber and he got the sense that whatever was in there, wanted it that way.

The filmy residue of horror and paralyzing terror was still palpable, but he felt a strange sensation as he moved toward the surface and away from the entrance. Rutker didn't look back until he was completely out of the water and a dozen meters up the tunnel. There was nothing to see of course but the feeling of being watched didn't diminish either. It was just that unnatural sense of terror that dissipated.

Rutker was relieved to gain the presence of mind to check on the other drone, the one he'd left behind earlier to guard his pathway from the main shaft. Nothing had triggered it in his absence, so he called it back.

He returned to the convoluted intersection with its overrun fortifications. Now he had the pieces of his missing drone, but he didn't know if he had enough to get any real intel from it. He tried to apply his mind to the question, but a wave of exhaustion washed over him, and he remembered that he'd been going at this for the better part of a day. He rubbed his eyes and thought through next steps. Water, food, a quick nap to rejuvenate.

He wanted to get topside to catch any sort of communication from Katherryn but knew that that would be a death sentence, especially in his present state. The best thing he could do was stay sharp and make his way to the colony before taking to the surface. Rutker lifted the drone parts up to get a look at them and something from that action triggered the drone's healing circuitry and it began to repair itself. By the time his catnap was over, he figured that it ought to be functioning enough to tell him some of the secrets of this enigmatic cave complex and maybe some of what took place here.

He repressed a yawn as he maneuvered the mech between two deformed hunks of rock infused metal, or maybe it was metal infused rock. He couldn't really tell. Whatever the material was, the two outcroppings would provide a modicum of cover. They also lay at the far end of the intersection, away from all four tunnel sections, which gave him the assurance that he'd at least be able to see any hostiles coming. As an added measure he deployed the drone, once again in sleep mode, so as to act as a sentry without being detected itself.

He was torn by the events of the day but specifically the last hour. The memory of tidal waves of terror washing over him as he drew closer to the submerged chamber was only replaced by the fleeting image of the man or apparition in the tunnel beyond the pool where he first descended into the catacombs. They felt sorrowful. He remembered his breathing and it escaped in shudders as he realized how wound tight he must have been.

Ripping the top off a sealed packet of some form of nutrient dense hydration formula he slurped the contents, not really bothering to taste it. He was surprised when it turned out to be sweet and somewhat tangy. Not bad at all, he thought. Nothing like the gruel-in-a-sock, ready meals he had to force down by the end of the second Battle of Turnedring Spires.

The last defense that finally broke the spearhead of the Delvadrid Expansionary Force with their Kirgen goons and Thune made weaponry. The only thing more revolting than subsisting on what was essentially wood pulp and animal fat was the thought that every ship he crippled or mech he destroyed was built upon the backs of a dozen slave worlds that stretched between Portal *Xandraitha* in his home system and Portal Charbides in the dark and frozen Delvadr Belt, home to the war machine that served the Primacy. Their estates scattered amongst the more hospitable systems they'd conquered. Which, of course, explained why the diplomatic envoy had chosen a much more circuitous route to the Treaty Ceremonies hosted by the suitably impartial and overwhelmingly more powerful Pentarch of Gefkarri on its little known home world of Tek. That also explained how they ended up waylaid by pirates on a planet unfamiliar to them.

The more he dwelt on some of the circumstances, the more skeptical he was that there wasn't some connection between, not the Delvadr Primacy and their pompous, peacock Lords, but the Thune Corporate and the supposedly impartial Gefkarri Pentarch.

He realized his thoughts had wondered far afield when a yawn escaped his lips again. He blinked away the sleep and rubbed his face but knew it was a losing battle. He managed one last glance toward the main shaft and then forced himself to glance in the direction of flooded chamber but that was about all he could do. He leaned back and was asleep in seconds.

Eight

To Dream of Dreaming

19.004329 AC (After Construct)
Age of the Half-Orc War

D'avry woke with a start. The campfire was reduced to a glowing mound of coals. Volkreek and Farn were snoring softly into their hooded cloaks. The shape of a man sitting on the rocks, alert, dividing his attention between scanning the river and hillside appeared to be that of Liggo, though D'avry wasn't sure how he could tell.

He realized he'd been dreaming. Dreaming of walking amongst long dark caverns, too perfectly carved to be natural. They were angular with complicated machinery running everywhere like mineral veins through granite. His architect's mind struggled to comprehend the labor it took to build, let alone the method of their construction. The tunnels stretched for miles and intersected randomly, yet as he descended the structure gave way to chaos, with tunnels and long chambers careening like veins in a gigantic organism.

The darkness was silent, yet somehow charged with foreboding. Every once in a while, the collapsed cavern roof would reveal stars in the night sky, seemingly familiar but in orientations that could never exist where he was from. And the most amazing thing of all was the moon. Not only did it have vibrant blue and gray streaks running from the poles nearly to the equator but it had its own, slightly smaller satellite. He sensed that it was not just a dream. He had not rested in the time that he was searching in the caverns.

Searching... He realized now that that was what he was in fact doing. What, or who, was he searching for? And then he remembered why he had woken so suddenly. From the darkness, a terror, yet he never actually saw anything. Something, somehow darker than the blackness of the tunnel, reached out to suck him down into the depths and consume him. D'avry had woken up just in time...

He struggled to recall every detail while at the same time forgetting as much as possible about the dark force; the terror waiting in the darkness. There was something hauntingly familiar about it, but he couldn't bring himself to search much deeper. He was okay with contemplating the tunnels and the foreign, otherworldly machinery. The sheer scale of the construction. He'd remembered pools of cavern water, the shafts to the surface, and something else.

Something and someone...A monster made of metal but with the manor of a man. A large creature, the size of a cave troll, but it had been nimble and somehow tentative? As if it were afraid of something bigger, even scarier. D'avry couldn't imagine what it could be that the monster was afraid of. Maybe the terror in the darkness, but what could eat metal?

Obviously, acids like those taken from crag wyrms in the mountains high above his homeland, but actually *eat* a creature made of metal? And one the size of a troll? That was impossible. Still, he was drawn to the creature and knew that it was important in some way. D'avry determined that there were still a few hours before the first rays of daylight. He would simply keep searching. He closed his eyes and found himself in a different place entirely...

Nine

Dust Bowl

31.12504 AC (After Construct)
Age of the Thinning Veil

Perpetual silence, perpetual night, infinite solitude; these were ideas that seemed to spring from the ether and grow root. A sour smirk crept across Deven's face. She felt the rough texture of the wood planks beneath her feet, warped from years of exposure. To what? She hadn't the vaguest idea. The concept of sunlight here was utterly foreign.

She didn't bother looking behind her. She knew it would be more of that eerie mist, blowing from somewhere to nowhere in the breezeless night. Searching for the source of the tired moonlight would be equally futile. It was impossible to discern. Glancing down, she noticed the lightly-tanned skin of her hands looked like dirty porcelain under the malnourished light. It made her feel sickly.

She frowned and her eyes flicked up toward the hill, boards creaked underfoot as she shifted her weight. Her first instinct had been to wander the town, discover its secrets, but now she just wanted to go. Surely there would be something up there, an estate maybe, or a governor's mansion, a monastery, something. But this thought was dashed by another certainty, that there was no point. There was no one here. Laundry lines hung barren, chimneys lay cold and smokeless. The town existed out of existence.

Standing around and doing nothing wasn't going to work. Perhaps from farther up she would have a better idea of the town itself, perhaps there was a pathway leading somewhere else? Somewhere less... depressing.

Deven started walking, and then picked up the pace, stepping a little faster, until she was jogging and then running and then tearing down the planks at a full sprint, arms pumping, wooden planks speeding beneath her feet. Down the boardwalk to the end she flew, the wind rushing through her raven hair. She leapt easily to the next landing, sprinted a little way and then bounded, planting a foot on one wall, and then the adjacent one before springing back to land atop an awning that moments ago had rushed above her.

She felt a surge of adrenalin and a little pride at the effortlessness of it. Taking two skipping steps along the shingled slant of the awning she sprang across the gap formed by a narrow alley. Catching the eaves of the two-story structure beyond, arms extended, feet planted, she bounced with the momentum off the wall, gripping the roof tight so that her body pendulumed on that axis. She let her momentum carry her up and landed on her toes where her hands had been moments before.

Just then, a shingle slipped away beneath her foot causing her to lose balance. She windmilled, one leg flashing out behind her as she bent at the waist to shift her weight back over the roof's edge. And then, just as quickly, just as simply, she pirouetted, bringing her errant leg back to safety and dropping softly to her bottom with her legs hanging over the edge.

Deven sucked in the cool air, feeling her pulse rush, and looked beside her at the place where the shingle had slipped away. But rather than wood slats or tar, there was... nothing. Blackness dotted with the faintest sprinkling of lights, as if she was looking through the rectangular hole into the night sky itself. That was impossible of course. Yet above her was nothing but the vaguest wisp of clouds. If there were stars there, she could see no sign of them.

Deven reached her hand toward the empty space but hesitated, and then she reached down anyway. Where the shingle had been, she was unsurprised to find was empty void. Her thoughts went back up the hill again, toward the upper village. There must be something there that could unlock this mystery, make some sense of the purpose of this place.

A thick raindrop splattered on a shingle nearby. And then another on her head, its coolness rolling down her scalp and then down her forehead. A smile erased the scowl she had been wearing, and she turned her face skyward to feel the cool drops on her skin. This felt a million times more real than the derelict structure she was sitting on.

The rain kept on until Deven and the rooftop were drenched and glistening dully in the muted light. The smell of wet wood, of a first of season rain, caressed her senses as her hair flattened against her face and the shoulders of her hooded sweatshirt. Still, she was transfixed by the hole in the shingled rooftop as raindrops splattered around the edges, and yet others fell cleanly into the nothing void between them. She did not know quite what to do with that knowledge. It, just like this place, defied logic.

She glanced again up the mountain, hidden beneath the gray-on-gray jungle of boards before her. She stood up on the gently sloping roof. Slipped a baseball cap from her daypack and pulled it down tight until she could just see below its bill. Heading toward the upper village she made her way to the roof peak, walking along its spine until it ended at the landing of a stilted structure just beyond.

There she followed a ladder to yet another landing, the mist seeming to part before her as she continued toward an alleyway where large crates were stacked, conveniently leading to another landing higher up. She continued this way, farther and farther up, eating up the ground between where she had started and her theoretical destination. The rain didn't stop and neither did she.

An hour passed though there was a timelessness to this

place. She might have thought that this was purgatory and that she would carry on like this into eternity but a gnawing feeling in her stomach informed her otherwise. If she was hungry, then she must find something to eat. Also, she was beginning to feel some fatigue in her muscles and would have to, at some point, rest, though the idea of rest seemed disquieting, it seemed wasteful. It felt to her that there was nothing that she wanted to do more than to solve this riddle and be gone, elsewhere, anywhere.

The rain continued but with less urgency. Deven, spying a suitable porch pulled herself up and sat, feet dangling over the edge as she looked back down upon the rooftops below her. From her pack she grabbed an orange, a handful of butter crackers and a chunk of sharp cheddar she didn't remember packing. Looking down from this vantage she could just discern the boardwalk where she'd begun her trek, only now it appeared to be something closer to a pier that stretched into and was surrounded by that same drab mist that coursed like a living thing through the shadows of this place abandoned in time.

She washed down her snack and half-jumped at the presence of a raven eyeing her from the railing little more than an arm's length away. Raindrops rolling down its head and beak it cocked its head and ruffled the feathers on its neck and wings to shed the water. With that, oddly, the rain seemed to lose interest and carried on elsewhere.

Deven had only just recognized that the bird had something tied around its neck when it sprang from its perch. Dropping to within inches of the rooftops below then arcing lazily back up the hillside, still skimming dangerously close to the structures as it climbed. It finally came to rest on the peak of a precariously leaning three-story building a few hundred yards further uphill.

This sparked a thought. Deven removed her hat, turning the bill to view the front of the black cap where a purple, black and gold stitched image stood out from the wet fabric. The image was of a raven's head.

Growing up in Bowie, Maryland, most of her friends and in fact, most of her family were Redskins fans, but she'd loved the Ravens. Loved the underdogs. Continued to love them even after they won a few playoff games. It just seemed right to her. Just like when she enlisted in the Marines. There were scholarships waiting for her. Academic as well as athletic, but again there was no denying what she knew in her heart. She wanted to defend her country. Defend democracy. There was a heritage to the Marines that she could identify with, an honesty to their ethic.

She'd enlisted, trained, and deployed within months and soon found herself on the other side of the world. She'd loved it all even up to that dull, dusty morning a few miles east of Ramadi, Iraq. A routine patrol had ended in screaming and twisted metal, dust, and fire and the staccato crack of 7.62 and 5.56 rounds. First came the popcorn bursts of M4's and then longer peels as the squad machine guns growled, laying down suppressive fire.

Deven had no recollection of what happened directly after the firefight started. She'd woken to shouting, ringing in her ears, numbness everywhere and then as the dullness faded into awareness and pain, a jolt of shock ran through her as she saw what she'd only felt vaguely before, that she was pinned beneath the wreckage of her overturned transport. She didn't even know how that was possible, but even in her muddled mental state it was evident that she would be unable to belly away to cover. She was stuck. Exposed. She kept thinking of what they would do to her when they found her, an American soldier. A woman.

Time distorted, seconds felt like hours, flat on her back in the dust, with a grenade clutched to her chest. She didn't know where it'd come from, but she had it and that's all that mattered. Pin pulled, it was just sheer will and determination keeping her conscious and awake enough to keep the safety lever held in place.

In time, the sound of *friendly* rifles began to dwindle and fade. The sounds from the ubiquitous pressed-metal 7.62's, too, slowly began to diminish in frequency, though they were still scary close.

Occasionally, she'd hear the sharper crack of a solitary high-powered round. Not an AK, but a sniper rifle, she thought. She was worried about the commotion drawing closer again, but the sniper rounds were coming from not far off, maybe the second floor of the apartment building across from her. Or maybe on the rooftop of the store beside it.

She found herself wanting to sleep and willed herself back into the present, into the pain. Instead, she tried to swallow and waved a fly away from her face without shifting her body weight. The fly came back but with reinforcements. There were five now, doing flybys, landing on her forehead, her lips and then playing chase.

Deven heard a croaking groan and was shocked to realize it was her own voice. She reprimanded herself for being so careless. She needed to focus on something else and stared up at the growing haze threatening to wash out the beautiful cobalt from earlier that morning. It was being crowded out by smoke and dust. And heat. The heat was coming on and the sun was just cresting the edge of the apartment complex, chasing the shadows up her waist. It was on her hands now and the grenade. It would be in her face soon. Blinding her, dehydrating her quickly in her present state, unable to do anything about it.

Another crack and the faintest rustle of gauzy drapes in a second story flat just twelve- to fifteen-yards away. If the sun was up any farther, she wouldn't have seen it. She concentrated on the information being presented. The rifle was suppressed, she realized, otherwise she'd have known it was closer. She blamed her shock addled brain for not figuring it out sooner.

There was no hesitation. The rest of her squad was at risk

and clearly had not yet pinpointed where the shots were coming from. She held the grenade close with her left hand allowing her right hand to drop, feeling pins and needles dully as blood returned sluggishly to her fingertips. She would need all her strength to make the throw.

Shaking out her hand, flexing and closing her fist a couple times, pain seared through nerve endings as she peeled her glove off with her teeth, one finger at a time. Her whole body throbbed with waves of pain, seeming to crowd her vision with every pulse. Deven struggled to shift her weight, ignoring the crunching noises she couldn't tell if she heard or felt. She was thankful for the numbness in her legs, but still hot bile rose in her throat forcing her to breathe through the pain and the panic.

I have to improve my angle, she thought. Fighting through tears she shifted again, an inch at a time and struggled to take a full, shuddering breath. The sun was warm on her neck and chin now, but somehow, for her efforts, she'd managed to line up the throw. She didn't have long before she wouldn't be able to see her target. As she transferred the grenade to her right hand, she felt the warm metal, smooth and heavy, satisfyingly so. She whispered a quick but honest prayer then let the latch fall.

One...two...three, she counted noiselessly before lobbing the grenade overhand at the window, the only way that she could throw it. Bright sunlight obscured her view of the target at the end of the movement. Even as it left her fingers she panicked, what if she missed? Or worse, what if she had been mistaken. Maybe there was a family up there, hiding from the attack?

The grenade landed just inside the window's ledge. A one-in-a-million shot. She heard a clatter of movement from inside and then it exploded. The buzzing in her ears raged on as the seconds crept by one after the other. She laid back, face heavenward, tears welling up in dirty pools on her grime-streaked face. *What had she done?*

Hurried footsteps scuffed from her right and stopped short as the body of a would-be assailant crumpled beside her. His face wet with perspiration, slack, his open mouth pressed against the dirt and dust. The rasp of bile returned, and her stomach convulsed. It crept up the back of her throat with the smell of sweat and dust and the acrid scent of explosives wafting from the diesel soaked dirt. Her eyes dropped to the growing blossom of crimson on the man's chest.

A staccato burst and another insurgent rushed from the storefront, rifle spraying wildly as he was dropped, his feet flying up as if he'd reached the end of a chain. She heard nothing but knew, somewhere out there, someone was looking out for her. They had her position sighted in and were doing the job they'd been sent here for. Just like she had. Deven took this to mean that the enemy sniper had been killed with her grenade. She prayed again but this time it was a simple thank you.

After that, the sounds of AK's had trailed off and the shouts of her squad mates came methodically up the street from behind as they cleared building by building, alley by alley. She hadn't seen her rescuers but woke in a hospital bed nearly a week later. Grateful to be alive, and yet regretful that her tour had come to an end. As bittersweet as service had been, she wasn't looking forward to going home.

Deven snapped back from her reverie, forgetting where she was for second. Pulling her legs up over the edge of the deck she rubbed the hard aluminum alloy and carbon fiber beneath the fabric of her driftwood joggers. *Ah, the new metal me*, she thought as if seeing her legs for the first time.

As it turned out, she had not been able to keep much below the knee of either leg. But, in a weird way, she was okay with that. She'd done her part. And the U.S government had done theirs. After months she was, well, maybe not good as new, but maybe better in some ways? It was a weird thought, she knew. No one would understand it, certainly not her sisters and *definitely* not her mother. Feelings, especially inconvenient ones, were not her specialty.

A small but familiar pang of guilt knotted inside her as she thought, not for the first time, that she wished it'd been Alice, her mom, who'd died rather than her dad. Deven's lip curled a little as though the thought itself had a sour taste. She knew, theoretically anyway, that it was okay to have feelings. That's what the counselor had told her anyway. She just wished that she could turn them off. Not feel anything. It would have been better to have lost those in the war. Seems she'd lost all the wrong things of late. First her dad. Then her legs. She'd give anything just to relive her sophomore year of high school on a perpetual loop. Never have to relive the rest of it.

Just then a motion caught her eye from below. At first it seemed just the movement of the fog alternately obscuring and revealing shadow but then, the shadow moved. In a blink it spanned a gap she herself would have found impossible and then in spurts it exploded forward and seemed to re-congeal at a stop before springing forward again.

Deven could make out only a vaguely human shape from this distance, it seemed like a shadow but somehow sketchy or wispy, like vapor, if that were possible. The shape spurted forward again but this time on to a rooftop that was familiar to her. Here it stopped and looked around almost as if searching for something, when it seemed to find what it was looking for and turned to face the hillside, scanning, searching, in Deven's direction.

Skin crawling, she eased herself back from the ledge, careful not to move quickly or alter her silhouette from the shadow's viewpoint. She slid back to where she could just see over the edge of the deck to where the shadow crouched on the rooftop. Suddenly, the creature stood and issued a breathy, howling growl that was answered in coyote-like yips from all throughout the lower village. Roughly a dozen or more by Deven's count. The shadow dropped to all fours as it crept along the roof's spine, looking for further traces of its prey.

Deven didn't need to see anything more. She searched her mind but had no frame of reference for what the creature was. But it *was* clearly hunting for something, was not alone and somehow it seemed to have picked up her trail. She estimated that it was maybe half a klick away. She moved as silently as she could, imagining the other creatures collapsing back on the first and forming a line, like a search posse, fanning out and pushing toward her position. Forcing her further upward. What would happen when she reached the upper end of the town, the very top? Was there safety there or just more emptiness?

Deven swallowed hard and scanned the structure for another exit. There was a loft at the back with a high window that might prove viable. She sprinted to the back of the warehouse-like building, uncertain and uncaring of what its purpose had been. Nothing about this place made any sense. She leapt up the narrow stairs with a fear induced burst of speed. But the window was too high. Biting her lip, Deven stepped back and scanned the room for anything that might help her reach it.

"C'mon, c'mon, c'mon, c'mon..." She cast about nervously and then, just like before, crates nearby could be used for a boost. "That'll work."

The glassless pane swiveled at its midpoint on barely serviceable hinges. If she could get out and hang from the sill, she might be able to reach out far enough to her left to catch the bare edge of a walk just above. The way the window opened made it impossible to stand on the sill to reach the roof easily. So, she slid out and scooted as far as she could to the left.

Reaching as far as possible, she was still a good three feet from the walk and a good foot below it. She'd have to leap for it. Deven's stomach sank. She didn't bother to look down. That might cause her to freeze which would only prolong the inevitable. Instead, Deven focused on the ledge, but her eyes betrayed her.

Dammit, she thought, cursing her lack of discipline. Where an empty alley would have been, there was just the flowing, ever-present mist. But something odd struck her about it. She dared a glance back down and saw that when the flowing mist parted, instead of revealing the exposed walk below, it revealed the same nothingness from before. The same impossible emptiness from where the shingle had slipped away. Great. Instead of hitting the deck, she'd fall through the mist into an endless void...

She closed her eyes, took in a long, deep breath, and let it out as slowly as she could. Swallowing to work some moisture back into her mouth, she accessed the rock hard core that had gotten her through the IED explosion that day in Iraq.

Swaying right, she rocked back to the left and sprang from the wall. Her left-hand finding purchase even as her right caught the blunt edge and dropped away leaving her hanging by fingertips. Her stomach tried to climb to safety as she swung wildly, but with a calm but determined pull, using her momentum on the back swing she reached above the ledge with her free hand and grabbed the foot rail. And then, again on the swing back, pulled herself the rest of the way up. Against every urging she refrained from climbing all the way over and instead, sat on her heels, clinging to the danger side of the softly creaking rail.

Deven paused, waiting to hear the shrill howl of alarm from below, but nothing came. Staying low, she shuffled silently as far to the right as she could, to keep the warehouse building between her and her hunters. Satisfied she was out of sight, she slid, finally, over the railing to relative safety. Deven eased her way along the walk until she could just make out the spot where she had first seen the creature. Now, where there had been one, she easily counted four. Jumping and re-congealing in ragged spurts, they leapt huge gaps or cleared single stories from boardwalk to roof's edge.

They were still quite a way below, but it would take them little time to catch her if she were spotted. She needed to draw them off her trail somehow. She had no idea how. She was not trained for this, even if she knew what she was dealing with. Deven closed her eyes and breathed out again slowly. It would come to her.

She slunk over the rail and studied the creatures as they searched. She spotted two more off to the left. They *had* formed a line of sorts, as an organized unit they were each clearing buildings, scanning walkways. They hunted with the prowling swagger of apex predators, certain of success, just biding time until they stumbled upon their quarry.

What had caused the first creature to signal the others? Deven had left nothing behind. There was the misplaced shingle but that was far below. The only other thing out of sorts was the raven she had seen earlier. She still wanted to follow that bird but now wondered if there was a connection between the bird and the hunting creatures.

She studied the creatures again and noticed a peculiar pattern. They seemed to go wherever they wanted but always stayed clear of the fog. Once, Deven even saw a creature skip to the side as the mist ebbed closer to it. They never ventured into an alley way or space between the buildings.

She was surprised. The creatures, at first, had seemed to be inhabitants of the ghost like town, but now seemed to her as alien to this place as she was. The faintest hint of an idea had formed in the back of her mind, but it would be a while before she was willing to implement it. She turned her attention back toward the hillside. It was getting steeper here and she would have to be cunning to avoid detection from here on out.

Ten

To Dream of Waking

Lance Corporal Deven Garraway woke to the smell of disinfectant and the gentle whir of monitoring equipment. TV shows and subdued conversation bubbled in the background. It was bright, but hazy shapes and colors were all that came to her at first. As the collage of shapes coalesced into meaningful images, she realized she was in a hospital. Not a field hospital. Or even the facility at the forward base. She'd been in there for an exhaust burn when a temporary generator had rattled off its mounts and threatened to rip it's fuel line.

No, she was somewhere else. Maybe Walter Reed back in the States? Her waking caused some bustle, and it was short order before her doctors were at her side and at first asking questions like, what year it was and what was her mother's name. Then, after satisfactory responses they ushered in an administrative officer who began to fill in the details about how her squad had been ambushed, how her Humvee had driven over an IED, that she had somehow managed to neutralize an insurgent sniper and had been in varying states of consciousness ever since.

Then one of the doctors, an older gentleman with a shiny bald head and tan lines from his sunglasses, broached a more serious subject. He explained to her what she already, somehow, knew about her legs but went on to express that she had suffered severe trauma to the head and neck as well. It'd taken several surgeries, but the fused vertebrae in her neck were healing, as was the fracture to her skull. She was disturbed by the discrepancy between what she knew, what she remembered and what had occurred in her dream. The dream that seemed to be so real but from a point in time that seemed well *after* the present. But if she'd suffered trauma like what the man had described then it seemed that it was to be expected.

The intervening months found her getting fitted for prosthetics, doggedly hammering out her exercises in rehab, submitting applications to a number of schools and basically keeping herself too busy to think about anything else. Least of all to get caught up in the inanities of her mother and sisters' drama. She was accepted to several schools but chose Stanford since it was on the West Coast and as much as she loved her family, she just loved them better from a distance.

Unfortunately, she wouldn't be able to attend classes until the fall semester, so she opted to take some of her undergrad coursework at De Anza Community, a few minutes south in Cupertino. That would allow her to get a job and an apartment and just generally get a sense of the area. Within a month of her acceptance, she was in Silicon Valley, attending the first of her remaining six months of scheduled rehab in her new home. Even though her disability benefits helped her pay the bills she knew, much like a shark, that she needed to stay moving to survive. She had discovered a veteran friendly coffee house a short distance from her new studio apartment where she could stand or sit as needed while taking orders and running the register.

Thoughts of the events in Iraq came unbidden, interrupted her nights, and often found her staring vacantly at customers standing in front of her, but not *too* often. Not often enough for her manager to bring up that delicate topic with a recent amputee and war veteran of a still ongoing engagement.

Thoughts of the gray town and the hunting creatures had passed largely from memory. That is until one evening, after a warm September afternoon had brought in the cool damp air from the coast and a sense of Fall as she remembered it from her childhood, even though California was a far cry from Maryland when it came to changing of the seasons. Still, she thought back when her father was still around to catch her lacrosse and basketball games.

She was walking home from Inkling & Co. after a full day of classes followed by a four-hour shift filling in for one of the baristas, Kemper, who rarely found his way to class or work when the swell was up. Apparently, the swell was up. "A little lumpy but shoulder- to head-high from the south-southwest with an intermittent larger and longer period northwest that would clear the lineup every forty minutes or so," she would find out later. She had no idea what that meant but Kemper was easy to talk to and easier to look at, even if he was a shameless man-whore.

It was after the walk home, when she had chosen resolutely to take the five-story flight of stairs rather than the elevator. It would be the first time that she had attempted it. Even after the long day she felt like she had it in her. And besides, she was tired of being treated like a cripple. Her vivid blue eyes, raven black hair and athletic figure made her pretty, and somehow that just made it worse. It made her an oddity and an endless source of curiosity, and no one quite seemed to know what to do with her. Within her five-foot-sixish frame she carried an endless reservoir of tenacity and determination into everything she did. *All go, no quit,* as her dad used to say.

It was this tenacity and determination that were the fueling fire behind her as she mounted the steps to her studio. And maybe thoughts of her dad who had been there for every challenge she'd faced while growing up. Every insurmountable object, until now.

The first flight was okay. She paused shakily before engaging with the next flight as it doubled back to the second-floor landing, which she did successfully. By this time, she'd already done the mental calculus to know that this would be an impossible task. However, she found that she was unable to stop herself.

Fifteen minutes later found her on the third floor with every opportunity to exit the stair well and wobble to the elevator but when she should have gone straight, she veered doggedly left, tears of frustration brimming in her eyes but choked back just as viciously as she stabbed her prosthetic feet, one after the other at the next set of stairs.

At the landing the tears were no longer held in check but flowing freely down her face and onto the concrete floor. Between floors, she was hostage, not to her failing legs but to her inability to accept anything other than victory. Her inability to be anything less than exceptional. Her fanatical determination to beat her body into submission and surpass all barriers, mental, physical, or otherwise.

The sounds of cars on the street below rumbled meaninglessly in the background. Her own breathing echoed in the stillness. The glaring lights and floor to ceiling windows made her an amoeba in a Petri dish if anyone had cared to notice. Anyone would have rushed to help but strangely, at that time, on that day, in that place, no one was around. Just her, the echoing *thunk* of each step and the insurmountable distance between her and her objective.

She let go of the rail she'd been clutching with both hands and grasping her thigh, lifted her right leg onto the next step. Pulling the railing toward her she stood on that leg using all of her strength as she pulled her body against the railing, face pressed against the wall for support, and shot her left hand down, clutching the fabric of her pant leg, she pulled until her toe just cleared the lip of the next step. She continued, excruciatingly, for two more steps when the muscles in her quivering leg just quit. Failing to hold her weight she crashed against the steps and then down, a tumbling tangle of body parts as she rolled down the steps striking her face hard on the concrete landing below.

A blinding flash jolted through her, and for a moment, she was in a crumpled heap, not on the floor of the stairwell in her apartment building, but on the washed-out planks of an alleyway in the gray town. The wispy, black, vaguely humanoid shape of a hunter standing on the edge of an awning above her. Its oversized, clawed hands twitched restlessly at its side. Its burning, red-hot coals for eyes, scanning the village beyond, searching, hunting…for her.

Just beyond, a couple rooftops away was another, and another further on and quickly Deven saw that there were dozens scattered throughout the town, not just the handful she'd seen before. The shadow closest to her glitched out, springing forward and re-congealed on the rooftop above the awning and then glitched again and away. The others followed similarly, pressing steadily up the hillside.

And then, just as fast as it had begun, it was gone. And she was alone under the harsh white lights of the stairwell, racked with sobs of frustration, humiliation and not the least bit of fear.

It was the next day, when Kemper, suspiciously eyeing her poorly concealed black eye, casually asked her if she would join him at a 'hang-out' with some friends in Santa Cruz. Surprising them both, she'd said yes.

It was at that moment when she knew that what had seemed a quirk of memory, twisted by trauma, was actually something else entirely. She didn't know what, but her vision from the night before, and earlier that year, resonated intensely and intimately within her. Spending time with someone she enjoyed but had no delusion of actually having to *count on*, seemed, somehow less consequential. Before she might have seen it as a waste of time, but now, strangely, she felt a sort of comfort in it. No expectations. Just… companionship. She smiled at the reflection of herself in the glass of the pastry shelf as she removed her apron before heading home to get ready.

In the coolness of perpetual evening, as a dreary rain splattered on the washed-out planks of a battered pier, a dark figure stood. He took in the frozen-in-time avalanche of rough-hewn planks that was the town proper as it spread away and up the hillside.

Assessed the lurking, flowing mist under and between the structures that shrouded the mountain beyond that must form the underpinning of the town itself. The slender figure sniffed the air but puzzled at the lack of substance to it. No scent of food or wood fire, or waste that would come with a town of this size. He scanned the empty windows and doorways as they glistened in the muted silver light of a puzzlingly absent moon, and then, was surprised to see a solitary girl. Far in the distance, she sat on a ledge, eating an orange. He quietly pondered the oddity.

Suddenly a ripple, in the fabric of reality as he perceived it, snapped and spread outward from the lower village somewhere between them. The sensation was not precise, but it was certain. He watched as an errant shadow, first disappeared and then reappeared strides away from where it had begun. He didn't recognize the form but knew danger when he saw it.

Unconsciously, his right hand gestured smoothly from side to side as he slowly began to fade from view, but then paused in the awkward space between, there and not there. Two more blips and then a third. Their invisible circles spreading out, intermingling, and then fading like stones thrown into a pond.

Most of the time when he found himself in a strange place it was due to something he'd done or been compelled to do. Now, he could only assume he was in a dream, as this place certainly could not exist within reality. He didn't know how to get back anyway. He would, in this dream, do the same as he would in reality: whatever needed to be done.

Out of curiosity, he slipped his hand into the overlapping folds of his jacket and felt the now familiar smoothness of the crystalline gold-veined window, fastened, impossibly, into his chest exactly where his heart should be. He felt the tingle of energy that was associated with the object that now lay inside that space. Another impossibility, an ancient book of magic with a flaming orcish arrow stuck fast into its cover; suspended in the infinite void contained within him. It hurt his head to think of it but it at the same time managed to dissolve his clearly uninformed opinion of what *was* and *was not* possible.

He shook his head to clear away the competing thoughts and fastened his attention on the space where the girl had been. Absently he realized that the rain still fell from unseen clouds while the ripples kept coming; intermittently, and then, after a longer pause, one or two more. He sensed and saw that they were scouring the structures at the base of the town, hunting for the girl possibly, though he couldn't conceive of why or who she was, what they were or where in the whole of existence this place belonged. A place out of time. Words, or maybe concepts, popped into his head: *Unity, Bond, Age beyond Ages.* This, too, was a new occurrence since the appearance of the lantern door in his chest. Uncovering the ways in which the artifact residing there, a literal melding of the powers of dark and light, interacted with and influenced his magical abilities was fascinating, but he'd still failed to gather any meaning to it thus far.

D'avry shifted restlessly from one foot to the other as he contemplated the situation, but then a vague awareness tugged at his attention. He felt an unfamiliar weight in the inside pocket of his jacket. His expression went flat. He knew what it was before reaching in and pulling it out to glimmer in the soft silvery light of the moonless sky. A simple coin. And yet, so much more.

The compulsion twisted in his gut, and he braced himself for whatever lay next. The Astrig Ka'a did what *it* alone willed, but strangely, this time he sensed a new dimension to it. It had always been an early season snow when he'd planned a parade. A stampede when he'd wished for a steak. But now, he sensed a hesitant sort of suggestibility, like that of a mustang who after a long afternoon of throwing its cowboy had finally lost interest and become pliable.

D'avry removed a leather strap that'd been wound about his

wrist and slipped it through a hole in the center of the heavy coin. As he tied it around his neck to form a necklace of sorts, he felt the familiar ripple and was now looking at the town from uphill as it spread out below him. He realized, too, to his immense displeasure, that he was staring at the jumble of weathered rooftops from behind a long, black beak.

Suggestible, apparently, but not controlled. Movement to his right drew his attention and he was staring at the girl from earlier, just a few feet away. Rain rolled down his feathers and into his eyes causing him instinctively to shimmy and ruffle them to keep them dry for flight. He realized, too, that this was also a posturing gesture before a suitable mate, but then quickly checked his bird instincts to focus on the important things at hand.

He didn't notice that the rain had ceased at that moment. He found it hard to pull his eyes from the dark-haired young woman still staring at him, her blue eyes round with surprise and curiosity. But then he sensed again the blip and pop of more of the hunting shadow beings as they gathered in the town below from some dimension beyond.

I have to warn her, he thought, but there wasn't much he could do in his present form. Leaping from the railing, he plummeted downward, slowly extending his wings to gather lift as he adjusted a wingtip to arc slowly left across the rooftops, well away, but close enough to the shadow things for the girl to take notice. He hoped she would anyway.

D'avry continued his arc and then as he grew closer and closer to the rooftops, he realized he was going to have to actually work at this flying thing. Beating his wings powerfully he let instinct instruct his actions and with a fair semblance of skill began to climb. *Whooshing* over rooftops he climbed higher and higher until he was what he judged to be a few hundred paces further up the hill than where the girl had been. However, when he looked back, she'd gone.

A wretched cry rang out from below and hung in the air, echoing across the mist shrouded hillside. It was followed by similar clipped responses from its counterparts. Still, the blips kept coming, their ripples clanging and bouncing throughout the town until D'avry thought he'd grow seasick from the commotion. Still, the girl was nowhere to be seen.

Eleven

The In-Between

19.004329 AC (After Construct)
Age of the Half-Orc War

D'avry awoke again and groaned. Everything on his side ached from sleeping on the hard, sand covered rock. A bone deep chill presided over the host of other aches. He hated camping this close to water. You just couldn't get away from the cold. He looked to see that the sky was clear and bright. However, here in the deep vee-shaped valley it would be another hour before sunlight touched this stretch of beach.

D'avry blinked the sleep from his eyes and was surprised to find that while being preoccupied by his list of miseries, he had missed a scant heat emanating from somewhere behind him and the faintest suggestion of cooking fish. He rolled over and was delighted to see the glow of a campfire, hear the crisp crackle of newly added wood, and just make out the faintest scent of sizzling river trout on a spit. This was heartening. The absence of Gearlach and the Librarian was not, however. Volkreek, who prepared the trout over the fire, flashed a half-hearted smile in D'avry's direction which somehow managed to summarize the state of things exactly. It said, 'Good morning! We're all probably going to die.' D'avry gave a curt nod and looked further past the ranger to Farn, who was quite a way off, sitting on a rock and staring down at the staff as if it had just given him a thorough beating and was threatening to do so again. D'avry would have to intervene soon or the priest was likely to turn himself into something nasty and irreversible. D'avry was not knowledgeable in the ways of magic by way of books of spells, but Farn's approach seemed to be inviting disaster in his estimation. He noticed also that Liggo seemed to be among those missing. The last thing that D'avry noticed was that the boat, which was still present and accounted for, was, however, sitting mostly submerged where they'd left it, in the swirling eddy pool that was away from the deeper waters rushing past the adjacent shore.

The waters were clearer and calmer now than they'd been the night before but looming in the back of his mind were the competing terrors of the present where they were being hunted by an undead Orc Warlord and the haunting dreamworld's he now found himself traveling while he slept, with their own distinct brands of terror and mortal peril.

He closed his eyes as his stomach tightened, slowed his breathing, and found his hand drawn to the crystalline window in his chest. As he touched it a tingle flicked through his senses causing the hairs to rise on his legs, forearms, and neck. There definitely was a power there. He sensed the dark and light of it, felt danger running through it like the steel of a zither string. And yet, there was something comforting to it, his thoughts drifted to stacks of worn, leather-bound tomes warmed by the morning sun that painted the library atrium of the academy in pastel pinks, yellows, and oranges.

He let his mind wander and faces began to emerge from the mist of memory, but not all of that memory was his own. He remembered things past and also things yet to be. He felt the thread straining between these people, stretching centuries and eons, separated by chaos. Sometimes the faces were shrouded, out of focus, and sometimes they were close enough to make out the details of wrinkle lines, eyelashes, pores, and then D'avry blinked in shock.

It was her! One of the faces was the girl from the gray town. He'd only seen her up close for a moment, but he was certain. Another face replaced hers, and it too was close. It was that of a man in his mid-forties. Soldierly of bearing, sinewy and hard but with a tempered intensity, at once father-like and weary, as if carrying the scars of a multitude of atrocities. This face was somehow linked to the metal monster from the caverns. And then, they were gone.

Volkreek crouched before him, granules of sand grinding softly together beneath his leather boots. D'avry looked into his eyes and saw that they were tuned in to the growing sense of danger that was now bubbling furiously into D'avry's awareness. The sun was still creeping down the hillside behind him but there was a certainty of violence on the softly flowing breeze. He gave a slow nod of affirmation and in one fluid motion pulled Volkreek to the ground with his left hand while his right, which was about to repeat the blending spell from before, did something completely different instead. Something that felt natural but entirely new. He'd never performed this manipulation but as it completed, Volkreek's momentum pulled them down, *through* the sand and stone of their campsite as if the two plunged through the surface of a pond. Their bodies sank further into what should have been choking dirt and rock as they twisted to look back toward the surface and were startled to vaguely see the ground a few feet above them. Arrows crisscrossed from multiple directions but skittered off the rocks where they'd been only moments before.

Volkreek and D'avry continued to look on in shock as roughly a dozen goblin-like creatures converged on the spot. The creatures also looked about in astonishment. One of the bug-eyed, hairy creatures, with two shrunken heads dangling from his shoulder armor paused and sniffed the air. He motioned across the water and down toward the confluence. Without a word, the party bounded down the shoreline in that direction. D'avry marveled as he saw *through* the river, which was also transparent in a way that was impossible under normal circumstances. He now saw an identical party shadowing the movements of the first but from the other side of the river canyon.

It was then that he realized that he'd been holding his breath this whole time. He turned to Volkreek and realized he'd been doing the same but was clearly near the end of his abilities. D'avry didn't know if it was possible to drown in this state but intuited that there was something that he could do. Bringing both hands to his lips, he slowly blew out. The action formed a bubble of sorts which, defying all logic, stayed contained within his hands. He offered it to Volkreek who without hesitation swam forward to take the bubble and breathe from it. And oddly, it seemed to work.

D'avry did not feel the frantic impulses of running out of breath as he imagined he should, but Volkreek apparently did. In fact, he wanted to explore the bounds of this new surreality, to swim in the river flowing above him to see if he would need to breathe there or could continue to exist outside the need for air. However, Volkreek was not so comfortable and in fact appeared to be running short again, the bubble had diminished to less than half of what he'd provided only moments ago. D'avry repeated the steps to create the bubble, while Volkreek finished the last of what he held before carefully taking the next.

D'avry then motioned toward the tree line, believing that surfacing there might keep them hidden from this newest threat. Volkreek nodded agreement and they both swam through the strangely transparent rock and dirt in that direction when something caught D'avry's attention. A small flicker of light like that of a glow-worm was visible in the underground, near the trailhead as it funneled into a space just wide enough for two people shoulder to shoulder. He swam toward the light and as he drew nearer, he felt that tingle of magic in it and something more. It had the feel of purpose. The sureness of fate. D'avry had learned long ago that with the Astrig Ka'a, there were no coincidences.

D'avry stared at what appeared to be a small wooden chest buried at the base of a flat sided boulder. It could only be about two feet below the surface. D'avry, again intuited that he would not be able to capture it in this current state, so he grabbed Volkreek's sleeve and swam to the surface just uphill of the trail, a few feet into the foliage.

Exiting the underground to the pine needle laden forest floor proved awkward as it didn't quite act like water, and they weren't really buoyant. It wasn't until the last tip of a toe had departed the below grounds that the earth felt solid. They both lay on the forest floor, breathing and listening for more of the unknown creatures' party but also processing what had just happened.

The feral look in Volkreek's eyes, as always, communicated volumes. Like:

What on earth was that? Where did all of those creatures come from? Do you think Liggo has been captured or killed? What about Farn?

D'avry caught all of that and more. The biggest question: did Gearlach find Trask or had N'Bruyyh stolen him back and was now on his way to uniting all of the orc clans in an ultimate battle against mankind? He didn't know the answer to any of these questions. He did know that they needed to find the rest of their party. Liggo and Farn first. That jogged something.

Why hadn't the wards been triggered? Either they didn't work, or Farn had dismantled them, or if he'd done something wrong and destroyed himself and the staff, they would have dissolved. That was a somber thought, but it didn't ring true in his heart. The priest had been there on the beach only moments before.

He sensed differently. In fact, there was a vibration of sorts that he could feel — like two flies caught in a spider's web. The vibrations were frantic but faint. One was close, maybe a mile away and the other… it was coming from *inside* the mountain. The goblins had to have an entrance to their lair that was inside the perimeter of the wards. Which meant that they'd be coming back unless they returned via some other hidden entrance elsewhere.

D'avry shot a glance in Volkreek's direction and was not entirely surprised to see that he seemed to be on the same page already. His eyes narrowed as he speculated about the unlikelihood but then he remembered the box by the trail. Turning on his heels, he made his way over to the flat-sided boulder and out of a whim slid his hand across the surface. It yielded a faint but discernible inscription in an unfamiliar language that quickly faded away. He repeated the gesture in order to lock into his memory the shapes and figures for later and then grabbed a stick and started digging feverishly. Volkreek joined in and in short order they were pulling the small wooden chest from its resting place of years innumerable. D'avry was surprised that though he was unable to see through the box while in the underground space, it appeared to be unwarded. Inside, he found a small, plain looking dagger, a generous bag of silver and gold coin minted under some long gone principality, and a ring.

The ring was made of a lustrous white metal, finely crafted, and inlaid within the rectangular setting was an oval shaped jewel. The stone was pearlescent and multi-colored, and it glowed softly, emanating a cool energy that he could somehow discern now. What was its purpose or power? He was unable to determine that at the moment and would have to sort it out at a more convenient time. Besides, it was too small to fit him even if he'd been brave enough to try. For now, his friends, as well as himself, were in grave danger.

D'avry didn't know where to start. Somewhere within the perimeter of their wards was a cave entrance but they hadn't found it when they were inspecting the area. It must be cleverly hidden indeed. He didn't know much about his companions, but they appeared to know what they were about. D'avry thought through his various spells and a few little tricks he'd learned over the years and really couldn't come up with any toe hold on how to crack this quandary. Volkreek on the other hand had returned to the scene of the initial contact and was working his way backward from where he'd seen the arrows coming from, which was all within the tree line but from many different angles. He walked amongst the trees, studying the ground, noting some disturbance in foliage here or faint footprints in the soft soil there, in general there was very little to go on. It was as if they just appeared from nowhere. D'avry's eyes were drawn upward. Had the goblins come from the trees themselves? Volkreek caught D'avry's gaze, and he, too, began to scan the tree trunks for signs of transit. There were none to speak of, but slowly, D'avry could string together a pathway through the branches that seemed plausible for a goblin sized creature but still couldn't ascertain an originating point.

Minutes passed and all that seemed to come to them was the sound of the river below and the faint whisper of wind in the treetops, when suddenly, a cawing noise broke the silence of the forest and a black shape lighted upon a treetop ahead of them. It squawked and fluttered away, dropping something as it drifted away on the breeze.

D'avry knew what it was before it touched the ground. It would be a coin. Plain, surprisingly heavy and with a hole in its middle. He ran up to the spreading oak, noting its impressive girth, it would easily take three or four grown men touching fingertips to reach around the entire circumference. Standing at its base, on the uphill side, he found what he'd expected to. He reached down and picked up the coin. Volkreek eyed him suspiciously but as was to be expected, said nothing. He seemed to take the new occurrence as commonplace.

Looking upward from where the coin had dropped, D'avry saw a substantial branch, prominently placed beneath what appeared to be an opening where the trunk had been split some years before, perhaps by lightning. The tree appeared to have survived and thrived in the intervening years but the cavity, from what D'avry could see from below, remained. If this was indeed the entrance to the goblin lair, he understood now how it had been missed. *Up is down* he thought, and the idea stuck in his mind as if placed there. Not unlike the words that continued to pop into his mind frequently now.

Unity. Bond. Balance. Framework. Focus. And yet other words like *Crossing, Age beyond Ages.* He couldn't comprehend their meaning yet, but he was certain that the Astrig Ka'a would reveal what it wished, when and only when it intended to. For now, if indeed there was an entrance above, their path seemed to be laid out before them. They would enter the goblin lair, attempt to locate their missing companions, escape intact and then, again, attempt to locate the rest of their party. Oh, and also avoid being captured, tortured and killed by a genocidal orc warlord. He was seriously hoping that Gearlach was having luck hunting down the librarian, Trask, before any irreversible damage could be done. D'avry was frustrated at the luck that had caused the party to be scattered, but he couldn't see leaving Liggo and Farn to their fates and he didn't see the odds of survival getting any better with a smaller party. It was small enough.

With renewed determination he looked back to the tree to find that Volkreek had already scurried up the massive oak and was reaching down for him to join him on the branch above. From the excitement that was evident in his eyes, D'avry knew that this was it. He grabbed the outstretched hand and in short order was standing atop the branch beside the mute Thadding fighter. The two were similar in stature, but Volkreek was heavier of muscle, indeed, D'avry had been surprised at how easily he had pulled him up to join him. He hoped that the skill and strength between them would be enough to free their friends. For that's how he now thought of them, this ragtag band of adventurer's whom he'd known now for barely more than twenty-four hours. D'avry could still sense the other two, deep in the heart of the mountain, still separated but getting closer together. He marveled at this newfound ability. There was amazing power there, but still much to unlock. This new sense didn't tell him how to get to where his friends were, but it may still be useful.

He had no sense of Gearlach or Trask, which concerned him greatly. Either they were dead, or they were being shielded by some other force or entity, or perhaps it was just distance? He couldn't be sure. He didn't understand these new powers, didn't understand their extent or their limitations, but one thing at a time. He looked now at the opening, at the split in the towering tree. There were steps carved into the sides of what was a partially hollowed out section of the tree trunk forming a tightly spiraled staircase. Volkreek cast his eyes heavenward for a quick second as if soaking in one last breath of free air, which hopefully would not be their last. D'avry realized he had unconsciously done the same.

Without saying a word, Volkreek drew his blade, his bow still slung tightly on his back. Pointing with his free hand to his eyes and then down into the darkness of the entrance into the goblin's lair, D'avry realized that this was the first direct communication he'd ever had with the fighter. He understood the request, suddenly realizing that any gear they'd had was still laying scattered about the campsite, if it hadn't already been carried off by roving bands of goblins or other creatures. As such, they had no lanterns that they could use to explore the caves. A pretty significant problem.

D'avry performed a truncated version of the hand manipulation he'd used to generate the flame column at their first meeting. This generated a small, heatless ember he held in the palm of his hand. He motioned for Volkreek to present his blade. Arching his eyebrow, his green eyes glinting with interest he did as requested. D'avry placed the ember on the tip of the double edged short sword and was surprised to see a muted ripple of rune-work run like a wave from point to hilt and back again.

This was an effect that was not anticipated, though very little surprised him anymore. He'd suspected that there was some minor enchantment to the blade since that would seem consistent with the rest of the party. Nothing of the magnitude of what he'd sensed from Gearlach's weapon.

The draw of that stone contained within the charm still gave D'avry goosebumps when he thought about it, though he didn't know why. He couldn't describe the sensation as good or bad, it was just a reaction like the invisible force exerted by a lode stone.

Volkreek moved the blade around gingerly to ensure he didn't lose the ember, but it appeared to be part of the blade now, just a glowing point of light at the tip, but the blade did seem to carry some residual luminescence, though faintly; the lightest of tracing along the lines of the blade and the runework that had been heretofore invisible. As he turned to the entrance, though, the luminescence increased slightly as though responding to the will of the bearer.

Volkreek, pulled the sword back and the light diminished to an almost imperceptible level. A smile could be seen beneath the reddish-gray riffles of his beard. His green eyes flicked over to D'avry and then back to the entrance as the sword's light grew again with intentionality. He took the first two steps, and then pushing the blade further into the darkness below him, quickly slid out of sight.

The warlord's skin crackled under the flames but seemed to repair itself as fast as it was eaten away. He looked down at his hand, the green flame crawling across charred flesh, stripes of red viscera showing in ragged streaks from beneath. The flames slithered in undulating waves up his fingers, hands, and forearm.

His ears were full of the sound of the rain and thunder and the rushing waters, but his nostrils were choked with the stench of his own blistering flesh and that of the oddly metallic-smelling fire.

Goriahh's magic was an abomination. *He* was an abomination, he mused, grinning darkly, splitting skin that healed back in the following instant. Twisted voices echoed in a miasma of homicidal urges inside his mind but were silenced by purpose. Hell *was* chaos, but it could not so easily overwhelm an ordered mind.

Nonplused, he cast his gaze skyward. The rain pelted his face, scoured his body but could not quench the flame. It would burn out in due time, he knew. He waded shoreward, the waters, steaming and hissing with his passing. As he reached the sandy cobble, he turned to consider his boat and crew and more importantly, the quarry they'd lost down the supposedly *impassable* section of river.

It had been a good plan. Thwarted by the very forces that had been bent to give him aid. *Attack swiftly during the chaos of the storm. Attack with fire and with fear.* However, the storm was overkill and created a new path for his prey to flee down. Fire had turned on those who wielded it. Fear did nothing but energize the flight of their prey. Folly.

It had been a mistake. Mistakes were painful. He felt that pain. He felt *nothing but* pain. Goriahh had failed to mention the side effects of immortality. But then, N'Bruyyh was no fool. He'd known there would be a cost. Great success required great sacrifice.

He scanned the tree line with eyes that pierced the shadows, the superior eyes of an orc. Beyond the embankment, the portage trail was there somewhere. He knew who's boot prints he'd find there as well. Well, he wouldn't find any boot prints in this rain. Though, even now it was beginning to diminish and with it the violently whipping wind. Within minutes, they both would likely fade into a more seasonably appropriate drizzle.

He breathed in the scents of the forest, tasted them, sussed them out from among the spores of burnt flesh and metallic smoke. His enhanced sense of smell, too, was all orc. N'Bruyyh didn't have to wait to follow the man's tracks. He could follow the scent of fear, and his sadly human otherness. *So out of place in the wild.*

"Humans..." he spat the word as it bubbled into his subconscious. He'd lost the others, but they would be drawn back to this man in their futile attempt to thwart his plans. Trask and this pup from the east, Gearlach. They'd both die, but in *his* time.

N'Bruyyh knew where the man was going anyway, roughly at least. But he intended not to take things for granted, like that idiotic storm. Another unnecessary flourish from the mind of that half-breed bitch. Instead, he waited for the rain to lessen and considered what came next, the *sign* from the heavens. The long awaited herald of the rebirth of the age of Dakremesh-Gul-Etten-Ga-Meshundhuul. A tool, nothing more. An opportunity.

He would use the superstitions of his people to bend their will to his. He could care less about ancient prophecies. Prophecies were for people who lacked the vision to do. After he was done, they would say that it was the gods that had ordained it, Dakremesh himself. But *he* knew it would have been all his own doing that re-forged the orc clans into a unified people, into a fearsome weapon. A weapon that would rend the skies and the land and all who stood before them.

After a time, N'Bruyyh came to a bend in the canyon. Here tall slabs of rock extended into the sky in a half-circle, like the inside curve of a bow. A tree specked island at the very top split the river into two identical falls that plummeted to the rocks below. Some of that water, though, wisped away in the buffeting winds, tousling softly like lovers tresses.

The warlord took in the scene before him, marveling at its

beauty, and smiled inwardly at the thought that this jewel of nature would soon count among his possessions. He spotted the white fur and great curled horns of a mountain ram drinking from the water's edge and watched as a large bird circled high above. The dark shape glided casually on the winds and then after a while descended down to within feet of the waters before finally lighting on a boulder, paces away and directly between the great orc warrior and his view.

The creature resembled a vulture, with glossy golden eyes and gore caked about its beak. Suddenly a grotesque crunching noise emanated from the bird and its leathery red neck snapped backward revealing a cavity in its chest which then tore into four distinct sections, yawning wide, peeling back with sickening pops and crackles of bone and sinew, looking like some kind of hell spawn flower made of feathers and flesh.

A deep sucking sound emanated from the void within the mutilated carcass and then green, bubbling bile burped up and dribbled slowly down the nearside folds of flesh. N'Bruyyh's face showed no expression.

"You're flare for the dramatic is unamusing," he told it.

"As is your prowess beneath the blankets." A vaguely feminine voice responded acidly, the voice emanating from within the twisted cavity. The creature hopped from one foot to the other before settling back down onto its rump. Bile spewed up again in an oozing wave and drooled into a growing puddle at its feet.

The warlord cracked his neck left and right and then slowly stretched a muscle in his back, one eye squinting with a twinge of knotted nerves. He continued, join to line above "Your storm flooded the gorge, allowing the band of men to escape. I told you it was unnecessary."

"So, too, lighting yourself and your crew on fire," the carcass responded.

His eyes narrowed, "Sabotage. Trask's capacity for

spitefulness apparently eclipses even his own legendary knack for self-preservation."

"So, you failed to get Trask and failed to kill that whelp of a drougehnn."

"I will hunt down the librarian... and Gearlach will come to me."

"True. I have seen it."

"Ox dross. Your foreknowing is for shit. That's why we had Trask. But we won't need him anymore after the Herald of Dakremesh rends the mountain and yields its splendor."

"And your greatness shall be rivaled only by your opinion of yourself! Don't forget who got you here—"

But the creature was unable to finish before N'Bruyyh, with a flat-sided swing of his great blade launched it in a squealing, bubbling arc, off the boulder and over the rock edge to the rapids below.

"Wind bag..." he muttered and then trotted off, sheathing his blade and attempting to shake off the fire that had yet to die out but still clung steadfastly to the flesh of his arm. After a moment he abandoned the effort, settled into an efficient jog, and disappeared into the trees as he followed the trail of his quarry.

Twelve

The Winding Path

The darkness of the forest seemed to close in around D'avry in the absence of his companion and of the glowing blade. This struck him as odd as it was still early in the morning and the sun had broken over the ridge while they were still hunting for the entrance. But now it seemed unable to penetrate the canopy above and a hushed silence had descended upon the grotto like a blanket. D'avry hurried along behind Volkreek, whipping up a new ember, half to see and half to sooth his nerves as he began the descent.

The staircase broadened as it wound downward and quickly the smooth warm browns of tree roots was replaced by the cold gray stone of the mountain's core. It continued down, meandering further away from the near vertical descent at the beginning but in no meaningful direction as far as D'avry could tell, especially in the absence of any landmarks. The two continued deeper, the staircase seeming to continue without end until around a corner it presented a small landing that protruded out between huge clefts of rock on either side. The landing appeared to open out into a great chamber shrouded by deeper darkness.

The gritty shuffling noises that had accompanied them for well over an hour now seemed to lose immediacy in this new space. The faintest of echoes told him that what had been largely just a tunnel through the rock was opening into something greater here. Volkreek extinguished the light of his blade with a thought. He'd had time to master its mechanics on the long path down. D'avry did the same, though he was still bound to the rules of conjuring as he'd known them which required a quick series of hand movements to complete the spell, essentially returning the flow of energy back to its invisible source.

They listened in the darkness. Somewhere nearby in the void there was a dripping. Further on, below them and far to their left, the faint clatter of a stream? Contained within the noise there was something else, like the quiet groan of an axle. D'avry immediately imagined a water wheel, but to what purpose down here? A faint shuffle nearby and Volkreek's blade blossomed to life and *whooshed* through the air following blurred movement up the wall.

It was a translucent gray creature with huge black saucers for eyes and suction cup like fingers on its feet and hands. *Somewhat frog-like*, D'avry thought, first thinking that they were kind of cute in a disgusting sort of way and then remembering that some frogs were poisonous and had tongues that extended many times the length of their own bodies. He felt suddenly less relief at this realization.

The roughly dog-sized creature scurried up and out of reach before spinning and staring back at them, seemingly content to observe from a distance. Beyond it, there was another, and another beyond that. Pretty soon D'avry could make out nearly two dozen, scattered about the walls above them and spreading away from where they stood on the landing. They were all still, seemingly transfixed by the light of Volkreek's blade. Soon, he counted fewer. He hadn't noticed their going but the number of pairs of black eyes staring back at them was growing less and less until it was just the one. The closest set of eyes above them.

"Do you know what they are?" D'avry asked. Volkreek shook his head, his eyes still fixed on the creature. Then the light blossomed, growing in intensity to reveal a massive cavern disappearing into darkness both above them and far away to the left as the cavern floor descended gradually down.

The light revealed a winding path following, and occasionally crossing, a clear stream as it continued off into the distance. What D'avry had discerned earlier did in fact prove to be a water wheel, roughly twelve feet across and of a construction that allowed it to pull water from the stream and deposit it into a vee-shaped trough near the top of its arc. That trough formed a small canal that spanned the distance to the closest wall on rickety looking wooden crossmembers. Once there, it meandered left and right following the folds of the wall before eventually disappearing from view. He spotted it again in the distance but much, much further away.

D'avry realized that he still had a sense of his companions, and it was indeed further down into the belly of the mountain, though not exactly in the direction that was visible from his current vantage point. He couldn't see any more of the creatures but the one that had ventured closest was still little more than a dozen feet away. At this point, having seen no signs of hostility, he was largely of the mind that maybe they were friendly or at least, ambivalent.

He looked to Volkreek who still had a suspicious air about him, darting glances occasionally in its direction. Finally, Volkreek looked to D'avry and then cast one last glance up at the wall climbing creature, shrugged noncommittally and then turned away toward the path. Instantly, the glow from the blade diminished to just enough to guide their feet and to keep an eye on their new friend. They pecked their way down the trail to the stream and were indeed followed by the gray, translucent creature lurking just out of reach. D'avry decided Lurker was a fitting name for it and it's kind.

The path along the stream, much like the winding staircase from the surface, continued for innumerable hours. Towering cavern walls seemed more like those of a deep canyon, though there was no sign of sky or stars. Occasionally D'avry did catch a glimpse of some luminescence in small clusters high up on the walls themselves. He thought that he could just make out shapes that seemed to him like very large toadstools, but he couldn't be sure. He found himself growing weary with the unending travel, though the going was much easier than it'd been at first.

Soon the path widened. It appeared to be a switchback in the trail, and it reminded him of the landing they'd first encountered at the bottom of the initial staircase. He wondered if it were possible that there could be an even greater space before them and how such a large cavity could exist inside of a mountain.

Volkreek sensed it too and reduced the glow to a circle just a few paces across so as not to give away their position to anyone or anything beyond their immediate area. They'd seen no other signs of life down here beyond the lurkers and the well worn stone of the pathway. And, of course, the water wheel at the head of the trail.

D'avry and Volkreek examined the extents of the clearing, exploring the boulders that formed its periphery, and found the remnants of a fire circle but the ashes were cold, and it had not been used recently that they could tell. D'avry was growing concerned. Better than half a day underground and so far nothing had really been as he'd expected. He had imagined that the caves would have been tighter, shorter, more riddled with danger and that they would have stumbled upon a hive of goblin activity. But so far there was nothing to suggest that the goblins had even passed this way other than his enhanced perception that told him his friends were still ahead.

Even that was concerning since it seemed that the two signals, for lack of a better term, had still not come together, and in fact did not appear to be any closer than when D'avry and Volkreek had started. He began to worry that maybe he was sensing something else, but that didn't feel... true, he guessed. The source of the signals or maybe signatures(?) was definitely his friends. And they definitely felt as though they were in peril. Theirs was not an enjoyable journey.

He didn't know how he knew what he did, but he did. He realized his partner might benefit from this information as they were *his* travelling companions after all.

"Volkreek." D'avry started, "I can… *tell*, that they're alright."

He had his attention. A curt nod conveyed his understanding. D'avry, again was surprised at how the man seemed to take almost anything in stride.

"I can also, *tell*, that they are further ahead in these caverns. I can feel their presence."

Once again, Volkreek nodded his understanding. Indeed, he seemed to have anticipated this as well.

"But… they're not getting any closer. We're not catching up to them."

At this, Volkreek blinked, his brow furrowing slightly.

"I believe they're moving. I'm beginning to get the sense that, maybe they weren't captured to be kept or used, but perhaps to be *delivered*… like, as an offering, or a gift."

This last was news even to D'avry. He hadn't developed this line of reasoning from the facts at hand, it was pure intuition, but somehow more than that, it was…certainty.

Just then, D'avry felt the familiar pull, like that of the Astrig Ka'a, but the energy he now associated with the lantern door in his chest where the combined artifact of the book of spells and the perpetual fire of the orcish arrow hovered, suspended. Now, he felt the pull of the *darkness* within that artifact. And it was disturbingly strong.

Something jostled his memory. It was the darkness within his dream the night before and he was surprised that he hadn't thought about it since. He supposed he may have been just pushing it out of his mind because of how terrifying it had been. Even now a tight surge of panic clenched his gut. That terror had seemed as much its own thing as the darkness had, and then he remembered something else.

The wave of panic he'd felt when he'd heard the drums as the band of orcs descended upon them in the storm earlier that day. He couldn't see how they had anything to do with one another, he was certain that they did not, but the effect was not dissimilar. Was it possible, that the terror he'd felt in the dream cave was magic as well? He felt like that was important for whatever reason, but the moment was the moment and needed to be addressed.

His friends were being taken somewhere, he couldn't be sure where exactly but he was beginning to have a suspicion. And this new angle with the presence in the darkness. It was a lot to take in... Even though he knew that they should press on, doubling their efforts to catch up with their missing companions, there was a piece of him that just felt stretched too thin, like charging blindly forward was a recipe for disaster.

He caught Volkreek's shoulder as he was about to continue his inspection of the landing. The hardened fighter jumped a little which struck D'avry as amusing and odd. He stifled a smile and hoped the arcane lighting wouldn't betray his efforts.

"We should wait here for a moment," D'avry told the ranger. Volkreek's eyes darted down the trail toward his friends and back to the mage, he stroked his beard nervously. Concern, and impatience were evident on his face. And there was something more. *What was it... fear?* That was new. In the short time he had known him, and given the circumstances they'd experienced, it was surprising. To this point, in the face of every crisis, he had been implacable. Resolute and quick to act. D'avry's mind jumped to an uncomfortable conclusion.

"You feel it, too. Don't you?"

Volkreek's gaze dropped and quickly snapped back up to meet his own. The muscles unconsciously flexing in his jaws. He nodded slowly, almost imperceptibly, but to D'avry it was clear consensus. The sense of dread, the sense of a building darkness, it was not just D'avry's hyper-sensitivity.

D'avry felt stuck. There was an idea just outside his comprehension, banging on the walls of his mind, but it would vanish the moment he turned his attention to it.

Thirteen

Feit Kar'zuum

Slowly, the sound of a low, groaning wind could be heard in the farthest reaches of the greater cavern. Blinding light sprang from Volkreek's blade, and he held it aloft as he turned to face the noise. Bright as it was it failed to penetrate anything but their immediate surroundings as the space inside the cavern was just too great.

Still the groaning continued and indeed seemed to be steadily building as more and more wind could be heard pouring forth from other areas of the open space, as though there were many such canyons entering a very large basin beyond them. The wind gained volume as it grew closer, whistling now through the rock structures below. Volkreek looked to D'avry for direction, but it was clear that he was just as clueless as himself. Wind began to stir around them now, whipping up little twisters in the dust, and no sooner did they begin to feel the hint of a breeze but the temperature began to descend markedly.

That breeze turned into a steady, sustained wind which continued to build, clawing at loose clothing, biting exposed flesh. The wind further on grew and grew until it was all they could hear. Like a massive waterfall the sound filled the space, the temperature, too, dropped to the point that D'avry's own breath issued forth in quick puffs of vapor, increasing with his heartbeat.

Both men pulled up their hoods, bringing their cloaks and jackets in tighter around them. Soon they were shielding their eyes as the intensity of the wind doubled and then doubled again. D'avry, now forced to cover his face with his forearm, suddenly realized that the lurker was nowhere to be seen. That seemed an ill-sign. At that moment he realized, too, that the light from Volkreek's blade had diminished somewhat and he was struck by the fact that in the churning wind he'd thought he'd seen the faintest silhouette of a person.

The wind ripped through the space with renewed force and it was clear that he would need to do something or they might possibly be whipped to death, or frozen, or both. D'avry dared a glance towards Volkreek. His companion was struggling now, a look of terse determination etched upon his face. He was gripping the sword with both hands, shaking with the effort of illuminating the small patch of stone around them.

D'avry's eyes widened, and he quickly had to blink away the sand and grit. Even as he brought his left hand up to wipe his eyes with his sleeve, his right hand began moving to form shapes within shapes which he then used to write invisible symbols and characters in the swirling air before him. Still blinking the dust away, his left hand now joined the other and in a more elaborate construction than he'd ever designed before he continued feeding the flow of the magic like billows to a flame, intuiting each next step to form something of which he still did not quite know the end result.

The invisible characters now began to form the slightest trace of luminescence as his hands moved through the air, undulating like drunken dancers, streaming shimmering trails behind them. The images lasting longer and glowing more intensely as he continued, his hands whipped feverishly and then in one final movement they clasped tightly together at his chest, clapping together. And then, flying quickly outward, a sphere of calm and light expanded and then stopped as if meeting some invisible line of resistance.

He calmed his mind and concentrated, pushing the sphere further still until it encompassed the two men with only an arm's length beyond before the calm reduced to the chaos that was still building around them.

The maelstrom seemed to be no longer something off in the

distance but rather was centered directly on top of where they stood. He was certain that if he'd not begun the enchantment when he did, they would indeed have been ripped apart, shredded by sand grit and frozen in place to the very spot. Now, with the barest space between them and the storm, it was clear that there were indeed forms of people or creatures contained within its rushing winds.

D'avry had many ideas of what this could mean, but none of them were good. It compelled him to focus more intensely, calming his breathing and his heart rate to channel and augment the flow more effectively. *Billows to flames,* he thought, and poured on more and more energy.

Out of the corner of his still stinging eyes, Volkreek was getting close to the end of his ability to continue and yet the intensity of the windstorm just outside their sphere of protection did not seem to wane. He began to question how long he himself would be able to continue to hold the sphere in place. They would have to move to a more protected location if they were going to survive.

Volkreek was sweating and shaking and the look in his eyes had gone from intense determination to something bordering on desperation. D'avry motioned with his head toward the switchback just ahead. *Perhaps there was a fold in the cavern wall where they could tuck in, bring the sphere in tighter in order to expend less energy or mana?* D'avry's mute companion didn't bother to respond with anything more than a shuffling sidestep in that direction.

And with that, they pushed toward the trail. The pressure of the windstorm against their repelling magic felt akin to pushing the carcass of a tree through the breaking waves of an incoming tide. It took monumental effort to get started but once they did it was almost as if there was at least a tiny bit of momentum moving with them. They continued to push down the trail, through another couple switchbacks, not finding what they were looking for when the trail, turning back yet again, narrowed and seem to almost recede into a sheer cliff.

D'avry had the impression that they were now quite a ways below where they were when winds had started. He guessed that the wide spot in the trail had actually been an overlook, though it seemed an impossible idea hours below the surface of the earth. They pressed in close to the cliff, shoulder to shoulder as the wind drove against them in unrelenting fury.

A hundred yards further on and sweat was pouring from them both. Then the rugged texture of the wall behind their backs turned suddenly smooth and D'avry's fingertips found marks on the surface that were clearly crafted. His heart leapt as he felt a long vertical line which seemed to him to be the outline of a doorway.

The sphere's intensity faltered as he felt a gust of wind whip the fringe of his long, leather jacket and looked down to see that with that sensation was the faintest trace of a grasping hand, he pushed the sphere out in a burst of intensity and before him a womanly apparition with glowing blue eyes stood in the air just an arm's length away. Only, she didn't recede into the obscurity of the wind as the others had. She wanted to be seen.

D'avry's eyes were locked on hers. Volkreek as well was frozen in place as her hands came up to press upon the invisible boundary of the now feebly glowing sphere. As her hands touched the field, halos of blue lightning splashed outward, and her eyes widened with indignation.

D'avry felt the pressure from those hands, felt her rage at being denied that which she sought. His mind went to the window in his chest, and he drew from its power even as the intensity of the windstorm swelled up around them.

The woman's eyes glimmered blindingly in the darkness. A miasma of hair like liquid black pearl swirled around her — an inverted halo with the tortured faces of the damned straining through, plasma waves of blue fire crackling outward.

The assault of light and noise was all consuming. Sweat beaded on D'avry's forehead and neck as he poured one last burst of energy into the defending calm as his hand found the freezing cold metal circle of a door handle.

He yanked it open, and he and Volkreek tumbled backward against the press of darkness and hate. The door slammed shut with an echoing *thud* and a spell of binding issued from his lips in a form of magic and in a language he'd never studied before. The door held fast, though he wondered how.

His look of shock was lost in the totality of darkness. The squall hammered at the outside. The woman shrieked in rage and with her a chorus of hate filled chanting boomed, rising in volume and intensity until, even inside, D'avry and Volkreek had to cover their ears. But then, slowly at first, it began to lessen. And, within a matter of minutes, faded to virtually nothing and then disappeared completely.

Volkreek and D'avry continued to lay there on the floor, sucking in ragged breaths from exertion and exhaustion and terror. The darkness in the chamber was complete but neither bothered to try to generate light. They didn't need to look at one another. Neither was quite ready to vocalize what they'd just experienced. Perhaps hoping that if they didn't speak of it, it might not haunt their dreams for the rest of their lives. Neither was quite ready to explore and possibly usher in some new danger in their current state.

D'avry wasn't sure what was on the isleman's mind but his was flooded with a thousand thoughts, not the least of them being, *what, under the moon, was that windstorm all about? Who was that woman? And the apparitions with her, what did they want!*

His mind again went to the window in his chest. He felt its contents, the book of magic with the flaming arrow in its cover, tumbling, suspended in an impossible void inside him. The subtle energy of it pulsed softly, almost as if it were a nexus of energy, like a focusing point, which he understood all magical or enchanted items to be in some degree or another. And then he understood a subtle difference he'd never considered before, which was that some items could *focus* magic, but maybe others could *attract* it?

He didn't know what this information meant to their current situation but as was usual, he filed the information away for later use. Meanwhile, they now had a new danger to consider as they pursued their friends. He didn't know how they could continue in the larger cave structure without drawing her attention again, The Mistress of the Storm. Would they need to turn around?

A meager light blossomed, as from a firefly and D'avry looked over to where Volkreek was gathering himself together, dusting himself off and standing shakily. The ragged look on his face told a thousand tales. He was weary, worried, dejected, afraid, the list of emotions went on and on, but it was all there written on his face and in the slouching set of his shoulders. Beyond anything else, he looked much like a wrung-out rag, like a rope frayed to the point of snapping under tension.

D'avry understood this. It was the expenditure of magic. It was likely that Volkreek had never been called to be a conduit in such a way before. Even though the enchantment of the item did most of the work, it exacted a high price upon its user in a situation such as they'd just faced. The ranger might have aged two years in an exchange such as that. The fallacy of magic was that *all* mages were old. The truth was that *some* mages were old, but *most* had looked old long before their time.

He shook his head wearily and motioned for the ranger to sit.

"No, Volkreek. Just, take it easy for a bit. You need your strength and there's...really nothing we can do at this point."

The finality of the statement struck D'avry. That was legitimately the state of the situation. They'd lost Trask, they'd lost Gearlach, and now they'd lost both Farn and Liggo. The mute ranger, collapsed down onto his butt with his hands hanging limply from his knees. His head hung low, he looked back up at D'avry and there was moisture in his eyes that glistened in the soft light of his blade. He wore his frustration and concern like a millstone around his neck.

"Eat. Rest. We'll figure out a way to get to them. If indeed they are, as I'd worried, being taken to the orc warlord, then my concern has now become my hope." Meaning that they'd most likely be kept alive and that the companions, who before were being scattered to the winds, now at least might all be converging on one spot.

D'avry said this last, his voice barely above a whisper. Volkreek nodded, his lips pressed into a thin line of solemn acceptance. He made a weak attempt to reach for a satchel on his hip where D'avry had earlier seen him forage for hard tack, but then he paused and gave up. Leaning back upon the light pack, with his chin resting on his chest, well hidden beneath the scraggly reddish-gray locks of his beard, he closed his eyes. His breathing slowed quickly, and in less time than it would take to sing a lullaby, he was fast asleep.

D'avry mused on the fact that Volkreek had somehow managed to keep his day pack in the midst of the chaos of the goblin attack earlier that morning. And then, he too, drifted off. But the world he visited now was not a shadow of his own, but a very real and tangible one.

Fourteen

Rude Awakenings

00.000001 BC (Before Construct)
Dawn of the Construct

Rutker awoke to find sensors clamoring throughout the interior of the mech. A man in a hooded trench coat stood just fifteen meters before him, near the closest tunnel intersection. He had no idea how long he'd been asleep and for a moment wasn't actually sure where he was. But reality came back into focus in less time than it seemed.

He looked again at the hooded figure. How long had he been standing there? And was there anyone with him?

He sat up straight, bringing his leg down from the dash where it'd been resting, and placed it into its stirrup. Looking through the signals hammering to get his attention, he quieted each one with a glance of acknowledgement. He found the life form scan, it's periphery greatly diminished by the close quarters of rock above, below, and to every side.

According to his sensors, the man was alone. He also appeared to be unarmed and yet, seemed strangely unafraid. The man's gaze was drawn to the lower tunnel and Rutker took the brief second to study him further. He was wearing leather, square-toed boots that laced up below the knee. Black billowy pants tucked in above them but were mostly obscured by the man's long jacket which was also dark and of a sturdy cut. From the look of it, it had seen many miles. As did he, since it looked as though he'd been sleeping in those clothes for some time.

Rutker couldn't guess his age but figured something in the early-twenties. The man's face, much like his physique, was thin and angular. It was not until he slid back his hood that he saw that the man had mid-length, sandy blond hair. Rutker was delighted to find that the man appeared to be human. *That's reassuring at least*, he thought. There was always a high degree of uncertainty when dealing with xeno's. It was easy to start an intergalactic war over a simple misunderstanding. *And I'm trying to stop one*, he thought tiredly.

Rutker pulled his wandering thoughts back into the moment. He was a little unnerved by the fact that, by the man's mannerisms, it was almost as if he was able to see through the canopy of the Novak's shielding. His eyes darted to the display to confirm that the shielding was in fact still opaque (which was the systems default state). Out of curiosity, he signaled the system to clear the shielding and was surprised at how much more of the outside world was revealed. It felt vulnerable, though he knew that the armor, of course, was still functional.

The man's chin tilted up at the action, as if confirming a suspicion, he'd had. But who didn't know what a mech was? Did he think that the Novak was just a battle drone or sentinel? Rutker's thoughts were drawn back to when he'd first entered the cave and had seen the apparition on the other side of the pool. That was starting to make a little more sense now. *But what was this guy doing down here?*

He checked his HUD again. The drone he'd stationed there had not been triggered though it was apparently still online. Quickly pulling up the feed he searched for activity but there was none. The man had not come from that direction, he surmised. The other direction of this tunnel was blocked, and Rutker knew what was down the tunnel to his right.

He was having a hard time imagining that he'd come from there. For one, he was bone dry. For two, it'd take a much greater man than himself to pass that way with his sanity still intact. Now his curiosity was truly piqued.

He opted to get the encounter moving. Besides, he was running very short on time, and found himself growing increasingly agitated at the thought of missing any more chances to touch base with Katherryn.

He toggled the external speakers,

"Hello. This is Captain-Major Rutker Novak of the Epriot Collaborative Defenciary. I'm operating in an ambassadorial capacity, on a mission of peace. We were forcefully landed on your planet."

The man looked at him in confusion and then, performed some sort of elaborate hand gesture and motioned for Rutker to speak again, or at least that's what he thought he was trying to do. So, Rutker repeated the message.

"...so, you see, I'm really just interested in gathering my things and leaving."

The man nodded. "Captain-Major," he weighed the words as if examining them under a microscope. "Is this a dream?"

Rutker laughed out loud and then caught himself. He'd thought the man was joking but then second guessed himself. It looked as though the man was actually serious. Maybe he was missing some cultural nuance, or maybe he *was* a xeno. *Shit...* Rutker couldn't be sure, so he just continued on,

"No, sir. This is not..." and he shook his head, "...this is not a dream...are you, okay?" he asked, trying his best to communicate concern rather than what he was feeling, which was that this man was clearly insane or just messing with him.

"Yes. I believe I am." And then, after another pause. "Where are we?" The man's attention was drawn again to the tunnel heading to the subterranean chamber.

Rutker was becoming more and more uncertain about the state of the man's faculties. He called the drone back to a position that was close but just out of view while he covered by carrying on the conversation.

"Um, well, we're... actually, I have to confess that I do not know what planet we're on. Let alone, where on that planet we are currently located other than to say, southern hemisphere, biggest continent and approximately two-hundred-and-eighty meters below the surface in what appears to be a cave system, or mining operation, or a little of both I guess. To be honest, I was really hoping that you could tell *me*."

The man looked at Rutker, narrowed his eyes, cocking his head slightly. It was clear he was thinking deeply about the situation, and who knew what else. Suddenly, the man smiled broadly as a thought appeared to coalesce in his head.

"Show me your currency."

Rutker barked out a laugh, again struggling to contain his surprise.

"So, this is a stick up?" He chuckled again.

The man seemed dumbfounded by Rutker's question but then his attention again was drawn away, but this time, *not* in the direction of the eerie flooded chamber.

Then the man's hand flourished and the drone flew from around the corner to land on his outstretched palm. Rutker struggled with what had just happened. The odd figure then brought the drone up to his face, which Rutker assumed was to examine it more closely, but then the man's face filled the entire viewscreen of the interior of the mech via the drone's feed. The SortieNet did this all without Rutker's command. Once that happened, his eyes shifted to focus on the mech pilot as if they were face-to-face instead of meters apart.

"You need something from me. And I need something from you. I don't know what it is yet, but, in the meantime... I will take your flying eye. I understand that you have many, although, not as many as you once had. We will speak again. But, for now, do not return to the surface. You'll find that you can get almost anywhere you need to go underground. Lastly, your loved ones. They are being held, but they are safe. You truly do not know where this place is?"

Rutker shook his head, dumbstruck, mouth open, trying to

understand what just happened but before he could ask any questions the man continued,

"And you're certain that this is *not* a dream?"

He shook his head, seeming to realize the answer to his own question.

"Okay, we will speak soon. And, oh…" He shook his head apologetically, "I am Avaricai D'avry. Just a mage. Journey with Peace and Light, Captain-Major. Yes… and God speed!"

And with that, he appeared to cloak or phase or utilize some other form of technology that Rutker had never seen before which caused him to disappear from sight. Like a ghost.

His mind was still reeling from the encounter but given all of the information at hand, the fact that his drone hadn't picked him up, the fact that he was able to speak and understand Roganni with no visible assistance, the fact that he was able to not only detect that the drone was hidden in the tunnel behind him but to hack Rutker's controls *and* his mech…this all pointed to a substantial technological advantage. The man was much more than he appeared to be. And yet, he didn't seem to know where he was. And he kept asking if they were in a dream…

Rutker had assumed that that must have been some sort of failure in translation. It was the issue about Katherryn, Mads & Macq that really had him shaken. Had he seen the crash landing and been able to observe undetected? Clearly, he had cloaking tech; Rutker had witnessed that with his own eyes. This was all possible. It was also possible that he had followed him down the canyon, into the valley and into these caverns, though Rutker didn't know what vehicle he was using but it must have cloaking capability as well.

That would explain the rest… and the spooky feeling of being watched, though he didn't exactly acknowledge those types of superstitions. Not exactly anyway. Still, what he said about Katherynn and the boys… Rutker found it hard to believe. The

Xandraitha's defensive capabilities were very strong at a tactical level. In space, against cruisers, not so much, but on the ground level, with the pirates, *no...* he corrected himself *...mercenaries,* needing to keep the ship intact in order to acquire its cargo, it would be a stronghold.

But it was almost a certainty that they had a traitor in their midst, based on the lost Marine attachment. Rutker wondered how the man would know if something had happened at the ship after he had left unless there were others with him. Or he had surveillance in place... Yet, the man seemed intrigued by the drone, as if he'd never seen anything like it. There were just too many questions. He was confused by the meeting. What was the point? The man had said that Rutker needed something from him and that *he* needed something from *Rutker* but didn't know what it was?

The reluctant mech pilot rubbed his temples in fatigue and frustration. He was beginning to feel the desperate ticking of a time clock in the back of his mind. He considered heeding the man's advice to avoid the pirates above ground but that would make it impossible for him to receive a transmission from Katherryn; if she was able to send one at all. And that was *if* he believed the man who had called himself a mage. He also said they'd talk again. If so, Rutker didn't plan to be taken by surprise. And *he'd* be the one asking questions the next time.

Regardless of whether the mage was correct about the situation on the *Xandraitha's Hope,* Rutker still needed to retrieve the diplomatic packages. Either so they could leave and make up the lost time on their way to the peace talks, or so he could bargain for the lives of his family.

Rutker re-deployed the one drone that he had underground so that it could scout a path to the colony. Then he began picking his way through the tunnels, taking precaution to stay several levels below the surface and keeping a slightly slower pace so as to avoid making undue noise. As an additional precaution he ran on a very low energy mode with the baffles partially closed. It would reduce his energy signature and keep him from overheating, thanks to the cool subterranean air at least.

Fifteen

Spiderwebs

In less than two hours, Rutker believed that he was directly under the colony. True to the mage's word, the tunnels were prolific, and Rutker had no trouble covering that distance underground. As much as he wanted to go to the surface to scavenge and see what he could learn about the people that had been there and what had happened to them, he just couldn't spare the time. Another two or three hours and he'd be at the first drop location. He pressed forward, doing his best not to think about what could have transpired at the ship and whether his family was okay. He threw out a quick prayer in his mind. One of dozens over the last several hours.

Between the drone's and his own reconnaissance, he was able push past the colony and into the hills beyond. Surprisingly, he was able to maintain a similar pace to what he expected to have made on the surface running in stealth mode and having to hide every chance he got. The biggest benefit was that he'd had no encounters, just kilometer after kilometer of rocks, dirt, mud and darkness. And he didn't have to tempt fate by running with the baffles closed in the arid heat aboveground. That in and of itself was a blessing. It meant he'd have more in the tank for later. He knew that there would be a later.

He still occasionally ran across overrun barricades, and he still found no remains of those who fought there. But, nearing on thirty-one hours on planet and he was finally closing in on the first diplomatic package. At this point he'd extrapolated heavily from the drone data he'd received earlier and what little he'd been able to gain while below ground. It was getting to the point though, where he would have to surface in order to close the final distance. Part of him was relieved but the rest of him was reluctant to leave the relative safety of the cave system. That's what he'd realized was the case. In the valley proper, there had been a considerable amount of mining tunnels. But elsewhere, so far, the surface of the planet seemed to be riddled with natural caverns and interconnecting tunnels as a feature of the terrain. Even as he neared this first destination, he reminded himself that there was still one to follow.

His mind dropped back to the encounter in the cave with the so-called mage. There was just so much about that situation that he couldn't get his mind around. What did he mean, that he needed something from Rutker and that Rutker needed something from him? He wondered if it wasn't possible that he was in fact the driver of the mech that knocked him into the cave in the first place. Knowing that he couldn't navigate the smaller spaces in the mech, he'd gone in on foot. That'd explain why he'd hid initially. It could explain how he'd know if the crew and Rutker's family had been captured, if indeed that were the case. Or, even if it was a lie, it'd give him more impetus to find the packages as quickly as possible. That would allow the man who called himself a mage to follow Rutker and nab them once he had them both in hand. Or make a trade for his family. This was plausible but he still couldn't tell if it was likely. It felt like a puzzle that was intentionally meant to mislead you into trying to solve it the wrong way. Like life.

That was the most likely explanation given the information he had to work with. Now, what was the *least* likely solution? That the man was what and who he said he was? That he indeed did not know what planet he was on or whether or not it was real or a dream? That the powers he demonstrated were in fact magical in nature, even though that was impossible. And that the two men truly did need to rely on one another for some reason that had yet to reveal itself?

Rutker preferred the first solution. And yet, the man did not seem to wish him any ill will. In fact, he seemed to be able to control Rutker's equipment against his will. Why wouldn't he have just forced Rutker to find the packages if that was what he was after? And why'd he steal the drone? Surely he had his own, or at least access to a far superior variety, given the tech he'd displayed.

That was a solid 'check' in the column of the impossible or at least the improbable. What else did that conversation imply, that he was an interstellar traveler but didn't know how he'd got there? Where did he go when he disappeared then? Or the dream thing. He'd assumed that the man had included himself as part of the context for the dream, that he was dreaming as well, but what if, when he asked him if it was a dream, he was asking Rutker if *he* was dreaming? That would imply that he could somehow insert himself into someone else's consciousness, into someone else's dreams.

The tech he displayed seemed to make that a possibility, though, again, it was not a technology Rutker had ever seen. And if he was from somewhere where magic or what looked like magic was an actual thing... Rutker's brain was really hurting now. The thought experiment so far seemed to have fallen flat and failed to guide his decision. Instead, he just continued to work his way toward the surface.

Rutker paused the mech two levels below the surface to eat, drink, relieve himself and limber up. The hydrating fluid he'd sucked down had a minor stimulant. With a little improvement in his circulation he was feeling sharp again, at least for the time being. He was beginning to think that being underground for all that time had stifled senses. Stepping back into the mech his gaze drifted back again to the scribbled graffiti above the dash and his hands traced the letters.

What cost, my soul? He could read it easily now.

Okay, it was time to go. He sent his solitary drone up through the glory hole that opened out into the fresh evening air above. The drone moved slowly at first, soaking in every signal it could from as far below the surface as possible. As it came up with no significant lifeforms or electronic signatures nearby, it rocketed upward to just below the treetops and performed the same routine before repeating the process one more time at an ultimate elevation of one hundred meters.

Rutker breathed out a deep sigh. He now had access to the majority of his drones. They were quite a ways off, still circling in random arcs about the area where they had lost contact. He received a massive download of information as well as a hyper-detailed view of the colony. He would be able to perform his investigation without even having to step foot on its streets now, but that would have to wait.

It appeared that the mech drop ship had been abandoned in place and all but one mech were able to be mobilized out of the area to engage in the search. That, or the bay that was stuck furthest into the fractured roof of the cave below was empty, but that seemed unlikely. That meant that there were at least three mechs roaming the area, in addition to whatever came down in the original wave.

The drones provided footage of the Elite mech that had dropped in behind him. It was a sleek looking Maelus, gen five at least. Rutker was beginning to feel a bit honored at all the attention.

It clearly was cloaked from electronic signals but, unlike the mage Rutker had encountered underground, it was not actually invisible. A sigh of relief escaped his lips. However, after conducting a quick set of scans, it jumped out of the area heading due north. That was disconcerting as it could have gone anywhere but it chose a destination roughly in the vicinity of the jettisoned package.

But that was most likely an educated guess utilizing the descent path of the *Xandraitha's Hope* as it 'crash landed'. Still, he'd have to keep his eyes peeled since he couldn't count on picking up its electronic signature on his sensors. He did think it odd that the Maelus pilot didn't assist the others and so he wondered whether or not they were actually on the same team. More likely that that kind of work was below his station. Still, the question was intriguing…

Having the information he needed, he peeled out six of the drones to the west. They would take a long circuitous route back to his present location so that he could conduct a more thorough investigation and also scope out the next drop zone. He then sent three to the south end of the valley, where they'd turn right and follow the others at a distance. Three more went west to scan that area for hostiles before turning north.

The remaining drones he left in place to maintain a presence. That was except for two that he sent below ground to pick up the path he'd taken to get to this spot. It served two purposes: One, it disguised their path back and two, it allowed him to see if he had been followed. If he thought he had the range he would have sent more back to the ship, but he didn't and it was not information that would further the mission, either to save the truce negotiations or to save his family. Retrieving the packages was critical to both.

Sixteen

The Chamber

19.004329 AC (After Construct)
Age of the Half-Orc War

D'avry awoke on his shoulder again. This was growing old. Sleeping on rocks, not eating, being chased by horrible things, each more horrible than the last, losing everything he had or found, and now, he couldn't even sleep when he slept.

When he closed his eyes, he found himself in other realities, trying to solve bizarre riddles and just generally attempting to get a grip on what was going on. First, the mechanical monster in the tunnels — more tunnels — and then the girl in the gray town with the shadow creatures and him being turned into that blasted crow and then being stuck in the tunnel again, only now discovering that the monster was actually a *man* in what appeared to be an impossibly elaborate suit of armor!

That guy was even more clueless than he was, if that was possible! But what he'd said was amazing; that he wasn't even sure what *planet* he was on. *There was life on other planets!* He only knew that planets were different than stars because of his extensive education. These 'wandering stars', he considered now; was it possible to travel between them and meet other people just like himself? Were they all populated? Not all islands were populated, but a disproportionate number of islands that *were* populated had cannibals. Were there cannibals on other planets? D'avry swallowed, not relishing the idea of being eaten by cannibals on *any* planet.

Then he imagined explaining his findings to his peers at the academy. They would have laughed him all the way through the streets and to the outer walls and then left him there. Then he remembered the flying eye, the drone or viewing device.

He fumbled around in his jacket until he held it in his hand. He caught a whiff of his own morning breath and wrinkled his nose; he'd have to work up some tea in a couple minutes. He performed the hand manipulation to generate the ember of light and somehow knew that this was not necessary anymore, he could just *will* it. Things were changing fast. Faster than he was comfortable with. His thoughts were drawn back to the device, as if it were the embodiment of these changes.

He had brought something back from a dream! He paused to consider the gravity of that idea. Sometime soon he would have to sort out the changed new ways of the Astrig Ka'a. To chronicle these abilities. For all he knew, he was the only person ever to wield magic in the way that was available to him now. But, as usual, now was not the time for such activities. Besides, he had no writing instrument, no parchment... and no tea! He sorely hoped the ranger was a tea person.

D'avry rubbed the grit from his eyes and then felt something on his upper lip. He wiped it away and was surprised to find a broad swath of crimson on the back of his hand. He reached up cautiously and felt his nose, but it was in surprisingly good shape considering the events of the last couple days. He thought again about the flying eye and wondered if there were some residual effects to its use, or maybe it was just a side-effect of the interaction between magic and machinery? Though D'avry could hardly see how this device qualified as that. There were no gears or levers, for one. If, in fact, it was a machine, it was to machines of this world as a catapult was to a spoon.

And how did he know all those things about the man inside the monster? There was a big difference between what he understood as intuition and actual information. It felt like stories were just being poured into his head. Like he was dreaming them up, but what he was dreaming was fact. This sounded very much like madness.

He wondered if this is what the prophets felt like. Sometimes a vessel, sometimes a mouthpiece. But of who's God was *he* a prophet? What prophet didn't know whom he served? The idea twisted in his mind over and over until he had to just put it away. Where were the great stories now? The piercing insights?

He decided to change gears and return his focus to the viewing device, the flying eye. It was entirely metallic in nature, about the size of a large orange and it was the color of brownish-gray earth and not reflective in any way. Also, it had strange angular patterns impressed into its surface but with no writing or symbols to speak of. He dropped his hand and the drone remained floating in the air. It was truly a marvel to behold.

But why had he taken it? He had intuited that it was a viewing device. *What an oddity*, he thought. But it was intriguing. He often felt compelled to do things, but this wasn't one of those times exactly. It wasn't the *Pull*, it was just... a hunch. But, somehow more than that. This would fulfill a greater purpose. Just like the ring he and Volkreek had found. *Something for later.*

On a whim, he allowed the drone to float off into the chamber, feeling its intentions, somehow entering its... mind was not the right word. Structure? Like a list of commands. D'avry let the essence of it wash over him. He intuited it's workings, it's needs, its...in puts(?) — the way that it consumed information, what it saw.

His mind ached from back to front and he had to pull back and breath. Calming his mind, soothing the frenetic craving that the machine had imprinted on his psyche. D'avry assumed a meditative posture, legs crossed, hands forming an open pyramid before him. The aching in his mind eased and he reached out again, enveloping the device with his will.

The drone floated purposefully toward the far wall and now he saw what it saw, zooming in to detail that was impossible with the human eye. Then, to his amazement, the viewing shifted colors. At once the world was cast in jade and emerald and then just black and white, but oddly inverted.

D'avry scratched his head unconsciously. The different views were fascinating, but he wasn't sure what benefit there was until he viewed one that was multi-colored, from yellow and red to deep blues and purples. This view gave a perspective on the room that was very different. When the eye looked back at D'avry he saw himself represented in red, yellow, and white, which contrasted distinctly with the blues and purples of the walls and floor around him. Volkreek, too, was lit up in reds and yellows, still crashed out but sleeping on his side now with his head on his pack rather than reclining as he'd been earlier. His face and hands were bright but his clothes slightly less so, and then the floor was a deep blue. D'avry followed the eye throughout the chamber, inspecting it now in more detail, alternating views frequently.

He felt the now familiar trickle of blood on his lip and relaxed his mental hold on the object. He found that the less energy he expended controlling it, the less his head hurt and subsequently, the less it seemed to harm his body in the process.

D'avry breathed and then shifted his attention to the chamber itself. It was tall, maybe five times the height of a man, and there was a square dais in the middle with a raised step and a large shallow bowl in the middle. It seemed to D'avry like one used for scrying, though it was very large and low. *That's intriguing,* he thought.

As he approached the back of the room there was a recess about two paces deep which was flanked on either side by large, fluted pillars. In the center of this recess there were three stone chairs. The center one was larger, taller and sat just a little bit behind the other two. This may have been a place of learning, or judgement, or both. Or perhaps it was an oracle, though it only smelled of old dust, not the sulphureous vapors that were so common to the caves of far-seers…

He allowed the flying eye to finish it's rounds and saw that there were hallways off either side of the recess and so he directed it down the left one first, which ran for a short distance before turning right and then doubling back on itself, feeding into a smaller chamber. This chamber ran parallel to the recess but was much longer, perhaps almost as long as the main chamber was wide. There was nothing here but a hallway opposite the room which looked to tie back into the main chamber, presumably the other corridor he'd seen already.

D'avry scanned through the different views and was interested to see a slight discoloration on the back wall of the chamber, centered directly in the middle of the room. Where everything else was purple and indigo, a rectangle the size of a small doorway was a slightly lighter blue. Flipping views caused this structure to disappear entirely. He could only see it using the rainbow spectrum. He would need to view this for himself. With that, he guided the eye down the remaining hallway and was unsurprised to see it return to the main chamber from the door on the right.

D'avry decided it would be good to inspect the anteroom but walked first to the dais. He reproduced the conjuring spell which created a small point of light and it hovered in the space before him as if affixed to a rod. Whenever he moved, it moved with him. That was new. He was surprised to find that since the turning of the Astrig Ka'a and the creation of the lantern in his chest, *all* of his magics had improved. Or maybe that was an incorrect term, *evolved*.

What before had been little more than parlor tricks most of the time were now quite effective, if not formidable. He would have to take care to not outride his horse, so to speak. It would be easy to grow overconfident with this newfound power. And yet, the opposite could be true. They had, after all, held off the mistress of the storm, though it was clear that she was much, much more powerful and would have won that encounter given time.

D'avry considered these things as he also noted that the

light he'd created, while visible in most of the viewing modes of the drone, was completely invisible in the spectrum view. *Why was that?* He didn't know what to make of it but continued his inspection of the dais regardless. If indeed it was a bowl for scrying it was very large and very low to the ground, only a couple handbreadths above the step on which it sat. Indeed, one could easily step right into it, which seemed odd as well. He noted these and other peculiarities as he made his way to the back, to where the chairs stood.

They seemed simple enough, almost crude, but the stone they were crafted from was not the same as that from which the room had been carved. The chairs also lacked the small ceramic tiles which decorated much of the space — the front of the chamber — in red, golds and ambers, struck through with bold black lines, while the back half was set in blues, greens and whites and struck through with silver lines that were bordered by gold. The dais served as the dividing line between the two. *Maybe a land and sea motif?*

D'avry wasn't sure of the significance of the contrasting color arrangements but imagined it was probably important to those who had created it. Any other trappings or fixtures had been removed, either when the place was vacated, or by looters in the intervening years.

With nothing better to do and nothing but time, he made his way further back. Walking down the right-hand corridor this time, he found himself in the anteroom again, this time in the flesh. It was much as he'd seen it through the lens of the flying eye. He searched its corners and its entire perimeter and found nothing of interest and then he brought his attention to the space where the shape had been located in the back wall.

D'avry felt drawn, not to the space but to something beyond it. He could sense a vague but unfamiliar energy which he assumed must be an artifact of some sort, hidden behind the invisible door. His hands absentmindedly traced the outline of the window in his chest and as he closed his eyes, he was able to see the room, not through the eyes of the drone, but in his *mind's* eye.

In this way, the room was covered in faintly glowing characters and symbols all of which seemed to emanate outward from what was clearly the doorway into the secret chamber beyond. D'avry had never seen anything quite like it. Except at the portage trail near the river. When he'd found the ring. The runes were similar. Maybe not the same, but close.

He looked back at the hidden passage. It was about a head shorter than he was tall, which would require him to stoop to enter, but he'd have to figure out how to open it first. He looked more intently at the symbols on the walls and found that he was utterly at a loss to ascertain their meaning. In addition to runes there were pictograms, a bizarre blend of typically disparate cultural cues. Still, the images were possibly even more difficult to decipher, as maddening as that was.

Some appeared to be the faces of men with headgear, others could be serpent-like, yet others just seemed to be blocks and lines, one in particular was an eye with angular lines surrounding it, but still no meaning was evident and even his growing powers seemed impotent. It seemed strange to him that he could communicate with the viewing device, which was as foreign an object as he'd ever encountered, likely from another world, but he was not able to even decipher a single symbol in this room. His language spell, too, fell woefully short. Perhaps if the language was spoken rather than written?

Still, there had to be a way into the hidden chamber.

Seventeen

The Seeing

It was an hour of frustration, tracing lines, scouring the wall with the viewing device, pushing on blocks, touching symbols in various orders, tracing lines between the symbols that seemed similar, but nothing worked. He considered all of the methods at his disposal and the only one that came to mind was the shifting spell he'd used when the goblins first attacked him and Volkreek on the riverbank. He didn't exactly know how to cast that spell as it had mostly just come to him in the moment. He tried now to recall the movements of his hand, though recalling what he'd done in the chaos of the attack was not a simple task.

As he considered a few of the motions, he found that for the first time he was able to truly feel how they manipulated the flow of the magic. He was careful not to put too much intentionality behind the motions so as not to create something unintended. He breathed, calming his mind, considering the movements, and began again.

He completed the sequence. Nothing exploded, he hadn't been turned into a star-nosed mole, so he tried again. This time, with intention. And the world flipped upside down. Or, more correctly, he flipped upside down. And where he had been standing on the floor of the anteroom, he was now standing above it and the anteroom was upside down below him. It was also hazy, as if viewing its reflection through the surface of a gently rippling brook.

He had accomplished the effect of the spell, but now, rather than floating inconveniently in the space as had happened at the river, his feet were planted on the exact same spot, as though he were merely a reflection of himself standing in a puddle. He was now on the opposite side of that thin dividing line between what was air and what was solid. Inverted.

He shook his head in disbelief but walked slowly forward nonetheless. He found that he could walk freely rather than swimming through the void like before. This was much preferrable. His attention turned to the chamber behind the secret door, and he saw into it the same way that he could see the anteroom, from below.

The space behind the door continued for three or four paces before opening into another chamber that was only large enough for three or four people and that, uncomfortably. On the back wall hung a tapestry but that was all that appeared to be in the room. At least as far as he could tell through the somewhat blurry image. So, he stepped forward, standing where he wished to stand in the room, and reversed the spell.

Immediately the world flipped on its head and he was right side up, standing in the small chamber behind the secret door. That was much easier than what he and Volkreek had gone through to extricate themselves from the shifted space before. He would need to come up with a name for this spell and for the space below the surface, but for now it'd have to wait. He wanted to understand the secret of the hidden chamber, and hopefully, eventually understand how to open the door.

Once oriented to the space he looked around, the light he'd generated still followed him, even through the in-between space. The tapestry was artfully crafted and before it stood a short pillar a handsbreadth to a side and which came up roughly to D'avry's shin. He realized now that this was the artifact that he'd felt from outside. It appeared to be made from the same stone as that of the chairs in the main chamber. It seemed natural to him to kneel down and sit upon his feet to inspect it more closely, so he did so.

But once both hands rested upon its surface, visions exploded into D'avry's mind. A myriad of sights far and wide, some he recognized and others that he did not and in between he seemed to fly above the surface of the land from the vantage of a kez'pur's eagle. His mind burned with the sudden onslaught of imagery and his hands dropped. The images ceased almost instantaneously, and he was left in the silence with nothing but the sound of his own breathing and his beating heart. After the initial rush of information, that was a profound silence.

D'avry looked around quickly to assure himself that nothing else had changed in the intervening time and was reassured that this was the case. The room was still simple and without adornment. The tapestry appeared the same, holding the same colors from the larger chamber, with the reds, orange and ambers to the outside edges, interspersed with light and dark browns and grays which seemed to emulate land and rock features, he thought. Down the middle were blues and greens at the bottom which then blended into blues and whites toward the top, seeming to suggest forests and lakes and then sky and clouds.

D'avry, drew in a long breath through his nose and straightened himself, sitting at attention with his hands upon his knees as he'd been instructed to at the academy so long ago. Feeling ready, he reached forward again and touched the pillar. Again, the images flashed, only now he seemed able to control a bit more the flow and the direction. He was able to, he thought, identify his homeland. His thoughts brought him in close and indeed within seconds he sped down and into the familiar halls that interconnected dormitories and lecture halls, laboratories and common areas of the Ko'zed Ha'graffi'tumn, the Academy of the Brothers of the Solemn Path.

As he drew close, he was surprised to find that the people he saw bustling around never came into focus and the closer he got the blurrier they became. He continued his searching and found himself in the main library of his discipline, only his status as an under-lord allowed him access, and yet now he walked freely through its aisles and upon it's many leveled catwalks and the iron bridges that crisscrossed the atrium spaces between as it rose up stories upon stories, books and bookcases filling it's walls all the way up. At the highest point of the tall chamber ancient timbers gathered to a single point at its peak, and here, even he had not been allowed entry. Until today that was.

He moved with a glance and stood upon the grated floor, something he'd always thought peculiar since all the brothers wore robes. He wrinkled his nose at the thought. It was only due to the majority of light coming from above and the requirement to use an individual lamp for your studies that allowed them to retain a modicum of modesty. He brushed the idle musing away from his mind as he drew closer to the books he'd been forbidden to learn from but was heart broken to see that much as the people were blurred by proximity, so was text, and even images, like those seen on the few paintings afforded space in the towering hall. Dejected, he drew his presence back into the sky and sought out the last place on earth he thought he would ever go voluntarily. He was there in less than a minute.

Before him stood a burnt-out husk of what had been, once upon a time, a magnificent spreading oak. A place where he recalled two lovers had made a promise which would never be allowed to be fulfilled. For a runaway queen-to-be, this would be the call that bought her back her birthright. For a heretic, who'd chosen love over the brotherhood, this had been yet another betrayal. A moment of dying. Of giving over his own will for that of the Astrig Ka'a. It hadn't even been his choice… though the now Queen of T'Serkus would likely not see it so.

Even before he had decided to move on, the tree and the still scorched earth around it began to recede. He drew himself back, moisture fresh in his eyes, and began searching in earnest for what he was looking for.

D'avry refocused his thoughts and the world blurred beneath him until a territory surged into focus. The Northern Sweep. Deep in the territory claimed by the orc tribes. Which tribe ruled what lands at any time was irrelevant. Theirs was a tumult of authority deposed, gained, lost, re-claimed, and lost again. Mankind sought no treaties with the orc for even when necessity outweighed mutual contempt, the tribe whose limited trust had been gained would be replaced by another, or crumble within and be replaced by someone new with different ideals and allegiances.

The orc were powerful, but powerfully divided. The thought of a united orc empire was truly terrifying to all other inhabitants of the sphere of the world. D'avry calmed his nerves and continued his search. He had gathered from his interactions with Gearlach and his nemesis N'Bruyyh, that the warlord had gained a sizable territory, only he did not know where he was from to begin with. Searching this way would not likely yield results. He decided it was best to work backwards. He had met the company of adventurers in a steep river gorge that he also could not place, but he might be able to return to the caves where he and Volkreek were currently stuck and go from there.

D'avry allowed the images in his mind to wander back to the mountains where he had first met the companions. He had an idea of where the cave system might be, roughly anyway. But then he saw the milky azure waters of a river and was certain. He dropped closer to the ground and flew up the river some way.

He recalled that the company had looked to have been freshly deposited from significant melee the night before and to D'avry's surprise, he found a place that seemed to match. It looked to have been an outpost on a wide section of river that could have been considered a lake, with a short but wide series of falls below it. Structures here still bloomed with tendrils of smoke. It clung to the sky as if unwilling to leave, the layers so thick at times that D'avry had to fly low just to see.

The destruction was profound. The remaining carnage baffled reason. This didn't look like a battle, it looked like wholesale slaughter. Ramparts were crushed, towers toppled, the surrounding village razed so that barely a stone lay atop another. It seemed likely to him that the party, after rescuing the librarian had taken refuge here or perhaps had stolen him during the attack. Either way, that had not gone so well for the inhabitants of the town or the keep.

D'avry pulled back to a vantage high above the smoke, above the mountain tops that, though not so tall as the ones further south, were still sizable. Far off to the east, the trees were thinning and gave way to a broad swath of hills that continued beyond sight.

D'avry realized this mountain range bordered the disputed lands. An area that formed a kind of buffer zone between the two races where no established colonies should have existed. This is what he'd been taught but no longer appeared to be the case, as small patches of haze dotted the landscape. He couldn't be sure if they were orc or human habitations from this distance and felt that he should be getting back to formulate a plan with Volkreek, though, he was sure that he had already constructed a plan at this point.

Sliding back toward the cave he saw the mountain now for its true size and was shocked to see that it was likely an extinct volcano and that it was truly massive, easily dwarfing those in the surrounding range. The snowline was barely visible beneath a thick blanket of clouds that became patchy and extended east, and far to the south. The area to the north was sunny but it was still early in the morning and much of the landscape was bathed in large blocks of shadow.

D'avry navigated toward the mountain and then turned east. He knew what he was looking for now. An orc outpost closest to the eastern slope of the mountain whose name now came to him from his studies, Tal Kar'zuum.

There was a deep spirituality associated with this mountain. It translated to Ghost's Crown as the peak, as viewed from some angles, appeared to have three jagged spires which resembled a tiara. Ghost was a loose translation though; the idea was more like that of a banshee, he mused and then his blood ran cold. He recalled his experience within the mountain with the screeching, rage-filled apparition and the violent winds that were at her command, the legion of the damned that served her. *Who had lived to tell of the mistress of the storm?*

D'avry proceeded but with caution now as even though he knew that what he saw was only in his mind, he did not understand the mechanics of how this magic worked. He did not want to give away what he was up to if that were possible. Drifting along the foothills his eye caught a road through the trees that dotted the foothills that made up the base of the mountain. He followed the road north and east and indeed there was an outpost ahead, denoted by a low blanket of haze. It was not overly large, which was good. He couldn't imagine the goblins venturing far from the caves, let alone the tree line and definitely not during the day.

He flew forward with greater impetus but did not have to get very close to the village to see that the structures were mostly tent-like, which was consistent with what he knew of orc construction. The figures were blurry, such as was the case at the academy, but these were clearly much larger than a human and even their beasts were large, appearing to be wide-horned, wooly oxen.

D'avry had seen what he came to see but before he pulled away, he saw something that he did not want to see. In the center of the village, before a large tent with a broad deck, were three tall poles. Each blackened from top to bottom, and on two of these poles were lashed forms of what D'avry could tell had been humans. *By the bodies!* His heart jumped into his throat before he remembered it was impossible for his friends to have travelled this far, and again, not this far from the mountain with the goblin parties unless it were night.

He remembered then that he had been able to sense their presence when he and Volkreek were following them into the caves, but, while using this artifact of the oracle, he found that he neither carried with him the light source nor was able to sense the presence of his friends. However, he was certain that while they were far ahead of himself and Volkreek now, possibly at the other end of the large basin or even into the tunnels beyond, they were most likely still underground. He didn't know how they'd catch up just yet, but now he knew where he thought they were headed.

There may be a standing bounty for humans or word may have spread that N'Bruyyh was looking for a certain party. Either way, his friends would most likely find themselves drawn to the top of one of those poles if they were unsuccessful. He cast a quick prayer for the souls of those who'd gone before them. He thought, too, of the other companions, Gearlach and Trask. *One thing at a time. Find Liggo and Farn, and then find the other two.*

D'avry let go of the pillar and instantly found himself back within the hidden room, his light source glowing silently in the space before him. He checked quickly and was pleased to feel the familiar signature of his two friends again. It felt as if they were somewhere near the far end of the caverns, either the end of the basin or in the tunnels that he assumed would be there. Not quite to the surface, not yet.

They had until nightfall to make it to the other side of the mountain. It was impossible. D'avry's stomach grumbled, and he remembered he hadn't eaten since the night before. He was trying to decide whether to exit the room through the tiny hallway or phase out through the in-between space the same way he'd come in when the scrying bowl came to mind.

What was the purpose of the bowl if the true device was here? D'avry knew that there was something that he was missing. He looked around the space but there was nothing but the tapestry. He inspected it again and realized that the center section covered in blues, whites and greens was bracketed at the top and bottom by a shape that looked not unlike the scrying bowl. In fact, it appeared as though the wind and water that was represented actually *flowed between* them. D'avry thought about this for a minute. He wasn't sure that he could formulate an opinion yet without now investigating the bowl. It was about time to wake Volkreek anyway if he wasn't already up.

Eighteen

The Portal

D'avry decided he didn't have time to work out the specifics of the secret door and worked the phasing spell. Again, he found the world flipped upside down beneath him and blurry as though viewed through water. He walked past the anteroom and straight ahead to the large chamber, past the stone chairs and right to the base of the raised dais and the large bowl.

Volkreek was awake now and looking not only worn out but dejected as well. D'avry realized he must have woken to find that he was alone and assumed that he'd been abandoned. D'avry felt a pang of grief for the fighter and reversed the phasing spell.

Instantly he was upright in the real world. Volkreek sprang to his feet, blade extended and emanating light that filled the room. His eyes were wide with surprise before he realized that it was the mage and softened a little. The sword remained steady though. Maybe he wondered if D'avry was a ghost as well?

"It's okay. It's me."

D'avry put his hands out in a gesture suggesting he was unarmed and that he meant no harm. The sword dropped a little.

"You were out hard, so I've been investigating the chamber and I think I know where our friends are being taken."

With that the man's eyes lit up, followed by a skeptical tilt of the head and a raised eyebrow that suggested he couldn't quite reconcile how the two statements were related. But the sword dropped a little bit more. He swiped at his upper lip with his free hand, indicating D'avry should do the same. When D'avry did he came away with flecks of dried blood from earlier when he'd been interacting with the flying eye or drone, he believed it was called.

"It's nothing. I'm okay," he said brushing it away and then leveled his gaze on Volkreek. "I don't think we can catch them on foot, but we may not have to. That is, if we can figure out how this works," D'avry said, stepping back and looking down at the bowl and then back to Volkreek.

"There is a hidden door in the anteroom behind this chamber. It has all sorts of magical protections on it to keep it hidden. I had to use the spell from the river in order to get past it and found a room with an artifact that allowed me to see places all over the world. Or at least I think that's how it works. In any case, there is an orc outpost on the other side of the mountain." D'avry went to point and then realized he had absolutely no sense of what direction was what this far below ground.

Volkreek's brow furrowed as he finally lowered the sword, placing it on the ground to retain the light. He dug through his well-organized rucksack to produce a small leather cylinder about the length of his arm. Removing a plug on one end, he produced a waxed papyrus map which he laid on top of his pack. D'avry walked over to see it.

It was of good quality and detail, though nothing approaching what he'd had at his disposal at the academy. It was fair enough though. D'avry observed that the far-right side faded into obscurity just beyond a north-south mountain range denoted as Talles dal Nata'ruun. Near the upper third of the range was a prominent mountain with a peak like a tri-point crown called Kar'zuum Tal. That's where he believed they were. Indeed, the banshee spirit, the mistress of the storm, seemed to confirm that suspicion with an exclamation point.

Volkreek traced a blue line from further northwest down to the mountain and pointed to a spot on its western slope which D'avry assumed he was suggesting was where they were at now, or at least where they'd been before entering the cavern. Without the connecting fork of the river visible on the map it was hard to tell exactly, but he was pretty certain that Volkreek was correct.

D'avry followed the blue line up the river to an outpost called Fort Talles Murdt near a lake named imaginatively, Long Lake. Beside the point on the map was a small sketch that somewhat matched what might have been the west-facing wall of the keep that he'd seen using the artifact in the hidden chamber. That was, if it had still been standing.

D'avry felt a deep sadness as he thought of all the people there who'd had destruction rained down upon them by the orc warlord, N'Bruyyh. *Undead orc warlord*, he corrected himself. That thought caused him again to wonder at the origins of this band of adventurers. He had many questions, but unfortunately, Volkreek was not likely to answer any of them. Gearlach would be the one with all the answers, but would he tell? He did not seem the type to give up much beyond that which he felt inclined.

The ranger traced his finger over the mountain to the eastern slope where it opened to a broad swath of chevron-shaped ticks which seemed to indicate low foothills. This area made up the entire upper right-hand corner of Volkreek's map and had no name assigned to it but the descriptor: *Orc Territory*.

The map did not show the orc outpost that D'avry had seen but he could estimate roughly on the map where it would be. He pointed to that location and then pointed in the general vicinity that he believed the cave entrance to be on the far side of the mountain. There truly was no way that they could cover that distance without cutting through the mountain itself.

From where they'd camped on the river it was nearly a vertical climb to exit the valley and there were at least two more significant valleys that they'd have to cross or they'd have to go further up on the slope of the mountain itself, which given what they'd experienced in the cavern and the mountain's namesake, he was certainly in no hurry to go scampering around further up on its slopes. Volkreek shook his head, took a deep breath, scratching at his beard absently.

D'avry stepped back over to the bowl, circling it, and looking for any signs of how to operate it and whether it was just for viewing or if it could be for something far better than that – actual travel. That was what he hoped was the intent, though the tapestry had shown two bowls. One on either end of the flow of air and water.

He scoured the dais and the bowl and could find nothing. Finally, he sat back and looked around the chamber itself, boosting the luminescence from his own light source to search for any clues. He didn't see anything helpful, but he did see that the flying eye had floated off into an upper corner where it'd been waiting patiently for direction. Closing his eyes, he recalled it with a thought. Volkreek jumped back a step as the drone swooped down from the ceiling. It floated down to land in the palm of D'avry's outstretched hand.

D'avry looked back at Volkreek with a shrug. "It's a long story," he said as he slipped the viewing device into the interior pocket of his jacket.

Volkreek looked at him appraisingly but, as usual, said nothing. D'avry continued to scan the room but noticed nothing out of the ordinary except for a small hollow in the recessed wall between the pillars. He hadn't noticed it before but in all fairness, it was very plain and nondescript. It sat about head high and was only about two feet tall by one foot wide and less than that deep.

Upon further inspection there was a square depression in the middle that appeared to be meant to hold an artifact or something to that effect. Immediately D'avry's mind snapped back to the pillar in the hidden room. He had not at the time considered that it wasn't fixed, but just stored in the chamber and meant to be placed here in order for the assembly to function properly.

He didn't know if he could bring anything with him when phasing but then he'd never tried. There was a first time for everything. He did, after all, have a much better capability in the in-between space than he had when he'd first discovered the spell. It was worth a try.

"Wait right here," he said with a wink, to which Volkreek's response was a hard, thin-lipped smile.

D'avry quickly shifted back into the chamber, finding it easier and easier to do so, and now, it seemed he didn't even have to swim or walk, he just moved through the space. Once there, he saw that the pillar sat in a similar depression. He grabbed the pillar but then his mind exploded with a riot of swirling geography, and he was forced to let go in order to just remain upright.

He tried again but this time he pulled the sleeves of his tunic down over his hands and grabbed it that way. He then wrapped the obelisk-shaped artifact in the low edges of his jacket, carrying it much like a baby in swaddling.

Volkreek jumped when D'avry phased back into the main chamber only a few feet away. He rolled his eyes in exasperation.

"Sorry," D'avry said, walking back to the recessed pocket in the wall. He placed the artifact in the depression and turned around to find that the bowl was filled with a slightly luminescent liquid that rippled blearily, splaying dull shimmers of light across the ceiling and walls of the chamber. It was beautiful. It made the space seem somehow more grand, more... holy, D'avry thought.

The liquid in the bowl remained transparent but somehow still cloudy as if the light emanated from the waters themselves. D'avry realized that he may have to navigate again by touching the pillar, but when he did so, there was no effect at all. He walked over to the bowl and touched it but there was still no change. The only other thing he could think of was that perhaps the chairs had something to do with the room's functionality.

He walked back to the chairs and choosing the centermost one, sat down.

This was the effect he'd been looking for. He was able to see the surface of the earth in his mind, only now, he felt or... comprehended(?) a new layer to its functionality. He could sense other such places as the chamber they were in. Other places throughout the world and he understood that they were for travel as well.

He wasn't sure how, but he could also sense that travel was possible to other locations, except that in that case it would only be one-way. So, there was a way to catch up with their friends and, if they knew the locations of the other oracle chambers they could travel great distances if need be. That was if the corresponding chamber was functioning like this one now was.

D'avry attempted to navigate to the next oracle chamber and found that there was one to the north but that it was a considerable distance, closer to the top of Volkreek's map. Nowhere near the outpost that they were trying to keep their friends from being turned over to. This would have to be a one-way trip and perhaps D'avry could explore the oracle network at some later time. *Always later.* He sighed inwardly.

He focused now on the eastern slope of the mountain, finding again the road that led to the outpost and working his way back. He still could not ascertain the location of the cave entrance and judging by how well it was hidden near the river he would not be able to locate it from an aerial view. They would have to intercept the goblin party or parties when on the road.

D'avry navigated to a point that he considered far enough away from the mountain's slope to not miss the goblins entirely and not too far down the road so that they ran the risk of meeting up with any orc patrols. This idea was suddenly beginning to sound much worse than when he'd originally conceived it.

It was inevitable that they would come face-to-face with the orcs again. He had just hoped to do it with the full party, and maybe with a lot more help if they could find it. As it stood, he did not have a plan on how to retrieve his friends. Right now, it was enough just trying to locate them and trying to catch up.

D'avry navigated further until he found a suitable location where the road ran along a stream on one side and had a short cliff wall on the other, with a flat area above that. This at least could give them the advantage of higher ground and possibly improve their chances of scouting the party out before being seen themselves. Just past this spot the road turned and there was a broad, shallow ford which might act as a natural barrier if things turned hot. D'avry had spent very little time in his life planning ambushes. In fact, almost zero. *Oh, well,* he thought, *it will have to do.*

He navigated a little ways further until he was on top of the bluff, near a copse of small trees that looked rugged and gnarled and which had almond shaped, pale green leaves. He didn't know what they were, but they seemed to provide a fair amount of cover. He moved a little further still to a place that he felt would be out of view and where he and Volkreek could safely exit a portal, if that was how this tool even worked.

With the location on the bluff above the road still positioned in his mind, he opened his eyes and found that Volkreek was standing near the bowl, looking intently at the image reflected in its shimmering waters. He looked up at D'avry with an expression of anticipation. He didn't seem to care that they were literally jumping in the path of possibly two separate goblin raiding parties.

D'avry wasn't sure how this next part worked but he stood up and the image remained in the basin. He breathed a small sigh of relief. He didn't want to give away that he really had next to no idea what he was doing, he didn't think it'd help the morale of his tiny rescue party.

The most natural thing that he could think to do at this point was to just step right up and onto the bowl. He motioned for

Volkreek to join him on the dais and after grabbing his pack and sheathing his blade, pulling out a medium-length hunting knife to replace it, he did so.

Nineteen

Disputed Territory

D'avry motioned that they should step forward at the same time and Volkreek nodded his understanding. Both men stepped up onto the bowl and found that nothing changed. It wasn't until they continued forward as if to step through to the other side of the dais that they found themselves standing in the sparse grass of the bluff overlooking a rolling landscape marked by thickets of mixed trees, some leafy and some that looked to be various kinds of pines. The cool mountain breeze carried the scent of the living forest and the sunlight on his face felt to D'avry like he'd just been released from a prison, which, in a way, they had.

Both D'avry and Volkreek turned to find that the portal was gone. They were out of the cavern and there was no going back. Volkreek turned again looking across the stream and down the road as far as he was able. His knife disappearing, to be replaced with his bow. He folded back the leather flap on his quiver to provide access to his arrows. Breathing in deeply through his nose, his eyes continued to scan the area for hidden dangers.

Several miles to the north the faintest wisps of smoke were visible, and he darted a glance at D'avry with a slight raise of an eyebrow. D'avry shook his head slowly, responding to the unverbalized question in a barely audible whisper.

"Not friendly."

D'avry took in the air again. Savoring the feeling of freedom, it jarred him to recall the condition of his friends and their lack of it.

He turned to Volkreek,

"Now that we're here, we should put a plan together."

The ranger looked at home in this environment and ready to take on orcs or goblins or whatever came their way.

"I'm really not very experienced in full-scale battle. My abilities as a mage have always been more scholarly and even then, I've mostly just got by on luck. Actually, that's the basis of my magic, pure chance and the whim of the universe, so, in this instance, I'm just trying to say that we need to have a plan that doesn't involve going toe-to-toe with what may be two separate goblin raiding parties and whatever orcs happen to be in the area."

Volkreek looked back at him blankly, clearly unamused. D'avry took this to mean, 'Get over it. Rise to the occasion or get out of the way.'

D'avry considered what he assumed to be his companion's rebuff. He was right in a way. There was nothing that could be done to change the circumstances. It was time to commit to the cause or walk away.

D'avry didn't have to choose really, it was more of an acknowledgement to himself that this was the course he was committing to. After years of just accepting reality, he found it hard to make decisions that might actually shape it. Any plans he'd made in the past were doomed to failure because of the Astrig Ka'a, but now it seemed the forces of the universe were moving *with* him rather than pushing him around as they pleased.

"Okay. So, here's what I think, and you just nod yes or no."

Volkreek nodded yes with an amused smile on his face. D'avry continued, "We don't know where the goblins are coming from, but we think it's up the hill somewhere further south along the road, correct?"

Volkreek shook his head slowly but in the affirmative. He seemed to be not willing to go all-in on this one but was in general agreement. D'avry nodded back and stretched his senses to ascertain where his friends were now. His sensitivity told him that they were in fact further south from their present location, which was a good sign. Additionally, he could sense that they were close in proximity but not necessarily together. That was maybe not so good.

"Okay, so, I can confirm that Liggo and Farn are south of us. By a few miles at least." He pointed as closely to the direction of that impression as he could.

"It doesn't feel like they're travelling in the same party. I'm concerned that the parties aren't actually together. They may be in competition with one another, but I can't be sure of that. In any case, fighting one group doesn't mean that the other will join in. They may, or they may just go around. Both situations have their problems."

Volkreek nodded somberly and then waited for D'avry to continue.

"We are assuming that the goblins will travel along the road to the Orc outpost. And we're assuming that they will do this at nighttime, since they aren't big fans of sunlight."

Volkreek nodded at both of these statements and then seemed to backtrack on his opinion. He searched the air for a second, as if recalling past events or something he'd heard around a campfire then nodded side to side as if to indicate a 'maybe' on both counts.

D'avry was confused. He'd taken those statements as foregone conclusions.

"Maybe I can use the flying eye to pinpoint the location of the goblins? But if they don't come out until the sun goes down then we'll have little time to intercept them, rescue our friends, locate any weapons that the goblins will have taken from them and then, we have to hope that the one we save is still in good enough shape to fight and help us retrieve the other one. Or something like that..." His plan seemed to be dissolving as quickly as the words left his mouth.

D'avry looked to Volkreek but he was no longer engaged with the one-sided conversation. Instead, he was looking past him, back toward the mountain. D'avry followed his gaze and there, up the slope near a series of rocky gorges that resembled a huge slash of a bear's paw, smoke was rising. And not a little smoke. One large column rose from each of the five slashes in the mountainside.

This did not look like a couple goblin parties stealthily meeting with an orc outpost. This looked like a signal fire for something much more substantial. Maybe some sort of event, like a seasonal trading festival or something of that effect. Maybe his friends weren't taken for a specific bounty but instead for barter. That meant a whole lot of goblins would be up in those rocks and a whole lot of orcs would be coming to take part in the festivities. D'avry's heart sank. He looked back at Volkreek and, as usual, it was clear he'd put all the same pieces together. They were too late.

Twenty

By Silver Moonlight

31.012504 AC (After Construct)
Age of the Thinning Veil

Spending time with Kemper and his friends was a welcome release. There were drinking games involved and though Deven's time in the Marines had prepared her extensively, she found that she had to moderate her intake somewhat since the loss of her legs. One, she just wasn't drinking as much outside of that environment. Two, she didn't have the same body mass. She was almost exactly ten percent lighter now. This was one of many things that she dealt with now on a day-to-day basis.

It was nice to spend time with people that didn't know her from back home. She'd been so much more focused, so much more rigid; the exact opposite of her sisters. It was as if she were the only one with her father's genes. The Marine Corps civil engineer was ever diligent, ever protective and seemingly incapable of doing anything without structure. He was also Deven's biggest cheerleader and go-to shoulder to cry on when things worked out worse than expected.

Tonight, however was going better than expected. Even though she still had her walls of skepticism firmly in place where Kemper was concerned, he was playing the gentlemen and had listened intently to her stories and about her hopes and aspirations. There seemed to be more beneath the gnarly surfer persona than he let on.

He and his friends were very interested about her time in the middle east, though they were careful not to address the incident that had altered her life, and appearance, forever. She, however, shared the story of her own accord, hoping that through repetition the sting of it might dissipate over time. Somehow, she got through it while staying upbeat and optimistic. Showing off her carbon fiber and aluminum alloy hardware like a badge of honor.

The only question came from a blond haired, stocky kid they called Claypool. He had the look of a skate rat but was enrolled at the UC up the hill and it was his misguided parents who had co-signed the lease agreement on the Stockton Avenue crash pad.

In the silence after she'd explained how she'd woken up in a hospital after passing out from blood loss his only question was, "Can you still surf?" This caused her to pause. She'd never been asked that before. Actually, she'd never surfed before other than body boarding at Virginia Beach in the summers when she was younger, and once in North Carolina.

"No. Not yet, but I'm sure there's a way. I still need to build up some muscle strength first," she said, rubbing her aching quad muscles and cringing.

This caused her to flash back to the night before and the series of events in the stairwell. It reminded her of the bruises under her make-up, the soreness in her legs that would be twice as bad tomorrow, but mostly it reminded her of the creatures in the gray town.

They were real. She knew that they were real. Even though that place felt like it existed in a dream, it didn't feel like a dream when she was there.

"Dev... dude, are you good?" Kemper asked, a look of genuine concern on his face. Deven looked around and everyone who'd been staring at he suddenly found interests elsewhere.

"Dude? Seriously? Anyway... yeah. I think I'm just going to step outside for a minute," she said and started to walk toward the door before being reminded that that activity was still a work in progress. She caught herself quickly with her forearm crutches, saving herself at least the embarrassment of landing on her face in front of the dozen or so people she had only just met. Pushing forward quickly with her crutches, face flushing, it took Kemper jogging a little to catch up.

"Hey, Speed Racer, slow down," he pleaded. "It's fine... you just faded out for a moment there. Probably just the microbrew that Coop brought. I think he bottled it himself, and to be honest, it might not be just hops in there, you know?" He chuckled a little, presumably trying to disarm the moment a little.

She didn't stop. Her mind was racing and being embarrassed was only part of it.

"Deven. It's really not a big deal," he told her. She paused; the cool night air had an added bite so close to the water's edge. She felt as much as heard the low roar and rhythmic crash of high tide waves against the rip-rap cove just yards away. The salty air carried the smell of kelp and a thousand other fragrances from the roiling ecosystem that was the Monterey Bay.

"Kemper, I'm ready to go home... if that's alright."

Kemper nodded, looking a bit like a scolded puppy.

"Yeah, sure." He nodded, shoving his hands into his faded denims. "Let me just tell the bros and I'll bring the car down. I'm still parked way up the street from when we got here."

With that he jogged off, sandals slapping on the asphalt as he went. A couple minutes later yellow, saucer-like head lights belonging to a mid-70's BMW 2002 jittered into view. It'd been restored, all the chrome trim removed and lowered a little, but it still maintained the shoe-box good looks of the original model.

Kemper pulled up to where she was standing at the wooden railing overlooking the crashing waves as they burst into white walls of mist before raining down in fat droplets on the concrete 'jacks' that protected the sandstone wall. Deven's legs screamed in agony as she plopped herself into the passenger side bucket seat and slipped her crutches into the tiny space that passed for leg room behind her.

It had the smell of vintage foam cushioning and the engine

droned through the thinly insulated firewall. Kemper revved the engine and it crackled with an exhaust that was clearly less civilized than the rest of the restoration.

"Do you mind if we take a short cut? Skyline drive is worth the extra miles," he said, a mock-sinister grin upon his face. She shook her head but waved him on as if to say, *do what you gotta do...*

That had been a mistake. Kemper railed the winding asphalt like it was Laguna Seca, slamming gears into the corners and then rifling through them on the way out, stretching out every last rpm to redline before shifting again. It was dark winding through the towering redwoods, but he seemed to know every curve like they were related.

She was terrified, her heart pounding in her stomach, but after a while the terror faded, and it was almost fun. She still didn't trust him entirely, but at least he could drive. They got to the top of the hill and Kemper again crashed down the gears coming to the stop sign for Skyline Blvd. He paid it only the vaguest respect as he rolled through, turning north towards San Francisco and burying the pedal again, chirping the tires and causing Deven's head to bounce off the headrest of her seat.

"Jeez, Kemp, this is a back road, not Le Mans," she groaned.

He turned to her, driving and shifting without paying attention to the road for what was possibly the longest three seconds ever and then revving the engine in time with two quick raises of his eyebrows, he turned back to the road but turned off the headlights.

"What are you *doing*?" she screamed, but then went silent as the quick shift to darkness faded. Trees and fields and bushes began to stand out in bright silver light making the road quite visible. It still wasn't even remotely safe, but it was captivatingly beautiful. The hill side and the patches of redwood trees gave way to rolling fields of tall grass which then dove back into trees and winding corners again.

The world being instantly transformed into monochrome black-and-white was a kind of sensory deprivation that heightened all her other senses. The engine rose and then chunked down under compression and then began building again. The car vibrated constantly, giving feedback as to the texture of the road and the rpms of the engine and the world just seemed to move around them as though on an old black-and-white movie screen. It was trance-like, hypnotic. But then, as they were accelerating out of a corner something was standing in the road just dozens of yards ahead.

It was there and then it was gone. Kemper slammed the brakes and then let off which caused the little car to fishtail tightly and then snap back into line.

The spell was broken, and they were both ripped back into the moment.

"What the hell was that?" Kemper exclaimed craning his neck to look back over his shoulder. "It looked like, I don't know, like big foot or something."

Deven was silent. Kemper looked back again to see if there was any last evidence of the encounter but there was nothing. Whatever it had been, it was gone now. He turned back and heard Deven scream.

"Look out!"

What he saw standing in the middle of the road, he couldn't quite piece together, it was like a tall man, but blacker than the shadows between the moonlit scenery behind him. It almost looked like his eyes glinted with light but that had to be wrong, a reflection off glasses or something. But Kemper did not have his headlights on...

He thought all of this in a fraction of a second, even as he again slammed on the brakes, downshifted and fishtailed under the force of the load. He still wasn't going to make it in time and the part of his mind that couldn't reconcile running someone over with the fact that they would in fact be running off the road took over and that's what they did.

The vintage rally car veered to the right, screeching hard and then shot over the shoulder and down the hillside, narrowly missing ancient, old-growth tree trunks, while bashing through fallen branches and ferns before burying the front end under a fallen tree suspended a couple feet off the ground. The safety harnesses and bucket seats did their job but the two were shaken.

"Are you alright?" Kemper asked Deven as his scrambled wits reconvened with his surroundings. She couldn't hear him through the screaming engine whose throttle was pinned but with a drivetrain that'd been forcibly disconnected. He tried to yell again before it occurred to him to turn off the ignition. After doing so, he asked again, "Are you alright?" he repeated. Deven nodded, taking mental inventory of all the screaming sensations clamoring for her attention, but none of them seemed to say broken or bleeding or not working.

She was about to reply when the words caught in her throat. A black figure appeared just outside the driver's side window. Her mouth was moving but the words wouldn't come out. She couldn't move, she couldn't warn Kemper that he was in danger. She could only watch as the door flew open, and Kemper, who was still looking intently at her, trying to understand why she couldn't speak, was pulled from the vehicle.

A strangled cry came from outside the car and Deven knew that there would be nothing that she could do for him. She'd seen these creatures before. Seen how they moved, seen their clawed hands, or paws or whatever they were. They were hunters…

Her hands fumbled uselessly at the five-point racing harness. She was in shock, but she'd been in life-or-death situations before, and her instincts and training kicked back in. She worked the clasps on the harness and then went for the door, but it wouldn't budge. Pushing on it with all her might, she still couldn't get it to move. It was smashed shut in the impact with the fallen tree.

Just as she went to push a third time a figure appeared on her side of the car and she recoiled, slipping over Kemper's seat and onto the underbrush beyond. She couldn't gain her feet, so she crawled and slid under the tree and down the hillside on the other side, tumbling onto a level patch of dirt and loam in a heap.

Deven sat up, scanning the darkness for the creature. Scattered shafts of moonlight pierced the canopy above. One shone on the creature. It was on the fallen tree, about thirty feet up slope. Her mind flashed to watching the creatures' blip across the rooftops. There was no escaping what would come next. She couldn't even walk unassisted. Deven struggled to her feet, in a low crouch, thighs burning, she waited, arms at the ready like an Olympic wrestler. She would die fighting. Just like her father.

Twenty-One

The View from Above

19.004329 AC (After Construct)
Age of the Half-Orc War

D'avry looked again at the hillside, at the rising columns of smoke, and desperation settled in. He was certain that there was nothing that they could do to save their friends. He looked back toward the orc outpost and saw that a matching column of smoke was now beginning to press into the sky. A response. They had seen the goblin fires and confirmed that they would meet. They were all doomed.

Volkreek was not so easily discouraged. He brought his hand to his face, pointing at his eyes with index and middle fingers and then pointed with those same fingers at the cliffside and the goblin fires, seeming to suggest to D'avry that he should use his flying orb to get more specific details or at least to see if he could locate their friends.

Nodding, D'avry reached into his jacket and produced the device. It sprang forth into the sky, zipping out of sight within seconds. Too high for any human or orc to see, and definitely too high to be seen by a goblin with their eyes more suited for darkness than broad daylight. Volkreek looked at him with upraised eyebrows as if awaiting the response to a question. D'avry responded.

"Give me a moment. I have to get the viewing orb into position, and I have... to..." He stopped mid-sentence.

There were many more than a few bands of goblins on the hillside. There were beginning to be hordes. The area below the cliffs was an anthill of activity on a large, gently sloping steppe of several acres. And off in the distance, to the south and further east, there were more columns of smoke ascending into the sky. Presumably more orc outposts.

This was, actually, D'avry had no words for what this was. It looked like highlander games but for the creatures from every human child's nightmares. Orcs and goblins were enough, but what if there were others? Trolls? They were not social creatures; he couldn't imagine trolls joining in for bartering and a round of lawn bowling. Volkreek huffed his impatience and D'avry paused to provide a report.

"There are many, many more goblins than we'd thought. Easily hundreds. Four? Five? And now there are other signal columns coming from the foothills beyond. More orc outposts I imagine. This looks like some sort of seasonal gathering maybe... for trade and who knows what else.

"Volkreek, I don't know what we can do. Even if we had Gearlach and Trask with us."

The ranger shook his head. It was clear that he would have no part in leaving his friends to be tortured or eaten or face some other terrible fate, even if the sake of humanity was in the balance. D'avry considered this. Their prospects were terrible to begin with and even worse with their forces scattered. They needed all the help they could get. D'avry wondered at the dream encounters that he had been having and if they played any part or if that was, as usual, some other insanity all its own.

D'avry's stomach growled loudly again. "Volkreek. Why don't you round up something to eat and I'll continue to spy on the enemy camp? Perhaps I can locate our friends, and maybe I can understand how the goblins are so bold outside during broad daylight. We'll be at a disadvantage at nighttime, but maybe we could have some luck during the day..."

The fighter nodded and paused as if he meant to communicate something else, but then turned and padded off along the bluff away from the road. D'avry slid back into the small grouping of trees against the hillside, where the portal had been. He wanted to avoid any unwanted attention if he could.

The flying eye required a greater level of concentration to see detail and view in the different modes when it was so high up. He sat down cross-legged, flipped up his hood and closed his eyes. Additionally, he decided to invoke the blending spell as a precaution. Better safe than sorry. Within seconds, the mage faded into the grass, rock and shrubbery.

Looking down from above, the view was largely trees but not of the immediate area he'd expected. Had the drone drifted off further than he thought? Also, it appeared to be stuck in a viewing mode that caused everything to appear monochrome and dimly lit. He was going to try to adjust the mode when he saw movement below and zoomed in, but then it was gone. The road was still here in the trees, but it too looked different as well.

Again, D'avry saw the movement. Now it was below the road and there was some commotion. Unable to see much more because of the trees, he decided he would chance it and brought the drone down through the canopy.

As the orb entered the forest, he was startled to realize that he wasn't viewing *through* it anymore, but in person. Looking around he found himself still seated, but in loam and the dried needles of a much larger and older forest than he'd inhabited on the bluff. And it was night.

The aroma of the forest was very strong but not unpleasant. Dusting himself off, he rose to his feet just as something or someone came crashing down the hillside, landing in a haphazard heap on the dirty forest floor. D'avry's eyes flashed wide as he realized it was the girl from the gray town.

Now her raven hair was mussed up and littered with dry leaves. She panted as she struggled to stand, her eyes casting about wildly, searching the hillside above. D'avry reached forward but then froze. He'd followed her gaze up the hill and that's where he saw one of the dark creatures from the gray town standing atop a fallen tree.

The girl gained her feet and crouched as though she would fight it bare handed. He felt more than saw the creature as it descended, popping out and popping back in to view in rapid succession. It covered the distance in the span of a couple heartbeats and dove claws first at the girl.

Before he realized what he'd done, D'avry sprang forward, tackling the girl to the ground but instead of the impact he'd expected, they seemed to fall right through the forest floor, swinging in a tight arc into the in-between.

The girl struggled away and fell to her hands and knees, the real world appearing as though through a fresh layer of ice on a frozen stream. She saw the dark creature land on all fours several feet away. It spun, searching frantically for its prey, it's glowing red eyes flashing as it cast about. Raising up on hind legs, it sniffed the air suspiciously before blinking out of existence itself.

The girl turned to look at D'avry, crab walking backwards, pushing feebly with her heels, when she suddenly seemed to realize that she was unable to breath. Her eyes bulged and she cast about frantically, looking for something, anything to save her. D'avry reached out but she recoiled even more.

He could imagine how terrified she must be with no frame of reference for what was happening to her and quickly brought his hands to his mouth and blew out a bubble of air, extending it to her but there was no resolving the situation with the girl. She scrambled back and looked as if she'd turn to run but then seemed to lose what strength remained in her and as she rolled over to her hands, they slipped out from under her, and she just crumpled to the blurry floor of the upside-down forest.

D'avry, uncertain what happened to someone who drowned in the in-between, rushed to her, grabbing her face in both hands, he breathed directly into her mouth. She didn't respond. He knew she didn't have much time and he didn't see any other options; they'd have to return to the surface and face the possibility that there were more creatures out there. His hand reversed the gestures of the phasing spell, and he felt the familiar whoosh as they swung right-side-up. Only this time, it was not the moonlit floor of the forest of giant trees, but the daytime, and it was back on the bluff at the base of the banshee's mountain, in lands inhabited by orcs and goblins and possibly trolls. Probably trolls. He shook his head with the depressing thought. *What have I done?*

The beautiful girl with the dark hair from the gray town lay unmoving in D'avry's lap, he went to brush some of the leaves and needles from her hair when her eyes blinked. Large pupils dilated to adjust for the light. She stared up at him. Her eyes were intensely blue as they reflected the overcast sky above before growing wide with fear and rage. She rolled away, again attempting to scramble to her feet.

"Who…" she panted out, "who are you? What have you done with Kemper?" and, "What was that *thing*?"

Again, she seemed to have more fight than strength in her as she sank down onto a hand and one knee. D'avry looked at her as though for the first time. Her shoes were an ivory colored sewn cloth whose toe and sole seemed to be of some material which was like leather but not. Too, she wore tightly fitting tan britches like a boy and had a black, hooded, long sleeve shirt which, again, was made of an exotic cloth that was not quite wool and not quite linen. D'avry also noticed that her fingernails were painted the color of blood, which matched her lips which were also painted or stained.

He wondered if this denoted some class of Conjurer he was unfamiliar with as she was unarmed but clearly familiar with fighting. It was then that he noticed the glint of metal between her shoes and pant leg. It wasn't armor, it was her leg itself and it was a stunning piece of work. He looked at her again. *What an unusual person…*

The girl screamed at him, causing a handful of birds to spring from the branches of a tree nearby. D'avry put his hands up in a gesture of peace and thought through the gestures for the spell of tongues that he'd used with the man in the cavern.

"I mean you no harm," he said, and his words sounded foreign, but he found that he could understand them well enough.

"Oh, yeah? Tell that to Kemper!" she screamed, her eyes brimming, she choked back the tears and then shuddered out, "What have you done with him? Is he... is he *dead*?" she asked her voice lowering to almost a whisper.

D'avry felt the magic flowing through him in an almost constant flow now. It was mercurial, subtly energetic. He was just a conduit, so he let it flow and returned his attention to her.

"I don't know this Kemper," D'avry stated, attempting to match her tone. "I showed up, much by accident, and there you were. You looked hurt, and there was that thing. I thought it meant to kill you, so...I tried to stop it." He shook his head, thinking back on the sequence of events.

Deven didn't look convinced.

"What happened? What was that place? Everything was... upside down!" she asked and then looked around, realizing for the first time that they were perhaps very far away from the scene of the incident. "Where are we? Where have you taken me? Did you *kidnap* me?" The questions tumbled out of her as she grew more and more frantic.

"Shhhhh! We are still in danger," he whispered emphatically, looking around and gesturing for her to calm down. "Unfortunately, I may have saved you only to bring you into the path of greater danger. And I don't rightly know how to get you back. Not that you want to go back necessarily either, considering what hunts you there," he said, and then thinking of something else. "How did you get to the gray town? Is that the place that you're from? They don't seem the same, exactly,"

D'avry asked trying to piece the puzzle together in his mind.

Maybe he could finally get some answers for once. The man in the tunnels had been surprisingly unhelpful. Every answer generating still more questions.

The girl's eyes widened and then squinted with suspicion.

"How do you know about that?" she demanded, "I've never told anyone. Are you *following* me? What do you want? Oh, my God, what is happening to me?" This last directed heavenward.

This wasn't working. D'avry decided it was time to start from the beginning.

"Let me start with this — my name is Once-Brother Avaricai D'avry, Under-Lord, amongst other things. I am a mage of sorts. Admittedly, not a very good one." He flashed an uncertain but disarming smile.

"My companions and I..." he said looking around as if he'd misplaced them, "...um, well we've gotten separated. Mostly. I still have one. He's hunting, I think. We have set upon a quest to stop an orc warlord from taking over the other orc tribes and plunging the entire sphere of the world into war. I do not think that humanity would survive that encounter. Oh yeah, and the orc, his name is N'Bruyyh. And he's undead. Which is to say he *was* alive before my companion, Gearlach, killed him, but then he was resurrected by some dark force of which I'm still uncertain as to its origins." D'avry searched the air for a moment, thinking that he needed to return to that line of thought very soon. He continued, "Regardless, N'Bruyyh tracked my companions down the river, the Nem Kar'kar, I believe it is, and amongst them was a librarian, not barbarian, which, I wouldn't blame you for thinking." He chuckled at his own joke. "The librarian, which I'm sure means something else in his culture, goes by the name of Graeburn Trask. I didn't like him very much — very intense. But he can kind of see the future, so you can see how N'Bruyyh..."

"Enough! Enough with this fantasy *bullshit*. What was your

name again?" she asked rubbing her temples, trying to massage away the nightmare.

"D'avry."

"D'avry?" she repeated and he nodded. "Okay. D'avry. Um, did you say...orcs?" she asked, looking pained to be entertaining such nonsense.

He nodded, a tight grimace playing across his face.

They had to be close in age, she thought. He looked like someone from one of her classes or from the coffee shop, though he definitely had more of a transient vibe going on, kind of Rasta meets renaissance fair. *Very Santa Cruz*, she thought. Not bad looking, but completely insane.

That caused her to think of the situation with Kemper. Her eyes clouded and she had to shove her hands into her hoody to keep them from shaking. She was so mad, but she didn't know who to blame, it was just so senseless. And insane.

How did that creature come to be there? Was it hunting her, just like in her vision of the gray town? *Was Kemper's death her fault?* She looked back to the madman in the trench coat, he was still blathering on about orcs and goblins, but he had been there. He had seen it too. And where was the place that he had taken her to? It seemed, actually, it had the same dreamy, otherworldly quality as the Gray Town had. And where was she now?

She looked up at a yellow sun that she couldn't differentiate from her own. She drew on the skills she'd learned in the marines and from her father. There were green buds on some of the trees and green grass but not many flowers, so that was a giveaway for spring, early spring anyway. It had been late summer just minutes ago. She blinked at that, nodded her head politely and continued to sort out what she could.

The sun was not quite directly overhead. There were pine trees around so she was in a temperate zone, probably mid-latitudes but she couldn't tell if that was north or south. If she watched the sun for a bit it would tell her what direction was west. And the direction of the shadows near noon would tell her what hemisphere since the sun would be transiting from nearer to one of the poles toward the equator.

Moss, too, she thought. Deven looked around and sure enough the pine trees had a bright, bushy green swath painted up their sides. Moss didn't always tell the truth; it grew where it was moist. Sometimes that was north in the northern hemisphere due to more frequent shadows. Prevailing wind had something to do with it. The sun would tell her. She could just wait. Or...

"Which way is north?"

"...so, then Volkreek launched his arrow with the line attached... I'm sorry, what?"

"Which way is north?" she asked, eyebrows raised and then smiled a thin expectant smile.

"It's that way," he motioned with his left hand in the direction that followed the range of mountains, "You're not listening, are you? I have a tendency to talk when I'm nervous. Not that you're making me nervous, just, well, this is a very precarious situation. Our friends have been taken by goblins. Those goblins are signaling the orc outposts for a gathering," he said this pointing to the spires of smoke rising from the craggy bluffs to the south of them.

Deven turned to look behind her and was surprised to see that there were in fact large columns of gray-white smoke rising from several outcroppings just a few kilometers away... To the south. They *were* in the northern hemisphere. At least she had *that* much sorted out.

She was struggling to keep the onslaught of disparate information at bay. She looked at the smoke. Goblins? She looked out into the valley and it was clear that there were hazy smudges scattered about the rolling foothills before her. Those certainly could be settlements. Maybe she was in Canada? She glanced up at the sun, her sun. The horizon looked the same.

The sky looked the same. The pieces just wouldn't go together. Here it was early spring. There it had been summer.

"What year is it?"

"Miss Deven. I understand that you're confused but..."

"What *year* is it!" she demanded,

"High Kantian or domestic?"

"Excuse me, what?"

"In High Kantian it is estimated to be Nine-thousand-one-hundred and twenty-three, by the way of the tri-oval, if you believe that nonsense," he waved it away dismissively, "... domestically, it is four-nineteen Grantholan. The year of the Dung Beetle. And it is kale, snow pea and radish planting time. Ooh, and asparagus," he added, gazing off into the middle distance as if envisioning a steaming plate of vegetables, or a hearty soup. In fact, that's exactly what he was doing. His stomach grumbled in sympathy. It was doing a lot of that lately and growing tired of being ignored.

"Are you hungry?" he asked.

"*No*. I'm not *hungry*! I want to know what year it is, and I want you to make sense and I want..." She flailed her arms and rolled her eyes, the veins were bulging in her neck, "Ughh! What's the use?" She flopped back onto her butt and started crying, her head buried in her arms.

D'avry looked on in sympathy but had nothing to offer. What could he say, he'd just yanked her out of her reality, into another one that she knew nothing about? He could sympathize. If anyone could, he could.

He gave her a minute. She pounded her fist into the damp ground, repeatedly and then seemed to lose steam.

"Deven, I'm truly sorry about your friend. I really am. I don't know what those things are, but they seem like they're looking for you. Do you know why?"

She shook her head, not bothering to look up.

"I know something is at work. I saw you in the gray town. I

was the bird, if you can believe that? Well, probably not, so just never mind about that bit. But there is, well, the great drama that's playing out in my world. I see similar things in other worlds. I don't know how they're connected but, the Astrig Ka'a is trying to guide me, I think."

She looked up, her dark eye make-up running in smeared streaks.

"It's, uh, well, it means Luck Magic. It guides me and it's given me certain powers. Like the ability to speak other languages, such as yours right now, or this —" He flicked a deft wrist and fire blossomed in his palm and then he quenched it. Like most mages he could have a flare for the dramatic and fire always pleased a crowd.

Deven's eyes lit up at that. She still looked a mess, but she seemed to have temporarily forgotten her woes. She studied him more intently and with less hostility than before.

"So, what I was saying is that I travel between places. It used to be just here in Relde and some of the farthest isles, occasionally as far south as, well, that doesn't matter. Now I travel to *worlds*. It used to be in my sleep, but my power is growing. Very fast. Too fast. And, well, I think the Astrig Ka'a has brought us together. I just don't know what for." He looked at her and breathed a heavy sigh.

They went back and forth for some time, she skeptically asking questions, he gently prodding for more details about her homeland and that of the gray town, the latter of which she had little to offer other than what he'd witnessed himself. She explained to him about the drive up the mountains which led to a long discussion about the technology that she took for granted in her world, that he could only conclude was in fact another world, like the one the man in the tunnel had alluded to. He explained to her about how he visited other worlds in his sleep, or in this case, accidentally, and how he had been an unwilling participant in the machinations of the Astrig Ka'a. He showed her the lantern door in his chest and her mouth dropped open. She reached out to touch it before modesty caught up with her and she paused, unconsciously chewing a fingernail instead.

"Well, you got one on me," she said lifting up first one and then the other pantleg to reveal the aluminum alloy and carbon fiber prosthetics that started just below her knee. It was D'avry's turn to be speechless. He had expected that her legs had been crippled in some way, but the materials were so foreign to him, and the craftsmanship was utterly amazing, and he had no idea that it went so far.

"How, if you don't mind me asking, did that happen? And it's fine if you, in fact, never mind. That was rude of me," he said, suddenly flushing.

"No, it's fine. I'm trying to tell the story more so I can let it go, and just, get used to it." She went on to recount how her squad had been ambushed by insurgents with IED's and RPG's and then pinned down by sniper fire. She had to spend a significant amount of time explaining what everything was, from tanks to helicopters, to the various types of firearms, as well as what a grenade was and how there were dozens of different types of those as well.

"Well, that is truly an amazing story. You're very brave. But, as I was trying to tell you earlier, you are probably in as much danger here as you were at that time. I don't know what the creatures were that were hunting you but there are still a great many dangers in my world. Not the least of which is the fact that roughly four-hundred or so goblins have convened on the hillside behind us, and an untold number of orcs are coming to join them — we've seen their fires.

"We really are in great danger, and our plans take us further into enemy territory to take on a creature that I don't know how to kill exactly. And, to make it worse, according to Gearlach, the half-orc warrior whom I believe is still trying to find our librarian friend, there is supposed to be some kind of *cosmic* event that is to unfold in the next few weeks.

"Timing and details are rather thin, but it is this event that will help N'Bruyyh usher in a new reign of terror, a united orc army. I wish there was some place safe that I could take you, but I fear that even if I wanted to, the rules still evade me. The universe still seems to conspire to send me or take me where it wants me to go." D'avry said this with a shrug and a conciliatory smile.

"I feel truly terrible for you and for your friend, Kemper, was it?"

Deven nodded again blinking back moisture, "I don't know, maybe he, maybe he got away?" But the look in her eyes said she knew he did not.

"Miss Deven, you don't know why they're after you, or how you found yourself in the gray town?"

She shook her head. 'No'.

"And forgive me for asking but, are you able to walk? You still seem pretty shaky."

"I had crutches. They have handles and they support at your forearms. I'm still using those most of the time, but I'm getting stronger every day," she said this, but her mind flashed back to the incident in the stairwell just two days before. She shook her head. "D'avry, I have nothing to go back to. I've been telling myself for years that my family would come around but after we lost my dad, well, we've just grown apart. So, even if we could go back, there's no point is there? The hunters will just find me again and I can't defend myself, even if I had an M4, I don't know if those things can be stopped.

"That one just ripped Kemper out of the car like he was a doll…" she said, staring off into nothing. "I can't go back. I don't see how this place is any more dangerous than where I was," she said, her blue eyes staring intently into his. "But I don't think I can cover the ground that you and your companions intend to cover. Do you have horses here? I could try to ride a horse. I've done it before, just not... with these," she said offering her foot and studying it as if for the first time.

"I would like to make myself useful, though. You believe humanity is in trouble. I would still be in the Marines if it weren't for my accident. I'm a fighter at heart and I know a thing or two about warfare. At least, our kind of warfare. But I can be helpful. Plus, I think that the technology that I'm familiar with can help. Like gun powder. And some types of medicine. Things like that."

D'avry closed his eyes. He had not expected her to want to join the battle. He had no idea how they'd avoid detection, let alone free their friends if that were even possible. He didn't even have a weapon for her let alone something she was familiar with other than a hunting knife, and beyond that, what could a woman do against an orc? Short of magic anyway.

But, with that idea, something struck him. What was the artifact that he and Volkreek had discovered at the river camp? It could be dangerous to try to unlock its secrets without very detailed and methodical experimentation. But they did not have the time or the proper tools to perform such work. Then again, since when had he ever been anything but willing to explore something to its final destination? Perhaps it was because it wasn't just his own skin he was worried about.

Twenty-Two

The Ring and the Wolf borne

"Miss Deven?" D'avry asked, opening his eyes, and then forming his hands into a steeple that he pressed against his lips, something he did when he was thinking deeply.

"I may have an item or two that could be of use to you but, I'm hesitant, very hesitant, to offer them to you as I do not know their origin. However, I do not believe in coincidence so I think that it may make sense to explore the possibilities, given our circumstances, but with as much caution as we can afford. Which, in truth, isn't much."

She looked back at him questioningly. She still had bits of leaves and dried redwood needles in her hair and stuck to her hooded shirt. She looked like a ragamuffin, but she was stunningly beautiful in spite of it. And the peculiar markings of her people, dark red fingernails and lips, though exotic and strange, seemed to make her more womanly, seemed to accentuate her beauty even while her metal legs and warrior demeanor made her seem less of a woman and more a force to be reckoned with. Yes, she may have the tenacity and the wit to unlock the secrets of the ring, D'avry thought.

D'avry reached into his jacket and produced the dagger, almost shocked that he hadn't lost it already given his recent track record. The blade was safely contained within its simple leather sheath. It had a belt loop and a leather thong that Deven immediately fastened to her thigh after slipping her belt through its loop and refastening the buckle.

Deven pulled the roughly foot-long, double-edged blade, flicked it on end for a downward strike and then quickly flicked it under, allowing it to rotate on its center mass, the handle never leaving her hand but floating between palm and fingers.

It was fast and fluid as if she'd *always* owned the dagger.

D'avry's brows went up but he remained silent, letting her inspect the beautifully crafted weapon. She admired it's sleek, efficient shape, the subtle fuller groove down the middle of the blade, the ever-so-slightly crescent shaped bronze guard, tawny-colored leather handle and counterbalanced pommel. She flicked both edges across her thumb before scraping the fine hairs on the back of her arm with one of the edges and seeing that it cleanly removed them, nodded admiringly and re-sheathed it with another deft flourish.

"D'avry, this is a remarkable blade. You just found this?" she asked incredulously. "Well, in any case, thank you. It's beautiful. Any chance you have a whetstone and some oil? I don't need them now, but I will if this is my only weapon."

"No, unfortunately, but Volkreek will. If he ever makes it back..." D'avry was legitimately getting worried now as it'd been several hours. He shook off his concern knowing that the fighter was both stealthy and capable. He'd find his way back.

D'avry then produced the ring from the bag he held within his jacket. As it came out into the wan light from the now overcast sky, it seemed to have a brilliance of its own. D'avry felt the drawing that he'd experienced the prior day, with Gearlach's great axe, and his own staff. This ring had similar power to it.

Indeed, vaguely, in his mind's eye he could see waves of arcane energy collapsing and expanding like light through a prism as it moved. He studied it, turning it this way and that, certain that if he could just catch it at the right angle it'd reveal its secrets, but to no avail. He finally, hesitantly, motioned for Deven to extend her hand. She naturally extended her left before blushing slightly. It clearly would only fit on her ring finger. But she wouldn't put it on her knife hand.

"Just do it," she said impatiently. "It doesn't mean anything and it's the only finger it'll fit. It's fine," she provided.

"Here, maybe you should do it anyway. It's... a powerful

artifact. And I haven't the vaguest idea what it does. It could be invisibility, it's *that* powerful. It could be luck; it could be suggestion. We won't know until you try it. It doesn't feel evil, not a dark magic, so I don't think you have to worry about killing or maiming with a glance." He laughed nervously.

She looked at him, concern etching her features. She took a deep breath, closing her eyes, and slipped the ring onto her finger. Nothing happened.

It felt cold, though it'd been inside D'avry's jacket, and he'd been holding it for at least a couple minutes. She looked at it on her finger. It was silver or white gold or some similar precious metal. Clearly the size suggested that it was for a woman, but it was kind of chunky, almost square, with smoothly rounded edges and hairline gold lines bordering the outward face edges. Other than that, she could see nothing remarkable about the ring and it appeared to do nothing special. She wondered if maybe D'avry was wrong about the ring. But he seemed so certain. Time would tell she thought.

"Nothing?" he asked.

She nodded affirmation.

"It could be you. Maybe because you come from a non-magical place. Maybe it's just different for you. I don't think we can count on that, though. I think we will need to be vigilant and pay attention to every little idiosyncrasy. Tell me if you feel anything strange and at the first sign of trouble, remove the ring at once."

She nodded again and just to be certain she attempted to remove it now and was alarmed to find that she could not. She tried harder and still it would not come off. She shot D'avry a look.

"What is this? I can't get it off. D'avry did you do something? Just tell me," she pleaded.

D'avry looked back in surprise. "N-no. Of course not. It won't come off? Are you sure, did you try spitting on it?"

She raised her eyebrows, looking much as if he'd just passed considerable gas. "Ewww. No."

She tried again with little luck.

D'avry blew out a breath and grimaced, "You may be stuck with it for a while, until we can figure out what it does and then possibly we can figure out how to get it off. This is the problem with unknown magicals. I mean, I don't think there's much that we can do for now…" D'avry added lamely.

"No. It'll be fine, I'm sure…" Deven responded. "We'll just get it figured out. But how will I know if it's doing anything?" she asked.

"We may not notice at first, or it may be painfully obvious. It's obviously not invisibility… It's possible that we just made difficult going even more difficult. But we won't know until we know…" he replied shrugging.

D'avry looked around again worriedly and then closed his eyes. He was surprised to find the drone right where'd he'd left it, hovering a couple hundred feet in the air above the Goblin Games or whatever it was that they were preparing for.

"D'avry. What's the matter?" Deven asked.

"I'm checking in on the flying eye, or um, drone, I guess. Do you have those?" he asked.

Deven's brows knitted, and she nodded before speaking, "Uh, yeah, we have those. How do *you* have those? That's technology."

D'avry explained that amongst the limited exposure he'd had to other worlds it had been hers, the gray town and a planet that had a lot of tunnels in it where he'd met a man that rode around in a large suit made of metal.

"A mech?" she asked, awe in her voice. "They're like tanks from my home world but instead of riding on wheels or tracks, they're actually more like an extension of the driver. Well, I guess like you described it, a suit of armor, but one that could be much larger and that moves under its own power." She shook her head in amazement, "That's awesome. I'd love to see it," she said, looking at him again with wonderment, not quite sure what to make of this peculiar person with his fantastic stories and bookish demeanor, who at the same time was clearly more than capable of living off the land and dealing with its dangers...

"Yeah, well, I'm still learning the extents of these new abilities and new things seem to be happening all the time. As far as moving people from one plane to another... that wasn't on purpose. Much of the time I don't know if it's a new ability or still something to do with the luck magic, the intent of the Astrig Ka'a.

I do need to find Volkreek though. I'm starting to get worried. And I need to find our other companions. Give me a moment," he told her. He sat down cross-legged, flicked up his hood and closed his eyes again.

D'avry used the drone to reconnoiter the goblin encampment. He found that the goblins wore black, sack-like, hooded robes and covering their eyes were goggles of a sort, made of leather with perforated metal screens. The screens were punctures or slits or combinations of the two and D'avry realized that they must work to limit the amount of light their eyes were exposed to.

In light of this, he imagined that daytime would be a *much* better time to conduct a rescue mission, due to their limited visibility. But they'd have to do it before the orcs showed up, since orcs saw better in the day than they did at night, much like humans did.

D'avry continued to scan the camp and watched as a stream of bodies flowed in and out of the various caves and down to the steppe. They were setting up tents and makeshift stables for livestock, of which there were mostly goats, but then further away there appeared to be dogs or wolves and then beyond that D'avry caught a glimpse of pens that were covered. He focused the drone on the covered holding pens and was shocked to find that they were filled with humans. It was many more than just the two he was looking for, perhaps two dozen or more from what he was able to see.

D'avry steadied his breathing, calmed his mind in order to ease the interface between man and machine. The view switched to the vivid, multi-colored spectrum and suddenly the goblins, animals and people stood out red amongst fields of yellow, green and blue, with exception now of the fires which appeared white.

It dawned on him that the spectrum-view was linked to temperature, though how it did that he was at a loss to comprehend. That feature had not been so obvious in the cave where everything was cold and they had had no fire, only the magic light of D'avry's spell and Volkreek's blade. Still, he would not be able to make out much of anything through the timber roof on the pens. The timbers appeared blue-black and the bodies beneath, white hot. He would have a difficult time just counting the people within. Identifying anyone would be impossible.

He switched views again and zoomed in as far as he could, but it didn't help much. The group of people were mostly men of fighting age, which D'avry thought was strange until he recalled the battle upriver at the keep called Talles Murdt. Some of these men may have been captured there or they had been washed downstream or tried to escape ahead of the battle. Perhaps they were just merchants and guards? That would explain why the prisoners were mostly men and not women and children as well.

Just then, D'avry though he caught a bald head in the midst of the people gathered in the second pen. He revised his estimate, the number seemed closer to twenty or thirty. There'd be no way that he could save them all. *And was that Farn?* And if so, was Liggo with him in the same pen or in one of the other two?

With black hair and beard, he would not stand out among a bunch of filthy captives. D'avry moved the drone to get a better look but still… *No, that might be Liggo in the third pen,* he thought. He would just have to go see for himself.

D'avry zoomed out and returned to the spectrum-view which he thought would make it easier to spot bodies in the forest so that he could go find his long overdue ranger friend. He navigated the drone northward the couple miles toward where he and Deven were located presently. D'avry was shocked to see that there were bands of what appeared to be goblins foraging in the forest not a mile from where they were sitting.

None seemed to be heading in their direction and he'd not seen anything that looked like an orc party. But as he got closer to the creek crossing, in a wooded area adjacent to the creek, about a half mile further on, he saw a cluster of dots and his heart skipped.

There was a larger dot which seemed to be pursued by several dots, some smaller and some oddly shaped. As D'avry zoomed in and switched the view he could tell that goblins were pursuing something through the woods. But some of the goblins were moving very fast, and then D'avry realized what the wolves at the camp had been for. The goblins were *riding* them. At least some were, as there were goblins on foot too.

D'avry chanced it and dropped the drone in closer and saw that indeed it was Volkreek that the goblins were pursuing. He was running, stopping to turn and fire shots with his bow and then resuming flight.

By D'avry's estimation, he did not have long before they'd be on him. D'avry swung the flying eye in behind the wolf borne goblins and navigating the trees expertly, he struck, driving the orb into the back of the head of the one furthest back. The rider flew forward over the front of his mount and was immediately pounced on and mangled by the wolf before it ran off into the woods, shaking its head furiously to remove it's bridle.

Wow, that worked! D'avry thought. *I wonder how much more the device can take?*

He didn't want to destroy such a valuable tool, but the demands of the present needed to be met. D'avry sighted in on the next wolf borne and did the same, only this time knocking him into another rider as they navigated over a narrow escarpment. He couldn't hear their screams but watched as they bounced off one level of rocks to another and was confident that they'd not be pursuing further.

He switched back to spectrum-view and saw three more wolf borne ahead but now they were circling the man, who'd stowed his bow in favor of the hand-and-a-half blade. His free hand held the hunting knife, blade down in a defensive position. The lead goblin raced in and D'avry urged the orb forward, for as soon as Volkreek had engaged the leader a second rushed in from behind.

D'avry's struck the second rider from behind, launching him forward and off his ride but he still came up with axe in hand. Volkreek was engaged with the leader as the wolf growled and snapped while its master waited and threatened wildly with a wicked sword and shield. The wolf lunged forward and the third wolf borne charged in from the ranger's right flank, but a flash of movement caused D'avry's pulse to jump, as he'd seen movement like that before.

The shape blinked from one spot to several yards away and then blinked again. A sneakered foot collided with the charging goblin's face, and it was knocked free of its ride. The new combatant landed lithely next to the fallen creature and a silver flash opened the goblins throat before the figure blipped away again. Too quick for the wolf, who snapped at thin air and then shaking its head, ran off into the woods.

This left the dismounted goblin and the lead wolf borne. Volkreek, seeing the lead goblin's attention drawn to a second enemy, dove in with both blades. The sword plunged into the wolf's chest while the hunting blade slashed deeply into the goblin's thigh. It screeched as the wolf toppled but didn't quite reach the ground before the long blade had been freed from the wolf's body and now freed the goblin's head from its shoulders.

D'avry watched in amazement as the last goblin was taken off its feet from behind and pinned to the ground, a tawny leather handle protruding from its chest. Volkreek didn't blink an eye. His sword found its sheath and the bow was once again in his hands. He charged up the short rise in the direction from which he'd come and loosed two arrows at its summit. Reaching for a third, he found his quiver empty. D'avry swung the flying orb around and found that there were still three goblins pursuing on foot.

He smashed all three in one swooping s-turn and then peeled off to a higher altitude to see how many more were in pursuit or still alive and might possibly be able to get back to the main contingent. All he found was a dozen or so cooling bodies, highlighted in green and yellow, scattered about the trail for the last half mile.

Indeed, where the final battle had taken place was only a quarter mile from where he and Deven were now. D'avry sprang up from his seated position and was racing down the path toward his friend. It seemed like an interminable amount of time but was only a couple minutes when he rounded a fold in the hillside and found the hollow where Deven and Volkreek were staring at each other coolly, surrounded by the bodies of goblins and a wolf.

D'avry was breathing hard. So was Volkreek who'd just done a marathon, dodging, fighting, and running for his life. He'd done all this with a stringer of rabbits tied to his waist, which undoubtedly is how the wolves had caught his scent. Otherwise, he doubted Volkreek would have been caught unaware.

The mage looked at Deven. She stood tall. In fact, there was something different about her that he couldn't quite place.

Maybe it was just the fact that when he'd seen her earlier she was barely able to stand, let alone walk. How had she even got this far?

"Deven, are you... okay?" he asked, though she seemed more than fine.

"Yeah. I'm really good, in fact," she said this while wiping the dagger blade off on a goblin's cloak before sheathing it. D'avry recognized the handle from the melee and realized that it *had* been Deven who had joined the fray.

"I think the ring, that must be what it does, or at least that's part of it. I can walk! I don't know if it's given me strength or just some significant amount of healing but, I can walk!" she repeated. "And even more than that, I can move, really, really fast. Almost like, I think it and I can be there. Just for short distances though but, it's, it's..." her voice started to break up a little bit and she blinked away the moisture that was gathering in her eyes. She swallowed and took a big shuddering breath before continuing,

"It's really, really cool." She looked at D'avry and smiled. "The ring's power must be tied to movement, which seems pretty coincidental when you think about it. Lucky, even." And she looked at him knowingly.

Volkreek stood there during this exchange, looking first to one and then the other, his chin length blonde hair plastered to his head, splayed out like feathers at the ends where it wasn't drenched with sweat. He was stroking his beard thoughtfully with the other hand resting on the knife pommel on his hip. He looked last at D'avry, tipping his head in Deven's direction and raising his eyebrows as if to say, "*And, who is this?*"

D'avry stepped forward to provide introductions. "Volkreek. This is Deven. Deven, Volkreek. He doesn't speak," he said this last to Deven, but Volkreek just answered by opening his mouth wide to show the stub of a tongue and then closed it with a mirthless smile. Deven and D'avry just nodded their understanding.

Before either could speak, he gestured for them to pause. Palms out, he brought his hands together, one covering the other fist and he made a contrite bow to Deven and then turning to D'avry, bowed again. It took a second for D'avry to realize that he was thanking them for saving his life.

He looked back down the trail in the direction from which he'd come.

D'avry interrupted him. "I checked already with the flying eye. There are no survivors. And the wolves seem to be content to make their own way. Have you ever seen anything like it? These wolf borne goblins?" he asked and looked at the two that Deven had dispatched. They were like the others, wearing the black sack cloth and what D'avry thought of as snow goggles.

The ranger shook his head and grunted. The first audible response that had come from the man through all of his and D'avry's ordeals.

"Well, those are some hard fought for rabbits you have there. We should do something with those I think. We will need to strike before the sun goes down in order to gain some advantage on the goblins, and hopefully do it before the orcs arrive," D'avry suggested.

The fighter's attention snapped to him and D'avry nodded his head in the affirmative. "Yes, I think that I found Farn and possibly Liggo, but I can't be certain. I will need to get in close to be sure. Beyond that, I don't know. I can't say if Gearlach or Trask are with them, there are between twenty and thirty people in pens up there." This got Volkreek and Deven's attention, both.

"They have how many people locked-up up there? Thirty?" she asked. "We can't just take our friends and leave the rest," she stated as a matter of fact.

Volkreek looked at her and then at D'avry quizzically. It dawned on the mage that he hadn't understood a word she'd said this whole time, since D'avry had performed a spell of tongues for himself so she could understand him, not the other way around.

"He doesn't understand your language," he said to her and then fished in his tunic for the coin but remembered that it was somewhere off in the wilderness with the raven, and hopefully Gearlach, and beyond his wildest imagination, with Trask, but he somehow doubted that. He dug inside his jacket for one of the coins from the chest and pulled out a silver piece, minted in an era that he was unfamiliar with. He rubbed it in his fingers and thought of the necessary elements for speech and understanding, drew from the lines of arcane energy that glistened vaguely in his mind's eye, crisscrossing every inch of space around them. They must be very close to a nexus, he thought. Then realized it was the mountain itself. It acted as a kind of focusing point. Again, information for later.

D'avry rubbed the coin more feverishly, willing the strands of energy to bend into it, fill it, and become somehow enmeshed in its structure. He imbued it with his intentions and let the complex set, similar to allowing molten metal to cool and harden in a mold.

The coin was freezing to the touch, and he dropped it into his other hand and passed it back and forth like a hot potato for a couple of seconds.

"Ooh, be careful," he said, handing it to Deven who reached for it and then in shock, quickly did the same.

"Wow. That's reeeally cold," she exclaimed, eyeing the coin appraisingly. "What'd you do?"

"I crafted a spell of tongues and imbued the coin with it. It's magical now, I guess. I've never made a magical device before. Crafting was another school in the Academy. I was no good at it. I stuck with architecture. Buildings, walls. I was quite good at that. Magic, not so much. Well, until now anyway." He shrugged.

Volkreek was looking at Deven anew, amazed that she now spoke his language perfectly. Having a mage around was turning out to be pretty convenient. Farn may have been a far superior warrior, but D'avry was beginning to grow on him.

D'avry returned his attention to the issue at hand. "I don't know what we can do about the refugees. All of mankind is counting on us to circumvent a war. We just demonstrated that we're good for maybe a dozen or a little more between the *three* of us. There are *hundreds* up there," he said pointing toward the smoking scar on the mountainside.

"We have to get in and get out. The other problem is that the mountain has caves all over. I wouldn't be surprised if the party that Volkreek found wasn't even from the camp on the hillside. They may have just been a hunting party like the ones that captured Liggo and Farn. *And*, we may still have to find the other two. Lastly, we still have to find N'Bruyyh. We don't know where he is, but he wants Trask badly. He may even have him, in which case, all hope may already be lost."

The other two were silent. It was clear that neither liked the idea of leaving the captives to perish but they had nothing more to offer as there was still no definitive idea of how they were going to save the two companions.

"I'm going to go up there. I will use the in-between space to slip in unseen."

Volkreek nodded but Deven looked perplexed.

"It's what we did when I found you in the forest, when we were *inside* the earth but still able to see what was above us, or actually below us, I guess," D'avry stated but then seeing Volkreek's look of confusion at something he'd said, he backtracked a bit mentally and realized, Volkreek had no idea where Deven had even come from.

"Oh yeah, sorry about that Volkreek. Deven comes from another world. They don't have magic and there's these dimension-shifting creatures that are hunting her, so I brought her here, which all of a sudden sounds like a terrible idea," he said this last as he realized that he may indeed have jeopardized their mission by bringing Deven here. Even though he hadn't done it intentionally *and* wasn't entirely sure how he'd done it in the first place.

"I don't know how it happened, actually. I was trying to use the orb to spy on the goblin camp and I was just in her world all of a sudden," he said, shaking his head in befuddlement.

"Also, you should know that I visit another world in my dreams, and it's vastly more advanced, I think, than Deven's. I'm not sure why this is happening, but I think it has to do with when the Astrig Ka'a *changed,* and the thing in my chest," he said, rapping on the window with his knuckles.

"After this thing happened," he said referring to the lantern door, "I could control things that I couldn't before, but then it seems like things just got a lot more complicated too. I don't know if you knew all of that, about me, but that's what's going on," he finished, and it was like a heavy burden being lifted from his shoulders being able to tell the ranger all of that. He realized he trusted someone for the first time in a very, very long time. He found that he was happy and afraid all at once. It was an odd mix of emotions. He also felt a pang of fear about his companions being held in the camp.

Volkreek reached out and grabbed D'avry's shoulder in a gesture of support and just breathed a big sigh. He then dropped the rabbits and wondered off to find materials to make a small fire. Deven was looking at him and it was clear that she had many more questions but was satisfied to wait till a better time.

"There's more that we need to understand about the ring's powers. But I must see about our friends. Do you know how to skin a rabbit?" he asked.

The words had only escaped his lips when she interjected, "I'm not letting you out of my sight. I'm coming with you."

He looked at her, about to object, but thought better of it. He could tell there was no winning this argument.

"Last I checked there were parties in the forest. I will use the flying eye to scout ahead. Luckily, the pens are on the south end of the field. But the sun is high and indeed, it appears to be past noon. We have a couple miles to cover, and we will be at risk in the dark. So, we will want to get back as soon as possible." And with that the two stepped onto the trail and began the couple mile jog to the goblin camp.

Twenty-Three

The Captives

The drone proved useful, helping D'avry and Deven to navigate the forest with little issue, only having to stop a couple of times to allow a party to pass by unsuspecting. As they drew closer, trails leading up the hill to the cliffs above, and presumably the tunnels, stood out from between patches of hardy, high-altitude foliage. They were only a quarter mile or so away and there was a heavy stream of traffic.

Most were carrying tent materials and things to barter with. There were also many goblins working to set up tents in the field now, shrouded as they were in the black sack cloth, but few of these wore the armor of the raiders or of wolf borne. D'avry also noted that the wolf pens were only a few pens over from where they kept the human captives. He did not like the proximity.

He scanned the surrounding area using the drone again to be certain that they were clear before instructing Deven to climb a tree and perform overwatch. She disagreed but when he reminded her that she could not breath in the in-between space she paused. Flashing back to that first experience she asked, "What was it that you tried to do when you rescued me? Was that a bubble? Can you provide air for me?"

"Yes, but I need to materialize in the pen in order to find the other companions, if they're indeed here. That means you have to join me in the pen, and you will... definitely stand out," he finished.

"I'm coming with you. Even if I have to go underground," she said crossing her arms as if the question were settled.

D'avry breathed out.

"Fine. You ready?" She nodded yes and smiled though he

could tell she was more than a little concerned. He would have to find a way to tell her no if this arrangement was going to work out...

He performed a now much simplified hand gesture and the world swung around them until they were standing on the same spot but perfectly inverted. Both of them looking through to the bleary haze reality beneath their feet. He brought his hands to his mouth and blew a grapefruit-sized bubble and handed it to her. She grabbed it in both hands and gingerly pressed it to her lips, sucking in as she did so. After a second, she looked up. He gave her the thumbs up signal and she nodded, and they continued on toward the pens.

D'avry navigated to the closest pen, where he'd thought he'd seen Liggo, and was surprised that the same perception that he'd felt in the cavern, and earlier on the hillside, had returned. He was certain of both men's whereabouts. He found the man he'd seen using the drone, leaning back against wood posts that made up the south wall of the pen. Once underneath a spot directly in front of him, he motioned again to Deven and then reversed the spell.

The world spun and they were kneeling in muddy hay, surrounded by the smell of humanity. The man jerked suddenly with surprise. His eyes wide like a frightened packhorse. D'avry's finger shot up to his lips to urge the man to remain quiet. He did, and then his dirt smeared face cracked into a huge smile.

"What're you doin' here?" he whispered hoarsely, in his broken dialect, motioning for them to move in close. The others in the pen who heard the commotion looked on with shock and then with nervous glances between them. Indeed, many appeared to be soldiers though more than a few looked to be craftsmen or laborers by their clothing. His suspicions about them being refugees from the battle at the keep seemed to be tracking. Liggo looked at Deven and then to D'avry.

"*This* is your rescue party?" he asked bluntly, not intending to be offensive. "She's uh, you know…" he said conspiratorially. Deven rolled her eyes, her dagger materializing in her hand as she played at cleaning the dirt from under her bright red fingernails.

D'avry attempted to explain. "Don't worry. She can hold her own. Now, I've got to get Farn but are the others with you?" he asked, not wanting to say their names out loud considering that some of the captives may wish to barter for their lives with that information.

Liggo shook his head no. D'avry asked the next most important question.

"Can you walk?" The thief made a slow nod in the affirmative suggesting that he'd like to do more than just flee with his life if he had anything to say about it.

"Okay, sit tight."

But just as he was about to work on getting to the next pen, he heard a familiar voice from the other side of the rough lumber posts of the pen wall. It was from the next one over. A hooded figure was leaning against the posts directly behind Liggo. He dropped his hood to reveal a bald head with a ragged gash that had dried blood running down behind his ear and to his neck in jagged streams like lightning bolts. He turned, gingerly.

"Don't worry. I heard it all. Never thought I'd see you again…" It was Farn, with his wiry blonde beard and shaven head, but his eyes were hard as he smiled. D'avry could see his face was swollen on one side. For him the last twenty-four hours had not been kind.

"We're going to get you out of here," D'avry assured him.

"What about the rest? These are good people, and they don't deserve to die. Not like this." The priest whispered, hissing the last with an emphatic note of contempt.

"I can only take a few people at a time. The goblins will surely notice if all the humans are missing and when they come after us, we don't have any weapons. It'll be a slaughter," D'avry responded trying to inject some reason into the argument.

"Any that wish to go should go. Any that wish to take their chances should stay. As for weapons, we'll take them from the bodies of our foes. Though I'd like to have the staff and my mace back, and I know Liggo will sorely miss his knives," Farn concluded.

D'avry shook his head but then looked around at the captives. Many kept to themselves but of the ones who dared to look in his direction, he saw the fire of hope beginning to rise. He turned his attention to the main camp and extended his senses to see if he picked up on any magical objects. He saw nothing close and nothing that stood out, but he did find that he was drawn to a large tent that had been erected toward the center of the clearing.

That seemed right to him. It was probably the tent of some sort of overseer, either of the goblin horde itself or of the bizarre, which D'avry saw now was what the activities most closely resembled.

Just then a loud cry echoed from the sky above, followed by several others farther off. All the captives looked up through the timbers of the roof. D'avry saw what looked like crows or ravens but then it became clear that they were very large, and they bore something on their backs. Again, came a screeching cry and D'avry was surprised how large the creatures actually were. The things upon their backs were more goblins. D'avry looked at Liggo to see if he'd ever seen or heard of such a thing.

"Raven borne... Just our luck. We'll have to keep to the trees then."

D'avry decided it was indeed time to go and to be extra careful. He pulled the orb down to the treetops near the pathway they'd taken to get to the camp. It would diminish their ability to steer clear of roaming parties but having the flying eye be spotted by one of the ravens could be just as damaging, if not worse.

"Alright. I can take a couple at a time. We'll have to move fast. Volkreek is set up near a ford about three miles north of here. Deven and I were just coming up to recon the area but it's clear that we need to get out while we still can. Besides the raven borne, they also have wolf riders in the forest, though they seem to be few and far between," D'avry explained.

He also told them about the in-between and how he could use it to travel but that they wouldn't be able to breath except for the bubbles of air that he provided. He told Farn and Liggo to talk to their respective groups of prisoners to decide who was and wasn't coming and he sent Deven to the last pen to prepare the captives there. She walked across the small space and blipped out of sight, reappearing in the next pen over to the shock and dismay of the captives there. Many of whom seemed too weak to make much commotion. Liggo's eyes grew wide, but he said nothing.

Not all of the captives chose to go, which surprised the priest, but not D'avry. He understood that some people were more willing to wait and see what happened than to choose action with consequences. He lifted a tiny prayer for their souls, though he knew not who might be listening.

All told, there were thirteen who left the cages, which in D'avry's estimation left the cages looking exceedingly barren, but the remainder arranged themselves so as to be seen in order to provide some cover for the escapees.

When they'd all reached the forest, D'avry gave a thought to what Farn had said in the cages, about leaving their magically enhanced weapons. Continuing their mission without them seemed like a severe handicap. For now, but more so for when the inevitable showdown with N'Bruyyh took place. He was more and more certain that it would come to that.

D'avry found Deven within the group of refugees, tending to a man with a swollen eye and an ear that more closely resembled a shelf fungus that'd been run over by a wagon wheel. D'avry grimaced. The swelling would probably go down, but infection would be the man's biggest concern.

He used the orb to scout out a spring where the group could find water as well as healing herbs and then he pulled her aside. He asked if she felt comfortable navigating back to camp with half of the refugees and with the help of Liggo while he searched out the party's weapons. She agreed without hesitation.

He instructed her about the spring and chose a handful of the captives that were in better condition and who had a military bearing. One in particular was a bear of a man who had been a blacksmith, named Laphren. If they were going to go weaponless into the forest, Laphren looked like he could look after Deven as well as anybody. Plus, he was familiar with the herbs that D'avry sought.

The group slipped off into the trees and D'avry sent the orb ahead of them. He would use it to scout ahead and then signal Deven if there was any sign of trouble.

Left in the trees now were just Farn and five of the captives, who for the most part didn't have any military experience. D'avry had them continue into the forest a couple hundred yards and then hide amongst the boulders in a shallow ravine so that he could infiltrate the main tent and see if he could regain their weapons.

D'avry used the in-between to navigate to the tent where he'd sensed the magic. Whether it was the weapons or something else, he couldn't be sure. As he approached from below, he noted that there were no less than six goblins going about the business of setting up operations. In the middle of the tent was a large banquet table which D'avry assumed was where the goblin overseer would greet the chieftains from the various orc outposts who'd responded with signal fires of their own.

At the far end of the tent was yet another large wooden table arranged perpendicular to the banquet table. This one was empty as of yet. Behind it, though, he sensed what he'd come for. There were two large chests.

The one on the right was long and low, but the one on the left was more traditionally shaped and would come up to his thigh, though for a goblin that would be about waist high. To D'avry's perception the left-most chest seemed to glow faintly. He assumed it was guarded with some sort of enchantment, but he also found himself drawn to the long chest on the right. He decided to check it out first.

As he drew closer, the tingle on his skin told him that there were magical items inside it. He unphased from below and materialized, crouching next to the chest. From this vantage he was mostly hidden by the wide table.

He looked around quickly to see where the goblins were and that they were still busy with their preparations. Seeing that this was so, he performed a small spell of opening on the lock of the low trunk. It clicked loudly and D'avry cringed, he was out of practice, he thought. He held his breath to listen, but it didn't seem that anyone had noticed.

Lifting the lid slowly he was able to sense more clearly the items inside and it was in fact Farn's staff, and there was a velvet bag which he hoped contained Liggo's knives. He didn't bother checking because either it did or it did not, there was nothing left in the chest but various non-magical artifacts that appeared to be instruments, astronomical or otherwise, and still others he couldn't be sure of but didn't have time to investigate. He removed the staff and the velvet bag and closed the trunk lid, not bothering to lock it yet since that would just make the loud click again.

He turned his attention to the smaller chest. Closing his eyes, he saw the trunk in his mind, saw its metal reinforced edges and corners, the heavy hasp, he felt the crafted hardwood that made up its walls. D'avry probed the enchantment that sealed the box and the tension behind the spell. Gently tugging at it, he saw a glowing web-like substance that clung to the entire surface. D'avry opened his eyes and the trunk appeared normal again, though he could still observe the faintest glow.

D'avry closed his eyes again and once more the trunk appeared to be covered in the softly glowing membrane. He searched all around and could find no seam or weakness to exploit. He knew that this was not his main objective but there was that tug, the pull of the Astrig Ka'a which told him that this was important.

It'd better be. But… don't be greedy and blow the entire plan, he thought.

Grasping the staff in his hand, arcane energy coursed through him. He focused on the power of the lantern window and its contents, and in his mind he just softly blew the web of enchantment away. To his surprise it wisped away into nothingness, and there was the chest before him. He smiled inwardly but then reminded himself not to get too cocky. He was playing with powers that were still largely foreign to him.

Once again, he performed the spell of unlocking and the hinge popped open with a much more sophisticated mechanism that thankfully only made a soft *clunk* when it unlatched. He paused and looked around again but found the goblins busy still with their preparations. He took a deep breath and slowly lifted the lid.

Just then a loud cawing noise echoed through the camp, and he froze, almost dropping the lid. The goblins all turned to see what the commotion was in the camp but after a minute returned to their work when they realized it was just the raven borne who had landed a while before and now were going about the business of dealing with their unconventional steeds.

D'avry continued with opening the lid and found that amidst bags of coin and other objects crafted in precious stone and metals, there was a small robin's egg blue satchel drawn tight by a golden drawstring. He didn't know what was inside, but he knew that this was what he was looking for. He grabbed it, slipped it into his jacket and closed the lid ignoring everything else.

Locking both the trunks, he cast a spell that came to mind unprovoked. It was a spell of binding. And at its root was fire. He smiled again to himself as he thought of this tiny bit of justice for the captives in the forest, running for their lives, beaten, bloodied, some disfigured for life. He nodded at a job well done and then slipped into the in-between.

D'avry appeared next to Farn, causing the man to jump and blow air abruptly out of his lungs with a sigh of exasperation.

"What took you so long? I think the lead raven borne just arrived. He's heading for the main tent," he stated as one of the captives dropped from the tree branches where he'd been scouting the goblin camp.

D'avry swallowed hard. They did not have much time indeed.

"Go. We must be gone. Quickly," he urged, handing Farn the staff, though he didn't know what the man would do with it since he'd had precious little time to learn how to use it. He imagined he could club some goblins with it at least.

They made their way down the hillside a hundred yards or so before they heard the chilling cries of the raven borne clamoring in the camp. Within minutes they heard an explosion and saw the huge birds taking to the skies through the trees above them, a large column of black smoke billowing into the sky from the camp itself. D'avry smiled broadly and renewed his pace.

Scanning the sky, D'avry noticed that the sun was dipping close to the farthest ridge on the mountain's broad, sloping base. He realized for certain what he'd only speculated at before, that it would be dark before they made it to camp.

"Stick to the trees. We must not be spotted before we can catch up to the others," D'avry urged.

He only hoped that the remaining captives wouldn't tell the goblins which way they'd gone, though he didn't think that they had any idea since they'd utilized the in-between to escape to the tree line. Truth be told, D'avry was more concerned that the wolf borne would sniff them out.

Just then a huge shadow flew past, brushing the treetops just above them, but he heard no cry of discovery. Just a close call.

"Continue on, quickly," he told them.

While he did so, he checked in on Deven with the drone. It had been picking its way smoothly through the trees and seen no signs of trouble to that point. But then, as D'avry switched views to the spectrum, a handful of yellow dots appeared along a row of rocks about a hundred yards further up and to the left of where Deven's group was headed. It was an ambush. As he zoomed in, he could just make out what looked like a dozen or so heads poking over the rocks. He wiped the blood that was now streaming down his nose on his sleeve and continued on, jogging and manipulating the flying eye as best he could.

Deven and her group of seven soldiers, the blacksmith Laphren and the dark-haired adventurer with the thick accent — Liggo, she thought his name was — slipped through the trees making reasonable time. Not great time, she conceded, but this was supposed to be a quiet exfil and these things didn't happen quickly. *Slow was smooth and smooth was fast*, she reminded herself. They'd paused a few times as they scouted over the crests of hills and before dropping into an exposed ravine.

Once, they'd heard a wolf's cry in the distance and waited to hear it echoed but no response came so they continued on again. Now they paused yet again as large birds carrying goblins could be seen in the skies above. *What had the priest called them, raven borne?* She decided that she'd rather not see them up close.

As such, they were picking their way through only the densest sections of trees now. Deven was focused on the task at hand, leading the refugees to safety, but her mind kept wandering into the periphery. *What was this place she'd been taken to? How did that work in the first place, being transported, and why? What would her mother and sisters be going through when she turned up missing and her date turned up dead?*

That hit her in the gut. She felt bad for her family, but she felt terrible for Kemper. *He didn't deserve that. And who was this guy, D'avry, who could perform magic and seemed to be able to slip between worlds?* She had to accept that magic was a real thing here as she was able to walk and even more, and she had personally travelled through the dirt, roots and stone beneath her feet more than a handful of times at this point. *And orcs and goblins! Seriously, what the hell was that about?*

It was like she was in a dream, and for a brief terrifying moment she worried that maybe she was, or possibly still in the coma. But then the feeling passed as she felt the breeze on her cheeks and smelled the mountain air of the alpine forest around her, felt the chill beginning to settle in as the last rays of sunlight fled into the treetops above before disappearing all together.

No, this was real. As real as the gray town at least. If not more. And what were those creatures that were after her and why? Well at least now she felt like she could fight back a little better if she had to, thanks to whatever powers were associated with the ring that D'avry had given her.

All these thoughts and more clamored for her attention when a shadow flew up within a couple of feet of her, she jumped but then recognized it as D'avry's drone. It was a remarkable piece of equipment, even for *her* world. But right now, she had to worry about why it was *here*, with *her*. She motioned for the others to drop low, and they complied without comment. The heightened sense of danger and her projection of authority probably overriding cultural stigmas around a woman leading a war party.

As had been discussed before they embarked, the drone, after getting her attention, sped off in the direction of the threat and shot up vertically about halfway to the target. This gave Deven distance as well as direction. If there was more than one threat they were out of luck, as it hadn't occurred to either of them to set up a signal for that eventuality.

"Liggo!" she whispered. "Ahead and left in those boulders." She pointed with a knife-handed gesture in that direction. "D'avry signaled that there's something there."

The adventurer nodded, seeming to care less about convention when there was a job to do.

"Aye. I'll drop back and circle 'round. You keep on forward. Just a bit slower..."

With that he disappeared back down the trail and out of sight.

She motioned for the others to follow her and then ran forward to the next group of trees in a low crouch. Once they'd all caught up, she repeated the process, running to the next cluster, careful to not expose the group to view from above by the raven borne. Deven paused as she wanted to give Liggo time to surveil the enemy, whatever they were. Laphren, stepped forward and crouched next to her.

"What is it?" he asked in a soft rumble. Deven looked up, as even in a crouch he was a head taller than her.

"I don't know yet," she answered truthfully. "D'avry signaled that there was trouble ahead."

He looked thoughtful.

"The mage..." he said bobbing his head in affirmation. "Hmm." Laphren cracked his knuckles loudly. "I'm ready for some trouble."

It wasn't meant as a boast. She reckoned he'd lost much prior to finding himself in the human holding pens of a goblin camp. For him it was time to even the score. They moved to the next grouping and Liggo slipped back into their midst. Deven turned to face him.

"At least a dozen of them greenies," he informed her. "Maybe more..." he finished shrugging slightly.

She was impressed he'd scouted them so quickly.

"Well done. Okay. Well, we're obviously not sneaking past them, so we'll make it difficult for them to ambush us. I'll take half the group to the next couple trees. You take this group and after we move forward, you move to the area we just left. We'll do this twice. That'll put us about seventy-five yards away. On the third hop, you don't move. You'll wait while we move ahead one more grouping of trees and then, instead of following us, you'll break up the hill with your group and we'll charge their position from the other side. At least if we're going to attack them unarmed, they will have to defend on two sides."

Liggo looked at her appraisingly. "Might work. We'll take some arrows for sure. But it's to be expected."

And with that, she nodded once, motioned for a couple of the refugees and for Laphren to follow her and they headed out.

Both groups worked the plan, bounding forward twice before letting the first group get two hops ahead and then they both broke for the boulders. But when they got there, there were no goblins to be found. Further inspection showed that there was a tunnel entrance, but it was very small. In fact, too small for any but Deven, and her only maybe.

So, this party of goblins knew where the refugees were, and they were using a tunnel system to track them it seemed. That meant that they could surprise them at any point between here and their destination, at the clearing near the ford. Now it was beginning to get dark, too, and the goblins would gain the advantage. Even if they did not have a significant force, it would tip the scales of fate in their favor. Deven gathered her squad of refugees and they continued to press forward as best they could for the shape they were in.

Twenty-Four

Reunion

D'avry watched the encounter with Deven's team unfold as his group also pushed forward but much more slowly as the raven borne were thickest closer to the goblin camp. He continued to scan forward ahead of Deven's group with the drone, switching amongst views and paying special attention to areas with large rocks as they had proven to house tunnel entrances, on this side of the mountain anyway. D'avry thought he'd caught a glimpse of a head slipping back behind the rocks on more than one occasion but nothing beyond that.

With daylight diminishing, he now was having to switch to the 'green view', as he referred to it, since it seemed to be less affected by the low light. He wondered if this is what wolves and large cats saw when it was night.

As it grew dark, he was concerned that the goblins would come in greater numbers but that had not happened, yet. In fact, it appeared that the raven borne were trending back toward the encampment as the forest grew dark. Perhaps the birds' eyesight was not strong at night? And though the goblins could see well at night, he didn't think that they could see very well at distance. Maybe they were getting a much deserved break? He doubted that. They continued to press on anyway.

It was well after dark when they found the small clearing near the ford. D'avry breathed a sigh of relief. Finally, he had rounded up his missing companions and they could focus on finding Gearlach and Trask and stopping N'Bruyyh from taking over the other orc clans and then annihilating the world as he knew it. He still needed to understand the larger picture of why he was being pulled into other worlds but for now, this world had enough trouble of its own.

D'avry made his way to Deven to make proper introductions with the rest of the companions and plan for what he was certain would be a more substantial assault by the goblin hordes at any time. Finding Deven in the small crowd of freed captives he approached her,

"You all made it back safely. I'm relieved to see that. Thank you for your help with getting everyone out."

"Thank you for *your* help with the drone. We didn't catch the goblins that you called out, but we saw that they were there and that they escaped back into the tunnels. Do you think they'll be back tonight with greater numbers?" she asked thinking much the same as he.

"Yes, and with wolf borne I'd guess, and who knows what else. Hopefully not orcs. I've never heard of them fighting together but if there's a chance to kill humans, I think the orcs would seize it. I really don't know what to expect to be honest." And then looking over to where the companions were gathered, "Let's talk with the others and make a plan."

He said this, motioning for her to join him. She followed, trekking through the low mountain grass and wildflowers of the clearing. With the low light heightening her senses, the smell of the field was strong, of course so was the smell of all the refugees, especially after their flight to freedom. She turned to them.

"You all should freshen up, get some water and find staves or clubs or whatever you can use as a weapon. I have a feeling we're going to need it tonight," she told them. "You all are very brave, and you've faced a lot to get this far..." She trailed off wanting to say more but was at a bit of a loss. There was a good chance that several of them, if not all, could die before the sun rose. She breathed in, turned on her heels and blipped back up to D'avry's side, thanking God for the luck of a magical ring with such perfectly suited properties.

"You handled yourself well back there," he said and then

thought that it sounded a bit creepy, "From what I observed with the drone anyway," he continued lamely but was convinced that that sounded even creepier. "I mean, you're a natural leader. The men, they respect you. I've never seen men follow a woman in battle."

"Where I'm from, this is more common, but it's still not... it's still a big challenge. I'm glad they trust me. I believe I have a different sort of training for battle than they have. I think they will complement each other...when the time comes. And thanks. I know you wanted to get in and get out, but you did the right thing saving these people," she said this and rested her hand on his shoulder.

He felt the warmth of her hand through his jacket and was surprised when heat flushed up into his cheeks. He pushed the thought away, a flash of strawberry blonde curls flicking through his memory. There were important preparations to be made and indulging memories of lost loves and present... distractions wouldn't help. Surviving the night was the first priority. He tore his mind back to the task at hand.

He turned to the circle of islemen. "My friends, I'm so glad to see you all together in one place!"

Farn, Liggo and Volkreek turned as one from their mini-reunion to greet him. Liggo grabbed D'avry's extended hand and engulfed him in a huge bear hug, shaking him like a rag doll before setting him down and punching him on the shoulder. A deep mirth shone in his eyes, as if he'd escaped death's clutches and slapped it on the ass.

"I'm in your debt, master mage. Thank you," he said this in his typically barely discernible dialect. D'avry smiled and nodded, truly grateful the man was well and in good spirits.

Farn followed with a firm embrace, fist pounding D'avry's back, adding only, "You surprised me. I didn't think much of you with your odd clothes and arrogant manner." He leaned back, looking at him at arm's length. "I've almost changed my mind about the way you dress." And D'avry wasn't sure if he was joking or being honest.

"Will you be staying with us then, to find Gearlach and Trask and to bury that hell-spawn, N'Bruyyh and his witch?" the priest asked, a fervent fire behind his eyes.

D'avry nodded affirmation, but there was something tentative about it. He smiled.

Volkreek, as usual, said nothing but inclined his head toward D'avry in a gesture of thanks and D'avry, having spent the last day and a half with the fighter understood this to be the deepest appreciation for finding his friends. He locked eyes and nodded back. And then added, "And, in addition to the crowd behind me, we've a new companion. You've all met Deven?" he asked, pulling her in to the circle. "It's a long story about how she got here, but she's proved herself, at least in my estimation," he suggested.

Liggo nodded in agreement. "Aye. By my eyes and by the bodies..." he said, invoking an old seaman's expression which meant that what the celestials had ordained had come to pass. High praise indeed.

Farn rubbed his bald head and then scratched at his beard. The priest looked at him and then back to D'avry seeming to accept Liggo's endorsement, at least grudgingly. D'avry tried to discern the root of the hesitation, but then his thoughts were interrupted as he remembered the rest of the booty he'd pilfered from the goblin chests.

"Okay, let's hope there's something good in here." He dropped the velvet sack he'd been carrying since the rescue. In it were Liggo's knives, which Liggo was happy to get back. Additionally, there were a few other knives, a couple small axes, and Farn's mace.

While the companions were happy to have their weapons back, the remnant was a sad armory for the rest of the refugees. D'avry turned to them and let them know that they needed to arm themselves and find any food they could before the goblins came back, which would probably be soon. Volkreek tugged on D'avry's sleeve and pointed to a pile of weapons off to the side. It seemed he'd not only cooked the rabbits but had gone back and scavenged the bodies of the goblins for weapons and equipment while they were gone. D'avry slapped him on the shoulder, pleasantly surprised.

He called to Laphren, the huge smith, to disperse the weapons as he saw fit and then turned back to the smaller group to finish deliberating. In the small amount of time they had left they needed to find a more defensible position. And lastly, there was the other artifact in the light blue satchel. He could sense the magic in it now, and it was strong.

Unity, Bond, Balance, Framework, Focus. The words boomed in his mind, as if sung by a choir of rock giants. As the words washed over him again, he felt as though he was beginning to ascertain their meaning.

This jewel was *Focus.* The burning book and arrow currently residing within the lantern door represented *Balance.* It embodied good and evil, dark and light, enlightenment and senseless violence. His mind's eye slipped into the space reserved for viewing through the drone and yet another word bubbled to the surface. *Framework.* Somehow, the drone seemed to represent that concept, the idea of a framework. Or maybe it *was* the framework. Then what were *Unity* and *Bond.* Were these yet other artifacts that he needed to discover?

Suddenly a powerful new realization forced its way into his perception. *N'Bruyyh has what he needs.* The gravity of that thought caught his breath. He didn't know how he knew it, but it was as certain as his own breathing. And behind it another thought percolated through the chaos. *Gearlach is in danger.*

D'avry just wanted to hide away. He wanted to have time enough to breath, to take his time to understand these new powers that seemed to be increasing in scale and scope at a rate he couldn't even comprehend. It was all too fast. Too much. He breathed in a deep, ragged sigh and looked up.

The whole party was staring at him, varying degrees of concern on their faces. Deven the most, Volkreek the least as he'd seen more of the mage's antics over the last couple of days. D'avry realized he must have been staring off for longer than he'd thought. Again.

"N'Bruyyh has Trask," he whispered as if unable to fully voice the pronouncement, as if in that way it would somehow cease to be real. Collectively their faces dropped. Farn's hands went to his head and then balled into fists. He beat his chest,

"No! This *cannot* be!"

He shot a look that could freeze fire at Liggo and Volkreek who looked away, unwilling to meet his glare.

This was the first time that D'avry had seen the two kowtow to the priest. Usually, the balance of power tipped the other way in the dynamic.

"This must be fixed!" he continued, glaring now at D'avry.

"There's a chance." D'avry raised his hand, closing his eyes as if listening to something barely perceptible and then pointed roughly northwest. "They are five or ten miles from here, at most. The best way to reach them will be the trail on the other side of the ford. But there's more... Gearlach may be in great jeopardy. I don't know if what I sense is what *has* happened or what *will* happen. For now, you must follow the river trail to where it breaks north along the ridge for that will be N'Bruyyh's path."

He turned to look at the three companions and at Deven. "And one more thing...the goblins are coming. In force." He turned his attention to the raven-haired firebrand with the red lips and still smeared mascara. "Deven, you must take the others and make haste," he said this last closing his eyes and nodding his head as if answering a silent question.

"Wait a second," she flared, stepping forward, her brows knit in confusion. "You said that as if you're *not* coming with us."

"I cannot. I must tend to other things," he said still seeming to be halfway between the present and somewhere else.

"No... No, that's *NOT* how it works," she said pushing a finger into his chest. "You don't just bring me here and drop me off in the middle of some cryptic quest to save the world, *your world*, from annihilation!" she burst out but even as she said it, she seemed to be losing conviction. Deven had already committed herself, both to D'avry and also in her own heart. The statement hung in the air unanswered.

"I must go. The same forces that propel this world to the precipice seem to hang many other worlds in the balance. And each is dependent on the other. I wasn't able to see that until now, but I feel it," he thumped his chest where the door resided, "...in here. The Astrig Ka'a moves. It changes, and I with it..."

The others seemed ready to protest when Volkreek stepped in, hands up to both the thief and the priest. He strode forward, grasping D'avry's forearm and shoulder. He looked the mage directly in his eyes, at first searching, and then as his lips pressed into a thin line, he nodded, gradually at first and then decisively. Without a word, he turned to the campfire and began making preparations to move out.

Farn and Liggo just stood there awkwardly for a moment. Farn was the first to speak out, "Aren't we going to *vote* on this or something?" he asked, looking around at the others and then resting his gaze on the huge smith. "You. You're good with following this... girl? Into battle?" The big man shrugged. Farn turned again to Liggo, imploringly. "Have sense man."

The thief tilted his head and mimicked the expression of the smith. "You and I wouldn't be here if not for her. By my eyes and the bodies..." he repeated his sentiment from earlier, trailing off, "I will see this thing through. And if the celestials choose to deliver the enemy by the hand of a milk-daughter, well, I'm just a fool, far from Thadding, but I'll play my part."

And then he himself strode toward the refugees to assess and assist in their efforts to prepare for what would likely be a fighting retreat across the river, followed by a search for lost companions and ultimately a final confrontation with the enemy... if they made it that far.

Deven alone stood in the close space where the group had gathered only minutes before. Farn wandered off grumbling darkly, stabbing the staff into the dirt with each step.

"Is he gonna be alright?" she asked D'avry

"Who, him?" he asked nodding in the direction of the priest and then turning his attention back to her, noting, not for the first time, how the moonlight seemed to sparkle in her eyes. He cleared his throat and stared at the trampled grass. "No. Farn Gemballelven will not stop, I think, until he's resolved his quest. Which, for the most part, seems to align with ours."

"When will you be back?" she asked.

"When you need me most," he replied, cursing himself for sounding trite and wondering if indeed he did come off as a little arrogant and self-absorbed.

"And you don't think now qualifies?" she asked, still fighting a battle she knew she'd already lost.

She started to say something more, but then stopped and just looked at him. Studying his blue eyes, his thin aristocratic nose and the muscles tensing involuntarily where his jawline angled up to meet his cheekbones. She could tell that his concern over his friends was tearing him up inside and her heart broke a little. She lifted a finger to move an errant lock of blond hair from his forehead and guided it back behind his ear. And then she stepped forward and gave him a light but lingering kiss on his forehead.

Deven stepped back flushing slightly, her eyes downward as she busied her shaking hands by making a show of dusting off her pants before slipping them back into the pocket of her hooded sweatshirt.

"Deven?" He made sure she was looking at him. "Don't fight N'Bruyyh." Concern was evident in his eyes. "You're fast now, but he's strong, deadly, fears nothing... and he only needs to catch you once. And besides, it's my fault you're here. Just promise me you won't do it."

She considered his words. "Well, we have to catch him first. And besides, I'm tougher than I look... and I've got a team to help me do it," she said, smiling weakly and waving in the direction of the milling band of refugees, some of whom now carried freshly cut sticks as weapons.

"Don't let them separate. Farn will want to chase after N'Bruyyh but don't let the team break apart. You must save Gearlach first. He's beyond the trailhead to the ridge. I fear he doesn't have much time. Keep the team together. I will meet you at a time and place that eludes me as of yet. But I *will* find you. Count on that. And...I'm sorry. I didn't mean to bring you into all of this..."

He said this last and Deven could swear that she saw the faintest glimmer of moisture in his eye.

With that, D'avry brought the goblin jewel up with one hand before his face. Its pale blue facets sparkling darkly in the fading glow of the dashed campfire coals. He recognized it now as a talisman he'd read about known as the Puerch'k Talles, the Soul of the Mountains. He was mildly surprised that the same pale blue brilliance reflected now was the same color as the eyes of the banshee spirit they had encountered inside the mountain.

It made a certain amount of sense, though he didn't know why. Magic, it seemed had greater dimensionality to it than the narrow band of utility man fashioned it for. There was a connectedness, he thought. No coincidences...This thought struck a chord in D'avry's mind, and he, again, filed it away for later. He then opened the folds of his jacket and tunic to reveal the lantern door. His skin prickling as dried sweat met the chill night air.

Deven's eyes grew wide, much the same as the first time she'd seen the lantern door earlier that day. In the pale light the gold veins running through the crystal glass seemed to move of their own volition. D'avry opened the door with his left hand to reveal the miniaturized book and flaming arrow spinning freely, suspended in the impossible void. He placed the Puerch'k Talles jewel beside it and the two began to rotate in a shared orbit, two points within a five-sided shape. He closed the door.

Balance. Focus. The other artifact that he had would have to wait. He would not place it inside the lantern door with the others until he absolutely had to. He would need the *Framework*, but for now it served a greater purpose as a much needed second set of eyes.

D'avry looked at Deven, memorizing every line of her face, the soft flow of her dark hair as it framed her stunning blue eyes and ruby red lips.

Wow, it was really hard to focus with her around, he mused. And then he closed his eyes and when he opened them, he was looking out upon a vast sea of clouds. Wind whipped his hair across his face, blinding him temporarily. Over the noise of the rushing air came the urgent clatter and cackle of mechanical devices and the whistle of pressurized vapor.

Twenty-Five

As the Crow Flies

19.004329 AC (After Construct)
Age of the Half-Orc War

Gearlach crunched over rocks and pine needles in long, steady strides despite having been at this for hours. Following the raven that D'avry had somehow conjured up had not yielded much of anything but, each time he reached the spot where he'd seen the bird last, he would hear a screeching caw from still further on. Just when he began to wonder at the wisdom of this effort, he'd come across a pathway that led north and south along the hillside. The bird had gone south and so did Gearlach.

Soon the steeply sloping forest grew to near vertical and began to give way to more ragged features, with jutting rocks and steep cliffs and then, after a while, there was the sound of rushing water from below. He found that the southerly trail had followed the mountain's contours and was cutting decidedly east. He was now following along the river that had joined the Nem Kar'kar below where they'd sunk N'Bruyyh's boat and then, within sight of the confluence, effectively sunk their own.

The sounds of rushing water grew as the trail descended toward the river. Before long the river was nearly all that Gearlach could hear, making it difficult to follow the raven if he couldn't keep his eyes on it constantly. The large, dark-haired half-orc warrior paused as the trail turned to granite at the river's edge.

Fastening the leather flap over his battle axe where it hung on his belt, he knelt down to the water and took in a double handful and washed it over his face, head and the back of his neck. The cool water was bracing but satisfying. He did this twice more before cleaning his hands and forearms.

Satisfied that he'd sufficiently cooled his body, and feeling reinvigorated, he stood and took a look at the path before him. The trail here was barely distinguishable and was really a matter of hopping from rock to rock or clambering up granite shelves while keeping an eye out for rock stack markers in case it took a turn into the trees.

Off in the distance he caught a glimpse of the raven, circling above the trees, waiting for him to follow. It was the strangest thing he thought, before quickly amending it. Chasing the librarian who was in turn being chased by an undead orc warlord was a strange thing as well.

He grabbed a handful of dried berries and pine nuts from his pack and consumed them while resuming his pace from before, continuing on up the rocks beside the misting whitewater. Though it was still overcast, dark blue pockets were beginning to appear vaguely through the carbon gray sky before disappearing and reforming elsewhere. The sun was now past its peak and the bird seemed to have somewhere to be as it never stayed long enough for Gearlach to catch up to it. Regardless, he trudged on, not knowing if he was going to find Trask or N'Bruyyh first.

Night fell and still the bird had not stopped. Gearlach's pace slackened somewhat but he continued to push. The bird was his best and only hope of locating Trask before N'Bruyyh and maybe not even then. As he walked, he consumed the last contents of a folded leather packet; salmon jerky he'd bartered from one of the locals in the fishtown bordering Fort Talles Murdt, the keep on the Long Lake. That fishtown was now a smoldering pile of ash he thought remorsefully.

Wherever N'Bruyyh went, destruction followed. He thought about the librarian's words regarding a blood red sky, and an object of power. That was surely where the man was headed, but he himself had said that he didn't know where the object was hidden. So where could he be going? Unless he'd seen another vision or been given a sign... That would explain why he'd suddenly deviated from rejoining the companions and struck off on his own. He would have known that N'Bruyyh would follow. Especially after he'd sunk his boat and destroyed his crew. The undead warlord alone could have survived the dark magic inferno aboard the craft.

Gearlach had no idea how he would defeat N'Bruyyh. It'd taken everything he had to best him in one-on-one combat and he'd been certain to give himself every advantage. Now, N'Bruyyh knew he was coming, he'd be able to choose the time and place and he knew what to expect. That was something that they both had, knowledge of their opponent's abilities, their strengths and weaknesses. But the dark magic that aided N'Bruyyh now, that indeed, he'd given himself over to in order to achieve his ends, Gearlach did not know what power that'd given him or *if* he could even *be* killed... It may be that Gearlach's only hope was to defeat the power at its source, which he was almost certain was Goriahh's doing. A task he'd be glad to partake in.

She was at the heart of it all. She was responsible for the death of his mother. When it had been discovered that Goriahh was pregnant with the illegitimate child of Gearlach's father, the Archduke, he'd had her exiled. Gearlach had learned that Goriahh had lost the child and it was not less than a week later that his mother had come down with a sickness that the doctors could not identify. It caused her to grow weak, lose her hair and her beauty as if she had starved herself to death. Only she hadn't starved herself.

She was the toughest person Gearlach had known, man or woman. Before Gearlach had been born, she had guided royal surveyors through the frozen Dalneel Mountains and the treacherous Worman Pass for the establishment of the northmost boundaries. It was only her and two others that returned from a team of twenty-four, soldiers mostly. Indeed, that was how she'd met the Archduke and over the years she'd proven as much an ally as a wife as she'd negotiated treaties when he was at the front lines of a two-sided war and sussed out traitors amidst his cabinet. She had not starved herself to death, even over the soul crushing heartbreak caused by the infidelities of her weak-willed husband.

Gearlach knew that Goriahh was behind it and then when indeed the traitors, no longer in check with Madredh, his mother, out of the picture, allowed an assassin into the Archduke's chambers, Gearlach had fled the castle to save his own life but also to seek out vengeance against the woman who had destroyed it.

He'd suspected that Goriahh had been a practitioner of the dark arts, but this was the one instance where his mother had been blind to reality. She couldn't see the malintent of her half-sister and wouldn't hear of anyone speaking ill of her. Not even her own son. That'd been the only fight they'd ever had, at least after adolescence. He'd tried to tell her that he'd seen her leaving one of the upper tower chambers in the middle of the night and that he'd thought he'd seen the glint of a dagger before it had been concealed beneath black hooded robes. His mother had been more concerned about what he was doing up there at that time than anything he thought he saw…

Gearlach had spent years away from his homeland. Outside of the outer banks, few knew of the Isle Kingdom of Gaugh and less still of his kind, the half-orc, half-human drougehnn. Most that did know of them considered them a myth as the offspring of orcs and humans tended to be mule-like, in that they couldn't breed. The drougehnn were different in that way, and in others. The fact that they were largely peaceful by nature distinguished them from *both* races. In stature they were somewhat on the larger side, though half a head shorter than the average orc. And they were all of dark hair and dark eyes like the orcs, but they didn't have the fully protruding canine teeth and they were closer to humans in regard to intelligence, but even by that standard they were somewhat exceptional.

Because of these attributes, and due to Gearlach's exemplary education, having grown up in the Archduke's castle, he'd excelled in his pursuits. He'd found himself a ship bound for somewhere he'd never heard of and negotiated with the second mate to be brought on as one of the crew, though he had next to zero firsthand knowledge of a ship's inner workings.

His negotiation had included no questions as to his identity or where he'd come from. To most, he was a very big human, but even if they had their concerns his strength and intelligence made him indispensable on a ship and so any squabbles were squashed by the officers, until he had found his place among them and ultimately, had captained his own privateer ship amongst a small fleet of "merchants".

They were, like so many privateers, creatures of opportunity and found themselves to be raiders as often as traders. That was until a shipment of arms for trade with n'agrah pelts brought him far upriver to a human outpost in the disputed lands. The river was only passable in the summer months, and it was very late in the season, but the admiral had hoped to be retiring within the year and this deal would make that a reality. Gearlach's three-masted carrack, the *Long Tooth*, along with two caravel captains had accepted the mission. Only due to the outsized bounty attached to it.

Gearlach had been careless with fate. He knew that with the admiral's retirement there'd be an opening on one of the corvettes to fill the open space on the admiral's frigate. Gearlach wouldn't have chanced it except that he was likely the next in line to promote and the master of one of only three corvettes would do nicely. With that wage, it would only take a few years before he'd be able to strike out on his own to hunt down more directly the woman who'd destroyed his family.

The moment they'd navigated the crescent shaped inlet the

weather had turned sour. By that time in his life, he had suffered more than enough injuries to feel a change in the weather. On that day his shoulder was aching as badly as any time he could remember. At the time, he had shrugged it off, but a day later, when they had reached the halfway marker, the storm rolled in.

They pressed hard for the outpost and made it, wet snow stacking on the railings fore and aft. By the next morning they were land locked. The day after that, the outpost was burning and so were his ships. They'd held off the orc hordes from razing the town, largely thanks to the shipment of arms, but when the locals spoke about a half-orc enchantress who had emboldened the orc tribes to take more and more land, Gearlach's blood ran cold. An old wound had been made raw.

He asked around for more details and had come across a pair of travelers returning a fugitive, a rebel priest, to justice. Their party had been greater, but they'd suffered a heavy toll in the raid. As it turned out, it had been the priest who had saved their lives. Now the leader of the bounty hunters who'd had the contract was dead and the bounty himself had saved the remaining members' lives. The tables had turned. It hadn't taken Gearlach much persuading to encourage the three of them to join him in his pursuit of the necromancer and the chieftain that'd led the attack. In fact, that had seemed to be what the priest was after in the first place.

They'd tracked the orcs through the passes, back to their camp, but found only more carnage. It seemed a dispute between chieftains had been settled by the one chieftain mounting the other chieftain's head on a spike. They discovered two similar episodes and the chieftain had become a warlord and he'd grown bolder. He now had his sights set upon the next territory.

The one remaining survivor at the orc outpost they had found had told him the warlord intended to unite all the orc tribes. He'd laughed at the idea that *anyone* could unite the tribes, but then he'd also died with those words upon his lips.

Weeks passed as the four stalked the growing army of orcs, now morphed into something that they hadn't the faintest hope of fighting against. One of the men in Gearlach's small band was a thief and a spy. With dwindling supplies and growing odds, Gearlach dispatched him to ascertain whether or not it was possible to get close enough to Goriahh to take her out and still get out of the orc camp alive. He'd come back with disappointing news but with something else that was unexpected.

N'Bruyyh not only relied on the drougehnn woman but on a *human man* as well. The man appeared to be a captive but the orc chieftain, now warlord, consulted with him regularly. The thief-spy, Liggo, believed that he could get to the man and possibly get information that would be useful to their cause.

Gearlach had agreed to the plan, only they'd got more than they had bartered for. They learned of the warlord's plans to unite the tribes but also of his plan to raid the keep on Long Lake, Talles Murdt, as a demonstration of force. They'd also learned of an event that the warlord would use to seal the alliance with the other orc tribes.

Using the necromancer's magic, he had made a pact with the goblins of Tal Kar'zuum. They had a yearly festival where the orcs of the valley traded with the goblin horde. N'Bruyyh was going to lure the orc chieftains to the festival and seize their allegiance by force, using his growing army and that of the goblins as incentive. And, if that didn't work, there was some other natural event that was to happen in the next several weeks which involved an unknown artifact. But the man hadn't had any of the details on that yet.

They didn't yet realize that much of the information that they were gleaning from the man, came not as much from the orc warlord or his necromancer, but from the man's own visions of possible future events and from the signs that he interpreted. Using Liggo as a liaison, Gearlach and the man, a librarian by the name of Graeburn Trask, formulated a plan to free him, slay the necromancer Goriahh and if possible, the warlord as well.

Gearlach and his companions raced ahead to warn the people of Talles Murdt and to prepare for battle.

The trail was growing dark ahead of Gearlach and the moon had yet to crest the far ridge before him. His half-orc eyes had no trouble picking out the path, but he was running out of steam and needed to recharge. He was just thinking this when he stumbled on some loose rubble, slid several feet and caught himself, dangerously close to the edge of the cliff. He paused. It was time to stop for a break, eat, and then resume at a safer pace.

As he paused the night sounds came to him. The river descended less rapidly below and so sounded less angry than further down canyon. An owl screeched not far off up slope. The overcast sky had not cleared up entirely and as such, he couldn't determine if the moon was up or where it might be in the sky. His best estimation told him it was still early into first watch.

Just then, a low growl emanated from the forest, followed by several more scattered amongst the trees. Before long, it was at least a dozen strong and Gearlach knew he was in serious trouble. At first, he saw just their bright yellow eyes but then the lead wolf stepped forward, nearly as tall as a man, the others, only slightly less imposing. Timberwolves. In the lands of the orc, Gearlach must look an easy meal. He'd prove to them otherwise. The growling grew in intensity as they drew closer, ready for the kill.

Gearlach understood group tactics and knew that the alpha would dominate the attack but would be closely followed by aggressive subordinates. He knew, too, that to run was just to be mowed down from behind. He had to fight and move. Gain the high ground and use the terrain to guard his flanks.

The alpha charged and Gearlach swung his axe in a wide arc

meant to crush ribs as well as rend flesh and it did its job. He sidestepped just as the blade connected and then continued the arc all the way around, the blade impacting the next wolf just at the jawline near its ear. A death blow that knocked it into the third, but with no meaningful damage. But it gained him enough space to jump up to the next rock ledge where two more were already closing in.

The first lunged, snapped and jumped back while the other mimicked the attack. Gearlach knew this was a distractionary tactic. He spun just as the wounded alpha leapt from below. With its size, the beast received the upper-cutting swing from Gearlach's axe, but still took Gearlach off his feet. It took all the half-orc's strength with both hands on the axe haft to keep from impaling himself with the rear-facing crescent shaped spike. He heaved the huge wolf's carcass to the uphill side to regain his feet and to provide a barrier between himself and the pair of wolves trying to get at him after the alpha's attack.

One of the wolves leapt over the alpha's body and Gearlach rolled to his back, kicking the wolf up and over into the night air and over the cliff.

Three down. He'd left one alive on the lower ledge, one in front of him and the others were still closing in to form a tighter and tighter perimeter. There were now nine or ten wolves, but he was cornered, and they were snapping and snarling from just out of reach, waiting for him to turn his back or drop his guard. Gearlach was backing slowly to the edge of the cliff, his right heel hanging in free air as he twisted to fend off the wolves from left, right and center.

Just then, pain shot up his leg. One of the wolves had his right calf in its jaws and he smashed it with the axe haft to free himself but as he did so, another lunged from his left. Gearlach fell backwards but corrected in time to catch himself, catching the ledge with his free hand as he tumbled over. The wolf, scrambled to correct, catching its two front paws on the ledge as its back half landed in free air. It bounced the wrong way and tumbled head over heels with a yelp into the night air.

The remaining wolves closed in and Gearlach's hand broke free. He fell, the rock wall rushing past before he was able to land the spike of his axe into the granite. Sparks flew, illuminating the night, until it finally found purchase. Gearlach silently praised the magical enhancement of the axe. This was not the first time it'd saved his life. Still, he was stuck, clinging to the side of a cliff, with a pack of timber wolves snarling just feet above him, while his quarry and the deadly orc chieftain slipped away into the night.

Where was the raven now? Had it known of this predicament and done nothing or was its purpose just so singularly focused that this didn't even play. Regardless, he was effectively stuck. He couldn't hang on all night, let alone a few minutes more. Though he'd spent endless hours in his youth climbing the cliffs around the castle keep at Hellot Mon, that'd been a long time ago and besides, armored boots were not designed to be so delicate of placement. They'd provide little utility here.

Still, his toes ground into the rock wall, finding little purchase. Off to his right the cliff wall formed a tight corner and there was a thin ledge. His timing would have to be perfect, but it was all he had. He leaned far to his left and then swung his body the other way, displacing the axe point and swinging it in a tight arc overhead. He re-seated the point, sparks flying again, temporarily blinding him, but his feet found support.

He'd closed half the distance to the ledge and so he hefted again, left and then right, committing every ounce of momentum into the lunge that he could muster. He landed, feet planted, his cheek grinding against granite as he pressed flat against the rock face.

Snarling and crying continued above. Loose rocks trickled down around him. He was maybe five paces below the hungry pack of wolves. They seemed fixated whether or not they could reach him. This caused him to wonder if it was merely hunger that drove them or something else. He could imagine Goriahh laughing wickedly in the firelight of some demonic ritual.

Gearlach had no choice but to wait it out. He sat on the ledge and plunged the spike into the rock wall so that the haft acted as a sort of safety bar, keeping him from suffering the same fate as the other two wolves if he managed to get any sleep that night. He'd have to figure something out when morning came, and the wolves lost interest. If, they lost interest...

Twenty-Six

A House Divided

Deven jogged lightly along the path, a meager torch lit the trail ahead, but it ruined her ability to keep a vigilant eye skyward as they broke cover between the trees. She didn't expect to see the goblin raven borne at night as the birds didn't appear to operate well in the dark, but that didn't mean the resourceful creatures didn't have other means of operation. Maybe giant bats or some similarly horrifying creatures she had never heard of. This place seemed to be filled with them.

Behind her the other companions followed, mixed in with the now poorly armed refugees. They still maintained the loose groupings from earlier in the day, with the hulking smith Laphren and softly padding Liggo in the forward squad, followed by Farn, his group of refugees and where D'avry had been, Volkreek took up rear guard. The group was in no shape to be travelling the wilderness at night, but the trail was well defined and if all else failed, Volkreek's blade could light up like a starburst, either to illuminate a larger area or ward off any night creatures bold enough to take on the whole group. Sadly, the list of such creatures was probably not short. Not in *this* wilderness.

As if on cue, a horrific screech echoed from a distant cliff and the group shuddered to a halt. Laphren was the first to speak in his low, booming voice. "Wyvern. Sounds like it has its quarry picked out. Too far away to be any of us. We should keep moving."

Deven nodded, swallowing. She wasn't positive what a Wyvern was but knew it couldn't be good, judging by the smith's demeanor. She blipped unconsciously yards ahead before realizing what she'd done. She slowed her pace to allow the others to catch up and then returned her gaze to the trail, but not before catching the spooked look upon the faces of some of her team.

Not everyone knew what she could do as she'd only visited one of the cages in this manner and most of *those* captives had been either too weak or too timid to want to escape. And then, during the harried retreat from the goblin camp she had kept her movements organic, not wanting to give away her special ability until it was absolutely necessary. Like it had been in the fight against the wolf borne that had attacked the ranger, Volkreek.

The sounds of wolves howling in the distance behind them urged them on as they crossed another fork of the river. Here it was easily sixty meters across and interrupted by stretches of bushes and trees. The deepest sections were just below her ribcage and cold as anything she could remember.

The team was loud and clumsy as it splashed through the frigid waters, some losing their footing and getting dunked in the process. They really were a ragtag force. She needed to get them across, get them dry and get them fed but she feared that there would be none of that tonight. It'd be battle that warmed them, and survival that fueled them to continue onward.

Sudden splashing from behind gave over to howls and snapping of teeth as a pack of wolf borne slammed into the group of refugees. Volkreek's blade burst forth a halo of light and wolves and goblins alike froze, blinking and shielding their eyes.

Deven sprang into action. Shooting in and out of the oncoming horde, slashing, kicking and tackling goblins from their mounts. Farn didn't waste time trying to use the powers of his staff but instead wielded it along with his mace, crushing skulls of goblins and wolves alike.

The rest of the group lurched into movement even as more and more wolf borne poured into the water. Light and shadow swirled chaotically as Volkreek wielded his blade in a seemingly endless string of attacks.

Deven sent a goblin sprawling into the waters after dispatching his mount. One quick blip and its master, too, was added to the numbers of vanquished assailants. When she came up out of the waters, she sucked in a deep breath and was afforded a quick second to assess the melee.

Surprisingly, the refugees were holding their own after the first wave. Tougher stock than she took them for. Liggo flashed in and out of the splashing animals and creatures, his twin hunting blades glowing wickedly in the light from Volkreek's blade. At one point he burst from the water behind two wolf borne, plunging his blades into their chests and dragged them back beneath the waters again, while Laphren snatched two others from their mounts, smashed them together and then began bludgeoning yet other wolf borne with the goblin bodies as they piled into the icy river.

Deven caught motion from the corner of her eye and blipped backward just in time to get blindsided by another wolf borne. Luckily, she caught its shoulder instead of its muzzle. Still, it spun her in the water so that she was facing yet a third, charging directly for her and only feet away. She blipped away and back in time to catch the goblin with her dagger and yank it free of its mount. The animal just continued to charge on through the waters and away, leaving its rider behind. None of the wolves stayed to fight, which was a blessing.

All around her bodies of goblins floated away or sank beneath the surface or a little bit of both and still they kept streaming in from the shore behind them. Her team of refugees had dispatched three or four dozen at that point. Many of the men had traded staves for the goblin blades, double wielding them like short swords. The team was coming into its element.

Even as the onslaught continued, Deven found she was bolstered by the fighting spirit of the men with her. A pair of light-haired men who looked like brothers were fighting back-to-back, encircled by riders. She re-doubled her efforts and dove headlong into the melee, clearing out goblins faster than they could enter the fight. Some of the others were pulling back to form a defensive line. She poured ahead, blade flying, slipping in and out of the flood until fewer and fewer bodies crashed into the water. Until no more growls of wolves or howling cries of goblins echoed in the wooded crossing. Just the sound of the water rushing heedlessly by.

The men were all panting, casting about wildly not really sure that the battle was indeed over. Deven motioned for them to retreat across the ford to the other side and then she blipped quickly across from where she'd been fighting the onslaught to the far side, ahead of her team.

"Steal food from the fallen, if it's not enough we'll cook wolf. I don't know if it's any good but it's better than starving. I'll take two with me that have the strength to continue," she said between breaths. "We'll scout ahead for N'Bruyyh, Trask and hopefully our other companion, Gearlach," she said as the men assembled on the riverbank.

Farn spoke up. "I'll stay and set up wards and tend to the wounded. We should scour the banks for any of ours who've survived but maybe got washed downstream with the current."

His accent seemed to be more pronounced when he was tired or distracted, she noticed.

Deven nodded while she scanned the group, still breathing deeply, her teeth chattering as she began to feel the cold and the wet in the high mountain night air now that the adrenalin was wearing off. Counting numbers, they still had most of their group, but it was obvious now that they were down by three, no four, men at least. Men whom she knew by sight but didn't yet know their names.

"Yes, do that Farn. Find who you can, heal who you can and get them warm, dry and fed. They'll need their strength if we don't get to N'Bruyyh before he can gather his forces."

And then someone else spoke up, a lean young man with shaggy brown hair who looked to be no more than fifteen or sixteen years of age.

"Ma'am. I can go. My uncle, Edha, he knew he was dying. He couldn't eat. He gave me his rations for the last couple of days so I'm in better shape than most. Besides, I can run for miles. I was a courier for the Lieutenant of the Guard. I used to run messages between Fort Talles Murdt at Long Lake and Daracel. That's *two* outposts away," the young man said with pride.

"Can you fight?" she asked and immediately regretted her words. Clearly, he could. They all had only moments before. He looked wounded but answered, nonetheless.

"Yes. I can fight. I'm not much to look at but running for miles on your own in the wilderness, you have to be made of tougher stuff to survive. Bears... Bandits....I can fight," he said resolutely, his hands drifting to the twin goblin blades tucked into his belt.

Deven remembered now that the boy had begun the night with nothing but a reedy looking staff he'd foraged from the woods. He must be made from tougher stuff. Deven felt as though her own struggles were insubstantial compared to that of the lot before her. She smiled. "Of course. Thank you for your valor. Do you have a name?" she asked.

"Becken of Bechan, Ma'am. No relation of course, just sounds the same. We're not from money. The officers call me Beck. Or at least, they did..." he told her his gaze drifting off into middle space.

Laphren too stepped forward. He had a long, puffy gash from his temple to the corner of his mouth. It was still bleeding down his face and neck. His shoulder also seemed to be mangled, as if a wolf or two had got at him. He stepped forward weakly but with a grim resolve. Deven saw that his left leg had also had a rough go of it. Before he could speak, she shut him down.

"Laphren, thank you but you're not going anywhere until you get stitched up. In fact..." She looked around amongst the battered, bruised and beaten and found only Volkreek looking somewhat fresh and uninjured. "Volkreek, why don't you join Beck and me? Liggo is the only other companion that Gearlach will recognize or who knows what N'Bruyyh, or Trask look like for that matter, but he was also one of the refugees. I think it's best if all the refugees get something to eat and are tended to right away. Except for Beck here who has extenuating circumstances."

The bearded swordsman nodded assent. Laphren seemed as though he'd argue the point but said nothing, and simply nodded instead. After that, Farn stepped into the leadership role, assigning men to search for their fallen, forage, set up camp or just sit and keep an eye out if they were too injured to do any of the prior tasks.

Liggo came up to the small scouting crew. "I'm a better tracker than the rest. I'll come with you as far as the fork in the trail that D'avry spoke of. That way you'll know if N'Bruyyh is up the hill or still ahead. Safer that way."

He said this and then turned up the trail, not leaving it up for debate.

Deven shrugged, looked at the others and then followed. Seeing that one of the refugees had started a fire to provide the campsite with light, Volkreek's blade sprang to life, and he followed quickly behind. Beck was already on Deven's heels.

They didn't have to travel far, just two or three miles before they found the fork in the trail. It took Liggo a matter of seconds to determine that a very large and very recent pair of boot prints had taken the trail heading up the hillside. There was another pair of boots that were human, coming from the same direction. Judging by the stride of the first, Liggo determined that N'Bruyyh was still in pursuit or at least he was at the time that he had taken the path. The exact time of which he found harder to determine, but the edges of the imprints were crisp which led him to believe that it'd only been a matter of hours since they were made.

The imprints from the man's boots were of a similar timeframe, so whether they were made at the same time or not, it was still likely that N'Bruyyh had the librarian by now.

Deven looked up to see that the gray sky was clearing, and the moon was beginning to shine through the clouds enough that one might make out the trail well enough in the silvery light without the need for a torch. She made a flash decision.

"Liggo. Follow the tracks. Leave markers before and after any forks. Beck, run back to the group. They should be tended to and fed by the time you get there or at least close to it. Get them up and moving. We'll meet here in three hours." Realizing no one had watches she looked up to estimate where the moon would be in that time, "Or, by the time the moon is a handsbreadth above the horizon. Does that work?"

He nodded. She turned to the ranger. "Volkreek, you and I will continue on and look for Gearlach. If we can't find him in that time, we probably never will so we'll turn back and regroup here, it's callous but it's the truth." Then to the other two. "If we are not back by dawn, leave without us. We're either dead or following as soon as we can. Does that sound like a plan?" she asked and was greeted with nods of affirmation.

Liggo and Beck broke off without a word, each heading off in their separate directions. It was clear that each was confident in their ability to travel solo in unfamiliar wilderness. This gave Deven some small amount of comfort in breaking up the group. Something she never would have done with the marines.

Volkreek and Deven turned to face the western trail, which had already begun to transition from the rolling wooded hills that infilled between the two mountains to a rockier switchback dominated section directly between the two peaks. Here, the canyon grew steeper as it worked its way around a near vertical fold in the mountain just north of Tal Kar'zuum. The pair proceeded with caution. Volkreek kept the light low as their path became more and more exposed to the opposing side of the canyon and to the surrounding area.

Once again, they heard the Wyvern's raspy screech in the distance and for the first time they were greeted by muffled howls and growling from further down the canyon. At once their eyes locked. It was clear that they had the same question in their minds. Could this be the trouble that D'avry had warned about? Volkreek bypassed the switchbacks entirely and plunged down hill, sliding as much as anything else, with Deven close on his heels. Within minutes they reached the lower trail which cut right and began to follow the cliffs edge along the river far below.

Deven caught the fleeting shadow of a huge reptilian creature crossing the quarter moon that shone down upon them and her blood froze. She grabbed Volkreek's arm.

"Did you see that?" she asked as they ran, eyes wide with fear.

He just nodded and continued on. She had no choice but to follow quickly behind but kept the spacing between them very tight. Now they were racing across the rocks, leaping down the shelves and bounding boulder to boulder until Volkreek drew up short with Deven almost colliding into his back.

In the blink of an eye, he'd sheathed his sword and had his bow in his hands, arrow nocked and then with a loud twang he let the first one fly. In the time it took for her to register what was going on, he'd already sent two more into the hides of the largest wolves she'd ever seen. The beasts spun, clearly unphased and charged.

In an instant she charged as well, clearing the distance in three blips as Volkreek focused on the rightmost wolf, landing two more arrows in the creature's chest by the time she connected with the first wolf. Driving her blade deep into its eye, she lost her grip and bounced off the creature's broad back, high and left, to land with a thud on the rocks mere feet from the ledge and a seventy-foot drop to the rushing waters below.

Deven rose groggily as more of the wolves further down trail turned their attention from the cliff's edge and came charging toward her and Volkreek. She could evade them, but she was weaponless as her knife was still lodged in the first wolf's head. As she turned to see where Volkreek was, she saw him firing off more shots with the bow, but not before he'd flung his sword, spinning on its center, roughly upright, through the air toward the oncoming wolves.

An alley-oop, she thought, drawing on her years of playing basketball. It was a perfect set up, with two blips she caught the blade and on the third blip came crashing down hard on the closest wolf, severing its spine if not quite it's entire head. The creature dropped on its chin and tumbled under momentum. The wolf next to it dropped with a half dozen arrows protruding from its chest and one in its eye.

Volkreek's blade was a hand-and-a-half for a man, but for Deven's petite frame, it was a perfect two-hander. Again, the mute warrior focused his arrows on the wolves furthest from Deven as she battled tooth to steel with the remaining pack, first popping in here and then reappearing behind to hack at a leg like she was swinging for the bleachers, then darting to the other wolf before it had a chance to react. In this way she cut down the remaining two, with Volkreek's arrows sinking deep into the last creature's throat as she pulled the blade from its torso. Tumbling away, she blipped up onto a boulder to avoid a last bite from its bone crushing jaws before it died.

Before the creature hit the ground, a booming screech echoed through the canyon as something large and fast whisked overhead.

Deven stood in stunned silence. A shuffling noise behind her causing her to spin, but too slowly. As her eyes struggled to focus on the shadows of the hillside, she saw yet another of the massive timber wolves, airborne and about to collide with her, fangs first. Her hands shot up reflexively, but just before impact, another screech boomed.

This time the sound filled all of her senses and she was knocked off the boulder. The last thing she saw was a strangely hairy reptilian tail whipping through the air where the wolf had been as the wyvern blew by, snatching it out of the air. Deven heard a solitary huge whooshing of wings and a sickening crunch as the wolf whimpered and then went silent. This all happened in fractions of a second before she hit the ground, hard.

Wind burst from her lungs with the impact and wild lights shot through her vision. She felt the metallic taste of blood in her mouth as she rolled slowly onto her side, honking as she gasped for air. In seconds, Volkreek was there, helping her to her feet and looking around feverishly, making sure that there were no more dangers from wolves or wyvern's or who knew what else.

Just as he was beginning to relax his guard and while Deven was catching her breath, they heard a muffled yell from somewhere both close and far away. Deven tried to control her rasping breaths in order to listen. The two heard it again.

It was coming from somewhere just over the cliffs edge. Volkreek was first to dash to the ledge. Deven blipped weakly to within a foot of where he knelt and peered over, still straining to gather her wits and breath.

Again, a voice rose over the dull roar from below.

"Is someone up there?" The weak, breathy baritone called out. Whoever it was, was either injured or sick.

Volkreek looked at Deven urgingly. She snapped back to reality, remembering that the warrior was mute.

"It's us!" she wheezed lamely, realizing that that did nothing to help the situation. She tried again. "Er, it's ME and..." seeing

Volkreek looking at her in exasperation, "Volkreek! We're here to help."

"Is that Gearlach down there?" she asked quietly of her companion who nodded vigorously, a brief smile of relief crept onto his face but was eclipsed by worry.

"Are you okay?" she asked of the man clinging to the edge of the cliff nearly fifteen feet below where they stood.

"I'm alive, but everything's numb from the ass down," the man said. "I've been sitting here all night."

That was bad. Even if they rescued him, with the blood pooling in his legs for so long, he could have a blockage that could break free and lodge in his heart or in his brain. Effectively turning this rescue attempt into a funeral.

She looked down again to assess the situation and it appeared that the man had wedged himself against the cliff wall with the spike of his battle axe stuck into the wall itself. There was no way she was going to dislodge it. The man, she realized was massive, like Laphren, and the axe handle alone was nearly as tall as she was.

"Do you think you can dislodge the axe? I think I have a way to get you up here. But once you are on flat land, we're still not out of trouble. You could have a blood clot from the blood pooling in your legs for so long. We'll have to keep you curled up for a little while and slowly get you straightened out. Do you understand?" she asked, yelling over the riot of river noises from below.

"Yes. I think so. But I will fall as soon as the axe is free. Do you have a plan for that?" the man asked.

"Yes. Just trust me."

"I don't know who you are, but if you're with Volkreek and if this has anything to do with that mage, then I can trust you," he said weakly, an air of resignation in his voice.

"Here I go," he said and pushed the axe blade free and began to tumble forward.

Deven blipped down, grabbing him by the leather strap connecting his shoulder armor to his breastplate and blipped back up. Just not quite all of the way. Apparently, there were limitations to what she could do with her magically enhanced abilities. The two teetered on the ledge, Deven on her knees, her carbon fiber and aluminum alloy shins grinding on the granite as she strained to hold the huge man in place.

He, folded at the waist, half on and half off, struggled to find something to hold on to with his free hand. Volkreek appeared, grabbing both of them he began pulling with all his might. Just as his foot slipped and it looked like all three would go over, Gearlach's right arm swung overhand with the axe, digging the spike into the flat slab. With one mighty heave, he pulled all three of them safely from the edge while his legs dangled uselessly behind him.

The three crawled a few feet more to safety. Gearlach rolled over onto his back and Deven quickly grabbed both of his legs and pushed them up to his chest. After the exertion and his hours stuck on the wall, he was useless to stop her. The scent of sweat and of urine was strong, but Deven was certain she smelled little better having fought goblins and wolves and having jogged for miles in the span of a few short hours.

"Thank you for that bit of help at the end there. I'm still sorting out some of my abilities. But just take it easy for a minute. Let's get you sorted out before we do more harm than good," Deven said leaning with all her weight to keep his legs folded and pressed up against his torso.

She slowly let his feet touch the ground but kept his legs tightly bent at the knee to restrict the blood flow, grabbing Volkreek's bow and placing it over his thighs and shins to act as a sort of brace, completing the ligature.

"Volkreek, give him as much water as he'll drink. We'll do this as slow and safe as we can."

Gearlach just lay on his back, letting the girl do whatever she thought she needed to do. It seemed like she might be a healer of sorts and she was clearly a practitioner of magic by what she'd done with him on the cliff. He didn't think even D'avry could have done such a thing, but then, D'avry himself didn't seem to understand his powers entirely either.

After a few minutes, the numbness gave way to the unbearable throbbing of pins and needles, which slowly dissolved into the chill of cold granite and of the cool night air. He didn't blackout and die, so the girl, who was clearly a foreigner, must know a thing or two.

After talking with the two for several minutes it sounded like N'Bruyyh and Trask were just hours ahead and that they had at least a semi-capable party waiting for them just a mile or so up the trail. That was the first good news he'd heard in a while.

They still did not know the place or time for N'Bruyyh's attempt at assuming power, though it sounded like it could have something to do with a large goblin encampment on the eastern slope of Tal Kar'zuum, just across the gorge from where they were now. And they also did not know what this sign that Trask had been anticipating would look like or when it would take place. But, by his estimation, it had to happen soon in order to be useful for the orc warlord to use it against the other chieftains.

Just then, a raven appeared at the top of a slender, moss covered pine towering above them, dimly illuminated by the first straining rays of dawn. Must be time to get going, he thought, and it cawed twice in agreement. Gearlach shook his head. Between Trask's signs, D'avry's unorthodox manifestations and Goriahh's darkly bent interventions, he was certain that magic would be the end of him.

But then, looking at his new companions and the bodies of the timber wolf pack scattered about the granite slabs before him, he amended that thought, it might just be his salvation as well. Besides, there was still work that needed to be done. He stood on shaky legs using the battle axe to assist him, and with the other two, slowly began to make his way up the trail.

Twenty-Seven

Shards of Light

Deven, Volkreek and the looming Gearlach, entered the clearing where the gorge trail met the one connecting to the ridge. At first the clearing was empty but then a bird like trill echoed through the early morning air, followed by several echoed responses, and a handful of people began to appear from the surrounding trees. They wore ragged clothes and looked haggard and beat down but cheerful despite their appearance.

But to Deven, there were far too few. And she did not see Farn or Liggo amongst their number. Her stomach dropped remembering D'avry's warning. So far, everything he'd said had come true. The fork in the trail, N'Bruyyh and Trask, Gearlach in trouble and now it appeared that Farn had indeed split the group and gone after N'Bruyyh without them. By the looks of it he had at least a handful of the refugees with him, maybe five or six, depending on if they'd found any survivors the night before.

Laphren stepped forward, with Beck falling in behind him. They seemed to be the informal team leads in Deven's absence.

"Miss Deven. Good to see you back," Laphren said grinning broadly and crowded in for a bear hug.

Caught off guard, she had no choice but to accept it, though awkwardly, and then patted the huge man on the shoulder.

"Breathe... I need to breathe!" she said in an urgent whisper.

He stepped back quickly.

"So sorry, ma'am. It's just, with all the wyvern screeching and what not, we had feared the worst," he said quickly in his deep, rumbling voice, looking a bit uncomfortable for the break in protocol.

"Well. It was actually the wyvern that saved my life... the

pack of timber wolves were the real trouble," she replied.

The men all stopped and stared with newfound awe; whether at being saved by a wyvern or at defeating a pack of timber wolves was uncertain and perhaps irrelevant.

"Who is this you have with you? Is this the drougehnn, Gearlach, we've heard about?" Laphren asked and stepped forward as if to offer another hug but was stopped short by a cold glare from the newcomer.

"Yes. That is what I am called," the dark-eyed warrior answered, staring levelly at the other man, his black cape fluttering gently in the slight breeze. It was clear to him that Farn had felt compelled to seek after the orc while the trail was fresh and though he questioned the soundness of the decision, he didn't blame him for not waiting for his return. Letting the warlord slip away would be doing an injustice to them all.

"Now, who are these others? I see many fresh faces," Gearlach asked the smith, noting that he carried only a wooden staff with a blade affixed to the end to work as a rudimentary spear. Goblin weapons would be too small for him to wield. He saw also that the notching and braiding of the attachment was excellently crafted for as crude a weapon as it was. The man stepped back, and Beck stepped forward quickly in his place.

"Becken of Bechan, sir," said the skinny, brown-haired kid, though with a surprising air of confidence. He continued. "And, you've just met Laphren, the smith." Who nodded at the introduction. "These others are Stuki, Tajiwar, Timmanee and Doolayn. They're all soldiers of the keep who'd been stationed on the Long Lake dam when it broke. I saw you there. Thank you for your warning. If only the commander had given it the credence it deserved…" the thin young man added.

Each man stepped forward as his name was called. Stuki was a heavy-set fellow with receding, sand-colored hair, roughly shaven jowls and wide set, dark brown eyes. He bore a scar through his right eyebrow, with puckered skin suggesting it'd been severe when it had happened. He also had a bit of a limp but that appeared to be fresh from the previous night's activities. Gearlach noted that his large hands bore bruises and open wounds as if he'd done most of the fighting bare-knuckled.

Tajiwar, was short and slight of frame but moved with the energy of a coiled spring. His shoulder-length black hair fell to either side, framing dark eyes, a thin nose, and thin lips. His skin was so pale as to appear white, an effect accentuated by his eyes and hair. He worked his hands together nervously as if trying to warm them up, but then stopped abruptly, palm over fist and gave a curt bow and a grunting, "Hoke!" Then returned to massaging his hands while he mumbled something unintelligibly under his breath. It seemed evident by his demeanor that it was just a quirk of behavior and not intended to be derogatory in any way. Similar to Becken, he had twin, black goblin blades, but these were double-ended and held in sheaths at either hip. The top part of the sheath sandwiched the upper blade fully, making it safe but also quickly available. The goblin kind were devilishly clever, Gearlach mused.

Last were Timmanee and Doolayn. They appeared a matched set except separated by a decade or so. The younger, Timmanee, was lightly muscled and in his early twenties, while Doolayn appeared to have about twenty pounds on him and most of that in his arms and chest. They both had pale blue eyes and freckles that dotted their lightly tanned cheeks with pale, white-blonde hair. Both wore fur lined leather and elkhorn bracers and carried tomahawk-like axes at their hips.

They, like the others had the bearing of soldiers but just a bit undernourished as they'd had little to eat for the last several days, starting with the three-day siege at Long Lake, then being washed downriver in the dam collapse, then the journey through the mountain caves as captives and finally their harried escape from goblin cages on the eastern slope. Not to mention, punctuated by an assault by more than fifty wolf borne while crossing a high mountain river in the middle of the night.

Gearlach thought on these things, calculating odds of success based on the events during his absence. He still didn't like the results of the maths, but they were better than expected. That usually meant that there were unknowns at play. In war, odds never got better, they just evolved until one side was left standing while the other nourished the soil with their blood.

After introductions, both Beck and Laphren looked to Deven for instructions. She had been informally chosen by the refugees as their leader since their rescue, and Gearlach's addition to the mix wasn't going to change that. Gearlach, seeing the shift in deference towards the woman glanced at Volkreek, who just lifted his eyebrows in bemusement and looked away. The massive warrior looked back to the diminutive girl with her hood pulled back to reveal glossy black hair that glistened with the sun's rays which were just now breaking through the trees. They were running short on time. He didn't care who thought they were in charge as long as they got moving.

Deven called for everyone to join her and then she blipped up onto a large boulder to address them. Eight in all stood before her. They looked different to her now than the night before. They were now clearly a pack of warriors, especially with the addition of the massive half-orc warrior, Gearlach.

It might be a different time and place, but the look was unmistakable and the expressions on their faces were identical to the ones shared by her fellow marines the morning they prepared to enter Ramadi to suppress the insurgent forces there. *Let's hope this ends differently,* she thought to herself.

Deven crushed the idea quickly as it percolated into her subconscious. She pulled her hair back into a ponytail and finding she still had a container of mascara in her pocket applied two fat streaks just below her eyes and rubbed them in to prevent glare before going into battle. As she did so, a crow dropped down to the rock beside her, cocking its head before jumping up to land on her shoulder.

She glanced at it sideways and then seemed to accept the new addition to the party and returned to face the men assembled before her. She noted Gearlach's look of mild amusement but ignored it. If he had a problem with her being in charge, the time to address it had passed.

"Okay, looks like you're all armed and fed. I'm sure none of you got any sleep, neither did we. We're going to double-time it up the trail. I'm not sure how far but we'll just keep going as long as we have to. Liggo should be leaving us guide marks. Hopefully Farn doesn't disturb them in his attempt to catch up. I'd like to catch the priest and his team before they attempt to rescue the...um librarian, is it?" she asked turning to Volkreek and then seeing him shake his head and nodding to Gearlach, she quickly turned to the drougehnn who responded.

"That's correct. He's a Ghodt."

"A God?" she asked, incredulously

Gearlach just shook his head. "No, a Ghodt. Why does everyone have a problem with this?" he asked looking around to see if anyone else found this as unusual as he did and finding none, returned his attention to the girl.

"They see visions and signs and things like that. He's foreseen that there will be a great sign, possibly in the sky and that there will be some kind of artifact that accompanies it. That will be used by N'Bruyyh in some way to influence the other tribes to join him. He'll use it to bolster his claim that he is chosen by Dakremesh-Gul-Etten-Ga-Meshundhuul as a fulfillment of ancient prophecy, from before the advent of the splinter tribes and the law forbidding unification," he explained.

Deven nodded slowly. "Dakremesh..."

"Dakremesh-Gul-Etten-Ga-Meshundhuul. The God of the Sky Below the Earth," he provided looking at the others again for affirmation and seeing that they, too, were perhaps just as confused as the outlander. He shrugged noncommittally.

Just then, the ground and trees around them were bathed in a deep, crimson light. They all looked up to see a blinding red pinpoint slowly streaming across the sky, a trail of cloud and fire billowing behind it. The sky, and everything else, was painted shades of red as it carved across the expanse in what seemed like slow motion. From the direction of the movement, it looked as if it would pass directly over the peak to the north of them. Exactly in the direction of the trail that they were on as it headed up the ridge.

"The sign..." Deven breathed and then whipped her hood up causing the raven to jump up cawing and flapping into the trees.

"Okay, move out!" she barked and blipped up the trail before settling into a purposeful jog.

The others fell into place behind her, scrambling to catch up.

Gearlach followed last, his long strides easily matching pace with the others. Looking up at the sky he muttered something under his breath about explosions and being fried where they stood but continued nonetheless, unlatching the flap over his axe blade and resting his hand atop its haft as he moved.

Volkreek, as ever, just took in stride the events around him, though, secretly he wished D'avry were amongst the party. He felt better about their prospects than he had in a long while but with the mage around things just seemed to work out, even as they appeared to be falling apart... He chuckled softly to himself as he jogged with the others, looking around at the red glow that seemed to paint the landscape while the star continued its fall to earth.

Twenty-Eight

Mongoose Herring

00.000001 BC (Before Construct)
Dawn of the Construct

With the area clear, Rutker exited the cavern, slipping between the boulders that hid the entrance from the surrounding area. This was good, he thought, just in case he needed to beat a hasty retreat. Much to his relief, the drone had located the first package less than six-hundred meters from where the cave system exited to the surface. There was no underground access any closer, so he was forced to expose himself, but the other drones had been busy and he felt fairly confident that the host of mechs hunting him down were scattered to the four winds.

That was, with the exception of the elite mech. He could be anywhere, and he was last seen heading in this direction. Rutker crept slowly amongst the stunted trees. The fine motor movements of the sniper mech that bore his namesake playing a major role in what had kept him alive thus far.

In hindsight, he couldn't have been more lucky. If they'd had a more capable mech in the stable he probably would have taken it and given the opposition he'd encountered thus far, even if he'd won the first encounter with the *Osiris* and the *Dragoon*, the mechs from the drop ships, or the drop ships themselves would have scattered his remains across the valley floor. Not to mention the stealth capable *Maelus-V* mech that had dropped in behind him without his sensors even making a beep. No, the *Long Rifle* was a minnow amidst crocodiles. As long as he could keep his distance, he would probably be okay.

So, as happy as he was about the package being close at hand and him not having to travel very far, there was one disappointing bit of news. He wouldn't be able to reach it without going on foot. He'd have to ditch the mech about seventy-five meters out, in a rock outcropping that had a slight overhang from a shelf above it.

Colonel Dexx was right about one thing; this area was pretty broken up. Rock shelves jutted out of the earth like giant shards of broken pottery. It was nighttime but with the planet's two moons there was tons of illumination. Rutker opted to wear a set of coveralls he found tucked behind the pilot's seat that were designed to disguise his heat signature. That, plus his helmet, ought to do the trick as far as staying hidden from prying eyes, either within line of sight nearby or stationed orbitally and scanning that specific area.

He glided into the pocket and dismounted, glad to be out of the frying hot mech with its baffles still on as a precaution. Rutker grabbed a grappling line from a utility storage bin on its underbelly and ensured that the charge was full on his Rawling Midget. It had already saved his life once that day. He corrected that statement in his mind, realizing that that had actually taken place the day before. The hours were blending together.

All he knew was that he would have to climb down into a thirty-meter crevasse to extract the package, a roughly quarter-meter square by one-meter-long cylindrical chest. He didn't even know what was in it. Really, he didn't care. As long as the seals were still intact, that was good enough for him.

He just needed to get it and get a move on to the next location. Hopefully, he would be able to get back in time to save his family and salvage the truce negotiations. He'd settle for the former, but he didn't know what kind of life he'd be sparing them for if the mission failed.

He pushed on through the rubble field until he reached the edge of the three-meter-wide gash in the landscape. Of all the places to land, the package *had* to fall into a hole too narrow for the mech to enter and too oddly shaped for him to just use the grappling hook remotely.

Of course, this may have been a stroke of luck as had the cannister just been resting on the surface somewhere the pirates or let's call them what they were... mercenaries, could have found it already.

He looped his line around an available boulder and locked the carabiner to a climbing knot he had fashioned out of rote memory before realizing he'd done it. Content with the configuration, he connected his rappel device which was also an auto-ascender and tugged hard twice. Everything was taut.

He leaned back with his feet on the edge and began walking backwards towards the bottom of the crevasse. As he pendulumed below the plane of the surface, the cliff wall began to recede away from him slowly, to the point that he was suspended in midair for a couple meters or so before the contour of the wall returned and began to slope more gradually. Touching down, he followed it back further toward the opposing wall until once again the rock dropped off and he was forced to hang free for the second time.

Below him was the smooth gray exterior of the package as it rested, one end wedged between a couple of the small boulders that made up the floor of the depression. As his toes touched down, he got the sense that he wasn't alone and his hand whipped the Rawling up to place two quick rounds on what he assumed was a creature or one of the mercenaries, but the pistol ripped from his hands and was caught by a dark hooded figure standing a few meters away in the shadow of the overhang.

Just as that happened, the boulder under his foot shifted and he lost his footing, causing him to spin suspended horizontally at the end of his line.

I'm dead, this is how I die, he thought as he spun, his assailant swinging in and out of his field of vision.

The hooded figure chuckled and Rutker released his ascender, thudding painfully on the cobble floor, and struggled to regain his feet with the uneven footing.

"You're fine, Capt. Major. Relax... I'm sorry to have alarmed you," the hooded figure said in a vaguely familiar voice.

Comprehension dawned on the pilot and his face flushed with anger and embarrassment.

"Mage!" he growled.

"D'avry," he said, "Avaricai D'avry."

"What are you doing here? If I knew you could just blip in and out wherever you wanted, I'd have sent you to pick up the packages yourself!" he said rasping loudly.

But it was a lie. He didn't trust the man any farther than he could have thrown him, and so far, he hadn't had the chance, but was counting the seconds until he could.

"Rutker, right?" he asked, stepping forward and tossing the pistol back, which Rutker caught and pointed back at him. The mage continued forward unphased.

"This is interesting," he said, looking at the cylinder and kneeling down beside it, "What do you think is in it?" he asked, looking up with keen interest.

"Touch it. I dare you," Rutker replied levelly.

The man's hand descended slowly downward with his index finger extended, hovering within a fraction of an inch while he retained eye contact. Rutker pulled the trigger anyway and was disappointed but not surprised to find that it did nothing but make a clicking noise. It had been *too* good to be true.

"Before you attempt to harm me again, think about what I'm doing here. Have I not had plenty of opportunity to harm you if that had been my desire from the beginning?" he asked standing erect and dropping his hood to reveal shoulder length blonde hair and an almost regal facial structure. For the first time Rutker noticed that it almost looked like he was wearing eyeliner. *To each his own*, he guessed...

"Like I said before, if you can just pop around anywhere you want to go, why did I have to hunt for this package, why couldn't you have just brought it to me if your motives were so altruistic?" Rutker asked, trying to bite back the contempt that was creeping up with bile in the back of his throat. He was pissed. His family's lives hung in the balance. His planetary system hung in the balance and this man was popping in and out of thin air, asking archaic questions and just generally presenting himself as a gigantic ass.

"I don't know where I'm going, I just know that it's where I need to be when I get there," he said simply as if that made any fucking sense at all.

"Uh huh," Rutker replied, dead pan, while brushing his coveralls off and casually glancing at the charge on his Rawling before slipping it back in its holster. It was at zero percent, somehow, although it had been at one hundred just minutes before.

"So, what're you playing at here, mage? What are you after?" he asked, growing well past tired of the exchange.

"The sense I have is that this object holds the keys to the future of humanity, at least on this planet, which I now believe to be..." He paused as if receiving a download from some unknown source. His face went blank and then suddenly he reached up, massaging his temple and then his hand slid down to cover his mouth and he looked at the pilot with the most sincere expression of regret, sorrow, loss? Rutker couldn't really decipher what it was exactly, but he was certain that the man was not lying when he spoke next.

"Go find your family, Capt. Major. This object is of no use to you and time grows short," he said, and then, "I'm sorry...for both of us."

"What is it?" Rutker growled, fear gripping his insides as he ripped the capsule out from between the rocks and ensured the seals had not been ruptured, which was immediately evident.

"So, this is how it starts..." the man said muttering as he walked toward the red sandstone wall of the crevasse. And then he turned.

"The thing, in the cave... did it speak to you?" he asked and immediately Rutker knew what he was talking about. The terror. And at first, he was about to respond 'no' but then he remembered a snippet of the dream he was having before he awoke to find the mage standing there the first time.

He said nothing.

"Yeah. Me too." The mage said before turning and walking directly into and through the sandstone wall. Rutker was left alone, standing with his mouth hanging open.

Standing at the bottom of a hole, in the middle of the night on a foreign planet with his wife and kids possibly held hostage by mercenaries or blood thirsty Delvadr, after watching a man literally walk through a stone wall, he was beginning to question... well, everything.

Rutker didn't need to open the package to know that it was empty, and that this entire thing had been a ruse, but to what end? He determined to head back to the ship, but he'd be certain to let Colonel Dexx think that he was still hunting for the remaining package. While he was chewing on the possibilities of what sort of double-cross had occurred, his thoughts were repeatedly interrupted by memories of his dream in the caverns below the valley's surface.

In his dream, he was in the mech, back in the submerged chamber, standing at the bottom of the pool looking up at the graffiti lettering splashed across the huge hangar door. Only in his dream, he could read the archaic lettering. Just as he had imagined, the message did in fact read "Beware". Only now, instead of believing that it was a warning about what was inside the chamber, he was certain that it was a warning about something else. Something yet to come.

Rutker reached out to Colonel Dexx and filled him in on the status of the hunt and was provided with directions to the next location, which was about a ten-hour hike from Rutker's current location. He told him to watch out as they had spotted some inter-orbital activity and Rutker clued the Colonel in to the fact that he had had a run in with some mechs and that the so-called *pirates* even had drop ships at their disposal.

This seemed to give Dexx pause but he recovered quickly and urged him to return as quickly as possible and, "Oh, by the way…" not to break the seal on the diplomatic packages.

He assured him that he understood the gravity of the situation and that he would in no way jeopardize the treaty, that such an action would be tantamount to treason. He made that last point with perhaps a little too much emphasis, but Dexx didn't seem to register the irony.

Before signing off Rutker asked how defenses were holding up and if Katherryn and the boys were doing well. He didn't mention the fact that Katherryn was supposed to have contacted him every six hours and had not once reached out during the entire length of his excursion. The drones that were still above ground would have captured any comms regardless of whether or not he received or responded to them. There had been nothing. He seethed coolly.

Dexx told him he was short on time but that the pirate offensive had been surprisingly light and ineffective. Rutker was sure it had been.

The Colonel also told him that Katherryn, Macq and Mads were all doing their part, assisting with keeping watch and generally maintaining a low profile. That last part didn't sound like Katherryn at all. Now he was more certain than ever that something had taken place and he was just hoping that the three had not been harmed in any way. He couldn't see any one of them going quietly. *People would pay,* he thought darkly. *And dearly…*

Rutker signed off and increased his pace, using the drones to map at high resolution to enable the mech to move at over maximum speed. Additionally, he peeled out three drones to scout the next package location just in case he was wrong, but more and more he felt a certainty in his gut that this peace treaty was a sham and that more than likely there was some other sort of negotiation going on or would be.

Peeling out just one drone to scout the *Xandraitha's Hope* he thought would provide invaluable intel while minimizing the risk of discovery. Now he had to figure out how to reach the landing site.

When he left initially to hunt for the packages, he had taken an easterly path down a ravine that was gradually sloped, but beyond the gentle rise at the far south end of the plateau there really wasn't another viable path up, other than to climb one of the exposed faces either to the north or the west. He found it unlikely that anyone would expect that tack but unfortunately, it would leave him wide open to view from the sparse pine forest below. It would be stupid to do it, but he was fairly certain that that's exactly what he was going to do.

He looked up to the sky and with the enhanced view from his heads-up display superimposed upon the transparent shell, he could see something that had not been there before, a shadow on the surface of the larger moon. Doing some quick trigonometry, he concluded that the object casting it was in the night sky to the left of the moon and somewhere in the middle space. Distance was dependent on size. The somewhat blurry edges suggest that it was not particularly close to the moon's surface.

That implied that the ship was *super*massive. He focused on the space where he thought it ought to be and after a minute or so found a faint light that could have been a star, but he was guessing was not. His initial impression was that it could be a long ship and that he was only seeing the front, the smallest percentage of its profile.

He enhanced the imagery using the mechs substantial targeting capability and his heart sank with recognition. It was a Thune frigate. Most likely owned by the Delvadr Primacy, but he was beginning to suspect Thune Corporate itself could be a player and he had not yet ruled out the supposedly impartial superorganism known as the Gefkarri Pentarch. Although, he didn't know what an entity that was essentially a planet-sized, interlaced, and interconnected forest would want with his people or their planetary system.

The Gefkarri and the Thune seemed unlikely partners although they did share the same leg of what was a pretty out of the way section of the galactic warp corridor. It was only through Delvadr and Epriot owned territories that that entire arm of the galaxy was really exposed to the greater body. That's when he realized that *that* was the greater play.

It wasn't about the Delvadr or the Epriot Alliance but what was beyond them. He wondered if the Delvadr even knew they were being played. They were so pompous and self-absorbed he doubted it. But still, he couldn't see what it was that the Gefkarri gained by ruining its reputation of neutrality. That was largely what had kept it from being invaded and occupied for millennia untold.

Rutker's mind was still racing through the possibilities when the targeting computer informed him that the incoming vessel would reach planetary orbit in twenty-one hours. That didn't leave much time. *To do what?* He didn't know...

Twenty-Nine

The Herald of Dakremesh

19.004329 AC (After Construct)
Age of the Half-Orc War

The meteorite streaked across the sky above them and contrary to her initial estimates it slammed into the peak of the mountain with a blinding light followed by a concussive wave that knocked them all off their feet. The trees shook and pine needles fell, along with branches in some cases. A loud crack echoed and a pine tree just ahead on the hillside snapped part way up.

The *whoosh* of branches and pine needles through the air gave little warning before the party, who were just now struggling to their feet, had to dive to either side. Deven, who was closest, nearly made it thanks to her new ability but as the tree collided with another tree further downhill, it rolled and careened further to the north where Deven had fled.

Crashing to the forest floor with a whomping thud, one of the spring-loaded, bushy pine branches crashed down behind her and then swatted her into the air like a seal pup from an orca's tail. She blipped quickly away from landing on another broken pine trunk but still landed awkwardly on the steep slope, tumbling headlong and sliding for another fifteen feet before skidding to a halt in a dusty cloud.

As she sat up, tasting blood in her mouth (again), and blinking the dirt from her eyes, she heard a shuffle and a quick flapping noise. Her eyes came to focus on the crow, perched on a broken branch, roughly eye level, about three feet away. It cocked its head, squawked twice and then cocked it's head the other way.

"Some help. Now be a dear and pull me back up the hill," she wheezed sarcastically.

The crow leapt up into the air, flapping to gain height, and then glided to a spot further up trail.

Deven stood up and started scrambling back up the hillside to the trail thirty feet further up. Volkreek met her at the edge and pulled her the rest of the way. Eying her conspicuously.

"I know, I know. I'm a mess," she said, dusting herself off.

He gave a flat smile and raised his eyebrows as if to say, *I didn't say it, you did.* She just patted herself down and looked around to see if everyone else was alright, which luckily, they were.

"Well alright. At least now we know where N'Bruyyh is headed. Unfortunately, so does *everyone* and *everything* within a couple hundred miles. So, let's get to it." She turned and started trotting up the trail. The crow followed along, sticking close to Deven, Gearlach noticed. Apparently, it had found a new person to torment.

It took them a couple of hours but just as the trees were beginning to thin and patches of snow tinged red in the meteor's afterglow began to dot the landscape, they rounded a corner to find the trail ended abruptly at the precipice of a massive crater. Easily a quarter mile across, the uphill side was near vertical as it rose into gigantic spurs of rock that looked like castle spires.

The far end was another ridge, forming a kind of bowl which spilled down into a rubble filled run-out gully below. The trees beyond the opposite ridgeline appeared mostly intact but everything else within a half mile was flattened outward, making no mistake as to where the meteorite had struck.

That, however, would not be in question as a glowing red gash at the base of the vertical wall was a clear indicator of something non-terrestrial. Emanating out from that point was fresh gray-green rock that jutted out in columns before diminishing into larger and then smaller boulders below. To Deven, the gash in the hill resembled a large glowing cat's eye.

Down in the crater just a few hundred yards further she saw Farn's party or at least most of them and further on there were a couple other figures that she couldn't quite make out. But one was significantly larger than the other. It was a pair of them, and it looked to her like that had to be N'Bruyyh and Trask. If it was the librarian, he appeared to be in rough shape as the huge orc half pulled, half dragged him upward toward the impact site.

A flash of light erupted and Deven realized that it had come from Farn. Apparently, he had learned at least one thing he could do with the staff's power beyond creating defensive wards. The purple-white plasma ball hit the hillside just wide of the orc and he and Trask were cast to the ground with the explosion of fire.

N'Bruyyh stood quickly but the librarian didn't move. He must have struck his head, or just reached the limit of his ability to carry on after the punishing hike up the mountain. Deven wasn't sure which from her vantage point. Another fire ball erupted, and the monstrous warrior dodged to the right but was again knocked to the ground with the impact. Again, N'Bruyyh rose to his feet, but this time abandoned the librarian altogether, instead charging up the hill with surprising speed toward the impact zone.

Deven realized that while she was watching this unfold, Gearlach had already sprinted ahead and was into the crater, cutting a higher path by leaping from one jagged rock fragment to the next in an effort to cut N'Bruyyh off. It didn't look to her like he was going to make it in time.

Deven followed suit, popping from one spot to the next in a blur of movement, but there was a lot of ground to cover. What she didn't see was that newcomers had reached the crest of the far ridge. It was an orc war party, twenty strong, and with them were two even larger creatures. And then a rider strode into view, a woman on a large draft horse. She wore black hooded robes and as she crested the ridge, pulled her hood back to reveal long, black, braided hair that she pulled around to lay over her shoulder.

Her complexion was fair, though there was color in her cheeks from the exertion of the ride. She took in the activity before her as bursts of condensation billowed from her mount's nostrils. She observed coolly as N'Bruyyh charged up the hillside toward the glowing gash, the party below chasing after him, while a man wielding a staff hurled fireball after fireball at the orc chieftain. She also saw the other party on the far ridge making their way down into the crater, with two shapes cutting a higher line to intercept N'Bruyyh.

The woman looked up and spoke to the large creatures looming over her. They were nephalkund. Their long, thick arms dangling from stooped shoulders, ending in oversized hands with curled black claws. The creatures had dark gray-brown skin but were mostly covered in coarse gray-white hair. They had large fangs, but their faces were dominated by three rows of spider like eyes extending from where a nose would be all the way up to the top of their furry foreheads. The creatures also had two sets of horns, one pair that ringed their heads like a tiara, jutting out near the temples. The other pair turned down along the jawline to protrude outward and down in a tusk-like fashion. They were hideous and terrifying.

The two creatures wore armor that consisted of a square, studded breast plate connecting to shoulder pauldrons. Each creature carried a spear and a crudely shaped rectangular short sword which looked more suited to hacking than anything else.

Upon the word of the woman, the pair of nephalkund lumbered into the crater, cutting high and right on a path mirroring that of Gearlach and Deven. The rest of the necromancer's party, her elite guard, charged down the hillside, screaming and waving spears and swords as they moved to head off the human parties nearing the center of the crater and just beginning to work their way upward on the path that N'Bruyyh had taken just minutes before.

Farn cast yet another fireball, but the orc warlord seemed to run on fresh legs and could take an impossible amount of damage. He ran forward a few more paces while Liggo sprinted to Trask's aid. The remaining refugees, too, pushed forward. They were committed now, having escaped the goblins and understanding that a united orc and goblin army would decimate mankind. They rushed to form a defensive barrier around the librarian and the thief. There were only three of the refugees now. The others had been lost when they had run across an orc scouting party. Luckily there had only been four orcs in the party or things would have turned out differently.

A loud roar echoed from above and Farn saw a line of orcs rushing down from the ridgeline above. And something else he had never seen before. Two large creatures that were cutting to intercept N'Bruyyh as he made his way toward the impact site.

Liggo had said something about unnatural beasts in the orc camp one of the times he'd snuck in to communicate with Trask. They didn't fight in the battle at Long Lake, but then, neither had the drougehnn woman, Goriahh. Apparently, she had been staying back so as not to miss the sign if it happened during the attack or if something happened to N'Bruyyh. However, it looked to Farn that she had plans of her own, that may or may not involve the warlord.

The beasts descended the crater from the northeast. It was evident to the priest that Goriahh was indeed overseeing the action from above. He caught movement from the corner of his eye and at first was afraid that it was yet more combatants entering the fray, but it turned out to be Gearlach, *finally*.

The half-orc warrior was charging toward the impact area from the south, across massive boulders lining the base of the cliff wall, leaping from rock to rock. And behind him was the girl, the de facto leader of the refugees, with her ability to lurch forward using the magical properties of the ring that D'avry'd given her, she was only behind Gearlach for a couple moments before she overtook him.

That caused him to wonder where Volkreek was. Turning further still he saw that the man, along with the rest of the refugees were racing up behind him. They were going to reach his location only slightly ahead of the orc war party. This was going to get messy. Farn turned to face the orcs, he could do nothing for Gearlach if he were dead.

He recalled the spell for the fireball and began to speak low and loud. The air twitched in front of him and then sprang to life as a small blue flame erupted, growing in size as he continued to chant and then, as though pushing the ball of fire at his opponents, he shouted the final words of the enchantment and it shot forth at the charging line of orcs.

The plasma ball exploded at their feet, sending bodies flying and on fire. The action split the line in half but there were still more than a dozen racing toward them. That was a more powerful spell then he'd ever cast before, and his vision swam as he reached inside to do it again. He caught his breath and drew energy from somewhere inside himself, knowing full well that his life, as well as those of his friends and the men who fought with him, was on the line.

Again, he spoke the words and the air before him boiled before bursting into a fist sized ball of light and as it grew too hot to hold so close, he cast out again, only this time the ball of fire was intercepted by another from farther up the hillside. The green ball of plasma collided with the blue-white one cast by Farn in the space between the human and orc parties and each was thrown to the ground in a blinding explosion of light that echoed off the granite walls, causing large boulders to rattle loose and tumble freely down the gully.

Farn sat up to see another green ball careening toward them from the ridgeline. He thrust the staff upward and spoke the only spell he knew, though he'd never tried it before with the aid of the staff. The ball of flame crashed down on the party and blew apart into a thousand fragments, leveling the orcs who were now only twenty feet away as they attempted to stand from the previous blast.

When the light subsided, the humans were amazed to find that they were unscathed. The refugees shouted in triumph and charged the stunned orcs, still a dozen strong but clearly reeling from the explosion. Just then the rest of the refugee party, along with Volkreek, showed up. They rushed up the hill to take part in the melee while the enemy attempted to regroup. It was not a match up that the humans could ordinarily win, but with the orcs stunned, the odds were at least even.

Still, Goriahh was not willing to let the humans gain the upper hand. Yet another ball of fire rained down from the ridgeline. Farn scrambled to counter but missed. Goriahh's fireball exploded amidst the knot of combatants, levelling human and orc alike.

Farn's fireball failed perfectly, exploding into the hillside directly below the necromancer, causing her mount to rear up, tossing her to the ground and interrupting her ability to recast. The priest seized the moment. Again, he drew deep from within and issued forth the words to cast the spell. A fireball sprang to life, but it was noticeably weaker than before. It was just using too much magic too soon.

The fireball streaked toward the ridgeline, but Goriahh deflected it easily. She, however, did *not* appear to be fading. Instead, she reached up to the sky, screaming words in an unknown tongue and the sky above erupted with burning sulfur that rained down on the fighters as they struggled to gain their feet.

The priest struggled to summon a defensive shield but found he was unable to protect more than a pace in each direction. Stones of fire pummeled humans and orcs alike and all turned to batting the flames and rolling on the ground to extinguish their clothes and armor.

Thankfully the burst was short lived. Still, Farn could tell the battle was tipping in the half-breed woman's favor. Goriahh was stronger, she had the high ground, and the humans now were in similar shape as the orcs. The fighting resumed and Farn relegated himself to providing as much cover from her attacks as he could manage, which wasn't much.

Thirty

The Nephalkund

N'Bruyyh was just reaching the flat shelf at the base of the gash in the mountain where the meteorite had impacted. A warm crimson glow issued from it, bathing the landing in light though he couldn't perceive its source. Boulders the size of his head tumbled down from the rock spires above as explosions rolled continuously from the skirmish below.

Just then, a piercing pain lit up his side and he was surprised to see what looked to be a human girl staring up at him in defiance. He laughed and swatted at her, but she was gone. The blinding pain came again but this time from his shoulder. He spun and the girl was nowhere to be found. Spinning once more, he was blindsided by the half-breed Gearlach slamming into him and pinning him to the rock wall.

The huge warrior took the punishment, the still-charred and rotting skin on his face cracking into a horrific smile. Arching his body off the wall he spun to the side just as a battle axe whisked past his head and embedded itself in the rock. He kicked viciously into Gearlach's ribs as the drougehnn warrior was overextended. But then a burst of pain lit up the hamstring of his other leg, as it leaked putrid black blood on the granite ledge.

The wound dropped him, and he just caught a glimpse of the girl as she blipped away from a backhanded swing of his arm. From where he landed on the ground, he flicked out a hunting knife with his left hand to where he expected her to be next and the hilt of the knife struck her squarely on the temple, knocking her to the ground in a crumpled pile.

N'Bruyyh grinned and was slammed hard into the ground for exulting in his victory too soon. Still, though strong and fast, Gearlach lacked the weight to hold the warlord down and a quick knee to his ribs caused him to lose his concentration enough that N'Bruyyh was able to slip a forearm across his face. He ripped down viciously into the granite floor, dazing Gearlach and allowing the bigger orc to roll to his feet, though he was instantly reminded of the dripping black gash in the back of his leg. Indeed, blood, too, was pouring from his side and shoulder.

Gearlach struggled to all fours and N'Bruyyh, planting with his good leg, drove a hard kick, again, to his ribs. The drougehnn crumpled but managed to roll with the momentum and came to his feet in a low crouch, though clearly favoring his right side. The warlord squared off with him, rounding slowly, making a show of limping even as the severed flesh of his leg knit back stronger with each passing second. Another explosion broke loose an avalanche of rocks and the two were forced to dodge the onslaught as the rocks blew, rocketing past. The two locked eyes again but were interrupted by an unnatural roar that echoed off the rocks around them and was followed by two heavy thuds from the far side of the landing.

Standing at the far end were Goriahh's nephalkund beasts, the ones Liggo had warned Gearlach about. N'Bruyyh roared,

"Goriahh! What's the meaning of this?" But rather than wait for a response he unsheathed his massive sword from his back. It was fully as long as Gearlach was tall and looked to weigh as much as a man. Gearlach ran and dove for his axe still buried in the rock wall. N'Bruyyh paid him no attention but kept his focus firmly set on the creatures moving steadily toward him from the other side of the rock ledge.

Gearlach wanted to check on the girl, Deven, but knew there wasn't any time. He needed to deal with one crisis at a time. The creatures bellowed again and charged, lumbering toward the unlikely pair. N'Bruyyh dove forward as a spear came thrusting at him. He spun and snapped the spear with his two-handed sword before continuing the motion into an overhead swing meant to come down on the creature's thigh, but the creature anticipated the move and deflected the swing down into the ground with its own sword, and then backhanded the huge orc across the landing and into the rock wall.

The other creature was focused on Gearlach. It, too, lead with a spear attack which the warrior dodged, but rather than go after the spear first, he rolled forward and came up with a sideways swing that sliced deeply into the creature's calf and then leapt away before the creature could counter.

N'Bruyyh was groggily rising to his feet when he saw motion in front of him. Focusing on the charging creature just in time, he lunged to the side just as the multi-eyed nephalkund drove its horns into the rock wall. It bounced off and stumbled back, expecting to have impacted with the something much squishier. N'Bruyyh seized the opportunity, rushed forward, and jumped one-footed off the rock wall and came down with a huge two-handed swing only to be skewered by the monster with the broken end of its spear. The warlord crumpled against the creature's arm and shoulder, his feet still dangling in the air, his sword clattering across the rocks. The monster tossed the orc, spear and all, casually down the hill as it turned to face the glowing crack in the rock wall.

Gearlach, seeing what had happened to N'Bruyyh turned to sprint for the meteorite but was caught off his feet by the other creature's spear, causing him to fly across the landing like a rag doll. He hit the other wall and lay in a heap on the ground, motionless.

The nephalkund jumped up onto the ledge above the landing and strode over to the glowing crack. It reached inside and drew out a glowing chunk of rock with crystal nodules sticking out of it at peculiar angles. The creature stared at it with unblinking spider-like eyes, the shadows cast by the meteorite somehow making it look even more sinister than before. But, as it turned around with the meteorite in its hand, the second nephalkund swung its blade down hard, striking it just above the shoulder. The creature bellowed in pain, dropping the orb to the ground as it staggered to its knees.

With a second swing, the blade came around and lopped the stunned creature's head clean from its body in a spewing mist. The second creature looked down at the unmoving corpse and then turned to bend down and pick up the orb from the gory mess. But as it did so, long dark arms extended from the still glowing crack in the cliff wall. More and more black, spindly arms extended through the opening and spread across the cliff face like a cancer until it seemed like the light from inside the crack would be blacked out entirely.

The nephalkund turned at the commotion and roared in challenge, but black spindly arms still issued forth from the hole until a scrambled mess of blackness revealed itself, hanging in the air high above the corpse of the first creature.

The dense knot of darkness hung silently, towering above the massive creature, but did nothing. Again, the nephalkund bellowed challenge at the otherworldly form but only for a second as the sound was cut off by a knot of black spindly arms that stabbed down into the nephalkund's throat, followed by more and more until they burst outward through the creature's body exploding it into indistinguishable bits that showered down onto the ragged rocks below.

The now massive black nebula – a halo of spindly legs hanging down and all around, like a mad man's scribbling against the sky – hung there in silence. Then below, from the glowing crack, other void black creatures spewed out. These were wolf like in form and stood as often on two legs as on four. Their manner was that of predators or more precisely, hunters. Blipping large gaps from one point to the next, their glowing red eyes never blinked as they took in the scene before them. The void hunters spread out on the granite landing until there were half a dozen of them scanning and sniffing the air as if searching for something.

On the ridgeline, Goriahh mounted her tall, gray and black dappled steed and wheeled away. The meteorite clearly would not be hers. Her two beasts were dead, N'Bruyyh was likely dead and what remaining orcs had come with her were nearly dead as well and *even* if they prevailed against the humans, would be dead shortly after, from what she could tell of the newcomers.

What they were she did not know but she was certain that they were not of this world. Perhaps the powers of the meteorite had rent a hole between dimensions or maybe it had something to do with this place as well. Regardless, she would need to regroup with the orc clans that were left after the foolish battle against the humans of Long Lake. They were newly united, and nothing destroyed a fragile truce like losing a battle. Besides, the goblins would need to be told what to do now that N'Bruyyh was out of the picture. She snapped the reigns and the mighty horse lurched down the trail and out of sight.

Below, the remaining orcs and humans had stopped fighting and were staring up the hill at the thing hanging in the air before the glowing crack of the meteor. There were only five orcs left and they were in rough shape. Seeing that N'Bruyyh was dead and that Goriahh had left them, they scrambled up the hill, beating a hasty retreat. Volkreek drew his bow but Trask shushed him and made a motion with his hands to stop what he was doing and be quiet.

Two of the void creatures bolted in the direction of the fleeing orcs, blipping from rock to rock and cutting the distance in a fraction of the time it would have taken a man. The creatures ripped into the fleeing orcs before they reached the crest, shredding armor like papyrus with their huge black claws. The orcs had weapons drawn but it was a decisive victory, with barely a reprisal.

It appeared to the humans below that the orc weapons made little or no impact on the otherworldly beasts which now stood glaring down at the human party who were, even now, slowly backing away the way they'd come.

Of the humans, there were now only a handful; Trask who looked to be in no shape to travel. Liggo and Volkreek, faces smeared with dirt and blood, were catching their breath from the melee. Farn, too, looked as if he'd been rolling in the dirt, half his shaven head speckled with dust and blood, though it was unclear if it was through injury or contact with someone else. He leaned leadenly on his staff. Laphren, the smith, had taken a knee though it was unclear whether due to fatigue or injury. At some point he'd swapped out his staff-turned-spear for a very large stone-headed hammer, most likely having belonged to one of the many orcs he'd vanquished in the short while since entering the crater. He was the largest of the refugees, roughly eye to eye with Gearlach but that was still half a head shorter than most of the Orcs they'd faced.

Missing from the line-up was Becken, the young courier. Laphren had lost track of him when they'd collided with the orcs initially before being scattered by one of Goriahh's brutal fireball attacks. Gone, too, were the men with Farn and Liggo, and lastly, the four soldiers from the dam, Stuki, Tajiwar, Timmanee, and Doolayn. Sadly, it seemed freedom had not been long lived for most of the refugees.

A haze of dim red light still filled the sky and bathed the landscape, some sort of remnant from the streaking meteor most likely. But beyond that was eerie silence, until a raven's caw broke the silence and a black shape flashed across the reds and grays of the crater wall. It blew past the two void creatures, and they followed it up and over the eastern crest of the crater where Goriahh had fled minutes before. Two flashes of light shot up from beyond the hill and silence followed again.

Without a word, two more of the creatures sprang from the

landing below the hovering void creature that now presided over the carnage. They blipped across the edge of the crater. One of the pair howled wretchedly as it cleared the edge of the crater, the other on its heels.

And then, a few seconds later, two more bright lights flashed from over the hill and silence again stole over the area. Volkreek turned his attention back up to the creatures, where they seemed to be guarding the meteorite crater, and the whole of the basin seemed to echo with the sound of gravel, grinding under foot.

The two remaining creatures turned to focus on the noise and broke forth down the tumble of rocks, heading directly for the human party. Volkreek loosed two arrows in short succession and both seemed to pass through or miss their intended targets. Cursing he slung his bow over his back and unsheathed his short sword and as he did so, it issued forth a blinding corona of light.

The creatures broke ranks, splitting to either side, but continued nonetheless. Right then, the raven cawed from above, shooting down at the rightmost creature as it blipped to within only a few paces of the party. But, as the bird seemed about to impact the wolf-like creature, the raven morphed into the shape of a man who drove to the ground, arm outstretched, headfirst. As it looked like he would collide with the ground, he just shot right through the creature and disappeared as the creature burst into a ball of light similar to what they'd seen from over the ridge but much, much brighter.

Volkreek, seeing the birdman materialize, turned his attention fully on the remaining creature as it cut the distance in half between them but before it could close the rest of the gap it fell or was pulled into the ground below it. No light issued forth, but a muffled thump could be heard and then just silence and the sound of their own ragged breathing.

And then, in silence once more, the sky or the light around them seemed to dim as though the sun had passed behind a fast moving cloud. But there was no sun, just the eerie red glow from the sky above.

Trask looked back to the refugees and caught Volkreek's face. He was covered in blood and dirt and his beard appeared to be just one mass of red as it was matted with sweat and blood, and then he looked up at the heavens.

The librarian was reminded of his vision from days before and was thankful that it had not so far proved to be a vision of the death of the mute warrior, however, it was still a chilling sight and reminded him that things were far from over. There was still the existence of the huge, hovering beast that had appeared from the meteor crater.

When he turned to look up at the rocks at the base of the cliff where the creature had been he saw that it had in some way grown and that, beyond his ability to quantify it, the very light itself seemed to be dimmer around the beast. Indeed, even as he was taking this all in, the creature seemed to be getting larger, the black scribbles for legs, or tentacles, grew longer and seemed to grow in number as well, first doubling and then tripling from when it first arrived out of the gash in the mountain at the crater's epicenter.

Just then, a split in the space above them grew and light spilled through before being totally eclipsed by an object with a long, pointed mast or bowsprit. It was made of canvas and nets and metal rings, and it continued to pour forth from the split in the sky. Soon, the form of a ship hanging below what looked to be a huge, cylindrical balloon, exited from the rip in the heavens.

It was like no ship any of them had ever seen. For long, metallic, spider-like legs protruded from amidships, three to a side. Then the split seemed to seal itself up behind the huge air ship as long flag-like streamers slipped through the last bit of sunlit space before the tear in the sky disappeared.

Long *whooshing* sounds like bellows issued forth, and indeed steam could be seen spouting randomly from throughout the contraption as it slowed its momentum forward and began, gradually, to gain altitude. More creatures began to pour forth from the glowing crack as if in response. The void beasts' tentacled arms shot upward at the flying craft, much like a giant squid trying to pull a ship down to the deep.

The ships long spider like arms *whooshed* and whistled and moved forward to seize the blackout beast.

Farn, assuming the airship to be on the side of the good guys, launched a fireball at the void creature and it struck it on the side. The explosion seemed somewhat unspectacular in comparison to the size of the creature, but a few of the arms disintegrated and the airship seemed to gain at least a little bit of forward motion as it now seemed to be focused on driving the void creature into the towering granite face. More sounds of bellows and of steam could be heard, but now, too, could be heard the voices of men yelling and repeating commands.

As more dark creatures poured from the rock wall, Volkreek saw an explosion of light from the far left. He turned and was both relieved and terrified to see Gearlach, swinging his battle axe as it collided with another of the blacked-out hunters, causing another explosion of light. More creatures turned and headed his way, but Volkreek was already charging up the hill, his sword swinging in arcs above his head, light pouring forth as he tried to draw the creatures away from the drougehnn warrior. He didn't succeed entirely, but many of the creatures did in fact lock on to the activity and began to charge down the hill, popping in and out and closing the distance at an inhuman pace.

Liggo, too, had taken up the charge and was rushing side by side with his brother-in-arms, bolstered by seeing Gearlach faring better against the creatures than the ill-fated orcs had.

Thirty-One

The Eleven Sevens

Farn continued to launch fireball after fireball at the creature but as fast as he destroyed the arms, they grew back. Soon they were reaching down to where he was on the ground, the creature easily fighting a two-sided battle. He was forced to raise the staff aloft and form the protective barrier to keep from suffering the same fate as the nephalkund only minutes before. He was heartened to again hear the caw of the raven as it shot into view and up to the landing below, at the meteor site.

The bird flew to the side of the platform where a flash of light exploded, revealing the dark-haired girl with red lips and black streaks under her eyes, standing, eyes wide, with her long hunting knife extended before her. The bird morphed into the shape of a man as it collided with another of the void creatures, causing yet another blinding explosion of white.

D'avry was relieved to find that while more of the wolf like void creatures were spilling forth from the gash in the rock, the ground battle seemed to be holding steady at least — the humans benefitting from the magically enhanced weapons that the unfortunate orc party did not have. The battle in the air, however, was another story.

He turned his attention to the thousand-armed, light-sucking nightmare attacking the Eleven Sevens, Rogue-Captain Thrasher's appropriated airship.

D'avry slipped into the form of the raven, recognizing that, like so much else, this shape-shifting, which at first had been something that was the domain only of the Astrig Ka'a, was now something that he could do, even if it was in a more limited fashion. The form of a crow was within his ability now, the form of a caribou, though what good it would do here and now, was still beyond his grasp.

Flitting up to the foredeck of the Eleven Sevens he cast about looking for any way to attack the blackout beast now trying to consume the vessel. From behind, Captain Thrasher's commands were being echoed by his first mate, the stocky, balding, and aptly named Archibald Widesides. The handful of sailors jumped at his orders, fearing, perhaps correctly, the ire of the first mate more than any beast they could face.

The men spun brass riveted cranks controlling the articulating arms, while still others heaved piles of crystalline shards into the reactors by the shovel full, steam erupting from relief valves on pressured vessels that ran through every surface and pocket of the craft. D'avry's eyes swept the deck looking for any tool, or perhaps just waiting to get a download from the Astrig Ka'a on what to do next, when he caught the trio of pale, blue-robed mutants sitting calmly, cross-legged, on a small, raised deck just below and before the helm. Though calm, their eyes were rolled back so just the whites were visible. D'avry grimaced involuntarily.

While crystalized andromedum, D'avry had learned, fueled the reactors of the vessel giving it power, that was hardly what kept the ship afloat and functioning. Every airship, in addition to its crew and officers, had its mutants. They boosted and directed the energies of the ship, as much feeling the intent of the captain as following commands from the first mate. Beyond that, they weren't really good for much else. They didn't speak, didn't eat much of anything and really responded very little to any sort of external stimuli. But, once they set foot on the deck of an airship, they at once bonded with it and it would take an act of God to remove them. Flying an airship seemed to give them purpose and a medium through which to express their otherwise diminished capacities in a way that was just too difficult to live without. While a captain, may or may not go down with the ship, a mutant ever would.

"Hard to stern, you stillborn pup of a narwhal!" First Mate Widesides screamed, his poorly shaven lip quivering while spittle hung momentarily in the air following his command.

Helmsman Drol responded crisply, locking the wheel by pulling back on a ratcheting brake and then pulling first one long lever from full forward to half-back and then pulling another even longer lever with a smaller locking lever on its handle all the way back before letting go and returning to the first which he shoved forward, grinding twice before catching its connected mechanism, it lurched back into its original position.

Steam erupted in bleating whistles from all corners of the ship. Brass and copper pipes thudded and squealed with displeasure as large gill-like openings on the fore and aft of the vessel flipped to direct wind from some internal source, the opposite direction.

The crew lurched forward but continued about their business, most of which was operating the six large articulating arms that were currently holding tight and pushing back the massive void-like creature hovering in the pale red sky before them.

Its black, chitinous arms clattered against the sides of the ship and were wrapping around the bow, slowly tightening their grip while crunching and popping sounds echoed through the frame of the *Eleven Sevens*. Still other of the creature's arms reached upward and had cut alarmingly large gashes into the fabric of the airship's porridge colored, football shaped balloon structure, before wrapping around the beam-like hoops that supported it.

Master Caterwaul, the youngest of the ship's crew, worked the levers of the number five arm furiously as directed by the fearful Mr. Widesides, but his eyes shot quickly from the hard, pole-like arm of the void creature only yards away on the railing, to where the muties sat peacefully humming in atonal harmony behind him.

He'd never heard them do that before. In fact, he'd never heard of *any* muties doing that before. And then, he saw something else. The strange man in the trench coat that had appeared from nowhere and convinced Rogue-Captain Thrasher to take a detour from their crew approved destination to this gods forsaken place. The longshoreman watched as the man in his hooded jacket walked back to the muties and looked as if he was going to join them! *Blasphemy of blasphemies!*

Caterwaul's eyes bugged out of his head as his attention was drawn back to First Mate Widesides and what, even for him, was a record breaking barrage of insults, slurs, and insinuations of imminent doom. Which, given the present situation, was saying something. The rail-thin fourteen-year-old responded by closing his eyes tightly and lunging forward to grab another fistful of levers, one foot on the railing, and haul back with every ounce of strength before slipping left, towards the chitinous arm, to dodge a burst of blistering steam and then slide back to throw the levers forward and spin a waist level wheel blurringly fast, clockwise, before repeating the action yet two more times. When suddenly, the controls started moving of their own accord.

Widesides glared at him and was about to explode with fury when, as Caterwaul stepped back with his hands up as if to say, 'It's not me!', he realized that, in fact, it *was* not him. The first mate spun to see that the magician had settled in next to the mutants, eyes closed, and seemingly conducting an invisible orchestra while humming along with them in what sounded like some sort of haunting, multi-octave chant.

In fact, all of the crew that had previously been manning the articulating arms were standing down from their stations, just watching the machinery function on its own. The chanting grew louder and suddenly number five pulled back from the void beast before them and shot down to the ground below, grabbing a man with a staff and pulling him up to stand on the deck beside them, something that the number five should not have been able to do.

The man with the staff, eyes wide, looked around desperately, certainly panicked from being plucked from the ground and hauled over a hundred feet up into the air. But then he caught sight of the magician and seeing the spindly black arms growing in number and tightening their grip on the fore-end of the ship and the airframe around the balloon above, darted for the closest black arm and cracked down on it with his staff. The arm exploded in a poof of fizzling light and then the man charged forward towards the churning mass of armored tentacles taking over the front half of the ship.

Farn landed on the deck of what was clearly a ship, but unlike anything he'd ever seen. It was suspended by ropes and metal harnesses from what could only be described as a giant bladder. But he didn't have time to contemplate the whys and hows, because he knew that this was another of the bizarre manifestations that seemed to occur around the conspicuous mage known as Avaricai D'avry.

The fighting priest spun around to assess this new battlefront and saw, indeed, that the mage was at the center of the insanity, surrounded by three other bald headed, robed priests or mages, though something seemed off about them. But he could sense the magic exuding from them. He was beginning to benefit from the staff in ways that were not entirely linear. Such as now, being able to tell that the priests were performing some large and diffuse magic and that somehow, D'avry had tapped into it. He also was alarmed to sense a presence in his mind that was not his own. Again, he assumed that the mage was to blame.

A chorus of voices boomed in his mind. "Go!"

Farn didn't know quite where to go but he spun on his heels toward the fore of the ship and saw that one of the chitinous arms had a firm grip on the railing and was working its way toward the controls of the large mechanical spider arm that had plucked him from the ground and brought him here. Without a thought, he swung the staff down hard on the arm and it exploded into nothingness with only a few effervescent pops in its absence.

The fighting priest, seeing the effect of his handiwork, charged forward to repeat it. Bashing, smashing and otherwise beating the tentacles into submission. The ship shuddered upward as arms that had held it down snapped off and were re-formed elsewhere on the blackout monster.

Once again, the words, "Go!" echoed through his mind in roaring, harmonic chaos and the blood in his veins turned cold. He knew now what the voices were commanding him to do. He continued to slash at the arms even as new ones flopped over the railing looking for purchase but he knew that he was just forestalling the inevitable.

This was the kind of moment he'd always been waiting for. Or at least since the loss of his farm and with it his loved ones, the day he'd devoted himself to the cause of justice. Joining the Ekpos, the Fighting Brotherhood, he had learned the ways of casting spells from books in the hope of defending his homeland from the raiders from the south and from, sadly, the religious fanatics of the neighboring islands to the west and the mainland.

It had been the southerners who'd laid waste to his family's lands but, while chasing them back to the lands from which they'd come, it'd been his cousins from Thadding Main who'd captured him and because of his practice in the forbidden form of casting, were taking him back to receive punishment. The irony of receiving justice, for seeking it.

But, in this moment, after first saving his oppressors and then joining their cause, he now found that the price for receiving their friendship would be the greatest sacrifice that he could give. In the absence of the comfort of his family and even the reward of wielding the ancient tome of his forefathers, he now found that this was not so heavy a burden. He could do this for his friends.

Gemballelven Farn of Far-Thadding, of the brotherhood of

Ekpos, and now of the drougehnn companions, charged forward towards the miasma of swirling black...

Deven stared at the ground through bleary eyes. Her head pounded and her vision seemed to expand and contract with each excruciating pulse. She blinked away the haze as the sounds of clashing armor and explosions grew from background noise to something decidedly more intimate and upfront.

She slid her legs underneath her and sat there for a minute contemplating a massive bloody chunk of skull with two horns and a half dozen lifeless eyes staring back at her. Looking further, there were chunks of creature scattered everywhere. N'Bruyyh lay further on too. He appeared to have been vanquished, a pole-size spear protruding from his chest.

All around was chaos. Down below, Farn was casting balls of fire at a black mass of tentacles that appeared stuck in the sky, which in turn was attacking a zeppelin-like ship, in much the same way that the kraken would a seafaring vessel. And then she heard an anguished howl that clawed at the back of her mind like a thousand fingernails on a hundred chalkboards. The skin crawled at the back of her neck as she spun, her head swimming with the abrupt movement.

A blur of black popped into view and then surged toward her; red eyes gleaming, massive black claws extended. Before she knew what happened, she sprang from her crouched position and collided with the creature, dagger first and it exploded in a flash of light that reminded her of the flash-bang stun grenades from her military training. And just like in those previous times, she was shocked by how disruptive the blast could be.

Suddenly, another of the creatures appeared to her right but she found it difficult to respond in her current state. She turned, slowly, like in a dream, when a streak of black zoomed in from below, transformed into the shape of a man in black clothing that tackled the creature, causing it, too, to explode into a nova-like flash of blinding light.

The man, stood there for a moment. Looking like a warrior-angel in a trench coat, smiled at her and then in a blink flew off in raven form up toward the airship a hundred feet above them. *D'avry... That was D'avry,* she thought as joy, relief, and a tiny bit of coherence, which still largely eluded her, came swimming back into focus.

She blinked away the cobwebs and her warrior's mind calmly took control. The battle above and below was intensifying even as it seemed to be settling into a draw. Something nagged at her, *Gearlach!* What'd happened to Gearlach? She scanned the scene of the battle with the orc warlord, beyond the glowing gash in the hillside, and saw a body crumpled against the base of a wall of rock.

She was there in seconds, patting the massive warrior's cheek. "Gearlach." And then again. "Gearlach! Wake up!"

His eyes fluttered and then stayed open, the irises all black, the whites streaked through with bloodshot veins. One was entirely red.

"N'Bru..." he struggled out, "Where's... the— "

"He's dead."

The great warrior's face contorted, and he shot up into a seated position, casting wildly about the landscape, searching for the body to confirm for himself.

"Show me!" he said, as he struggled first to one knee, wobbling drunkenly, and then to the other before grabbing his great axe to steady himself and rise fully.

"He's just over there..." she said, pointing to a place where the body had been just minutes before. "He *was* just over there." Now all that remained was a large, black pool of blood and the broken shaft of a spear big enough to be a tent pole.

"By the bodies!" he exclaimed, a weary rage energizing the words as he spoke. "And Goriahh?"

Deven looked confused. "I don't know. I must have been

knocked out. I think I missed quite a lot," she said, motioning in the direction of the battle waging above them.

"Hmm. Yes, so it seems." He grabbed her chin gently and turned her head to look at the bruise blossoming at her temple. "You were lucky. But you got your licks in. Can you still fight?"

She nodded uncertainly. Surprised by the concern...and the praise.

"Then you should probably be up there," he said looking in the direction of the airship. "I imagine that's D'avry's doing?"

She nodded again. "I think so. Seems like a D'avry thing to do."

"Then you know what you need to do."

"And you?"

Gearlach looked in the direction of the far wall of the crater. "I have unfinished business. Now, go get the mage out of whatever trouble he's got himself into." And then he took a shaky step and then another, seeming to gather his strength and then started to jog toward the far crater wall either to hunt N'Bruyyh, or Goriahh or most likely, both.

Deven turned her attention to the battle above. The ship was now battling the creature like a thing alive, not in the wooden way that it had before, but intuitively, fluidly, as if it was a creature in its own right. But the blackout beast was still growing in size. Drawing on some unseen reservoir of power.

Suddenly, one long spider-like arm slid down from the ship to where the priest was standing, exhausted from his constant barrage. Deven realized that this was likely her only chance to join the fight. She bounded down the rocks, springing ahead in jagged surges just as the spider arm plucked Farn into the air. But she was too late. She whooshed past the priest's foot, missing by inches, and had to redirect to keep from breaking herself on the rocks below.

Farn flew higher and higher toward the ship and Deven realized she had only one way into the fight now. A chitinous arm swung into range and she blipped into the air, snagging it as it passed by. Several other of the creature's arms seemed to sense this outrage of defiance and swung blurringly into view.

Deven popped away, to an arm several meters away and higher up. She blipped three more times in quick succession, each one drawing her closer to the ship until, within a couple of hops, she was racing up an arm that was latched to the port side of the bizarre vessel. She leapt over the edge, spinning and slicing behind her just as a black, spear-like arm thrust her way and *poofed* into a blast of light when it came in contact with the arcane blade. She landed softly on deck and spun to take in the action.

The deck was chaos. A bizarre chorus thrummed in the air like a nuclear reactor filled with steam locomotives and a thousand chanting monks tripping on mescaline. Black spindly arms waved wildly, beating the deck and railing, grasping lines, and tearing holes, horrifyingly, in the balloon materials above. A flash of light caught her eye and she saw Farn, swinging his staff wildly. Smashing the creature's arms, blistering light exploding from each pass as they were destroyed.

An unseen arm knocked her aside even as she watched Farn get pinned to the deck. She shot across the deck in two hops and intercepted a piercing arm as it plunged towards his chest. He ripped himself free, rolled to his feet and swung the staff in a huge arc, exploding arms in a flurry of blazing light. He caught her arm.

"Protect the mage!" he yelled pointing, a zealot's wild light behind his eyes.

And then he rushed toward the front, swinging wildly, bashing the creature's arms, the ship rearing upward as the pulling, groping arms tore free.

Deven turned toward the stern of the craft and was horrified to see that indeed, the chitinous black arms were clattering in clumps, spreading like a cancer toward a group of people sitting cross-legged upon a platform before the aft deck. Her jaw dropped as she realized that D'avry was among them.

Deven surged across the deck. The void creature's arms shooting forward to pierce the oblivious foursome of mutants and mage. She slashed at an arm just before it struck, but another took its place, and then another. Deven hacked and hacked with her blade, but the arms surged forward, seemingly endless in number.

Soon, she and D'avry as well as the mutants were pinned in place. One of the mutant's blue robes growing red around a thick black spear through its torso. It's eyes, still wide, grotesquely white, it chanted louder, screaming unintelligible words, blood spewing forth from its mouth and dribbling down its chin to join the spreading pool below. But still the ship fought, the cacophony of disparate and chaotic noises growing louder with each passing second.

Farn pressed forward maniacally, driven by adrenalin and fear and fervor. A momentary window broke through the tangle of legs and he charged forward. Planting a foot on the rail, he raced up the wide, wooden bowsprit and sprang out into the empty air.

Black, spindly arms shot forth to meet him but were intercepted by the blurring brass of the airships mechanical arms under D'avry's and the mutants' command. Farn arched back as he fell. The staff firmly in both hands, trailing behind him as he plummeted to within range of the light-sucking void and slashed down with all his might.

For precious seconds, there was nothing. No noise, no rushing of wind, just...peace. Suspended in that space, Farn smiled, letting the staff slip from his hands, and then a burst of blinding radiance rent everything asunder.

A concussive wave buffeted the ship. D'avry and Deven, now free from the monster's arms rushed to the foredeck and looked over the railing to the crater valley below. All that was left of Farn, and the creature, was D'avry's staff, laying on a broad, flat slab of granite below.

D'avry's face was expectant, then slipped to concern and then settling into disbelief, finally sank into the heaviness of loss. His hands fell from the railing limply as cheers erupted from the crew, silenced quickly by the whip-sharp commands spewed forth by the first mate. The airship, after all, was gaining altitude at an alarming rate without the beast to hold it down.

Still, shouts of astonishment and of victory rang forth from crew and from the ground below. All were exultant. All but one. Deven looked around and found that she was alone. Again.

D'avry sat, legs hanging over the broken granite as he faced the last rays of sunlight spilling from under a pale-red sky. The chill wind scouring the fractured peak tugging at his shoulder length blond hair petulantly before dying down and trying again moments later.

The grinding of gravel under foot told him someone was there. "Did you get a hougan?" he asked.

"Yes, everyone was very appreciative. Kinda like a cheeseburger, I think. Probably better hot, but I'm not complaining...I ate two," she offered, rubbing her stomach, and making a sour face.

"It's not your fault, you know," she said, her hand resting on his shoulder as she, too, took in the fading rays. Her black hair flipping back in the wind revealed geometric lines of broken skin on her temple from a hard impact that was even now revealing green, yellow and hints of purple.

"Yeah, it was. I really thought the staff would protect him," he said. "I was wrong, and Farn died... I think. Or worse. I don't know what to think, " D'avry exclaimed in a rush of emotion as he swallowed hard and let out a long, ragged breath. His eyes dropped to his hands laying uselessly in his lap.

"I wasn't cut out for this," he confessed quietly as much to himself as to the girl standing next to him.

She sat down on the granite shelf, her hard metal legs *clinking* together as she crossed them, with her dirty sneakers, one over the other.

"I don't know if you were *made* for this, but you're clearly being *re-made* for it. We all are. Besides, if you can't do it, I don't know who could. Honestly, D'avry, I don't even know what you did back there. Did you see it?

"You were a bird and then you were blowing things up and you made a fragging steam-punk airship materialize from another dimension, or something. *And* you brought us hougans, whatever those are! You really were something."

D'avry grimaced as if in pain. "Well, it wouldn't have worked if it wasn't for you. You saved my life."

Deven shrugged off the statement. She went to rest her head on his shoulder, and then, wincing from the blossoming bruise on the side of her face, shifted a little before reaching her arm up on his shoulder and resting her cheek there instead.

"I think Farn would have liked hougans..." he said.

She brushed that same stubborn lock of hair behind his ear. "I think you're right. What're we going to do now?" she asked. "I mean, what's next?"

"I really don't know. You saw the creatures. They're here too."

She nodded.

"I don't know if they're part of... the machine," he said and she looked up at him, her brows knit.

"What do you mean?" she asked.

"I've been..." He paused trying to formulate the words. "... trying to put these pieces together. Why I have been going to these different places. What they have in common. What's the meaning of the Gray Town? And, well, I haven't figured any of it out, except one thing and that's that the first... the *important* time and place, is with the Capt. Major, the mech pilot, Rutker.

"The thing in the caverns. Something happened then. Or something is about to happen in his time. It changes everything. There's a machine in the sky. It's like a ship but it's bigger than... I can't even describe it. Something happens, there's a double-cross. A betrayal, and humanity as we know it is changed. Forever. Only now, something new is happening.

"The creatures from the crater and from that night when I brought you here. They aren't *from* here. That thing with the arms and the void walkers, they're so cold. Emotionless. Except I feel one thing from them. *Wanting*. It's like a hunger. They will stop at nothing to satisfy it."

He looked at her, the bruises, and scratches. Her battered knuckles and scuffed up sneakers. She looked tired.

"We're not safe here. We're not safe anywhere. I have to go back to the beginning, but I owe Rogue-Captain Thrasher a favor now. And there's something in his world that I need too. I fear we're out of time.

"I know I'm asking a lot and you don't even really know me, but... will you lead the men? Gearlach will not rest until he's found Goriahh and made her pay for what she's done to his family. But most of the others, I think they will follow you, and I need an artifact from Thrasher's place-time. It's a cypher. The Astrig Ka'a is revealing things to me—" but he wasn't able to finish.

"Wait, wait, wait. You're *leaving* again!" she burst out and punched him in the shoulder before catching herself. They were on the edge of a cliff after all.

"Take it easy!" he said laughing, rubbing his arm, only slightly terrified. Of the fall or of the possibility that her feelings might somehow be a mirror of his own.

"Deven. I know there's a lot going on here. *A lot* to unpack. I'm just afraid that, well, I've already stayed too long. I wanted to see you before I left but I just couldn't get my head on straight after things went down with Farn... with how things went," he said, shaking his head and looking at his hands. "Thanks for talking me through some of that, and for hiking all the way up here! I will see you soon, okay?" he said, as much as asked. He lifted her chin so that their eyes met.

And then he kissed her. And for the first time in years, his heart leapt in his chest and his stomach dropped, and then he was gone, leaving her with nothing but the wind and the sunset.

Deven sat there for a couple minutes, thinking. There was nothing to do but walk down, gather her team, the ones who'd come with her, and continue the quest. *Her new life....* Perhaps someday, she'd have someone to share it with. She smiled sadly and blipped off the rock and down the ridge toward the anchored airship, musing at the shimmering sunlight pouring through a rift in the sky behind it.

Thirty-Two

Homecoming

00.000001 BC (Before Construct)
Dawn of the Construct

The bluff came rising into view and Rutker slowed the mech, opting to slip in as stealthily as possible. The heat, even though it was nighttime, was, as usual, unbearable with the baffles on. A tiny, highlighted blip sprang up on his heads-up display and he instantly recognized the heat signature as that of a human being or something like it, standing at the base of the cliff.

Before he freaked out, fearing that he'd already been spotted before even getting within visual of the *Xandraitha's Hope*, the cool, collected part of his mind kicked in. He reserved judgement. He didn't get angry. He accepted that this was just part of the new reality that was his present predicament.

Let's just hear what the joker has to say, he thought.

Sliding in between a couple of sparsely treed boulder stacks, Rutker powered down the mech and cracked the baffles ever-so-slightly. He might as well multi-task.

True to form, D'avry came strolling up, nonchalant as ever. Acting as though there were somehow not in excess of two dozen mechs scouring the countryside looking for him, or for anyone, that was not one of *them*.

"Slow night at the circus?" he asked but it was clear that his new companion didn't catch his meaning. "Twice in one night. Must be important," Rutker suggested.

"Oh, most definitely," the mage replied, resting on a long wooden staff that he noticed had some sort of illuminated object impressed into the large, gnarled head. He was little more than a kid, yet he had an air about him...

"So, what's the plan?" Rutker asked, realizing that that must be what this was all about. "I need something from you, and you need something from me, right?" he asked, remembering the conversation from what seemed like years before.

D'avry looked at the mech pilot. There was something odd about his demeanor this time. Something had happened, Rutker realized. Some of the swagger had worn off.

"You've seen the ship, right? The really big one? We need to go there," D'avry told him bluntly, which only reinforced his concerns.

Laughter erupted and Rutker was shocked to realize it had come from himself. He shook his head and looked at the mage as though for the first time.

"You really are completely insane. Certifiable," he told him, but he couldn't deny the tiniest flutter of butterflies in his stomach. "What about my family? The truce? And how would we even get there?" he asked shaking his head and putting his hands in the pockets of his flight suit.

"You know none of that matters," the mage replied and before Rutker could explode, he continued. "Obviously, we're not going to leave your family at the hands of mercenaries, or your traitorous Colonel Dexx. But there are things at work that neither you nor I can even comprehend. There is much more to this planet. Things that have been in place for eons. Waiting for the right time. The right...people."

And before Rutker could speak a word, they were back on the valley floor, standing at the foot of the crippled drop ship. Rutker, D'avry and the Long Rifle.

"It's time we see the face of our enemy," D'avry said, looking up at the drop ship, taking in all of its alien foreignness.

Rutker's mouth was dry. He darted a glance at the mage, and then at the drop ship and then he turned to look heavenward to the point where he could just see the reflected light of the Thune ship, visibly larger now. The rage was building.

The calm calculations of his pilot's mind were being increasingly crowded out by rage over the magnitude of the injustice. And by fear. Fear of what would happen to his family and to his people if he did not go with this psychotic madman. There was no one else who could do it. Just him.

He looked at D'avry, still standing there in the double-shadow of the drop ship, made by the two moons of this alien planet. The cool night air kicking up gentle tufts of white sand against the side of the dwarfed mech. He nodded. "So, this is the plan then?"

It was D'avry's turn to nod, but his eyes were unfocused, staring at some invisible thing off in the distance.

"Yes. This is the plan."

—END—

Thank you for purchasing Dawn of the Construct, the first book in the Soul Machine Saga. I truly hope you enjoyed exploring the untold stories of Earth (and Epriot Prime) as much as I did. Of course, there's much more to come.

Please realize how important your experience is to myself and future readers of the series and share your thoughts on your favorite online site and also on my webpage, where you can participate in the community and stay informed about upcoming projects and events: https://enlard-author.weebly.com

FANTASY, SCI-FI, HORROR & PARANORMAL

If you prefer to spend your nights with Vampires and Werewolves rather than the mundane then we publish the books for you. If your preference is for Dragons and Faeries or Angels and Demons – we should be your first stop. Perhaps your perfect partner has artificial skin or comes from another planet – step right this way. If your passion is Fantasy (including magical realism and spiritual fantasy), Metaphysical Cosmology, Horror or Science Fiction (including Steampunk), Cosmic Egg books will feed your hunger. Our curiosity shop contains treasures you will enjoy unearthing. If you have enjoyed this book, why not tell other readers by posting a review on your preferred book site.

Recent bestsellers from Cosmic Egg Books are:

The Zombie Rule Book
A Zombie Apocalypse Survival Guide
Tony Newton
The book the living-dead don't want you to have!
Paperback: 978-1-78279-334-2 ebook: 978-1-78279-333-5

Cryptogram
Because the Past is Never Past
Michael Tobert
Welcome to the dystopian world of 2050, where three lovers are
haunted by echoes from eight-hundred years ago.
Paperback: 978-1-78279-681-7 ebook: 978-1-78279-680-0

Purefinder
Ben Gwalchmai
London, 1858. A child is dead; a man is blamed and dragged
through hell in this Dantean tale of loss, mystery and fraternity.
Paperback: 978-1-78279-098-3 ebook: 978-1-78279-097-6

600ppm
A Novel of Climate Change
Clarke W. Owens
Nature is collapsing. The government doesn't want you to know
why. Welcome to 2051 and 600ppm.
Paperback: 978-1-78279-992-4 ebook: 978-1-78279-993-1

Creations
William Mitchell
Earth 2040 is on the brink of disaster. Can Max Lowrie stop the
self-replicating machines before it's too late?
Paperback: 978-1-78279-186-7 ebook: 978-1-78279-161-4

The Gawain Legacy

Jon Mackley

If you try to control every secret, secrets may end up controlling you.

Paperback: 978-1-78279-485-1 ebook: 978-1-78279-484-4

Readers of ebooks can buy or view any of these bestsellers by clicking on the live link in the title. Most titles are published in paperback and as an ebook. Paperbacks are available in traditional bookshops. Both print and ebook formats are available online.

Find more titles and sign up to our readers' newsletter at http://www.johnhuntpublishing.com/fiction

Follow us on Facebook at https://www.facebook.com/JHPfiction and Twitter at https://twitter.com/JHPFiction